2018: *THE CONQUEST OF SPACE HAS JUST TURNED DEADLY!*

While America prepares for a return to the Moon in 2020, the Chinese land a military expedition at the lunar South Pole and in defiance of UN treaties: seize the Moon's subsurface ice fields and mineral resources for the People's Republic of China. African-American President Cordelier Price, thrust into her role as Commander in Chief by an assassin's bullet, must enlist the aid of defiant former NASA astronaut, John McGovern, to lead an international coalition and stake a counterclaim. McGovern, however, finds that he must share his command with a beautiful female Russian cosmonaut. Together they face traitors, assassins, and the Chinese military that will stop at nothing to end their quest. As the coalition's crew battle for their lives on the unforgiving surface of the Moon, China's true plans for global domination emerge, sending the world on a collision course toward nuclear war.

Books by Chris Berman

THE HIVE

RED MOON

STAR PIRATES

Upcoming books by Chris Berman

DAS BELL

ACE OF ACES

CHRIS BERMAN

Leo Publishing, LLC

This is a work of fiction. All names, characters, places, and incidents are either products of the author's imagination or are used fictitiously.

RED MOON

A Leo Book
Published by Leo Publishing, LLC
Florida

www.leopublishing.net

ISBN-978-0-9834735-3-4

Library of Congress Control Number: 2012931621

First released in 2010
Reissued in hardcover through Leo Publishing, LLC in 2012

Copy Editor–Robert Bignell
Cover design painted in oils by Montgomery Triz:
www.leopublishing.net/featuredartists.htm
Interior design–Marina Buryak

Printed in USA
This book is printed on acid-free paper

This novel is dedicated to former NASA Astronaut, Dr. Norman Thagard, whose expertise and technical advice in writing this story were very much appreciated. This story is also dedicated to every man and woman, from every nation--past, present, and yet to be born--who will set our feet firmly on the road to the stars.

ACKNOWLEDGEMENTS

I wish to thank everyone who has made this novel possible and in particular the following:

Dr. Norman Thagard for details of the interior of the MIR space station and permission to use the character of "Norman Thagard as "Norman Taggert," as the Director of NASA in Red Moon.

Captain Edgar Mitchell, Command Pilot for the Apollo 14 Lunar Lander, for his interest in this novel.

NASA-Apollo test pilot Scott McLeod's enthusiastic support for Red Moon and for his personal introduction to the Grumman Aerospace engineers, who designed and built the Lunar Module that took American astronauts to the surface of the Moon.

Mr. Robert Bigelow, founder and president of Bigelow Aerospace, for permission to use the name of his company and the concept of an inflatable lunar habitat in my novel.

I especially thank my wife and children for their support and enthusiasm.

Foreword by Dr. Norman Thagard, Physician, Engineer, and NASA Astronaut. The first US crew member of the Russian MIR space station.

"*Red Moon*" is captivating. I found myself reading it in very short order because I couldn't bear to stop reading. Although the action is almost nonstop, the characters are very well developed. With a background as fighter pilot, engineer, physician, and astronaut, I am sensitive to the point of loss of interest in stories that erroneously portray those professions and it is this quality that frequently turns me off to science fiction works. That was not a problem with "Red Moon." To the contrary, a great strength of the book is that, while fiction, it is very believable. The book is also timely. It is obvious at the time of this writing that the Chinese are serious about becoming major players in space. Their exploits of the past few years and their apparent plans for the future leave no doubt that the intent is to compete with and ultimately exceed the capabilities of the United States in human spaceflight. I recommend *Red Moon* without reservation. It is well-researched and well-written. The book should hold the attention of even the most jaded reader.

–Norman E. Thagard, M.D., NASA Astronaut (Retired)

INTRODUCTION

The battle for resources is as old as man. First between individuals, then tribes, and later nations. In the 1500s, with Spain's discovery of the riches of the new world, treaties and agreements were promptly drawn up between the nation states of Europe to equitably divide those resources, and just as promptly those agreements were shredded by cannon and musket fire as those nations battled each other on land and the high seas to possess them.

In 1998, the NASA spacecraft Lunar Prospector made a startling discovery. Water in the form of ice, accumulated over billions of years from comet impacts, might lie frozen below areas of the Aitkin Basin, under the soil of the Moon's South Pole, blanketed in perpetual darkness, frozen to minus 370 degrees Fahrenheit. By 2009, NASA confirmed the existence of water ice on the Moon, and in 2014 an unmanned Chinese lunar probe located the buried ice fields, one meter below the rubble-strewn surface.

For the conquest and exploitation of the Moon's wealth of titanium and aluminum ores, and the harnessing of the riches of the solar system, a readily available supply of water for colonists as well as fuel in the form of hydrogen and oxygen – the two elements of water – needs to be present. Whatever nation or nations control these resources will control the Moon, and control of the Moon is control over which nations are permitted access to space and who has ownership of the solar system's vast bounty.

This is the story of just such a battle in the near future to gain and hold the high ground in man's new frontier. It is a cautionary tale as well, for while mankind's technology advances at a fearful rate, man's acquisitive and aggressive nature remain as they were when his most deadly weapons were the spear and the bow and arrow. This is the story of *Red Moon.*

– Chris Berman

www.freewebs.com/chrisbfla

RED MOON

The gestures of the moon have faded
washed out through the busy urban street,
which shut the moon's warm features meant to greet.
Time morphing dark embroidery on skyline dinner banquet,
the one enchanting guests, indeed,
and used to make them want to eat,
to washed-out veil locking in disgrace glum host's face
. . .
by the same city rays which laid it.

No longer was the moon allowed to speak
true wondrous secrets that it used to hold--
trusting a young soul trapped within a corpse that's old
--whose sailors gloried under infinite, black blanket
reduced to present treatment from a heart turned cold.
They garbled precious secrets; distance bridged the bold.
Staccato sign left mindless passer not a trace of moon's face
. . .
while claret stained a moon, as would a wine leak.

~ **Marina Sergeyeva**
Upstairs
(Used with permission)

PROLOGUE

HE STOOD MOTIONLESS as the bitterly cold wind clawed at his flight suit. His mind was trying to will away one word on the paper he had just been handed: "not." "*The addition of this item has not been approved.*"

"Nikolai, I don't like it not one damn bit, especially how they waited 'til *now* to tell us."

"What is expression of the English: Ours is not to question why, ours is but to do and die? We are soldiers, you and I, *da*? So, we obey our orders even if we know they are given by idiots."

Major Roy Jackson took in a deep breath, feeling the inside of his nostrils ice up in the sub-zero air of a Russian winter. "Yeah, only it's a shame in my country that the idiots are in the American Congress who think our *friends* up there are going to obey treaties and play by the rules."

"Don't feel bad. *My* country's idiots went along with them."

Major Jackson looked at the message again, shaking his head, and called over to the Russian officer. "Hey, what are you doing?"

Colonel Schevyenskey had turned his back to the American to face the massive Soyuz rocket on the launch pad. Unzipping the pants of his flight suit, he took aim at the rear tire of the transport van that had delivered both men to the launch pad, soaking it with a steaming stream in the freezing air. "I'm pissing on the transporter. It is tradition since first done by Yuri Gagarin. Ever since then, all cosmonauts must do this before launch…for luck."

Jackson grabbed the zipper on his own flight suit and opened it. "In that case, I'll join you. We're going to need all the luck we can get."

Closing the front of his suit, Roy Jackson looked around, his eyes drinking in the snow-covered landscape, the green of the pine trees against the impossible depth of a blue winter sky. He did so with a deep sense of foreboding. It was a sense of finality that many men on the eve of battle felt, giving away possessions and writing final letters to loved ones. It was the hollow feeling in Jackson's gut that this would be the last time he would ever stand upon the world of his birth. Finally, he turned to Nicolai Schevyenskey, his breath steaming out in clouds. "Okay, let's light this candle and get the hell out of here."

* * * *

Colonel Schevyenskey adjusted the orbital path of the Soyuz-Salyut lunar station, watching the dirty gray half-illuminated sphere of the Moon swell before his eyes. Roy Jackson, a veteran of over a dozen spaceflights, sat next to him in the cramped quarters of the Soyuz. They had exited the Salyut station an hour earlier to prepare for the braking maneuver that would place them in a circumpolar orbit about the Moon. The Salyut, one of four that had sat in storage at the Baikonur launch complex in Kazakhstan for over forty years, had gone through a complete upgrade with modern computers and control systems. It was rolled out and launched into space on top of a mighty Proton rocket. Once in orbit, the station was mated to a NASA-built Antares rocket to hurl it out of Earth's gravity well and place their ship on a course for the Moon. In a separate launch from Plesetsk, the military rocket base in Northern Russia, Colonel Schevyenskey and Major Jackson piloted their Soyuz to the ungainly looking moon station, docked and then set off for lunar orbit.

After three days of watching the half-illuminated and cratered orb grow ever larger, it was time for the final braking maneuver that would take them over the lunar South Pole and the no man's land of the Moon's far side, blocking any radio transmissions from the Earth.

As the station closed the distance to the battered and pockmarked world below, sweat beaded up on both men, despite the chilly interior temperature of the capsule. In a matter of minutes, the station would be over the Aitkin Basin at the Moon's South Pole. Hidden below was a land that had been blanketed in everlasting night for billions of years. Somewhere on that dark rubble-strewn plain was the Chinese moon base and fuel production facility hidden in the darkness. Just minutes earlier, the radar detectors on the outer hull of the station sent a signal to the internal alarm system, bleating out a warning that they had been found by powerful Chinese search radar.

The space station, to which the men's Soyuz was affixed to, stood out like a brilliant point of light on Corporal Chang Wu's radar screen situated in the command dome of the Chinese base. He would need to wait only a few more moments until the spacecraft slid behind the southern limb of the Moon and away from the prying eyes of those on Earth. Wu again glanced at his screen. It was time. With the nod of his head, the base's senior officer authorized Wu to transmit a launch command to a bank of *Han* anti-satellite missiles sited 500 meters from the base's camouflaged dome.

As the Soyuz-Salyut spacecraft passed out of radio contact behind the Moon's far side, all hell broke loose…

"Jackson, I show a launch from South Pole! It is a missile! It has radar lock on our ship!"

Roy Jackson stared down at his display and desperately applied power to the attitude jets to alter their ship's path. "Damn it! I can't shake it! Hang on, Colonel, I'm going to try and outrun it!"

The valves on the Antares's fuel and oxidizer tanks opened and began pouring the ingredients of liquid fire on their paths down the engine's fuel lines. The pressure within the rocker motor's combustion chamber built with Jackson counting down. "Five … four … three … two … one … ignition!"

Pumps spinning at thousands of RPMs sent liquid oxygen and hydrogen on a collision course to a controlled explosion in the rocket's reaction chamber, and the main engine fired. At that same instant, the *Han* missile closed to within twenty meters of the craft, and a shaped charge in the warhead detonated. Like a shotgun blast, over a thousand, ten-millimeter steel balls closed the gap to the moon station at several thousand feet per second, slamming into the Antares engine, blasting apart the reaction chamber and starting an explosion that propagated through the Salyut station, pealing its outer hull back like the skin of a banana. Finally, the steel balls reached the Soyuz, shredding the capsule and slicing off the two extended solar panels like denuding a dragonfly of its wings. Colonel Nicolai Schevyenskey's last thoughts, like that of Major Jackson's, were of his family and his sincere wish that the politicians who sent them on this mission without defensive weapons would rot in hell.

Twenty minutes passed at the Houston Space Center. By now, the moon station should have been out of the Moon's radio shadow. Twenty-five minutes, then thirty, with desperate calls bleating into space. After more than forty-two minutes from the point that the station would have emerged beyond the lunar far side, a radio transmission broke the palpable tension at the space center. However, it was not the call that anyone wanted to hear.

In heavily accented English, a disembodied Chinese voice spoke with chilling finality. "Houston, this is the Chinese moon base calling. This is General Wang in command. We regret to inform you of an unfortunate accident with your spacecraft. It has been struck and destroyed by a meteor as it passed near our base. Our scans reveal no survivors. China deeply regrets the loss of your astronauts due to this very unfortunate matter."

CHAPTER ONE

The White House, Office of the President of the United States

President Cordelier Price sat in her executive chair, arms resting on the dark mahogany desk. Thrust into the role of America's first woman chief executive by an assassin's bullet that took the life of President John Richmond just eighteen months earlier, she was proving to America and the world that behind her smile and slim figure lurked a tiger that could go toe to toe with any world leader. Her first crisis in fact came within hours of her taking the oath of office on board Air Force One as doctors in San Francisco's Mission Hill Hospital reluctantly shut down the life support systems to President John H. Richmond's body. It was clear to the team of surgeons that the massive damage to his brain caused by a .30–caliber copper jacket bullet was beyond repair. In those dark hours, Cordelier Price took control of the "football," the launch codes to America's nuclear ICBM forces as the Taiwan crises exploded in the China Sea. In a well-planned operation that coincided with the death of the American President, an invasion force from the Chinese mainland set sail across the straits of Formosa as Chinese fighter aircraft attacked and bombed the nationalist island. While many in Congress pleaded with Price to stand aside, she did not and forced an end to the confrontation with a demonstrating of just how high the stakes were that the Chinese Communists were playing with. A Stealth bomber, flying undetected over the Chinese mainland, launched a cruise missile with a dummy nuclear warhead that landed within a dozen meters of Chinese Communist Party headquarters inside the walls of the Forbidden City. As soon as the impact was confirmed, newly appointed President Price made direct contact with the Chinese

Premier. Without threats and without bluster, she simply asked him, "When will your ships and aircraft be returning to the mainland?" She didn't have to issue an ultimatum; her actions spoke louder than words.

In her heart, Cordelier Price knew the assassination of her president and her friend was ordered and carried out by the Chinese as a prelude to their invasion. However, they had seriously miscalculated the will and strength of the first African American female vice president.

Burning with anger, her hand reached down to the football and caressed the launch code keys – the keys to open the door to Armageddon – and then she withdrew it and wiped a tear from her eye, closing the case that held death beyond imagination. No, it was not the innocent men women and children held captive by the Communist government that would pay, but some way, some day, those who ordered and carried out this despicable murder would meet their fate. Quietly, as if the ghost of John Richmond was standing before her, she uttered, "John, I will avenge your death, and I will make you proud that you chose me as your vice president."

President Price sat thinking of those terrible first 48 hours as commander in chief when the Senate majority leader and the Speaker of the House entered and sat in the two blue leather chairs that faced her. Cordelier Price's light brown, almond-shaped eyes usually held lightness to them along with her pleasant smile, but that day they flashed daggers at the two individuals who were now facing her.

"Mister Speaker, Congresswoman Feinman, I've just finished a letter of condolence to Major Roy Jackson's family, and I will be leaving tomorrow to attend a memorial service for him. I think it's harder on his family and the family of Colonel Schevyenskey to know what's left of their loved one's bodies will continue to circle the Moon for hundreds, if not thousands of years. Their grief will be without closure. *And*, I have you two *leaders* to thank for that. When we conclude our discussions here today, I will be calling the Russian President to try and justify why, against my better judgment, I went along with your committee's recommendation not to place defensive weapons on the moon station. And, I might add that several of your committee members seemed more concerned about preserving the interests of certain corporations with ties to the Chinese than the interests of America."

Senator James Carey was the first to speak, but he shifted in his chair, and his eyes would not meet those of Cordelier Price. "Madam President, we acted within the scope of international law and the 1967 Treaty of Outer Space. It was our conviction that the United States and our Russian partners, of course, would not violate that treaty."

"Even though you *knew* from intelligence analysis that the Chinese had in fact placed offensive weapons on the Moon?"

Senator Carey again averted his eyes, looking everywhere but directly at the president. "We…we've heard that tune before…weapons of mass destruction that didn't exist, overinflated intelligence estimates…we …we can't be expected to…"

Before he could finish, Congresswoman Feinman spoke. "Madam President, I've seen the Chinese report; they say a meteor hit the spacecraft…I've even seen their images of it. You can't hold our party and the Chinese responsible for their deaths!"

Cordelier Price had to press her hands together, compose herself, and steady her anger but still some of it rose to the surface. "Congresswoman, are you so *gullible* to actually believe that line of crap the Chinese handed us, or are you just wishing it was true to assuage your guilt for sending those brave men to their deaths?"

Reaching into an envelope on her desk, Cordelier Price pulled out a series of three 8x10 photo images. "These were captured by a surveillance satellite in geosynchronous orbit at an extreme angle of about 120 degrees to the orbit of the Moon. The Chinese didn't know about our little snooper, which did manage to capture this." She handed the images to Donna Feinman. "That streak of light at the very edge of the Moon's disk is the exhaust plume of a Chinese rocket being launched from their base. As you can see in the last image, there's an explosion that is partially hidden by the Moon but clearly visible against the blackness of space. Now, this is classified information, because if this gets out to the public, I may be forced to issue a declaration of war. We have no idea as to what the ultimate goals of the Chinese are, but we're not going to play our hand until we find out. Now, I am about to have a very difficult discussion with President Simonov, and I am going to assure him that the next joint mission, should he even agree to another joint mission, *will* carry a full complement of both offensive and defensive weapons... Do I make myself clear? And, one more thing, you are not to discuss *anything* concerning the *real* truth behind the loss of the space station. This is now a matter of national security, and I'm certain you are aware of the consequences involved with releasing any of this information. However, on a more personal note, you're both up for re-election. I believe your constituents would find it extremely troubling that you placed your desire not to offend the Chinese over the lives of those men. Now, please ... if you will excuse me, I have work to do."

Cordelier Price did not look up from her desk as the two opposition leaders left the Oval Office.

Moscow: 22:30 hours: Office of the President in the Kremlin

President Victor Simonov closed the spigot on a golden samovar that had at one time belonged to Czar Nicolas himself and returned to his ornately carved executive desk. He eyed his three advisors and the Russian Foreign Minister that faced him in dark red and gold trimmed chairs. President Simonov had ascended the ladder of power in Russia and won the presidency of the Russian Federation in 2015 by two means: his quick wit backed up with a keen intellect, and his great wealth. These assets helped put in place the first Russian president since Boris Yeltsin with a true commitment to broadening democracy. Victor Simonov was a "New Russian" who, as a young man, had taken full advantage of his county's break with communism to make a fortune in Caspian Sea oil development. From there, he parlayed his money into the international export market and a newly invigorated banking system in Russia. He had made a clean break with his predecessors with a policy of working with, rather than against, Western interests to build a better future for his county. Today, at age fifty-six, just slightly more than a year after the one-hundredth anniversary of the 1917 revolution, Simonov stood at the pinnacle of power of a new Russian capitalist dynamo that supplanted the rotting communist system. His future and that of his country and the world looked bright until July 20, 2017, when what nearly everyone in the aerospace and intelligence community "knew" to be a Chinese space station suddenly fired up its rocket motors and set a course for the Moon.

The date of July 20, the anniversary of the first moon landing, was chosen by the Peoples Republic of China to rub the American's noses in the fact that it was China, not the United States, who had returned to the Moon first. To make matters worse, in violation of the 1967 Treaty of Outer Space, the Chinese claimed the lunar South Pole ice fields as sovereign territory and set up a base that some suspected had a military component. That suspicion was confirmed 48 hours before with the destruction of the joint U.S./Russian moon station sent to begin countering Chinese domination of the Moon and to establish a competing colony and the deaths of its crew, American Major Roy Jackson and Russian Colonel Nicolai Schevyenskey.

President Simonov's steel gray eyes scanned the room, taking in the details of his advisors. Director Yevghenny Pavlovitch Golovko of the FSB, the Russian intelligence agency, spoke first. "It is my opinion and that of my colleagues in the FSB that we abandon this ridiculous cooperation with the Americans and go our own way to establish a Russian national moon base. Agreeing to forego defensive weapons on the mission because of arm-twisting by the American Congress over our wheat purchases not only cost the life of Colonel Schevyenskey, but also destroyed one of the four remaining Salyut stations in our inventory. What did you tell the American *woman* when you spoke, that this was the end of our cooperation? Are you so captivated by her charms or is it just her mastery of the Russian language?"

Simonov narrowed his eyes and fired back. "There is no hard evidence that this was an attack on our lunar space station, so I am not certain defensive weapons would have prevented this, although, the Chinese explanation of a meteor strike does seem to strain credulity. This accident also took the life of an American major, as you well know. I met him and his wife at Star City when he was training. He was a good man. Secondly, you will not refer to the American President as *that woman.* Yes, she is charming and yes, she does speak our language better than half of our own citizens, but behind her smile are teeth of steel. She stood nearly alone and forced the Chinese back from Taiwan while still reeling from the murder of her friend, President Richmond, a man who I will remind you diverted an American aircraft carrier to our aid in Vladivostok when the People's Republic of China decided to reclaim some of their so-called *lost territory.* And, lastly as head of the FSB, how do you explain that *you* never suspected the Chinese space station was in fact a cover for a moon landing or ever voiced *your* concerns before our moon station's destruction?" The Russian President tossed a slightly worn paperback book to Golovko.

"I'm sorry Mister President; I do not read the English language," Golovko said.

"Then let me explain it to you. This is a book of fiction written a number of years ago that predicted this very event. Perhaps we should replace your intelligence agents with writers of fantasy."

Yuri Zhdanov, director of the Russian Space Agency spoke up. "Even if we wanted to go our separate ways with the Americans, we cannot. Yes, we still have three Salyuts and any number of Soyuz spacecraft, but we do not have the Antares Space Tug to get the Salyut to the Moon, nor do we have any lunar landers or the deployable habitats to set in place on the Moon. We have half the resources, and the Americans have the other half…but…I have been speaking to my counterpart in Germany. The ESA wants participation in a moon base and will provide money, personnel, and most importantly crew modules for much larger missions. I think we must all agree to be pragmatic and put aside a bit of our nationalist pride. The Americans must as well, because right now China owns the Moon and by virtue of her claim, China can dictate to Russia, America, and the entire world just what we can and cannot do in space. I think this threat far outweighs any prideful egos we may all have. And, if I may respectfully add, do not be too hard on Director Golovko. The Chinese were masterful at their deception. I'm certain the American President is having a very unpleasant talk with her own CIA chief right now."

Wearing a dark green uniform festooned with medals, Marshal Nevsky, commander of the Russian strategic missile forces, leaned forward in his chair. "The Chinese caught us…caught all of us – Russians, Americans, the ESA – with our pants down. It happened before in 1941 when Stalin turned a deaf ear to those who were screaming that the Germans were preparing to invade the *Rodina.* We didn't listen then, and we didn't listen now; neither did the Americans to a *troublemaker* within their own astronaut corps. The former American Air Force Major John McGovern tried warning the world that this was exactly what would happen. He paid a price for his vision and honesty; NASA relieved him of his flight duties. After that, he resigned. I have his file here, if you would care to review it, Mister President."

Simonov reached across his desk, plucking the red folder from the marshal's hand and opened it. Looking back at him from an 8x10 photograph were the light blue eyes of John McGovern. He was a man with short-cropped sandy brown hair and a smile of self-confidence. Obviously, this photograph was taken before he had been bounced from the NASA program, for he was in his flight suit. The Russian President continued to scan the page, speaking quietly to himself. "Born in Stamford, Connecticut 1977, entered the U.S. Air Force Academy in Colorado, 1995, flew combat missions during the Iraq War, joined NASA in 2011, served on board the International Space Station twice and then was relieved of flight duties two years ago for spreading alarm about the motives behind Chinese activities in Earth orbit." One other piece of information: divorced fifteen months ago, shortly after resigning from NASA.

Simonov's eyes fell on the transcript of a speech McGovern had made. "Let me read his comments to a congressional commission on the future of space exploration, the conference he was specifically told not to address:

"*America today is once again about to commit the grave error of underestimating our enemies. We let it happen to us in 1941 when we dismissed the Japanese as an ineffective military power. We did it again on September 11, 2001, when we were still treating terrorists as criminals rather than the desperate fanatics they actually are, and so again we paid the price for our insular views. Today, we are about to make the same foolish error. Remember, China is not a friend to America. China has designs on economic and military domination of the world. They have been thwarted at every turn here on Earth, but the Chinese are pragmatic, patient and inventive. If they cannot dominate and project their power here on Earth, they will do so from space. The entire thrust of their claimed civil space program is in reality a carefully planned military operation. It is my firm belief that China's ultimate goal is to seize the resources of the Moon: that is, the frozen water beneath the lunar South Pole. This will afford them unlimited supplies of both fuel and oxygen to establish a trans-lunar space force and essentially chain the United States and the world's other space-faring nations to our planet. Should we then be permitted to engage in our own uses of space, it would be only with China's permission and only under their ever-watchful eyes. Ladies and gentlemen of this committee, I urge you to fund an emergency development program to establish our own moon base at the earliest possible opportunity. The freedom of the United States, as well as the world, hangs in the balance. We cannot call ourselves the land of the free with Chinese overlords staring down upon us and dictating to us as to what we are and what we are not permitted to do…*"

Simonov closed the folder, squared his muscular shoulders in his chair and then addressed the men in the room. "We Russians know how to come from behind. Peter the Great knew it, and we proved it in 1941 when we were nearly defeated by the Germans. We proved it again by placing the first satellite and then the first man in space. This time, the stakes are much higher, and the penalty for failure far greater. I've read your reports, and I have done my own research. If the Chinese remain unopposed and unchallenged to their claim of the lunar ice fields, then the entire world is held captive. We are essentially shut off from access to the planets and to the resources of the asteroid belt, and even our own space stations and communications satellites are in jeopardy. Right now, China holds the high ground, and we are left unprepared to stake our own claim to these resources. By the grace of God, we still have the Salyuts, the Americans are pushing ahead with their new lunar landers, and now we can expect cooperation from the European Space Agency. For now, this may be an alliance of convenience, but I believe this is our collective future, not to be thrown away as it was after 1945. I am going to call President Price back as soon as we conclude our meeting, and I am going to insist that this man of theirs, John McGovern, be placed in a command position of the next joint mission to the Moon. I believe his courage and his foresight has given him that right. President Price has assured me the next moon station will be fully armed and will be not only able to defend itself but to attack if necessary. Russia will never again be under the thumb of the Mongols as we were so many hundreds of years ago. If we need the help of others to remain free this time, then so be it."

The Russian President turned to his Foreign Minister and his friend. "Anton Sergeiavich, as soon as time permits, please make arrangements to meet with the principal ministers of the ESA nations to begin integrating their programs with ours. Now, it's late. I will place my call to President Price and then turn in for the night. *Spakonia Noche*, gentlemen."

As the men stood up and walked toward the door, Simonov caught the arm of his Foreign Minister and quietly spoke to him. "Anton Sergeiavich, do not leave just yet. I have something to discuss with you."

"Yes Victor Andreavich, what is it?"

Simonov waited until the last man, Marshal Nevsky, shut the door before speaking. "Sit down Anton. I have something to say to you, now that we are alone." President Victor Simonov withdrew a small key from his suit coat pocket and opened a door on his ornate gold trimmed desk. Reaching in, he withdrew three photographs and handed them to his long time friend.

The Foreign Minister shuffled through them and with a puzzled look turned to Simonov. "Forgive me, Victor, but what is it I am looking at? These appear to be telescopic images of the Moon, is that correct?"

"*Da*, they arrived by courier directly from Washington this afternoon, to my personal attention, bypassing the FSB and even your ministry personnel." A look of confusion crossed the Foreign Minister's face. Before he could form a question, President Simonov continued. "These images were taken by an American satellite. This was no accident. Do you see the streak of light just above the edge of the Moon? That is a Chinese missile launch. The second photograph shows the fireball when it struck our Salyut. The American President had these delivered personally to me."

The Russian Foreign Minister stared at the images, turning each over in his hands thoughtfully before he spoke. "Victor, you did not say anything about this during our meeting; why is that?"

It had been a long day and Simonov rubbed his forehead before answering. "The tentacles of the Chinese are long, and I believe they run deep into the *Rodina.* The fewer people who are aware that I know the real truth behind th*is accident*, the better. Of the all the men in this room tonight, I fully trust only you, and as for Golovko…I trust him the least. He hides all thoughts of his true intentions, and I do *not* like his eyes…yet…he is the Director of the Federal Security Bureau with powerful friends. I cannot have the man arrested on just my suspicions. However…if we follow one serpent, he may lead us right to the nest of vipers. Now, goodnight and let this information remain just between the two of us."

"*Da*, you have my word Victor Andreavich."

* * * *

The American Airlines MD-80 on landing approach descended though the heavy winter cloud cover that blanketed the city of Albany, New York. Former astronaut John McGovern felt the familiar tug of gravity, as if someone had just slammed on the brakes. In a sense they had; the pilot was slowing the jet for an instrument approach to the airport runway hidden below. The plane dropped through layers of cold gray clouds that seemed a perfect match to McGovern's mood. He was headed back to his Berkshire home in Great Barrington from a memorial service for his friend and fellow astronaut Roy Jackson. He and Major Jackson trained as a team, spending weeks working together aboard the International Space Station. They had even flown the final mission of the Space Shuttle Endeavour together before she was decommissioned and replaced with the new Orion launch system. McGovern was scheduled to take the new Orion up into orbit as her pilot, but just days prior to the launch he lost his flight certification. The official NASA explanation was flight fatigue, but John knew very well it was retaliation for speaking his mind to a congressional committee about the real danger China posed. Powerful people with vested economic interests in China made certain that astronaut John M. McGovern would be a former astronaut.

The pressures put on him after his address forced his resignation. He felt he had lost everything and in a sense, he had. Even his wife divorced him, citing his obsession with his imagined Chinese threat for ending his career and their life together. Only today, standing in the cold sunshine of the Colorado Springs Air Force Academy Cathedral, holding Roy Jackson's widow as she buried her head into his shoulder, soaking it with tears, did John knew for certain he had been correct all the time. The only thing he couldn't figure out was why NASA, the White House and the media were buying into the pure bullshit of the Chinese explanation of a meteor strike that left his friend and a Russian cosmonaut orbiting the moon like ground up hamburger. What really galled him was the appearance of President Cordelier Price, surrounded by a small army of secret service agents. When she spoke at the memorial, it was about the "accident" that took the life of Major Roy Jackson. John thought to himself that he used to have a lot of respect for this woman. *How the hell could she parrot the Chinese line about this being an accident?* This was no accident but a deliberate act of war.

Retrieving his winter topcoat and carry-on bag from the overhead compartment, McGovern maneuvered his slim but muscular frame down the narrow aisle and out the plane's exit door. As he stepped into the jet bridge, two U.S. Air Force officers confronted him.

Before he could speak, the first man, a handsome African American, smiled and extended his hand. "Major McGovern, I'm Lieutenant Colonel Miles Brown, and this is Captain Emery. I'm very pleased to meet you, sir."

McGovern looked the man over before extending his own hand and then spoke. "Excuse me, but it's *former* Major McGovern; I resigned my commission after I was forced out of NASA. Why don't you just call me John? And for the record, I've just had a very long and very difficult day, so if you'll excuse me, I'll be heading to the parking lot to go home."

"Okay by me, John," the man replied. "But with the way that snow's coming down out there, maybe you ought to take your time about hitting the road. In fact, it would very much be my pleasure to buy you a drink and shoot the breeze for a while."

"Listen, no offense Colonel, but since when did I develop a fan club in the Air Force that you two want to be my long lost pals? I just said goodbye to a very good friend and fellow astronaut today, and frankly I'm in no mood to be jovial."

Lieutenant Colonel Brown reached into his jacket, withdrew an envelope with the seal of the President of the United States on it and placed it into John McGovern's hand. McGovern took it, and turning it over examined the embossed presidential seal. It was the real thing all right.

"Major McGovern, the captain and I carry a high security clearance, and while I don't know what exactly is in that letter from President Price, I do know that they want you back. Back in the air force and back at NASA. Yeah, you were right and we were wrong. That's what the captain and I were sent here to tell you. They want you back for something important. That's all I know."

Sliding his index finger into the opening, John McGovern ripped open the envelope and began reading:

From the Office of the President of the United States, Cordelier Price, this eighth day of February 2018

Dear Major McGovern:

As President and Commander in Chief of the United States of America, I want to extend my sincere apology for the treatment you suffered for speaking your mind and trying to alert those of us in government to the danger the Chinese military space program posed. I would like to you to consider my offer to reinstate your rank as an active Air Force officer and to ask you as my fellow American citizen to consider leading a second mission to establish an international outpost on the Moon. Please consider this in the light of the destruction of our first attempt at placing a base on the moon by a Chinese missile. I am placing my confidence in you as a former military office that you will not mention the fact that we know it was not a meteor but a Chinese offensive weapon that destroyed the lunar space station.

I urge you to consider this offer in the manner it has been presented. Your warnings as well as your suspicions of the Chinese space program have been vindicated. I would consider it a personal favor if you would accept this offer in the manner it has been given. Again, I offer my apologies and my regrets for any way your government has wronged you.

Sincerely,
Cordelier D. Price, President, United States of America

McGovern held the letter for a long time, reading it a second time with a tumult of emotions forcing their way to the surface. Anger was the first of these to break free, and he nearly ripped the letter to pieces until the sense of vindication washed over him. He was still torn in two directions, with feelings of relief that he was finally being taken seriously and a desire for revenge now at war upon the battlefield of his mind when the Lieutenant Colonel again spoke.

"One more piece of information you should know Major: Jason Cumbers is out as Director of NASA, or at least he will be by sunrise. President Price is appointing former astronaut Norman Taggert as the new director. I believe that you and he have a great deal of mutual respect for each other. So, what do you say Major? Are you back on board?"

McGovern's eyes met Brown's as he took the measure of the man. *Wow*, he thought, *they're bringing back Norman as director? His support for me nearly killed his own career.* "Colonel, I'll have to sleep on it, but I will have a decision for you by early tomorrow morning. Yeah, it's still snowing pretty hard, so maybe I'll put up for the night at the Airport Hyatt. I won't be driving anywhere tonight. That being the case, I'll take you and the captain up on that offer for a drink. God knows, right now I think I need one."

One drink turned into a few more with John McGovern and the other two Air Force officers sharing war stories late into the evening. Morning dawned clear and cold with the sun reflecting of the blindingly white snow that had fallen the evening before, highlighted by a deep sapphire blue sky. A knock on McGovern's hotel door brought him back from the view out his window. Opening the door, he again faced the Lieutenant Colonel.

"Major McGovern, I have a call for you on this encrypted cell phone…It's the President, sir."

McGovern took the phone.

Brown could only hear one side of the conversation: "Yes, I read your letter. Yes...thank you very much. Really? I didn't know that. Well, yes I would be very happy to meet with you and Norman but no promises. Today? I think I'll need a change of clothes…Oh? I see. Okay then, I'll see you later today … and … thank you. It feels good to know someone is finally taking me seriously, but I feel terrible about the loss of those men. Yes, I agree. It must not happen again. And, I owe you an apology as well. I was at the memorial for Major Jackson when you spoke. I…. really thought that you bought the Chinese story about a meteor. Yes, I agree, better to have them thinking they put one over on us. I'll see you then…and thank you."

With that, John McGovern broke the connection and returned the phone to Lieutenant Colonel Brown. "It seems I have a supporter from an unusual source. Russian President Simonov insisted that I be asked to head up a second space mission. Ah...I need to go out and grab a change of clothes somewhere. All I have is what I was wearing back from Colorado."

"No problem about that sir, I have your majors uniform right here."

"Wait a minute, since when does a superior officer start calling me *sir* and bringing me my uniform?"

A smile broke across Brown's face along with a chuckle. "Well, sir, your rank of major is just temporary until you get to Washington. If you decide to take the president up on her offer, you'll be a full bird colonel by this time tomorrow, and you'll be *my* superior officer. And, no need to make flight arrangements, the captain and I will take you over to Stewart Air Force Base. There's a Gulfstream jet waiting to fly you down to Andrews for your meeting with the president…unless you'd rather strap into the back seat of an F-15-B?"

McGovern just shook his head. "No, a Gulfstream would be just fine. Let me get showered and changed, and we'll hit the road, okay?"

Beijing China, Office of Space Intelligence

It was a cold cloudless night with the nearly full moon shining down on streets, icy and wet from melting snow. The harsh glare from the mercury vapor lights overhead cast a glossy green sheen on the asphalt walkway leading to the office of Space Intelligence. Sung Zhao, his short-cropped hair still jet-black despite his fifty-one years, pulled the collar of his leather coat to close it more securely against the icy fingers of the winter's night trying to claw their way in. Zhao turned his head upward to gaze for a moment at the Moon, its light bathing his face and revealing a long, ugly scar that ran from just under his right eye to his chin. As a young intelligence agent, he had been unlucky enough to be within range of an errant piece of metal that sliced through the air at several hundred feet per second during the test of an explosive device that Zhao had helped design. The shard of aluminum buried itself in his right cheek, just missing his eye by millimeters, and disfiguring his face. It had been Zhao's plan that the device was tested for, but he would hear about its success or failure second hand from a hospital bed.

It was 1996, and the Americans like naive children had brought their Lovell Intelsat to China to be launched on a Long March rocket. The American team was to make certain that the highly sensitive technology of the satellite's guidance system was not accessed by any Chinese personnel. Zhao, a young intelligence officer, had different ideas. Through his perseverance and persistence with his superiors, they allowed him to put his plan in motion: Place an explosive device at just the right spot in the Long March to ensure its destruction without damaging the satellite. It had to be at just the right altitude. Too soon and the pieces would fall back to the launch pad for easy recovery of the satellite by the American team. Too late and there would be little of value left to salvage if anything at all. Zhao's device was set for 22 seconds after launch. The debris would fall on a village directly in the flight path of the rocket and likely kill hundreds, but Zhao and his superiors felt this to be a trivial matter next to the goal of obtaining the Lovell guidance system.

On February 15, 1996, the motors ignited on the Long March rocket as gouts of flame enveloped the launch pad thrusting the craft upward into a cold deep blue sky. At 22 seconds after launch, that sky erupted in an angry red fireball, blasting the rocket to pieces and sending flaming fuel and metal raining down on the nearby village, taking more than 500 lives. The crash site was declared strictly off-limits to the Americans for safety reasons, while a specially equipped Chinese team went in to salvage what they could of the payload. The next day, the charred and battered remains of the Intelsat was handed over to the Americans. When questioned about one hexagonal blue anodized component that was conspicuously absent, the salvage team leader just shook his head saying what they brought back was all they could find.

Two days later, as Sung Zhao lay in his hospital bed, his face swathed in bandages, two stern-faced high-ranking military officers entered his room and stood over him. Suddenly a smile broke across the face of one of the officers as he handed Zho a hexagonal device about fifteen inches long made of blue anodized aluminum. Despite the pain from the contraction of his ruined facial muscles, Zhao broke into a grin. Finally, China had gained an advanced American-made guidance system. Once their scientists could reverse engineer it, the device would be incorporated into a new generation of Chinese ICBMs. No longer would their rockets carry just a single nuclear warhead: now each instrument of destruction could carry up to eight independently targeted 250 kiloton nuclear warheads with an accuracy of less than a dozen meters to their selected targets. Sung Zhao, at the young age of twenty-nine, was hailed as a brilliant intelligence officer. Twenty-two years later, Zhao was again the driving force of a bold plan to claim the resources of the Moon and make certain that no nation but China would dominate space.

Zhao again looked up at the Moon, knowing his men, equipment, and weapons were in place on its cratered surface. His plan was just beginning to unfold. He returned his gaze to his office door, opened it, and entered to find the Chinese Vice Premier as well as the commander of the Chinese strategic missile forces waiting for him. It would be a long night as Zhao's plans unfolded and captured the imagination of two of the highest ranking Communist Party members of the People's Republic of China.

He bowed as a matter of respect to his superiors; however, Zhao, as well as the two ranking men in the room, knew that in this matter it was Sung Zhao who was in command. This was the greatest opportunity that had ever been presented to China to enhance its position as the dominant world power.

Vice Premier Gao Xi spoke first. "Zhao, your plan appears to be successful even beyond your first estimation. With the destruction of the Russian-American moon station, you have disrupted their program and sown the seeds of mistrust between the two nations. Perhaps you have derailed their efforts permanently or at least delayed them for many months. So then, what is the next move?"

"Before I answer that Vice Premier Gao and General Chen, I wish to assure you that apparently both the American and the Russians have accepted our explanation of the destruction of their craft as an accident. No fingers of blame save for a few discredited troublemakers point at China and those who have expressed doubts are not taken seriously."

General Chen, heavy set and balding, spoke up. "I had some reluctance and apprehension about your plan, but I can see now the destruction of their craft was done in such a manner so that no evidence of our involvement was discovered. The West and the Russians may have their suspicions but have nothing to confirm it was our missile that ended their mission. You have my complete confidence, Zhao. Now tell us about the next phase of your plan."

Zhao smiled with self-assurance, even if only the left half of his mouth turned up. The damage to the right half of his face had permanently severed muscles and nerves in such a way to make that side immobile. "By sowing havoc within the ranks of the Americans and the Russians, we have a window of opportunity to reinforce and expand our moon base without interference, and due to its location, without observation. We have scheduled three launches, each a day apart to bring added military personnel and new prefabricated sections for the expansion of our base. In addition, we have added extra weapons to increase our security. However, the next phase of my plan is one of humanitarian assistance and China's promise of nearly unlimited riches from space for the struggling nations of the Third World. We will build a manufacturing and transport system on the Moon to process the titanium, aluminum and rare earths that are abundant in the lunar soil with a solar furnace. With the use of a magnetic accelerator, we will send the processed materials back to Earth orbit. There, we will affix the packages of processed metals with re-entry shields to deliver them to the many struggling and resource poor nations of the world, earning China their loyalty and assuring world opinion will favor us and not the Americans or the Europeans or the Russians.

"The next phase will also include a demonstration of both China's technical prowess as well as our generosity. In less than four weeks, a very important resource and communications satellite in orbit over the African continent will suddenly cease to function, leaving the Pan-African nations desperate to replace it for financial data, crop, water current and weather data. The West will of course launch a replacement – for a price, however. Shortly after lift-off, the American craft will experience a catastrophic launch accident. China, will not only replace the African satellite at no cost, but we will assemble and deliver that satellite to geosynchronous orbit from our facilities on the Moon, as a demonstration of our technological superiority over all other nations. With good will and the riches of the Moon flowing to the non-aligned Third World, China will not have to fight for domination of space: We will be handed that position on a silver platter."

General Chen nodded thoughtfully but then added, "We are certain the Americans with Russian assistance will not give up so easily and try again to establish their own claim the ice fields?"

"Do not worry, General," replied Zhao. "That contingency has already been planned for. If, and when, the Americans launch, it will result in a *catastrophic malfunction*, in the words of NASA. Come closer gentlemen, and I shall enlighten you on the specifics of the plan. To execute it, we shall require the resources of a very specific military branch, but I think you will agree the plan is foolproof."

CHAPTER TWO

Washington, DC

Even as the U.S. Air Force Gulfstream jet's wheels touched down on the runway at Andrews, in the White House, President Cordelier Price and Norman Taggert were in deep conversation, pouring over John McGovern's government records. If John suddenly felt his ears burning as he exited the jet, he gave no sign of it as he headed over to a dark blue Ford staff car and on to the meeting with the president.

President Price was attired in a light gray wool blazer and matching knee-length skirt. At age fifty-eight, she still cut an attractive and petite figure, her coffee-colored skin showing only the mildest effects of aging. Norman Taggert, the first American to fly aboard a Russian spacecraft 23 years before, still had the classic appearance of the right stuff. His deep blue blazer adorned with a NASA lapel pin sat straight on his square and still well muscled shoulders.

"Yes, Madam President, his record is definitely not by the book. He's a risk-taker you know. On weekends, he'd head up to Daytona to race vintage motorcycles. All of his racing wasn't just on the track either. I remember making that call to the Florida Highway Patrol that got him off the hook after he was clocked at a 105 on SR-405 heading to Kennedy on his 49-year-old BSA Lightning. That was sort of a carryover from his academy days. You can see three disciplinary reprimands in four years. The only thing that absolved him in the eyes of the academy was his four-point-oh grade point average and his uncanny flying skills. His instructors said he could make a jet trainer do things the designers never dreamed of."

Cordelier Price listened to the new NASA director while holding McGovern's photo. *Handsome man,* she thought. Then she addressed Norman Taggert. "I see he's not afraid to take risks to save the lives of others either, even if it's not exactly in compliance with orders."

"Yeah, I'll tell you a little about his escapade during the early days of the Iraq War. He was flying an F-15, returning with his squadron from a strike mission, when he spotted an A-10 below him limping back to base. The A-10's pilot took ground fire and lost one engine. John sort of has a sixth sense and knew, in his gut, that pilot was just hanging out there like chum in shark-infested waters. McGovern broke formation to join up with the A-10. His squadron leader ordered him to remain in the formation. John claimed his radio went out and never heard the call. Just as he was leveling out, two Iraqi MiGs jumped the A-10 thinking they had an easy kill. John came screaming in on full afterburners and shot down both Iraqi fighters. If John hadn't gone to that pilot's aid, that man and his plane would have been nothing but body parts and scrap metal all over the desert floor. John did it again on an EVA outside the International Space Station. A French astronaut accidentally severed his safety line and began drifting away. He was told absolutely not to go after the man, but once again, John had ah…*radio trouble.* He had no reaction pack, but he unhooked his tether anyway, took aim at the man, and pushed off with his legs. He caught up with him and started throwing his tools and then extra removable parts of his suit and the Frenchman's, using the reaction force to propel them back to the space station. If John hadn't gone after him, the man would have run out of air long before those administrators in Houston would have come up with a *by the book* rescue plan."

Price looked over more of his file. "I see he was specifically ordered not to address that congressional committee about his views on the Chinese space program."

"Yeah, that was the one that put the nail in his coffin at NASA. I tried to bail him out, but I almost lost my pension over it. There seems to be some pretty powerful people, pretty high up that wanted to keep the lid on any anti-Chinese sentiments but then came the assassination of President Richmond and their aborted invasion of Taiwan. No one can prove the two are connected, but I'm sure *you* must suspect that they are, and now this damned accident with the moon station. It doesn't pass the smell test as far as I'm concerned."

"So, if you were in a potential combat situation, how would you feel about having John McGovern on board?"

"I'll tell you right now, Madam President, if I was in a situation where my life depended on my partner, there's no man I would rather have next to me other than John McGovern."

A look of determination crossed the face of the president, and she nodded in agreement. "Then I'll tell you this right now, Mr. Taggert, that was no accident. We have a satellite image of the launch of a Chinese missile from their moon base followed by the destruction of the moon station. We're keeping silent on this because if the Chinese believe that we think this was an accident, maybe they'll get sloppy and just maybe show their true intentions. The CIA thinks this goes much deeper than what we've seen so far. Anyway, your input just confirms my decision to offer John McGovern a command assignment on the next moon mission along with reinstatement into the Air Force with the rank of colonel. God knows he deserves it after what he's been through: losing his credibility, branded as some conspiracy nut, the end of his career and then his marriage. He was right all along. We owe this man a lot."

* * * *

John McGovern sat in deep thought then again looked at his watch. Thrusting his arm forward, the blue of his uniform sleeve slid back to reveal a solid looking stainless steel blue-faced diver's watch. However, it was the blue of his major's uniform that sent his emotions colliding in ways he never dreamed they would have 24 hours earlier. Just one day ago, he held the widow of a fellow astronaut as she wept over the loss of her husband and mentally cursed the stupidity of the American President for mouthing the Chinese line about this "*loss being a terrible accident*." Now, he was less than 15 minutes away from an audience with her, wearing the uniform he swore he would never put on again.

As the staff car entered the White House grounds and he and his driver were checked through security, McGovern considered what he would say to Cordelier Price once he was inside the Oval Office. Norman would be there as well. If Norman Taggert was now the director of NASA and he and the American President had set up a private meeting to urge his return, then something big must be up. John thought about his wife…no, ex wife…whose world came apart when John finally crossed the line with what she called his obsession with China's motives in space. After his speech to the committee, he found himself forced out of NASA. He resigned his commission in the Air Force but he still would not keep silent. Then strange things began to happen – credit lines were closed, checks from accounts that should have held plenty of funds bounced. Then Cheryl, his wife, came into her job at the banking center one morning only to be told to clean out her desk. Cheryl, a senior loan officer, had more than 12 years of exemplary service at the bank. Just three weeks earlier, she had been given an award for her work and now she was before the bank's vice president being accused of transferring a customer's money on a mortgage closing to her personal account. She stood in disbelief as her boss handed her the "proof" – computer records showing the transfer and her account balance, now 170,000 dollars higher. He told her to leave quietly and no charges would be pressed. Someone with computer skills and clout went to a lot of effort to end Cheryl McGovern's career.

Cheryl pleaded with her husband to shut up about the Chinese, but after the assassination of President Richmond, followed by the Chinese attack on Taiwan, John McGovern stepped up his attacks in print, on the net, and any venue he could muster, earning him the title "conspiracy nut" with mainstream media, as well as government officials who placed him in the same category as UFO abductees, Bigfoot and the Loch Ness Monster eye witnesses. With John and Cheryl's finances stretched to the breaking point, and McGovern's unwillingness to keep silent about a threat he felt could banish America from space, Cheryl filed for divorce. John packed up his collection of belongings and his three motorcycles in the back of a rented U-Haul and left Florida for the Berkshires of Massachusetts. There he settled into a small rented house on the outskirts of the town of Great Barrington. Yet, despite everything that happened, John would not keep silent.

His tenacity and single-mindedness had nearly cost him his life. In late October, he was riding his "thumper," a 1971 BSA 500 Victor motorcycle, when a car came alongside him to pass and instead swerved into his lane, sending McGovern and his bike off the side of Route 23 near West Otis. Only his skill, honed in vintage motorcycle racing, kept him from slamming into the galvanized guardrail. As he slowed to collect his wits, the driver of the car locked his brakes up, spun 180 degrees and headed back toward him at high speed.

That was no accident and not some kid out to put a scare into a motorcyclist, McGovern thought. *Whoever is driving that car is a pro, and he's out to kill me.* McGovern twisted the throttle grip on the ancient bike, putting to the test the recent rebuild of the BSA's 500 cc engine and transmission.

With a loud *braaapp*, the barely muffled exhaust note of the British single echoed off the pavement. *Can I outrun this bastard bent on ending my life?* McGovern was pushing ninety on his vintage bike as he tore into the turns on Route 23, racing to the junction with Tyringham Road. The chilled autumn air clawed at his face as trees draped in the reds and golds of fall merged and blurred into colorful ribbons on either side of the road. *If I can make it there, I've got a chance.*

Tyringham Road was much narrower and twisting than the main route, and he could cut up West Center Road, which was unpaved, the perfect environment for the scrambler bike. He checked his mirror and could see the car gaining on him, a Lexus 500 with blacked out windows. It was his 34 horsepower verses the driver's 300, but the marvelously light British-built single cylinder bike flew as if it had wings.

McGovern made it to the turn and leaned the bike so far over his left foot peg sent a shower of sparks across the blacktop. The driver of the Lexus spun, nearly losing control on the turn, then regaining like a professional driver. The Lexus was still on John's tail, but the twists and turns of Tyringham Road were playing in McGovern's favor, opening up the gap between him and his pursuer. Finally, the dirt road came into sight, and at the last second, John shot off the pavement at over 70 miles per hour, propelling gravel and dust. The Lexus missed the turn, tried to brake, and slid sideways smashing the rear quarter panel against a large rock. McGovern slammed on the bike's drum brakes and turned to go back after the driver, but he was quick, and raced off, back to Route 23 and the Massachusetts Turnpike.

John McGovern sat catching his breath, heart pounding. He pulled his cell phone from his belt and put a 911 call to the State Police. At first, he thought he was getting somewhere until he gave his name. An officer got on the line to say in a mocking tone that they would be sure to check out his story along with the Bigfoot sighting from last week.

When McGovern arrived home, there was a message waiting for him on his answering machine. The caller ID read: unknown number. John pressed the button and a deep monotone voice boomed out, "Next time, you won't be so lucky, big mouth!" After that, McGovern kept a lower profile as well as a loaded Walther PPK 9-millimeter automatic nearby.

John McGovern, his thoughts still dwelling on the incident, seemed oblivious to his surroundings, passed by the decorated rooms and paintings hung on the walls of the White House corridor. Then he was at the door of the Oval Office. A Marine guard saluted him and McGovern automatically returned it.

Norman Taggert met him at the door, extending his hand. "John, good to see you, especially now. I…I know how difficult this last year has been for you."

"As I know as well, Major."

President Cordelier Price stepped in front of John McGovern and extended her hand. His first impression of her up close was she appeared to be a much younger woman than her true age. She had a sincere smile that spoke volumes about her character. But, he knew she also had another side – the side of a tiger that would not back down. She took a calculated risk during the attempted Chinese invasion of Taiwan by delivering a dummy nuclear warhead right on the doorstep of the Communist leadership in Beijing. Painted on the replica warhead in Chinese characters were the words, "Boom, you're dead." Cordelier Price made it clear to the entire leadership of the People's Republic of China, who were assembled just 50 meters from where the dummy warhead landed, that the United States would not tolerate the forcible annexation of a democratic nation by the communists. As soon as she knew they had received the message, she placed her call to Beijing. She simply asked Premiere Feng when could the world expect to see an end to China's military exercise and told him not to confuse her presidency with past administrations. "Once the United States confirms the matter is closed," she informed him. "Our own exercises involving the testing of the improved stealth capabilities of our new B-2 bombers also will end."

Her last statement made it painfully clear to the communist leadership that American stealth bombers, quite possibly armed with nuclear tipped cruise missiles, were flying undetected and unopposed in the skies above China.

That ended the crisis on the spot and earned her a reputation that she was as tough as or tougher than any ten of her male predecessors. However, some sectors of the media give the nickname of "Dirty Harriett" and even speculated if she asked the Chinese Premier if, "He was feeling lucky today." Other members of the liberal anti-military mindset had far less complimentary terms for Price such as, a "trans-gender Oreo," a white man in a black woman's body. In a sense, she followed the lead of the late President Richmond when he committed an American aircraft carrier to lend support to besieged Russian forces. The Chinese leadership, after months of stalemate with Russia over ownership of the territory that bordered Jixi on the Chinese side, took matters into their own hands, sending hordes of Chinese troops and armor across the disputed border, attacking Ussuriysk and Artem before moving south toward Vladivostok. Surprised and outnumbered, Russian pilots in Mig-29s and SU-35s battling waves of Chinese J-20 fighters suddenly found the sky filled with American F-35s and F-18s backing them up. With additional Russian forces came a Chinese retreat and a negotiated cession to the hostilities, however, with old memories of the Mongol conquests of Russian lands in the 1200s and the Chinese incursions of the early 1970s, any spirit of trust between the two nations died the day of the attack.

President John Richmond took a lot of heat for his unilateral decision to intervene on Russia's side. American and Russian relations had been severely strained after 2011, but Richmond saw Victor Simonov as a new beginning for the two nations and felt he had to prove that encouragement and support for greater democracy from America was more than just talk. Chinese exports had fueled multi-billion dollar empires in the United States and now those empires were in jeopardy. In a matter of months, an assassin's bullet took the life of President Richmond and put Cordelier Price, his African-American vice president, into the role of Commander in Chief of the United States armed forces and as President. Now she was just inches away from John McGovern, taking his hand in hers and shaking it warmly.

"Major McGovern, welcome to the White House. I can't tell you how pleased I am to have you accept my invitation to meet. Believe me, I know how difficult your life has been since you began voicing your warnings about the Chinese. You've had some impact here. Purchases of Chinese-made goods by Americans are down nearly 10 percent once you got on your soapbox. This has made a lot of people very upset with you. Bankers and financial groups managing Chinese stocks and credit funds, huge department store chains bringing in cheap Chinese goods and shippers, who have seen a drop off in container business. I'm not surprised that someone tried to take your life four months ago."

McGovern, however, did look surprised. “So you knew someone tried to run me off the road near my home?”

“Yes we did. You should also know that the day after this happened you had a guardian angel watching over you. My orders.”

“You mean the FBI?”

“No, I mean a *company* angel: CIA. The tentacles of this go deep, and we’re finding out there are a lot of very well-heeled individuals willing to put their profits ahead of their country. I can’t be sure that certain individuals within the FBI haven’t been compromised. By watching you, we were hoping to gain a bit more information as well as keep you alive.”

McGovern took a deep breath and paused before he answered. “So you believe me. Thank you. But still, you sent those men on their mission without any defensive weapons.”

For a moment, Cordelier Price cast her eyes down. “Yes, that’s right. My fault. My fault for listening to a bunch of congressional representatives that seemed more intent on representing corporations with deep ties to the Chinese than their own country. They didn’t want to have us appear aggressive in this mission. They arm-twisted the Russians, too, jacking up their interest rate and delaying their wheat purchases until they went along with us on the no-weapons directive. I failed those men, but I will *not* repeat the same mistake. That’s why I wanted you here, and that’s why Norman Taggert is the new director of NASA. We and the Russians and the ESA are going back to the Moon in force, and we *are* staking our own claim to the lunar ice fields. We will not be dictated to by the Chinese, and we will not be bottled up on Earth because China believes it now controls the space between here and the Moon. I want you to spend as much time as you need with Norman Taggert today and brainstorm a way to get us back to the Moon in less than sixty days. If anyone can do this, you two men can. The Chinese are up to something, and it’s big. Our surveillance satellites show three launch vehicles ready to go at their Xichang space complex, one of which is a huge rocket that appears to be a copy of the old Soviet Energia booster. We believe they're all bound for their base on the Moon, carrying additional personnel and supplies for expansion. Gentlemen, the Chinese are on the Moon to stay, and we need to catch up and do it very quickly. I'll put the executive conference room at your disposal and all of the information you need to devise a plan…and, I hope, Major McGovern, you will accept the restoration of your rank with an immediate promotion to colonel. One thing more…I want you up there, leading this mission to secure our own share of the Moon's resources and to maintain our freedom and access to space. We did it once before as a young nation on the high seas, and by God we'll do it again in the vacuum of outer space. So, do I have your commitment?"

John McGovern had been fifty-fifty to the idea of coming back to the Air Force and NASA on his way to the meeting, but after meeting Cordelier Price, he didn't even think twice. "I'm in. Let's get this moving…and thank you…for everything. I know that Norman and I will get this done and on time. I already have some ideas, and I'm sure Norman does, too."

A warm smile broke across the President's face. "Okay then, I'll leave you two to start working on your plans. Remember, anything you need, just ask for it. Good day, gentlemen."

John McGovern, now Colonel John McGovern, sat with NASA Director Norman Taggert in the executive conference room, laptops out as well as accessing the White House's computer system. As the plan coalesced, it began to take on an almost MacGyver-like quality as both men realized where some of the hardware had to be obtained from, including the Smithsonian Air and Space Museum. Several hours and one large pizza later, a rough draft of a plan had been worked out. It would still take many more hours to check and recheck their figures before calling Yuri Zhdanov, director of the Russian Space Agency, and Heinrich Stohler of the European Space Agency to discuss the plan and get everyone on board.

The challenges were to get personnel down to the surface of the Moon, set up a habitat, and hold that territory at all costs until reinforcements arrived. This had to be done without getting China and this ad hoc alliance into a shooting war. It seemed to both men that the hardware would be far easier to work with than the politics of the situation.

The next mission to the Moon would no longer be one of exploration but a military expedition. To Norman Taggert, an avid student of history, the similarity to the confrontations that occurred between Spain, Portugal, England and France in the 1500s with the discovery of the New World was eerily similar. In that era of exploration, treaties and agreements were signed and sworn to, equitably dividing the lands of the Caribbean, North and South America, between competing European powers for equal shares of these new lands. However, it didn't stop the wooden ships of that era from blowing each other out of the water once gold was discovered. Now a treasure beyond value for any nation bent on the exploitation of space had been found on the Moon – water. Water from comets that blasted the Moon billions of years ago was still there as a kind of permafrost beneath the rubble of the Moon's South Pole, a land in perpetual darkness, where a temperature of minus 300 degrees had remained constant for eons. This ice would provide liquid water for survival of a lunar colony as well as oxygen and hydrogen for rocket fuel. Without this resource, a moon base would just be a very costly experiment, requiring constant replenishing from Earth. With water, it became a self-sustaining colony and the key to the unlimited riches of the solar system. Whoever controlled access to this resource controlled the economy and the future of the entire human race.

A second pizza had disappeared along with the sun many hours later. Still McGovern and Taggert worked long into the night, joined by a retired engineer from Northrop-Grumman Aerospace. The man, Warren McCann, was in his late seventies, and couldn't quite get over the shock of having two NSA agents appear at his door to escort him to Washington for a meeting at the White House.

McCann, wearing his reading glasses, was going over the drawings and calculations that were hastily put together by the two NASA astronauts. After studying them for about ten minutes, he said, "I agree, gentlemen, the development and testing of the new lunar lander is too far down the road to do us any good. If its development budget hadn't been cut back in 2011, we wouldn't be having this conversation, and China wouldn't be sitting on the Moon right now, claiming those ice fields. But…your plan? Yeah…I guess it could work, but holy smokes, who are you going to ask to fly a museum exhibit down to the surface of the Moon?"

John McGovern looked him in the eye with dead seriousness. "No one, because I'm going to pilot the Lander."

Norman Taggert then spoke up. "Yeah, that's about the size of it. A museum piece, but we've identified five of them…or at least four and a lot of parts. The two best-preserved lunar landers are LM-2 at the Smithsonian and LM-9 at the Kennedy Space Center. LM-13 and 14 are partially complete and LM-15 is a lot of parts sitting in a Northrop-Grumman warehouse on Long Island. Since you were involved in the original Apollo program, you'll be of invaluable help getting LM-2 and 9 flight-ready as well as updated with the latest computer and engine technology."

Warren McCann eyed McGovern with a look of disbelief. "You're serious, aren't you? You're actually going to fly a fifty-year-old….*exhibit* pulled from the Air and Space Museum down to the lunar surface? Do you have a death wish, Colonel?"

John McGovern leaned closer to the retired engineer. "Mister McCann, we have no choice. We got sloppy. We got sloppy, and we lost the Moon. We were all too busy shopping at Q-Marts, buying everything from toys to TVs to tires for our cars at bargain prices from the Chinese. We never asked where all those profits were going. Maybe we just didn't want to know, but now we do – a massive military space program. We were like cattle being fattened up for slaughter. Using the old Apollo landers is the only way of getting people to the surface, stake our own claim, and not be shut off to our access to space.

Norman and I have come up with a plan that will use Russian spacecraft and technology, an ESA docking module and the two most complete LEMs in our inventory, and we have to get it done in just 60 more days. China's going balls to the wall with fortifying their moon base, as well as some construction effort that we haven't quite figured out yet. We suspect it's a mass driver using magnetic rails to launch equipment or processed materials back to Earth orbit. This would be a clear demonstration to the world of Chinese technical superiority that would only reinforce their case at the UN that they should be recognized as de facto having sole claim to the ice fields. We've got to get there and fast to establish a counterclaim and hang on to it. Look, Mr. McCann, I know you signed a document giving you access to classified information when you got here, so in case you haven't figured it out already, the loss of our first joint attempt with Russia was no accident. The Chinese blew up the station. They're playing hardball, and we have to get in the game. This time we're bringing a bat."

The challenge seemed to breathe a look of youthfulness into the former Grumman engineer. "You know, for the past 13 years since I retired, I spent a lot of time dwelling on what could have been if we hadn't bailed on the moon program back in the 1970s. Yeah, count me in, and you can count on just about every engineer still alive who worked on the Apollo program." McCann shook his head and laughed. "You're going to have the oldest engineering staff in history. The design department's going to look like a senior's retirement home, but by God, we'll get the job done. Now, let's see the rest of your plans on just how you're going to get this half-assed cobbled up mission back to the Moon."

While the three men pulled up technical drawings on their computers and traded ideas, another plan, that of Chinese Space Intelligence chief, Sung Zhao, was coming together 22,500 miles above the Earth.

CHAPTER THREE

Space, Geosynchronous Orbit above the Continent of Africa

To call it a spaceship would almost give the collection of fuel tanks, structural tubing and rocket motors too much credit. That is, if you could even see it at all. It was black, black as the inside of a coal bin at midnight, coated with layers of radar absorbing material, the same stuff used to cover stealth bombers and fighters. Tzen Qui, a Chinese military astronaut, sat wedged into a space from which he could barely move. He was thankful that at least he was weightless. With his absorbent undergarment already soaked through, the lower half of his flight suit was damp with urine, filling the tiny cabin with the sweet acrid stench of a men's room at a train station. A few hours into his mission, Tzen Qui deeply regretted accepting a second cup of green tea. Fortunately, the mission's planners had seen to it that he was given plenty of laxatives and no solid food before lifted off from the moon base, or it would have been a lot worse. The pills they gave him killed his hunger and kept him alert, but still, he would have another three more days of torture on his way back to the Moon once his task was accomplished.

Tzen's mission planners were very accurate about programming his course. Now he could see his goal, silhouetted against the impossibly beautiful blue and white vista of the Indian Ocean, less than 23,000 miles away. It was the size of a bus, dwarfing his tiny craft. As it grew even larger, he felt like a guppy approaching a whale.

The Pan-African satellite gleamed in the unfiltered sunlight of outer space, its gold anodized panels and blue solar cells sparkling like some enormous jewel. Tzen Oui fired his thrusters to kill all but a tiny bit of his craft's forward motion. Slowly, he approached the satellite that provided all telephone, computer and video communication for the African continent. It also served the purpose of monitoring weather and crop patterns, vital to Africa's struggling economy. Its $2.8 billion cost strained the budgets of the participating nations, but it was deemed vital if those nations were ever to climb out of the Third World poverty pit in which their populations resided.

The object on the long boom at the front of Tzen's ship was about the size and shape of a brick with a plastic bubble in the front, filled with a jelly-like substance. The pilot fired his thrusters again and approached the satellite, closing the distance at a crawling pace of two meters per minute. He dared not strike the satellite too hard with the device and damage it, or the mission would be a failure. Slowly, ever so slowly, Tzen made contact with the satellite. His craft's aft thrusters gave a final nudge, and the brick made contact, bursting the thin walled bag of jelly. This caused it to instantly harden in the vacuum of space, gluing the device securely to its target. Tzen Qui exhaled so loudly that he startled himself, not realizing he had been holding his breath. He backed his craft away from the Pan-African satellite, and a smile of satisfaction broke across his face. He could go home to his base now – home to real food and a hot shower to wash away the stench of his bodily fluids.

Tzen turned his head to look once again at the satellite before engaging his main engine to loop around the Earth and return to the Moon, invisible to prying eyes and radar. In just seven days, if the timer functioned as designed, that magnificent monument to the technological prowess of mankind in the 21st century would be nothing more than an orbiting pile of scrap metal. Tzen's superiors would see to it that the only nation capable of averting financial disaster for the Pan-African nations would be China, earning his nation the world's gratitude and respect.

****

One day in Washington had turned into three that included a visit by

McGovern, Norm Taggert and former Grumman Engineer McCann, to the Smithsonian Air and Space Museum. The three men made a beeline to the Apollo exhibit, inspecting the LEM when they were pointedly told by a security guard to get away from the lunar lander until Colonel McGovern and NASA Director Taggert produced their credentials. The three men were quickly escorted to the curator's office. At first, the man, Jeffry Sobowsky, was incredulous that NASA was going to remove his prized exhibit and when informed of just why it was being taken away, doubted not only the sanity of the plan but of Taggert and McGovern as well. However, upon reflection, Sobowsky, a former military officer and pilot, had to agree it was the only way to get personnel down to the surface of the Moon right now. Then a sense of pride filled the curator as he realized that "his" LEM, for decades chained to the Earth by budget cuts that scrubbed the final Apollo missions, would fly at last. Sobowsky thought of the gold foil wrapped craft as some great bird of prey, finally set free from its cage to fulfill its destiny in the sky. The meeting ended well with Jeff Sobowsky choked with emotion when he learned that the man in front of him, Colonel John McGovern, would actually be the one to touch down on the Moon at the controls of his prized exhibit. As the three men departed, he hurried over to begin closing the exhibit wing to await the crew that would disassemble and remove the lander.

CHAPTER FOUR

Johnson Space Center, Houston, Texas

The early morning sun bathed John McGovern's room at the Clear Lake Hilton in shades of gold. It was 7:15 in the morning, and he and Norman Taggert would be meeting with NASA program engineers at 8:30. The Space Center was less than a half mile from his hotel, but with the attempt on McGovern's life and the destruction of the moon station, no one was taking any chances. A car would pick up the two men at eight, giving them just enough time for a quick breakfast. Putting on his uniform jacket, Colonel McGovern pulled a card from his pocket that he had placed there days ago. It was the ticket to redeem his car, still parked at the Albany Airport.

Crap, he thought to himself, *I was in short-term parking. This is going to cost me a mint. Well, I shouldn't complain. I have a government expense account once again, along with my dignity.*

Entering the Space Center was an emotional experience for McGovern. Fourteen months before, he had been forced out of NASA, all but disgraced for his belief that many in the space administration called delusional about China's real intentions in space. However, even McGovern was dumbfounded when the space station that the Chinese had just completed, fired up its rocket motors and set course for the Moon, deploying a lunar habitat, followed by a crew of three in a lander. In the weeks and months that followed, their base was enlarged and more personnel were added, bringing the permanent Chinese contingent to sixteen. Setting up the base at the Moon's South Pole just beyond the near side horizon allowed the Chinese to keep all of their activities hidden from any observers on Earth.

Two modified surveillance satellites sent into lunar orbit ceased to function before completing a full orbit to transmit any data back to Earth. Just two weeks before, NASA, working with the Russian Federal Space Agency, using a Soviet-built Salyut Space Station taken from storage and propelled by an American Antares rocket, set course for the Moon. Even if the United States and Russia had been beaten to the Moon by China, they were going to at least have a permanent presence in lunar orbit. The station could be manned by a crew of two with supplies and personnel shuttled between the International Space Station and the Moon using modified Soyuz spacecraft. This would have to do until Project Constellation would be ready, 18 months from then. It would be America's return to the Moon, but after running into delays and cost overruns, Russia was added as an international partner.

The *Ares I* was complete and had been serving as the crew and equipment ferry to the International Space Station since retiring the space shuttle fleet in 2011, but the much larger *Ares V* was behind schedule and overbudget. It would have been delayed even further without incorporating technology from the massive Russian Energia booster rocket. The Energia, with its 12 million pounds of thrust, was discontinued after the cancellation of the *Buran* space shuttle that it was designed to carry, but several were built and two were actually flown. Adding design components from the Energia shaved a year and several billion dollars off the project. Once again, as it was with the International Space Station, Russian participation became invaluable, sweeping many thorny political issues under the rug. The other key component to a return to the Moon was the Lunar Surface Access Module, or LSAM. This would be the craft that would touch down on the Moon and carry a crew of four. The new high-tech lander also would not be ready for another year, and that was being optimistic. The pace of development meant that the return mission to the Moon by the United States, along with Russian participation, would occur in July 2020, just in time to celebrate the 51st anniversary of the first Moon landing. Now, that timetable had been moved up from 18 months to 60 days, and in just moments, Norman Taggert and John McGovern would be addressing a conference room full of NASA engineers to explain just how this had to be done.

The eight NASA engineers all stood as a sign of respect when Director Norman Taggert and Colonel John McGovern entered the conference room. There were quite a few "welcome backs" accorded both men.

Norman Taggert spoke first. "Gentlemen, and uh…lady…good to see you again, Rebecca…as you are most certainly aware, there's been a complete shake up here at NASA since the loss of the moon station just one week ago. President Price relieved Jason Cumbers of his position as director of the agency and convinced me to come back, ending my…ah retirement, as well as my new career as an aerobatic pilot. By order of the President, that pleasure is strictly off limits now that I have been reactivated to this post. All of you are here today because all of you have taken a good deal of heat from the former director for thinking outside of the box. Well, let me tell you, right now we need people who think so far outside of the box they can bend down, pick it up, and toss it out the window. The reason we need creative thinking is we're going back to the Moon, and this time we're putting people down on the surface. Not for a visit, but to stay long term and we're not waiting 18 eighteen months to do it. We're going to do it in less than 60 days."

That brought a mummer to the gathered assembly of engineers. Bob Nagle spoke first. "*Sixty days?!* Even if we had the *Ares V* ready for launch, the *Altair* LSAM is nowhere near complete. If we pushed it with double personnel and 24-hour shifts, we couldn't shave more than four or five months off that schedule."

"I know that, Bob, and so do the Chinese. Now, you are all grade one security clearance, so it's about time you know. This news will confirm what I'm sure that you all suspect. The moon station was destroyed by an anti-satellite weapon, not a meteor. The Chinese have launched three rockets bound for the Moon over the past three days, and one of them was huge, packing nearly 14 million pounds of thrust.

They're engaged in a sizable construction project just this side of the lunar horizon where we can see them. But what worries us is what's going on below the horizon where we can't see what they're doing. It certainly has us concerned, as well as our Russian partners. Now in about an hour, we're going to video link to an engineering conference with the ESA and the Russian Space Agency to start to integrate our plans, because each agency holds a piece of the solution to make this happen. So, without any more comments from me, I'll let Colonel McGovern go over what he and I, along with one of the original Apollo engineers, have come up with. Taggert then motioned to McGovern to join him. "You all know John, and I'm sure you all know how he was treated when he tried to alert the space agency as well as his country to this threat. Well, now he's back at the behest of both President Price and President Simonov of Russia. John will address you about the plan. God knows he's earned it after the crap he's had to take. It'll be your jobs and the jobs of the Russians and the European aerospace engineers to make it work. It's our best chance and our only chance to grab a piece of the lunar ice fields and hang on to it."

With that, John McGovern stood up. He was not the kind of man who would rub it in about his correct assessment of the Chinese goals nor revel in satisfaction of his nemesis, Jason Cumbers' dismissal. He just squared his shoulders, made eye contact with everyone in the room and began. "We don't have a lot of time, so I'll cut to the chase with Norm's and my plan. It's the best we can do with what we have sitting on the shelf. Don't dwell on what we don't have, that won't help. Try to figure out how to make this work with what we do have. As before with the moon station, our plan is to use one of the Russian Salyuts that they have in storage. This time we're going to mount it to one of the two multi-docking port modules that the Europeans have built for their planned space lab and manned orbiting observatory. Because this configuration will be quite a bit heavier, we're going to need to use the Earth Departure Stage from the *Ares V*. There's one that's complete and one that can be ready in thirty days if we push it. This will get a crew of six into lunar orbit. We will again use a Soyuz as a transfer ship, traveling between the Moon and the ISS."

Rebecca Bennick raised her hand to interrupt McGovern. "Okay, Colonel, I can see how that can get us there, but how about getting down to the surface? We have nothing ready to land on the Moon."

A smile broke across the face of John McGovern. It was the kind of smile that crosses the face of a poker player when he lays out his hand and reaches over to rake in his winnings. "Actually, Doctor Bennick, that is already being attended to right now. Two of the original lunar landers from the Apollo program are being disassembled for shipping to a Northrop-Grumman Aerospace facility for refurbishment. They'll be made flight-ready with considerable technical upgrades, and we'll use these to get our crew down to the surface."

That brought an upsurge in volume in the comment of the engineers with junior engineer Roger Calloway looking just a bit incredulous. "Sorry if I'm just a bit skeptical, Colonel, but the remaining LEMs are over 50 years old. Actually flying them down to the lunar surface is a considerable risk."

"That's a risk that I'm going to have to take because I plan to fly one of them myself. As for the condition of these vehicles, two are pristine and have sat in the controlled environment of the Smithsonian Museum and the Kennedy Space Center for many years. Two others are mostly complete and are also in museums with temperature and humidity controls, and one is in parts, sitting in a warehouse at Northrop-Grumman Aerospace on Long Island. There's nothing wrong with these landers, and phase one is to upgrade their computer and navigation systems with 21st century components. Hell, my Ford has more computing power than the original systems in the LEM. Second, we need to upgrade the descent engine. The goal of the Apollo program was to put men down on the Moon in a fairly narrow equatorial band of latitude. We have to put our LEMs down at the lunar South Pole and probably in the dark. This will require a much longer burn time and, of course, more fuel, but we have much more efficient rocket motors today than existed in the 1960s, so I can't see any insurmountable obstacle to this. We just have to come up with the right motors and fit them into the original landers. The trick is to modify an *Ares I* rocket or a Titan IV to place the landers into Earth orbit to be integrated into the moon ship that we're planning. One more problem: We need to come up with some sort of habitat that can be dropped on to the lunar surface for our crews. I feel confident you'll come up with an answer for that one. Your job for the next hour or so is to hash out the best ways to proceed on this, and then we'll be joining the Russian and European engineers by video conference.

Fred Withers, now nearing sixty with his white hair contracting sharply against his black skin, spoke up. "After all the crap I took from the former director, I was going to be out of here next month with a new career with Bigelow Aerospace. They're going to place a series of inflatable space stations into low Earth Orbit. I'm pretty sure we can get them to modify their design to work on the Moon as a habitat for our people."

Norman Taggert chuckled and then added with sarcasm. "Careful, Fred, you've gotten out of your box again. I mean *really!* Using *private* enterprise in a *government* program? Okay, as soon as we're done here, please get on the horn to Bigelow Aerospace and discuss this with them. I'm putting you in charge of coming up with a surface habitat."

Over the following hour, a consensus formed between all involved that the plan could work. The coordination with Russia and the ESA was vital, but the part that was making everyone nervous was the use of 50-year-old lunar landers. George Metzger, the senior propulsion engineer, pulled up several choices of newer technology rocket motors that could replace the old hypergolic system on the LEM. At a quarter of a million miles from Earth, engine failure would mean no hope of rescue. Hypergolic fuels ignite on contact, eliminating the potential for an ignition system failure. This was a safety concern in the late 1960s when such systems were considered the only reliable choice, but the trade-off was that hypergolic fuels produced a much lower specific impulse or thrust, shorter burn times and added extra weight to the LEM. Since Apollo, rocket technology developed for the shuttle and a host of other spacecraft could ensure reliable ignition with far better performance, nearly doubling the LEM's "linger time" before having to set down. The flight path to the lunar South Pole would be longer, and with the landing area in darkness, there was every possibility that the lander might be fired on by the Chinese. Due to this, Colonel McGovern stated that the lander needed to be armed with some sort of defensive system and electronic counter measures.

It was decided that Fred Withers and Rebecca Bennick would be on a flight to Nevada at the conclusion of the meeting. There they would begin immediate discussions with Bigelow Aerospace on manufacturing an inflatable lunar habitat. Just as the final brainstorming session ended, Yuri Zhdanov of the Russian Space Agency and his engineering team were signing in to the video conference.

A smile crossed Norman Taggert's face as the Russian director's face appeared on the screen. "Yuri! *Kak dil-ah! Nu kak taviyet simmyah?*

The Russian director appeared pained. "Hello Norman. Yes I am fine and so is my family…but tell me, why have you not been arrested as yet for murdering the Russian language with your dreadful American accent?"

"I could ask you the same thing. Chemical warfare has been banned, yet you tried to kill me with your bag of two-month-old socks Velcroed above my sleeping nook!"

Director Zhdanov chuckled and broke into a wide grin. "Ah, those were the days, my friend, aboard Mir. You were quite the celebrity, you know. The first American to train at Star City and the first to co-pilot a Soyuz. We have seen each other far too rarely since those times."

"Well, with what's going on right now with the Chinese, I think we'll be seeing a lot more of each other and very soon. They launched three more rockets in the past three days."

A look of concern crossed Zhdanov's face. "Yes indeed. The first Chinese craft arrived this morning in lunar orbit and yet another lander was deployed along with an equipment module. The second craft will arrive tomorrow, and the third is a monster carrying a massive cargo section. Our observations confirm your suspicion of a mass driver under construction on the near side so they can fire mined ore back to Earth orbit, but you may not be aware that large sections of mirror are being erected near the mass driver."

McGovern spoke up. "Any ideas on what they might be doing with those?"

"Yes Major...oh I see…sorry…*Colonel* McGovern. Our engineers believe they are building a solar smelter, using focused sunlight to refine aluminum and titanium ore from the lunar soil into pure ingots for shipment back to Earth orbit. Their demonstration of their *peaceful* exploitation of the Moon will weigh heavily in their favor at the United Nations when they seek to legitimize their claim to the lunar ice fields. It is their activities beyond the near side horizon that worries me and all of us. It would appear they are fortifying their base as a military outpost."

Norm Taggert shook his head in grudging agreement. "God, I wish it weren't so. We're carrying our greed and our violence out to the stars. Two good men have already died trying to get a foothold for us." Taggert's introspective musing then stopped and focused to the job at hand. "We're not going to back down on this, not the USA, and I'm certain you're not going to either. We have a plan that will work. We're just waiting for Heinrich Stohler of the ESA to join us and we'll get down to details."

The wait wasn't long. Within five minutes, Stohler of the European Space Agency signed in. His English carried only a slight hint of his German heritage. "Ah, sorry for the delay," he said. "I wanted to review NASA Director Taggert and Colonel McGovern's recommendations for this mission. While the plan carries risks that at any other time would be considered unacceptable, I believe we have no other option. Our Chinese friends have just announced to the world that they will begin supplying pure refined and processed ores to some of the world's poorest nations as a gesture of good will. Not only have they gotten to the Moon first, they are winning the propaganda battle as well. Your idea of using the docking core of our Space Lab has merit, but I've not had any agreement from our French partners on this. They are very reluctant to release it for this project. I believe that their president would prefer to accommodate the Chinese, rather than confront them on this issue."

Zhdanov spoke up. "We know that President Laurent has just signed an agreement to sell the Chinese government pelletizing technology for safer nuclear fuel storage. It was reported to be worth 20 billion to the French economy. I think they would be very reluctant to jeopardize that deal. Although I expect President Simonov will call him directly to make an appeal for his participation."

Norman Taggert shook his head in disgust. "Here we go. It'll be back to calling fast food potatoes *Freedom Fries* again."

McGovern then added, "Maybe if the French knew it was missile launch that took out the moon station it would embarrass Laurent into an agreement on the project. We can't keep it a secret forever."

"No John," replied Taggert, "I know you have your battle sword drawn on this, but the longer we go without the PRC realizing we know they wasted our station and killed those men, the better off we are. You'll get your shots in."

McGovern shook his head in both disgust and anger over their loss. "When I held onto Roy Jackson's widow as she cried her eyes out, I *knew* that was no damn meteor and I *knew* for sure it was no accident. I'm personally going to kill the son of a bitch who ordered his ship destroyed. You can say what you want, Norm, but this is personal. Trust me, I'm not going to let my emotions cloud my judgment, but I'll see to it whoever killed Roy Jackson and the Russian colonel will pay for what they did."

As it would turn out, the French President was no fool. Once he was secretly made aware of the evidence that two heroic men in an unarmed ship had been murdered in cold blood, his attitude changed.

France was still recovering from Laurent's predecessor and the way the former leader and his party caved in to the demands of Muslim radicals. This included a reference to France saving on dye for their national flags by eliminating the colors of red and blue in favor of all white. France had already been paid for most of the Chinese purchase. For a few hundred million Euros, they were willing to part with their share of the docking module, along with one other concession – a French astronaut had to be part of the mission. Having no other alternatives, Russia and the United States agreed. Within 48 hours, the docking module was on an Airbus "Beluga," bound for the Kennedy Space Center.

One of the German engineers, Hans Horenburg, addressed his Russian counterpart over the video link. "If we all are to meet this timeline of 60 days, you will need to ready another Salyut station for launch. We have a few former East German engineers on staff that worked in the USSR prior to 1989. We can make arrangements to have them, along with anyone else you need, flown to Baikonur to assist with getting the craft launch ready."

Under normal circumstances, a strong dose of Russian pride might have resulted in a polite, "No thank you." However, with this situation being anything but normal, Director Zhdanov accepted the offer without hesitation.

The international meeting continued for another three hours with plans being made for the refurbishment of the two Apollo-era landers as well and the construction of new docking collars for the two spider-like crafts. Stress points and material specifications of the Salyut would be gathered and sent to NASA for adapting the EDS engine to propel the craft, and a call went out to the CIA in Langley, Virginia, to dispatch a high ranking official to meet with the French government to apprise them of the true facts concerning the loss of the moon station. If there were no insurmountable issues with Bigelow Aerospace in converting one of its inflatable space stations for use as a lunar habitat, then everything looked like it would be moving ahead smoothly.

CHAPTER FIVE

China: The Xichang Satellite Launch Center

Space Intelligence Director Sung Zhao stood under the hard yellow-orange glow of a sodium lamp illuminating the entrance to a secure blockhouse at the Xichang Military Launch Center. The freezing wind picked up and swirled a dusting of snow about his feet that had fallen earlier in the day. In the interplay of light and shadow from the single overhead light, Zhao's scar, running from just below his eye to his chin, was a crevasse, an ugly gash giving his face a ghastly mask-like appearance. Illuminated in the distance, entrapped in a maze of steel supports was yet another rocket being loaded with cargo and supplies, destined for the South Pole Lunar Base. It was nearly midnight. Sung Zhao lit a cigarette and waited in the bitter cold for his superior, Beijing's head of intelligence, Hua Kim Fong.

With the chilled earth numbing his feet and his cigarette nearly gone, a car pulled up in front of the building and disgorged Fong. He was quite tall as well as broad, giving ample evidence of his Korean ancestry. The man approached Zhao with a look that told him not all might be going according to plan. Sung Zhao bade him to enter the concrete and steel reinforced building so that they might converse in warmth as well as privacy. The interior's heat caused Fong's eyeglasses to mist over, and he pulled them away from his face to wipe away the moisture. A solitary technician sat reviewing a series of procedures on a computer monitor. However, when he saw the two men enter, he immediately stood up and grabbed his coat, exiting the building to wait outside in the freezing mid-February darkness. Turning to go, the man he did his best to avert his eyes to keep from staring at Zhao's ghastly scar.

Zhao bowed to his superior, and the two men sat in gray metal chairs across from each other.

Director Fong opened his thin case, produced a report and placed it in front of Sung Zhao on the small table, then spoke. "The Americans and their Russian partners are planning a second mission to the Moon. This time they have added the Europeans. I thought that you assured me destruction of their first attempt would sow the seeds of discord between Russian and America."

For a moment, the self-confidence of Sung Zhao seemed to drain away, but only for a moment. "Honorable Director. I had said the destruction of their moon station would most *likely* cause discord between the Russians and the Americans. If this has not happened, we have still bought ourselves many months to strengthen our position on the Moon. Our generous actions toward the nonaligned and oppressed nations of the world will assure us the position of sole possessor of the Moon's resources. Secondly, even with America, Russia and Europe combined, they cannot reach the lunar surface. Their lander, the *Altair*, is still over a year away from completion."

Director Hua Kim Fong considered this before speaking, but then he felt he should caution Zhao. "Sun Tzu said many hundreds of years ago to never underestimate your enemy. I trust that you have read *The Art of War*, Zhao? Our intelligence agents report that at both Washington's Smithsonian Air and Space Museum and the Kennedy Space Center, fully functional lunar landers from the Apollo era have been disassembled, removed and shipped to a Northrop-Grumman Aerospace facility. We must assume they intend to use these crafts to reach the lunar surface."

Zhao's face, normally immobile, registered a disconcerting look of surprise. Disconcerting as it only appeared on the undamaged half of his face. "*Ha*, these Americans are fools to believe that 50-year-old museum displays can match the capabilities of our superior technology. These antiques will serve as their coffins!"

"I hope you are correct, Zhao. Their determination and willingness to take this risk makes me believe they suspect or may even be aware that it was our missile that destroyed their first vessel and not a meteor. Our sources in Kazakhstan have informed us that the Russians have sent an engineering team to inspect and review the condition of their three remaining Salyut Space Stations. I believe they will try to reach the ice fields themselves in short order. You said yourself we do not wish direct confrontation with the West. Rather we want to be awarded our solitary rights to the Moon by world opinion and the United Nations. The Premier himself has voiced his concern that you perhaps chart a dangerous course for China."

Sung Zhao sought to control his annoyance of his superior, but the undamaged half of his face registered his resentment of his plan being questioned. Still, he thought of a response that would resonate with Fong's own nationalism. "Director Fong, over 2,000 years ago, the Empire of the Chin Dynasty developed the science of making chrome alloy for the swords of their warriors, making them the finest instruments of battle on the planet. It was not until the 1930s that the West discovered this technology. The Chin invented the assembly line, again not seen in production until Henry Ford incorporated its use. The Ming Dynasty was once the greatest empire on Earth. We invented gunpowder, rockets, and even paper and optics and medicines. The list of Chinese accomplishments is endless…yet, to the round eyes of the West, we were a simple, backward, peasant people. Even today, what is China to the West? A cheap source of labor to produce their products for their multi-national corporations! When China exercises her right to reclaim her lost province, held illegally by the so-called nationalist government of Taiwan, we are forced to back down and run like dogs with our tails between our legs. Mighty China! Dictated to by that upstart *black woman* of an American President? Yes, we chart a dangerous course, but one with the goal of reaching a shore of unlimited wealth. The nation that controls the Moon controls all access to the space about the Earth. China will reap the riches of the Moon and then the planets. China will be the master, and all other nations will crawl to her, begging for the scraps of our wealth. The world will be remade in the image of China. Those nations who oppose us will shortly find themselves chained to the Earth, unable to gain access to the wealth of space. They will be trapped in a bottle that only we can open. They will wither and die in poverty while China and all who swear loyalty and follow her will be prosperous beyond their wildest dreams!"

Hua Fong sat stunned by the force and the passion of his Space Intelligence Director, but then Fong was a practical man and would not be swept up in Zhao's nationalist vision so easily. "Zhao, your dreams for China are bigger than one world can hold, that is true, but you *must* be certain that we are not opposed by foreign forces on the surface of the Moon or in lunar orbit. We cannot risk the potential of a war with nuclear potential when we are in sight of our goals. Make certain this does not happen."

Sung Zhao, wearing his odd half smile, nodded in agreement. "Yes, Senior Director. You can report to the politburo that all in under control. At the conclusion of our meeting, I will be placing a call to our operatives in Alma-Ata. They will make arrangements with *certain parties* who will ensure this mission of the Western/Russian coalition will never take place. This you have my word on."

"I hope you are correct, Zhao, as there is more to this. The American, John McGovern, has been invited back to NASA and their Air Force. We believe he has been given command of their planned second mission. Our sources of influence in America went to considerable trouble to discredit him."

Anger flashed in Sung Zhao's eyes. "Then this *McGovern* will soon find himself with nothing but piles of scrap to command. However, if he continues to be a source of irritation, well, the world is a dangerous place. In his profession, there are many opportunities for McGovern to meet with an *unfortunate accident*."

* * * *

It was just before 11 p.m. when the video conference ended. John

McGovern and Norman Taggert had been working straight for the past five days with very little in the way of sleep. Both men stepped out into the mild air of Houston's winter night and were greeted by the soft glow of the nearly full Moon. Six months earlier, either man would have looked up at the brilliant orb that dominated the night sky and perhaps reflected on its beauty. Either man might have given thought to an American lunar return mission in 2020. That night however, both men's eyes were fixed upon that battered sphere with a sense of dread, that this object in the sky held something malignant and corrupt. John McGovern stared up in deep concentration until Norm Taggert's voice snapped him out of his thoughts.

"You're thinking about the mission, aren't you, John?"

"Yeah, pretty hard not to. Now we're down to 55 days and counting. I'd been thinking, back before this all started, I'd most likely get a shot at a moon mission. It would be one of the high points of my career, you know, following in Neil Armstrong's footsteps. Now I'm really going, and it'll be me putting a lunar lander down on the surface. Only it'll be a 50-year-old LEM, not the *Altair*, and I won't be coming in peace. I'll be dropping into a war zone, and I don't even know who my copilot is yet."

Taggert nodded in agreement. "I can't say I know how you feel right about now. I can't believe we're turning our Moon into a battlefield, but such is the way of mankind. I'm not even sure who'll be flying down with you, but I suspect it may be Major Vladimir Kutusov. He's certainly qualified, and he's a soldier. Listen, let's get you back to the hotel so you can get some rest. I'll get you back up to Albany on a military flight tomorrow morning so you can bail out your car and get your place closed up. Then I want you back at the Cape in three days to begin getting ready for this mission. Once we work out the bugs, you're going to head over to Star City for training on the Soyuz and Salyut spacecraft and space station, so, you're going to be one very busy man. Come on, let's grab my car, and I'll drive you back."

Northrop-Grumman Aerospace, Saint Augustine, Florida, 12:55 a.m.

Joe Gonzalez glanced at the LED numbers on his pick-up's audio system that showed he was on time for the 1 a.m. shift at the Saint Augustine Northrop-Grumman refit facility. It was a chilly morning in North Florida but he was thankful he was there instead of at their facility in New York, driving in to work in the biting cold that was blanketing the country a thousand miles to the north. Looking up from checking the time, the sight of the vertical tail section of a C-130 cargo plane parked on the apron caught his attention. It was an Air Force turboprop, and Joe knew that none of these aging medium duty haulers was supposed to be at his facility for any upgrades. In fact, the tanker that had arrived earlier in the day for an avionics overhaul had vanished along with the two F-22s that should have been clearly visible in the forward hanger from his vantage point. Then something else caught his eye. The cars of his night shift crew were backed up at the security gate with the individuals inside being double-checked, by not only Tom Corby, who had been the night shift gate guard for years, but also two armed U.S. Marines.

Joe Gonzalez waited in line and then pulled his Ford up to the security gate. Tom, along with one of the Marines, approached to his window, with the soldier playing a flashlight on Joe's face.

The man, a sergeant, motioned to him to roll down his window. "Sir, ID card, please." The request was polite but firm. Joe Gonzalez had been employed with Northrop for more than 20 years, and as the prototype supervisor, his position was the same as lead foreman on all retrofit and upgrade projects. Now, as he sat there with his ID badge out for the scrutiny of the Marine guard, his mind was in a state of confusion.

He spoke quietly to the regular security officer. "Hey, Tom, do you mind telling me what's going on here?"

"Damned if I know, Joe. About an hour ago, that C-130 landed with some Air Force and NASA guys. I suddenly found myself getting some extra help up here at the gate from these two Marines."

As Tom Corby finished his last sentence, the Marine guard handed back Joe's ID card. "You're good to go, sir. Head into the reception building and assemble your crew. The folks inside will brief you as to what's going on."

Once inside, the murmurs of his nightshift crew barely had a chance to escalate in volume when three men went to the front of the room to address Joe's team: one civilian in a dark blue windbreaker with a NASA emblem on it, an Air Force major and a guy that had to be pushing eighty.

The man with the NASA jacket cleared his throat and addressed the assembled nightshift crew. "Gentlemen and ladies, I'm Dominic Blancato, project manager for the American portion of highly sensitive space project. Now, I know you all have security clearance, but the major here is going to give all of you some paperwork to sign that spells out just how sensitive what we're about to discuss is and what sorts of penalties are involved for breaching any part of this security agreement. Is that understood?"

Each member of Gonzalez's crew nodded in the affirmative, signed the papers, and handed them back to the Air Force major.

"Okay then. Rather than telling you about everything here, let's head over to Hangar Nine so we can show you what we've got. Then I'll let Mr. McCann from Northrop-Grumman clue you in on the details."

John Morgan, new to Joe's team and about 22 years old, was wide eyed on the short ride over to the hangar. He was sitting next to his boss. "Gee, Mr. Gonzalez, what'd you think this is all about? You think this is like Roswell and they have a crashed UFO in there?"

Joe chuckled and shook his head. "I think you've been reading too much science fiction, John. But, we'll find out soon enough."

As the nightshift crew and their boss entered the hangar, a look of incredulity crossed everyone's faces. It wasn't an alien spacecraft that greeted their eyes but something almost as amazing. There, sitting in the middle of Hangar Nine was the LM-2 from the Smithsonian Air and Space Museum in Washington – an honest to God 50-year-old

Apollo lunar lander.

The elderly man from Northrop walked across the immaculately clean floor and stood beside a gold foil wrapped landing leg of the spacecraft. "Good to see you all here tonight. My name is Warren McCann, and I was one of the original lead engineers on the Apollo program when we were just known as The Grumman Corporation. I'm back at the request of the company after 13 years of retirement. I'm proud to say I was one of the thousands of men and women back in the Sixties that had the privilege of putting the first Americans on the Moon. Well folks, the reason I'm here tonight is to tell you that we're going back to the Moon. Not two years from now, according to NASA's timetable, but in less than 60 days. And, we're going back with this lander you see behind me, the LM-2, and with the LM-9 from KSC. The LM-9 will arrive here about two hours from now. We felt it best to carry out this operation under the cover of darkness. I'm sure all of you here are well aware that the Chinese beat us to the punch, and I'm certain all of you as Americans are mad as hell about their claim to *own* the Moon's resources. Trust me, that is not going to happen, and America is not going to wave the white flag. We're going back to the Moon, by God, and it's going to be your job as well as those of the other shifts to make both lunar landers flight ready in 45 days. You'll be tearing down every panel, every nut and bolt and pulling every piece of wiring out of both landers. You're going to update them with state of the art computer and radar imaging hardware, new high performance rocket motors and something the original Apollo landers never had – defensive weapons. You're going to have some engineers from Raytheon heading down your way in a few days to integrate modified versions of Patriot missiles that'll be carried by the LEMs. I hate to think of the Moon as the next battlefield, but you can be certain we're not going to get a friendly welcome, and we have to be ready to defend ourselves.

Your job over the next 45 days is to make it happen. All other work has been shifted to Northrop-Grumman facilities in other parts of the country. You and all the other shifts are authorized to use as much overtime as you need to work seven days a week, and you'll have anything you want delivered here in 24 hours or less with just a phone call. Oh yeah, and you're also going to have a bunch of us old farts keeping you company. Every one of the original core of the Apollo lander engineering team still alive, and that would be eleven of us, will be joining you. Now, we want you youngsters to be able to keep up with us, so my crew and I will try not to go too fast for you. Okay then, I'll turn this meeting over to Major Stollman, who'll discuss the integration of the weapons systems on the LEMs."

And so it went for another hour half. The drone of a second C-130 began to reverberate through the hangar, announcing the arrival of the second LEM from the Kennedy Space Center's Moon Landing display. With the meeting concluded, Joe Gonzalez stepped outside. As the aircraft descended toward the runway, Joe's eyes caught site of the brilliant, nearly full moon bathing the facility in soft, almost misty silver light.

The Moon, he thought, *we're going back to the Moon and, by God, I'm going to be a part of it. My crew and I are about to make history.*

* * * *

At the very moment that Joe Gonzales turned his gaze from the sky and went back inside Hangar 9, the next phase of Sung Zhao's plan began. Twenty-two thousand five hundred miles in space, the timer on the brick-shaped explosive device reached zero. Circuits closed as a minute charge of electricity reached the detonator. In milliseconds, the first tiny explosion began to propagate through the brick of C-4 material that had been planted days earlier by the Chinese space pilot. In the blink of an eye, the bus-sized gold and blue hexagonal satellite began to deform and bend at the center, as if some invisible force was in the act of snapping it in two. In less than a thirtieth of a second, the silent vacuum-shrouded blast tore the glittering jewel to shreds, leaving only a trail of debris to circle the Earth.

It was just after seven in the morning with the rays of the early sun slanting through the windows of the Nairobi National Bank. Akello Mbugua, a young woman with big ambitions at one of Africa's leading financial institutions, had just logged into the bank's secure network to begin her day. She was in an hour early, as was her custom. Akello had turned away from her monitor to arrange some papers on her desk. When she looked again, the screen, instead of displaying lines of international transactions, was blank. For over a half hour, she tried to sign back in, but to no avail.

At exactly the same moment in Dodoma, Tanzania, the Pan-African News Network's signal ceased to be received. Cell phones stopped working, and the newly formed African Commodities Market lost contact with the outside world. Africa, the last continent to begin to integrate fully into the 21st century, had forgone the kinds of redundant infrastructure of miles of telephone cable and microwave repeaters seen in the West, in favor of direct satellite communications. Suddenly, the member nations of the Pan-African Alliance, formed in 2012 to bring their Third World economies out of the economic basement, were blind, deaf and dumb. As the rotation of the Earth swept more nations across the African continent sunward, panic in government and financial institutions began to grow with the brightening of the morning sky. The nearly $3 billion multi-function satellite that served African nations from Somalia to Senegal had ceased to function. Desperate calls went out to the Hughes Aerospace Corporation to determine the nature of the problem. When the satellite couldn't be raised, a call went out to NORAD, the North American Aerospace Command. NORAD, in the days of the Cold War, stood ready to track incoming Soviet ICBMs. Now, NORAD's most important job was tracking the thousands of objects in orbit about the Earth, alerting nations to the re-entry of space junk as well as watching out for potential collisions between the cast-offs of the Space Age and weather, communications and surveillance satellites. NORAD's radars no longer showed a solid refection at the orbital location of the Pan-African satellite but rather hundreds of tiny pieces following the same orbital track. The only conclusion was the satellite had been destroyed by either a meteor or an errant piece of space junk. Once it was confirmed the satellite was gone, emergency calls went out from the member African nations to build and launch a replacement as soon as humanly possible, regardless of the costs involved.

By late afternoon, the Pan-African Nations were trying to pick up the pieces of their shattered communications system as financial markets collapsed. Not only did the satellite carry the electronic encoding of millions of bytes of information that represented billions of dollars in revenue, but it also was designed to monitor weather as well as agricultural growth and water currents for the harvesting of seafood. All those badly needed functions suddenly were gone.

Late afternoon on the African continent was early morning in Houston Texas. John McGovern had just dressed and made use of the in-room coffee maker. The television was on in the background, but when the CNN announcer began to tell about the loss of the Pan-African satellite, McGovern's ears perked up. He grabbed the remote and turned up the volume. Listening to the report, the idea that a meteor or a piece of space junk had taken a satellite out in geosynchronous orbit seemed absolutely absurd. A person stood a better chance of being struck by lightning while holding the winning Powerball ticket than having a meteor strike such a target. Again, the word *meteor* stuck in John McGovern's thoughts. *Too damn many coincidences here involving meteors. Someone deliberately destroyed that satellite, and I have a damn good idea I know who. I just don't know why...yet.*

* * * *

"General Wang, please convey my most sincere congratulations to the young officer who preformed his mission so successfully. The explosive device planted on the Pan-African Satellite eliminated the target."

Sung Zhao replaced the encrypted lunar communications telephone back into its cradle before turning to his subordinate officer. "So Chun, the plan advances with great speed and success. Have you contacted Admiral Shen as I have ordered?"

Agent Chun bowed to his superior officer. "Yes sir, I have. The admiral has dispatched the vessel with the equipment that you have requested. Everything will be in place before the date that your plan requires."

A smile on the undamaged side of his face acknowledged his satisfaction with his subordinate. "Very good. Well done. The date has not yet been set by the Americans, but all will be ready when it is announced. However, ten days from now, Captain Tso must be in position to perform a test of his weapon. Is that understood?"

"Yes sir. The commander is eager to see for himself the effects of the device."

"Good. You may go now, Chun. I will speak with you tomorrow morning."

* * * *

Colonel John McGovern's Berkshire home was still cloaked in a blanket of dazzling white from the snow that had fallen during his return from Colorado. That was eight days ago. *Eight days and a lifetime*, he thought. McGovern had gone from disgraced former air force officer and former astronaut, the butt of conspiracy theory jokes, to the visionary who seemed to perceive the future. Now, instead of living in the shadows, he was in the spotlight, reinstated and promoted by the President of the United States and leading the second moon mission. This time, not only leading it, but also flying a Lunar lander down to the surface and establishing a beachhead in hostile territory.

John's suitcases were packed with a variety of warm and cold weather gear. Two weeks at the cape and then three more in Moscow's Star City, going from tropical to near arctic in the month of March. Replacing the spark plugs on his three motorcycles, their cylinders filled with protective oil, he looked around his place. The warm pine walls of the A-frame house, his fireplace now cold, the damper shut and the photograph of his ex-wife put away. *Cheryl: The worst part of the divorce was how you refused to stand by me…to believe me and support me when I was sure I was right. You even tried to push me into psychological counseling, like I was some kind of paranoid nut case. Well, I was right all along, but it's too late for us now. Some wounds just don't heal.*

A dark blue Chevrolet with U.S. Air Force plates pulled up in front of his chalet-like home. As a junior officer exited the car and knocked on the door, an old but appropriate tune was playing in McGovern's head … *And I think it's gonna be a long, long time, 'til touchdown brings me 'round again to find … Yeah, that's me … Rocket Man."*

John locked his front door and took a long hard look around his surroundings, his eyes drinking in the beauty of the snow covered Massachusetts landscape.

"Are you ready to go, sir? I'll help you with your bags."

At the same moment that McGovern shut the passenger side door of the staff car, Sung Zhao's plan was entering its next phase, gliding silently below the waves, moving into firing position.

CHAPTER SIX

Florida, Kennedy Space Center

Colonel McGovern was relaxed, shaved and showered after a morning workout that included a three-mile run on the beach at the Space Center. He was wearing his usual lightweight blue pants and a white polo shirt adorned with a NASA emblem. McGovern projected the look of the classic astronaut – trim, athletic, in his early forties with slightly thinning sandy brown hair and endowed with a quick smile and confident walk. He was back to the man he was before everything hit the fan. He figured this meeting on mission planning should only last about 40 minutes and then he could get back to running simulations on the lunar lander. Even though the landers were being retrofitted with computers and electronics a hundred times more advanced than the original components, he would still be flying a spacecraft down to the surface of the Moon that was older than he was. The rocket motors on the LEM were undergoing retrofits and upgrades as well. In an ironic twist, the motor best suited to get the LEM to the surface was an updated version of the N-1 engine. There were about twenty of the new series available from the Russian Energia complex. The irony was that the N-1 was to have been the rival Soviet mission to the Moon at the height of the Space Race. In a way, it was a posthumous vindication for Ukrainian engineer, Sergei Korolev, that a piece of his massive moon rocket would at last make the journey to the surface of the Moon, McGovern thought.

There simply wasn't time to try to build a new landing craft from scratch. The two lunar landers for this mission had been taken from the Smithsonian Air and Space Museum in Washington and the Apollo display at KSC. There were enough parts for the two additional landers that were placed in storage and these would be fitted with the more powerful and less thirsty Russian motors. McGovern and his co-pilot would have about 28 minutes, double the time of the original rocket motors, to find a level area at the lunar South Pole and set down. With all those mountains ringing the basin floor, once below a thousand meters they'd be an easy target. There was very little margin for error, and added to this was the distinct possibility they would face interference in the form of military personnel from the Chinese moon base.

The best plan would be to land as far from the Chinese base and hydrogen production compound as possible and still get to the ice fields. He and his crewmate would have to make the "habitat" operational and possibly defend it from hostile action by the Chinese. Added to this was the fact that the lunar ice fields were in perpetual darkness at the Moon's South Pole. That would mean either putting the Lander down in sunlight and driving to the habitat in a lunar rover or using either infrared or radar to try to land what was essentially a museum exhibit on a pitch-black field of dust and rock covered ice.

This meeting had not been on the schedule but served as a 6 a.m. wake-up call. Norman Taggert's secretary had telephoned to say that he wanted to see him at 8:30 in his office to review crew selection. As far as John knew, the mission he was to command was to be crewed by a French astronaut, a Russian cosmonaut and three other Americans – William Curtis, new to the space program, and Mission Specialist Thomas Garcia and Gordon Vanders, the latter an old hand from the shuttle missions – all well-trained and experienced, not just in space, but the two of them had military backgrounds as well. Neil Armstrong may have come in peace for all mankind in 1969, but now that the Moon was the new focus of economic expansion, peace was becoming just a memory. Humans began doing what they have always done when it came to controlling resources that would dominate world trade, fighting for supremacy and here the stakes were very high. If China developed the resources and production on the Moon and blocked other nations, then the Chinese would succeed in putting the entire world in a box. Caught blind-sided, who would have guessed two years earlier that China would not only have a presence on the Moon but would build a mining and production facility in order to claim the Moon for the PRC? It made McGovern's head spin. He was thinking about this so much he hardly noticed he had reached Norm Taggert's door. A light tap on the glass was all that was needed to bring a response from the other side. Taggert opened the door and greeted McGovern with a warm but slightly hesitant smile. Taggert, the first American to serve a tour of duty aboard the Mir space station in the mid 1990s, still looked fit even though his hair was nearly gone. His handshake was still firm and his blue eyes still had the stars in them. It was said that any man who spent time in space, among the stars, carried them back to Earth in his eyes.

"John, good to see you this morning, thanks for coming down on short notice."

"Well, Norm, you're the boss on this project so here I am. What's up?"

The NASA director walked over to the coffeepot. "Coffee, John?"

"Ah, no thanks, I'm going to run a landing simulation, and you know how the guys in medical are. They'll be watching my heart rate, so I don't need any extra caffeine in my system to cause them to question my cardiac fitness."

"Sure John, I understand. Ah, how are the simulations checking out?"

McGovern's intuition said something was not quite right, so he decided to push the question. "Come on Norm, you didn't invite me in for small talk on the simulator runs or to buy me a cup of coffee, so what's up?"

Norman Taggert took a deep breath. "John, I'm project director of the American part of the mission, but I still have to answer to a higher authority, the President of the United States, and she has to keep our united front together with all the players – Europe, Russia, you know. We can't allow China an exclusive hold over the Moon, but this is turning out to be as much a political as a military mission. There are a lot of countries in the Third World; many non-aligned nations would just love to see China rub our noses in the dirt. They buy into the Chinese promise of direct aid and technology for their nations, once China secures its exclusive claim to lunar resources. The Chinese have been making good on those promises as well. They'll be sending refined ore back to Earth; it'll be placed in drop shields and parachuted to receiving areas in Africa, Asia and South America. We can't have so much American domination of the mission, so we're undertaking some … eh ... personnel changes on the mission. Captain Vanders is out. He's being replaced by a Canadian."

McGovern looked a little as if someone had hit him in the gut and his thoughts ran to his command of the mission. *Would I still be leading the expedition?* "Okay Norm, what's the situation? Am I out as mission commander?"

"No, no, of course not, John. You're still technically in command of the landing mission."

McGovern frowned. "*Technically* in command? What the hell is that supposed to mean?"

"Okay, okay, it means you are in command of the mission once you land on the moon. A decision was made to have the Russian cosmonaut command the mission from the Earth to lunar orbit."

"All right … I guess I don't have a problem working with Major Kutuzov. He knows what he's doing."

Taggert looked down at his desk and took a deep breath. "It's not going to be Kutuzov who'll command the out bound mission. It's going to be Cosmonaut Natasha Polyakova."

McGovern's face became noticeably redder as his voice got louder. Anger was slowly creeping into his emotions. Politics had gotten the first mission crew killed. "Who the hell is Natasha Polyakova?"

"John, she's an experienced cosmonaut who's been running a

department at the training center at Star City for the past three years and she has mission experience. In fact, her father is Doctor Dmitry Polyakov. He spent 438 days aboard Mir in 1991."

"Well unless she also got his flight experience through his DNA, I think that has very little to do with anything. What's *her* mission experience? Does she have any military training? This is not going to be a friendly expedition to the Moon, you know. For God's sake, I may have to put the lander down in the dark! Either that or drive for over an hour to the habitat! If that option's chosen, we may as well paint targets on ourselves as we go motoring across the Moon! The Chinese have an exclusive foothold, and I doubt they're going to have egg rolls and fortune cookies waiting for us when we land – more like guns and anti-personnel rockets. If we start getting shot at, I need someone sitting next to me that can shoot back!"

"She did an eight day mission four years ago to the ISS to resupply food and computer hardware."

"*Really!* Eight whole days? That's it?!"

"John, calm down," Norm tried to say reassuringly. "Back in the Apollo days, very few of our astronauts had more than two weeks total time in space, and today we have fully automated systems. There's not that much to do about getting from the Earth to the Moon except looking out the window. The computers will be doing all the flying. Besides, this was a political decision. Next week is International Woman's Day. John, we're not just fighting the Chinese for control of the Moon, we're fighting for the support of millions of people in many countries here on Earth. We have to show the world that their best interests lie with our international coalition, not with China. Besides, she was an alternate for the Russian Biathlon Olympic team, so she's a crack shot."

McGovern shook his head. "There's a hell of a big difference between shooting at a metal target and a human being whose shooting back at you."

"John, for ten days before the mission, the whole crew will be given intensive military training by Special Forces instructors, everything from firearms to mini rocket launchers and hand-to-hand combat. We are *not* taking any chances on this, believe me."

"Jesus! This sounds like a damn political cluster *you know what!* Kutuzov fought against Chechen terrorist as well as leading the Russian aerial strike force against the Chinese incursion into their Vladivostok territory in 2016. On the lunar surface I need a soldier with me, not some *girl* with political connections playing astronaut like this is some kind of damn game!"

Reassuringly, Taggert reached out to grab John McGovern by both shoulders. "John, it'll be all right. Failure on this mission is not an option, and we are not making you, the crew or anyone else some kind of sacrificial lamb on the altar of politics."

The redness and heat of anger began to drain from McGovern's cheeks. "So, am I supposed to think of something clever when I step out onto the moon? Something memorable like: One small step for Man?"

Taggert dropped his eyes again. "Ah .... Yeah, that's probably going to be one small step for a woman. It was decided that Natasha will exit the Lander first."

Taggert looked up again at John McGovern. He looked a little like a volcano about to explode.

Before he could get another word out, Norman added, "John she's here ... in the conference room. Maybe you'd better meet her, talk to her before you blow your stack. I don't feel great about this. I'm your friend, and I was your advocate when everyone was dumping shit on you. I have to walk a line here. Listen, just talk to her ... okay?"

McGovern, still fuming, looked at Taggert as if he had been sucker punched. Before he could say a word, the center's launch alarms began to blare. John McGovern had been so deep in his training schedule that he had completely forgotten that a Falcon-9 with an unmanned cargo module bound for the International Space Station was launching this morning. Quickly he put down his paperwork, and he and Norm

Taggert headed out the door to view the lift off. He was not even aware of the attractive young woman that exited after them and stood with her eyes turned skyward.

The brilliant yellow-white glare of the Falcon-9 rocket motors' ignition bloomed like a sunrise against the azure blue of the Atlantic Ocean. It took a full 30 seconds for the roar and thunder of the lift off to reach the people gathered outside the director's offices. In that time, the unmanned craft climbed on a tail for fire, breaking through the scattered low hanging clouds and arced out over the Atlantic Ocean. At one minute and ten seconds into the flight, the craft was a brilliant point of light racing into space and then, in a scene eerily reminiscent of that fateful day of January 28, 1986, the sky erupted into an orange fireball that continued to swell and grow, taking the form of a huge white mass, streaked with ugly shades of red. Falling from the explosion-spawned cloud were bits of debris – remnants of a few hundred million dollars worth of machine and cargo.

With tens of thousands of people both at the Cape and the surrounding towns and beaches staring at the spectacle in the sky, 70 miles out to sea, a glistening quartz and silver parabolic mirror on a stainless steel stalk began to slowly retract and sink beneath the waves.

"*Jesus Christ!* What the hell just happened?!" It was Norman Taggert's voice. It came through to McGovern as if he was in a trance, his eyes still glued on the expanding cloud that marked the final moments of the Falcon-9. Next to him, a voice filtered in – feminine with a distinct accent. "*Bozh Moi!* Was there a crew on board?"

John turned his head to meet a pair of blue green eyes the color of the Caribbean Sea, set into one of the most attractive faces he had ever seen. The face was framed with light brown hair and sat atop a slim but shapely figure. The woman was dressed in cream-colored slacks with a pale blue top that carried the emblem of the Russian Federal Space Agency. Colonel McGovern was momentarily taken off guard but he still had his wits about him.

"Ah ... no, no it was an unmanned cargo launch ... but it was carrying a lot of supplies up to the ISS," he said.

A look of relief crossed the woman's face. "Oh, thank God. My first day in America at the space center, and I am witness to a disaster. I am happy no one was aboard."

In John's mind, the pieces then fell into place and he asked, even though he knew the answer. "And you are …"

"I am Natasha Polyakova of the Russian Federal Space Agency. I am here to begin my training for the moon mission with Colonel John McGovern … Is he here?"

"Ah, you're looking at him … *Cosmonaut* Polyakova." Eyeing her up and down, his gaze centered on her pale blue leather Italian high heels. "Most of the areas you'll be working in have computer access flooring. Lose the heels; they'll dent the aluminum panels. Listen, I'd love to stay and chat, but we've just lost a cargo rocket here, and we have a hell of a mess to clean up. My simulations on the LEM are sure to be scrubbed for today. Norm will be jammed trying to figure out what went wrong, so, I'll see you at the LEM simulator tomorrow morning at 7 a.m. *sharp*."

As McGovern was walking away, she called out to him. "Wait … wait, where is the simulator … how do I find it?"

Without even looking back, he shouted, "Figure it out for yourself or ask directions."

* * * *

It was well past midnight when McGovern entered Norm Taggert's office. "Norm, I know you've had a long and difficult day. Any idea what happened to the Falcon?"

Taggert looked up from his computer screen set on a desk covered with hard copy telemetry readouts. "Nothing so far. Everything points to a spike in temperature and pressure in the second stage LOX and RP-1 tanks, like all of a sudden they superheated. This is nothing like *Challenger*. There, one of the SRBs blew out an O-ring and burned a hole through the fuel tank. The Falcon-9's first stage was performing perfectly. The second stage hadn't even fired at that point, so how in the hell did it superheat like that?" Taggert sat shaking his head. "Doesn't make sense. And I know what you're thinking, but no way could this have been sabotage. No one without clearance could have gotten within a mile of that rocket."

"Yeah, maybe you're right, Norm, but I mean the Falcons have had a perfect safety record up 'til now."

Taggert shrugged and then added, "So did the shuttles until *Challenger* and then *Columbia.* What do they say? Shit happens, but I don't think you're here to help me go digging through the telemetry of the explosion."

"No, I guess not. I really wanted to talk with you about my … ah … co-mission commander who I also just leaned is supposed to be my co-pilot in the LEM. Come on, Norm! They send a cosmonaut cadet that looks more like eye candy than a space pilot? Is she here for a beauty contest or to train for a mission? I have to tell you, I'm not happy … not one damn bit. This is a man's job getting down to the surface. Anything might happen. Having this *girl* along could jeopardize the entire mission!"

"John, I know how you feel, but you have to look at it from the political perspective as well. Did you see this?"

McGovern took the newspaper from Norm Taggert's hands and eyed the headline: *Chinese deliver on their promises.* Looking further down the page, he read on: *Today, the first drop shipments of highly purified titanium from China's lunar mining operation arrived via parachute to cheers on the ground in the African Republic of Chad. The Chinese Foreign Minister proclaimed this is just a taste of the future that China will make available to the developing nations of the world. This demonstration will weigh heavily in China's favor in its quest to have a claim on the Moon exempted from the 1967 United Nations Treaty of Outer Space.*

John tossed the paper back on Taggert's desk. "So it's about winning the hearts and minds, is it?"

"That's about the size of it, John, and the reason you're sharing command duties with an attractive female cosmonaut."

McGovern's face belied a sly smile. "Yeah, now that you mentioned it, Norm, I guess she is that attractive I mean. Listen, I'm going to hit the sheets. I plan to have her in the LEM simulator in the morning, and then we'll see if she's just for show or if she has any go. Anyway, don't go crunching your numbers for too long. You say malfunction, but I say something's fishy. I can smell it."

"You've been pretty much on target with everything else, John, so I'll keep looking for anything unusual that might rule out a mechanical malfunction. Oh, and as for your … uh *space cadet*, try not to beat her up too badly. I'm sure she feels as uncomfortable about being used as a political football as you feel about having her replace Major Kutusov."

* * * *

The view out the triangular window was claustrophobic. Every time she shifted the joystick, the extreme contrast between the pitch-black sky and the nearly blinding gray-white landscape made dizzying jumps through the view port. John McGovern looked away from the 24-inch LED display that replaced the myriad of analogue gauges between the pilot and co-pilot's windows. His gaze fell on Natasha's hand. Her long slim fingers were gripping the joystick so tightly they were blanching white at the knuckles.

"Ease off. Keep your wrist loose and try to use smooth corrections." He again looked at the display. Fifty years ago, during the Apollo program, such a display, reading out fuel consumption, altitude and turning radar sweeps into full color images would have been right out of a science fiction film. Still, as cutting edge as the computer and engine upgrades were on the LEM, it was still the pilot that had to bring it in for a soft landing and this pilot was in trouble.

McGovern called out the numbers. "One thousand meters down, 100 ahead, 700 down, 60 ahead, 500 down, 30 ahead … too long, we're going into the red zone!"

The low fuel alarm began bleating out a warning that less than 80 seconds remained until the tanks would run dry. Natasha's stress level began to climb as evidenced in mission control as her heart and respiration rate increased dramatically on the medical monitors. She began trying to bring the LEM down faster but it began to oscillate.

McGovern's voice began to climb in decibels. "Watch your pitch. *Watch your pitch!*"

The black and gray line of demarcation between the lunar surface and the sky began to slide up and out of view. Now Natasha Polyakova and John McGovern were staring down at the crater pocked lunar surface 100 meters below the LEM. The LED display screen showed the Lander was at a 45 degree angle and beginning to rise.

McGovern's voice grew louder. "Fire your thrusters and get us vertical again! *We're gaining altitude*!"

The Lander climbed to 800 meters before Natasha corrected the forward pitch of the craft, with the low fuel alarm still blaring. Then suddenly an almost pleasant disembodied female voice began to speak.

"Thirty seconds to engine shut down … 28 seconds to engine shut down."

Natasha's hand steadied on the joystick and the craft was now dropping vertically, just passing the 500 meter mark when … "Engine shut down in five, four, three, two, one…" The LEM, now without power, plummeted the last 500 meters to the lunar surface. Despite the Moon's one-sixth gravity, the fall was still the equivalent of 250 feet on Earth, the height of a twenty-story building.

The horizon shifted as the craft tumbled toward a fatal impact, the ground rushing up to claim them and … then, the lights in the simulator came on.

McGovern turned to his white-faced co-pilot and in a sarcastic tone addressed her. "Well, congratulations *Space Cadet Polyakova*, you managed to kill us both quite nicely. Oh, not as dramatically as when you crashed us into that mountain on simulator run No. 1, but it was a far more interesting way to die than when you put us down on the slope of a crater and we tumbled for a quarter of a mile to the bottom. *Very well done*."

Natasha Polyakova fixed him with a look that could kill, blurting out, "*Sabacka!*" She unzipped her cotton flight jacket and threw it on the floor, then stormed out of the simulator. McGovern just shook his head and waited for her to cool off before heading outside to speak with her. He found her on the outside balcony overlooking the launch complex with her back toward him. Even in the NASA issue jump suit, her attractive curves and light brown hair, blowing in the mild Florida breeze, were speaking subconsciously to his male hormones. However, he put any such thoughts aside as his life and the success of the mission would depend on her and for just those very same reasons, she would have to depend on him. It had been a late night for McGovern, brooding on the launch accident the day before as well as his irritation about the crew changes, still he realized he's been really hard on the cosmonaut.

"Listen Natasha, I …"

"Would you please address me as *Captain* Polyakova? I do have an official if temporary rank you know."

"Okay, Captain Polyakova … look, I'm sorry about my sarcastic comments in there. You're working with an unfamiliar piece of hardware, and I'm sure you being on this mission in place of Major Kutuzov wasn't your idea. The LEM is a difficult machine to master, but you have to be able to fly it both down to the lunar surface and then get the ascent stage back into orbit. Anything can happen on this mission. We're headed into hostile territory, and someone might get killed. If it's me, there's no reason you should die, too. You have to be able to pilot the LEM like a pro. Now, I know that you can fly a plane, and you've at least flown in space before. Let's take a break and hit it again in the afternoon. And … I'm sorry; I've reviewed the old tapes of the Apollo crews training on this very same craft. Considering this was your first session, you did a hell of lot better than some very well known *first-step-for-man* … astronauts."

Natasha Polyakova turned to look at him, the anger finally having drained from her face. McGovern was struck by her beauty: her large blue green eyes, delicate lips and heart-shaped face. "Apology accepted,

Colonel. I … did get us killed three times in the simulator. I'm sorry. I should have asked for assistance in balancing the thrusters. They are very sensitive. I feel like I have failed my examination. And you are correct. I did not wish to be here on this mission. It was seen as scoring important political points to have a woman in a command position. Many of those in the Russian Space Agency added, an *attractive woman*, as if I were here like a kind of decoration and not a trained cosmonaut."

A warm smile broke across John McGovern's face. "Well, they were certainly right about the attractive part, and I certainly understand you're here because you have to be. You're a cosmonaut, a member of a select club and you do have my respect. Come on … let's grab some lunch and try it again in about an hour. What do you say?"

CHAPTER SEVEN

The White House, Office of the President

Cordelier Price sat watching the big wet flakes of a March snowstorm fall outside her window. It wouldn't last, though, not in Washington, not this close to spring. Still, the blanket of white that covered the White House lawn returned her to her memories as a small girl living with her parents in the Tennessee Mountains east of Johnson City. Sometimes the snow would fall for days. She'd come into the house, wet and freezing from a day of sledding to the warmth of the fireplace and the aroma of her mother's cooking. *Days past,* she thought, *without the responsibility and the duties of the highest office in the land.*

She turned to see the Chairman of the Joint Chief's, Admiral Warner, and her science advisor, David Belowsky, waiting just outside the door to the Oval Office, and stood up to greet them. "Come in gentlemen and please be seated. I want to go over the information on our Moon mission and your opinions on China's latest propaganda victory."

Belowsky spoke first. "Madam President, the impact and public relations coup of having an actual mining and ore processing facility on the Moon is enormous. In terms of public opinion, we've been left in the dust. The effect this will have on the Chinese position with the United Nations as to whether China should be exempted from the 1967 Treaty of Outer Space will weigh heavily in their favor. We have to step up to the plate or rather get down to the lunar surface to prove that we have a right to be there as well or we're just spitting into the wind."

President Price's face, took on a serious look of determination. "I couldn't agree more and that's why we have been pushing ahead despite having to make certain *political accommodations* on this."

Belowsky replied, "If you mean the addition of the French and the Canadian astronauts and the replacement of Kutusov with a young woman, you should know that I heard from Norman Taggert about that last one and I can tell you, Colonel McGovern is not a happy camper."

The President turned to the Chairman of the Joint Chief's. "Jim, what's your take on the shuffle with the Russians?"

"This mission could end up like the last one, blown out of the sky. Major Kutuzov is a war hero and the poster boy of the new Russian military. Getting him killed could have some very serious repercussions. This Natasha Polyakova is a young cosmonaut with very little flight experience. She's high profile, though, but not in the way some factions in the Russian government would like. Several years ago, when the Russians were flexing their muscles with respect to some of their former Soviet republics, this Polyakova helped organize public protests against their actions. Under normal circumstances, she might have met with an *accident* … I'll leave it at that. But, her father was a highly well known and decorated cosmonaut – very high profile. The protest movement worked, but their current FSB internal security head, Golovko, never forgot it. It was his insistence that she be sent on this mission as a demonstration of women's equal rights and representation in our alliance. More likely, he's hoping that if this mission ends in failure, she'll be out of his and the government's collective hair for good."

The President shook her head. "Nice, send an inexperienced young woman into a potentially lethal combat situation. What about the French?"

This time David Belowsky, her science advisor, spoke up. "The French had originally wanted this man Rousseau on board, but instead, through some very intense lobbying on his part, Captain Remmy LaCasse managed to grab his spot. Once he learned that McGovern was commanding the mission, he said he owed him his life and he does.

He was the French ISS crewmember that John was ordered not to go after when the man accidentally cut his own tether. McGovern went after him anyway, claiming his earpiece went dead. As for the actual nuts and bolts of the mission, that's going just fine. Both lunar landers are undergoing refurbishment at a Northrop-Grumman facility in Saint Augustine, Florida. They'll have them ready in 42 days to be flown down to the Cape for launch prep."

Cordelier Price took on a look of worry about the last sentence. "Do we have any idea what happened to the Falcon-9 launch vehicle that blew up, Jim?"

Admiral Warner answered with some hesitation. "Ah … no. Not entirely. The telemetry showed a spike in the temperature and the pressure inside the fuel and oxidizer tanks on the second stage. When the pressure red lined, it blew the tank and exploded. It's pretty damn peculiar. There's nothing in the data or the design of the rocket for that matter that can account for something like this. It's almost like … no, forget it."

Belowsky looked over at him. "Almost like what, Admiral?"

"Well, I was going to say, almost like the results from one of the SDI tests with a high powered laser, but there's certainly no hard evidence of an outside cause like that."

Price nodded her head in agreement. "Still, Jim, have this checked out. We've been having too many accidents lately, like the destruction of the Pan-African satellite. There are several African nations whose economies have taken a beating since losing the satellite. Okay, the next order of business, how are you coming with mounting weapons on the Salyut and the LEMs?"

"I'll have a full report on your desk in about two days, but here are the preliminaries. Raytheon Corporation has been tasked with making a scaled down version of the PAC-4 Patriot Missile for use in space. They'll replace the fins with thrust vectoring and some tiny thruster jets for maneuverability. We've been assured by the Russians of receiving four to six rack-mounted R-77 missiles, again modified for use in outer space and we're trying to see if an AEGIS Gatling Gun point defense system can be integrated into the Salyut. As far as the LEM goes, we may be able to add some additional anti-missile defenses, but we're concentrating on ECM, you know, electronic counter measures and chaff … that sort of thing. Colt Firearms is working on something for use on the Moon. It's the CL-V-60 – "V" for vacuum – rifle. This gun has been extensively modified for use in a hard vacuum. That means the metal parts, ammunition, lubricants, the whole nine yards and sights as well as a trigger that can be used by combatants in spacesuits on the Moon."

Cordelier Price shook her head. "You mean that young lady and John McGovern? They'll be the first ones down to the surface. I hope to God we're not going to wind up fighting the first off-planet war."

"Madam President, we already are. The Chinese fired the first shots and killed two good men. But … there has to be more to this than just war. The Chinese aren't stupid. They plan for the very long run. There's a lot more to this, I'm sure."

To that, Cordelier Price could only agree. "Fine then, as long as I know things are moving in the right direction, and then I plan to personally address the United Nations just before the mission heads off to the Moon. Any name for the spacecraft yet?"

David Belowsky began to laugh. "Yeah, The United Spaceship Bitsa … because it's made of bits of this and bits of that, like 50-year-old landers, a French docking module, and a 45-year-old core component – a Russian Salyut Space Station."

The Admiral interrupted. "Actually the name decided upon collectively is the *Alliance*."

"Fine then. I plan to address the UN and our own citizens just before the departure of the *Alliance*. I'm also going to spring it on the Chinese as well as the world that we have hard evidence that an offensive missile from their base destroyed our first mission. Now, this is pretty distasteful for me, but we are fighting a propaganda battle as well as a military one. I would like the Air Force to prepare a photomontage and maybe some home videos of Major Jackson with his wife. I'm asking for the same from the Russians on their Colonel Schevyenskey. I'm going to give a tribute to these men as brave explorers who lost their lives in the service of humanity and then, I'm presenting the evidence of the missile launch. You can guarantee that the Chinese motion before the Security Council for sole access to the lunar ice fields will be DOA. Now, I have to get back to work. Please keep me informed of your progress and the mission status."

* * * *

John McGovern had picked up a turkey and Swiss sandwich along with an iced tea and waited for Natasha by the exit door. She came out with a plate piled high with shrimp salad and an iced tea without any ice in her glass. The two headed for one of the outdoor tables on the balcony of the NASA cafeteria then sat down at the pleasant light green table, sheltered from the strong sunlight by a blue and white stripped umbrella.

Natasha took a mouthful of shrimp on her fork, closed her eyes, and reveled in the flavor. "You know, I love the taste of shrimp, ever since I was a little girl and my parents would take me on holiday to the Black Sea. This is bit like it, you know. I love the sea air and the warm breezes. When I left Moscow, it was the coldest winter in the last 20 years and now … this is like paradise, with palm trees and the skies filled with birds."

John looked at his mission co-commander in a different light, no longer stoked with anger over the last minute switch that Moscow had pulled on him. She was like a young girl on her vacation, full of smiles and trying to make pleasant conversation.

He put his half-eaten sandwich back on the plate, took a swig of iced tea, and then spoke. "Can I call you 'Natasha'? Because I was really way off-base both yesterday after the launch accident and today in the simulator. I had no right to come off like that."

"Okay, Colonel, you may call me Natasha, and yes, I fully understand how you must have felt. Did your launch team discover the cause of the explosion?"

"John, my name is John, okay? Please just call me that. As for the explosion, not yet but they're still working on it. I have a theory that this was no accident, just like the loss of the first mission."

Natasha Polyakova's face took on a puzzled look. "What do you mean the first mission was not an accident? I have been told it was struck by a meteor."

Now McGovern became visibly angry, and Natasha at first thought it was something she had said. "Don't tell me you don't *know*," he said. "They sent you here for this mission, and you *don't know?* I guess that hardly surprises me that in a world where governments lie and cover up, that you'd be kept in the dark. That was no accident. We, I mean the USA, have hard photographic evidence that a Chinese missile took out the moon station, and I'm sure your government has it, too. They didn't tell you?"

Her eyes went wide, and she said something under her breath, shaking her head. "Somehow, this does not surprise me at all. I was briefed on my part of the mission by Federal Security Director Golovko. This is not unexpected to find myself in this situation. Golovko is one of the old guard, a holdover from the past. My comrades and I were a thorn in his side. After the imperialist factions of the government began an aggressive policy in 2013, I, and many of my friends, students and ordinary people, chose not to make a return to the past. We took to the streets to protest, we wrote articles, we got on television, even your CNN and the English BBC. We made them change the course of Russia, but it was … not without sacrifice. Many in the movement met with strange accidents. My fiancée, Misha, was killed. He came home to his apartment to take the elevator to his floor and ... the cable broke ... he fell to his death. The official explanation was a worn out elevator cable, but I know from others who inspected it and know in my heart that it was cut."

John McGovern could see tears begin to well in her eyes and felt it was best to keep her talking, and not to dwell on her loss.

"So how did you escape any reprisals, Natasha?"

"I didn't completely escape. Frightening telephone calls in the night. People denouncing me in the press as unbalanced. But my father is a very, very famous cosmonaut and a hero of Russia. Too many uncomfortable questions would be asked if I met with some kind of misfortune. Director Golovko must have felt this was his opportunity to be rid of me."

"Listen, Natasha, I know a lot more about what you went through than you might think. I was on everyone's case about China's real plans even before they launched their Moon mission, and I was screaming at the top of my lungs that they were going to cut us off from our access to space and the Moon. It cost me my Air Force commission, my career as an astronaut, my marriage, and it nearly cost me my life. Apparently, in America, there are many well-placed individuals with financial ties to China that didn't want me creating problems for them. Now, it's different. I'm only sorry it cost the lives of two good men to prove me right. Anyway, you *do not* have to be here. Now that you know the truth and you know just how dangerous this mission is ... go home and be safe."

Natasha squared her shoulders and took on a look of determination. "Go home and be safe? If I leave this mission, I'll never be safe again, and I will have no career, such as it is already. But, if we succeed, I will be a hero to Russia, and I'll expose all the liars like Golovko and his conspirators. And, there is more. I know Nikolai Schevyenskey's wife. I often spoke with her as she played with their children around Star City. I ...was convinced by those who should have told me the truth that his death was an accident. I owe it to his family to succeed. I'm not going anywhere, except back to the simulator."

* * * *

"Okay, ease up on the thrust, balance your pitch and yaw ... good ... good now just a little more power. Twenty meters to go, five forward, fuel is good at 120 seconds. Three meters to go ... one forward and ... touchdown .... The *Chika* has landed!"

Natasha took a deep breath and a smile of satisfaction broke across her face along with a giggle. "The *Chika*? Our lander is called the Seagull?"

McGovern laughed, too. "Sorry but that was the only bird name I knew in Russian except for *vorin* … ah crow … and I thought that you made such a graceful landing that I'd call us the Seagull. That was an excellent landing. Let's do another run through and call it a day. I have an idea. Tomorrow we're getting together with the rest of the mission crew for training. After that, we won't have any free time for anything. I saw how you went for those so-so frozen shrimp from the cafeteria. I know a place over in Cocoa Beach, right on the water, that has the best seafood around here. What do you say, want to go have dinner together?"

Natasha thought for a moment then nodded her head, yes. "I would like that very much, Colonel McGovern"

"Great, then I'll be over to your quarters and pick you up about 7:30 … and the name is John, just call me John, Natasha, okay? Now let's take it from the top again."

CHAPTER EIGHT

Lunar South Pole, the Chinese Moon Base

General Wang, commanding China's first lunar outpost, studied the terrain beyond the walls of the protective dome through a thick Plexiglas window. His view overlooked the black crater floor, which had remained in darkness for at least a few billion years. Below the regolith and boulder-strewn landscape was a layer of permafrost nearly half a kilometer thick and only a few meters below the surface. This was a treasure worth going to war over. This was the key to China's destiny and ultimate control of space, as well as the entire world's global economy. The far half of the Crater Scott in which the base sat was beyond the limb of the Moon's far side. That is to say, everything beyond a demarcation line 30 kilometers forward of the base was invisible from the prying eyes of observers on the Earth. For the first time since the advent of spy planes and surveillance satellites, a nation could carry out any activity with impunity, totally concealed from observation.

Wang watched as the powerful arc lamps came on in a new excavation section, bathing the surface with the first photons of light to touch the soil in eons. The lights were powered by a small nuclear reactor that had been launched from Earth just four days before. Along with the reactor came more men and more equipment and something else, something to ensure that no one, and no nation, would lay claim to these recourses. In metal crates, surrounded by space-suited workers were twenty 500-kiloton nuclear warheads. After China's blatant disregard for the 1967 Treaty of Outer Space, banning any national claim to a celestial body, the carrying of nuclear weapons into space seemed like a trivial infraction.

He watched the main computer display screen that depicted the arrival schedule for another lander then turned to his subordinate. "Lieutenant Tao, I see that Lander No. 4 has not touched down as of yet. Their schedule was to have been on the surface 30 minutes ago. What is the delay?"

Tao saluted and then bowed quickly as a sign of respect. "Sir, they are having some problems in the transfer of the cargo to the lander from the main module. This is a critical maneuver and cannot be rushed. The satellite components, which are being carried, are delicate and must not be damaged. We must bring them to the surface and join the two halves correctly to provide the illusion to the world that our manufacturing technology at our base allowed for the actual building of the device here on the Moon."

Satisfied with the explanation, General Wang made a short curt nod to his subordinate. "Very good, Tao. Have the technicians completed the last section of the magnetic track as ordered?"

"Yes, sir. All in place for the launch, in order to demonstrate the superior technology as well as the generosity of the People's Republic of China."

"Very well then, I must contact the project director and advise him of our progress. You are dismissed."

It was nearly midnight in the office of Space Intelligence when General Wang's call came through, scrambled by an algorithm program that encrypted his transmission to such a degree, that even the new high-speed mainframe computers, successors to the legendary Cray, would spend the next 50 years attempting to break the encoding. By that time, Wang thought, *China would not only rule the world but the entire solar system.*

The call was passed through to the director's office. "Yes General Wang. Excellent! No, I do not have a problem with the delay so long as it ensures our plan moves along the path of success. Yes, all will be ready here; the navy's initial test was a complete success – the target was destroyed. Very good. Our next contact will be in three days."

Zhao's subordinate, Chang Xi, could hear only one side of the conversation, but he could see from Zhao's expression that his superior was pleased with the answers he had received from the Moon. Zhao turned to Chang Xi.

"Everything is now in place for our master stroke in winning the accolades of the nations of the world. Even in America, we have received enormous support. In particular from their media. The media and press of the United States cast their president as a warmonger and loose cannon. They find our overtures toward peace, the sharing of resources with impoverished nations and our commitment to eventually supplying clean solar power, exactly what they wish to hear and to believe. They are very useful idiots, indeed."

Xi added, "The very influential film actors and musical performers of the West have been of enormous importance to us as well. I understand one of their popular female singers has made a recording to say that China is the savior of the poor, the healers of the Earth." Chang Xi began to laugh, "Their gullibility still amazes me, Director Zhao."

"Yes, Xi, this was the failing of the Soviet Union. When they attempted to amass world power and domination, they chose to bludgeon their opposition with a sledgehammer with predictably poor results. We, on the other hand, use a blade so thin and so sharp that the victim does not know he has even been cut until after the damage has been done. Very well then, enough talk. Contact Admiral Shen. Inform him that the Americans will launch in three more days. Then you may go."

* * * *

Natasha Polyakova stepped out on the balcony of the astronaut's housing complex. The evening was almost magical, having just come from a freezing Russian winter. The breeze from the ocean was soft and carried the warmth of the tropics as well as the scents of jasmine and hibiscus flowers. Natasha was mesmerized by the gentle swaying of the palm trees and the incredible spectacle of the sun, looking bloated and red, slipping beneath the broad expanse of the Indian River. Its rays colored the undersides of the evening's gathering clouds with a fiery paintbrush. She saw the car pull into the complex's parking lot with John McGovern at the wheel. It was a convertible with the top down. Natasha thought it was so American yet so appropriate for this beautiful evening. Her eyes focused on the man. His tall straight frame, broad shoulders, trim waist and easy manner spoke of a physical confidence, a magnetism that she could not help but be drawn to, but the stone that sat upon her soul caused her to close her eyes as if to will away the fantasy that was beginning to form in her mind. The knock on her door brought her out of her musings.

Opening it, she was greeted by John's warm smile and three roses. "Hi, Natasha. Here's a little peace offering from this morning's session. I actually do know a few things about Russian customs. You know, never give yellow flowers and never give an even number of flowers either."

Natasha smiled back at him. "Oh, thank you so much, John. It pleases me that you know something about my culture and respect it. Perhaps it's just a perception and perhaps one that is incorrect that Americans do not respect another's views and culture. I … thought at first you were like that, and I had set it in my mind to dislike you. I'm sorry I was wrong."

"Hey, no harm done. Are you ready? You're going to love this place."

"Yes, just let me get my jacket."

As she turned to go back to her bedroom, John was struck by how beautiful she was. Her white linen slacks clung to her figure in all the right places. The black sleeveless top she wore displayed her long, graceful arms. John was thinking that being so strongly attracted to a woman, whom he might have to make very objective life and death decisions about, was not such a good idea. He shook his head, speaking under his breath, "Why the hell didn't they send Kutuzov?"

"Excuse me, John. Did you say something?"

"Ah … no, just thinking out loud."

Natasha donned a lightweight white cotton jacket. Turning a full circle in the living room, she asked McGovern, "So, how do I look?"

"Like you just stepped off of South Beach in Miami."

* * * *

They had just crossed the bridge over the Banana River to the spectacle of white feathered birds and pelicans traversing the sky. To the east was the incomplete circle of a nearly full moon. The warm air blowing over and into the Mustang convertible was intoxicating with the scents of jasmine, sea grass and salt air. It was almost like moving through liquid.

"John, this is paradise. How lucky you are to live this every day. I love it and this car as well. I suppose your open car is the only way to travel here?"

He turned onto the picturesque stretch of road known as A1A and headed south. "Maybe you wouldn't have such a high opinion of Florida during the hurricane season, but, yeah, you're right. This *is* great, but this isn't my car. I borrowed it from a buddy of mine from the engineering department. My car, along with my motorcycles, are all locked up, back in snow covered Great Barrington, Massachusetts. I … ah wanted to get as far away from here and all the memories that go with this place as possible. Let's just say I was made to feel very unwelcome. But, if you think this is a great way to travel around here, you should experience this on a motorcycle. You feel like you're part of the wind, like you're embedded in the natural world. Sort of in harmony with the universe … I guess."

"Oh, that sounds wonderful. I'd like to try that sometime."

"Okay then, the next time I can get my hands on a bike, I'll take you for a ride. By the way, I'm taking us to one of my favorite places for seafood. It's called Coconuts. Not too fancy but they have excellent food and usually some pretty decent live music … and, it'll be a real Florida-American experience for you."

* * * *

Natasha finished devouring her scallops and then turned her attention toward the mysterious looking golden brown circular object on her plate. “Oh, John, you were right. This is so good! What is this next one please?”

“That’s a crab cake and you’ll love it.”

“And you are eating a *shark!?*”

“Better for me to be eating him than the other way around, don’t you think?”

Natasha laughed and then shook her head. “You have a good sense of humor, John. I like that. But … I can also see you carry a stone. It intrudes on your enjoyment. I can see it in your eyes. Do you feel like speaking about this, or is it too personal?”

“No, I can talk about it. It’s just that I didn’t want to talk to anyone … but, okay, maybe it’s better to get some things off your chest rather than keeping everything bottled up. I sure learned one thing though. When you start stepping on the toes of powerful people and putting their financial empires in jeopardy, you can forget about freedom of speech.”

Natasha frowned as she spoke. “So, I see our two countries may not be so different in the ways they deal with those who speak out.”

“Funny, I used to be able to say that in America at least they don’t kill you, that all they can do is make your life a living hell but I was wrong. Back in October, I took one of my motorcycles out for an autumn ride. The Berkshire Mountains are just incredibly beautiful that time of the year. I love the back roads up there. Anyway, I found myself being run off the road by a black Lexus. If it wasn’t for the fact that I spent a few years racing motorcycles, I would’ve died right there. Whoever it was saw they didn’t get me the first time and chased me down for miles before I lost them. But … they killed me in other ways. Before my divorce, they figured that if they couldn’t make me shut up, they’d make my wife’s life a living hell. She just couldn’t take it anymore, and I suppose that I just couldn’t keep my mouth shut about what I was damn certain of – the Chinese were aiming for the militarization of outer space and shutting us off, not only from the Moon, but from Earth orbit as well. These people, whoever they are, maybe Chinese here in the states or more likely Americans who value their bank accounts more than their country, tried to see to it that they closed my mouth permanently. American corporations spent close to a billion dollars promoting the 2008 Olympics in China. You think they'd spend that kind of money if they didn't expect to be getting huge returns on their investment? Think they want someone with a big mouth running around upsetting their applecart? Now that I'm proven right … well I'm the big hero, welcome home John. What I lost already … I'll never get back."

Natasha looked at John McGovern with a deep sadness to her expression and reached across the table to take his hand. "Did you love her … your wife, I mean?"

"Yeah, at least I thought I did. Still do in a way. She was just … not strong, I guess. I needed someone with the same convictions as mine to stand up against these people. I refused to compromise when I knew I was right and she couldn't handle it any longer."

"Is she still here … in Florida, I mean?"

"No, she moved back to Colorado, a long way from here. Ah hell, forget about all this doom and gloom. Tell me about your life in Russia. What was it like to have a celebrity for a father?"

Natasha's countenance took on shyness to it. "Umm, I don't really know. Dmitry was always just my papa. When he left for his mission aboard Mir, there was still a Soviet Union. I was just two years old when he finally came home. He was gone for almost a year and a half. Poor Papa, it took him so long to get his strength back. Then be became director of the Space Agency when we began working with the Americans. We had a very nice life. I lived with my parents in Moscow. Then I went to university to study aerospace engineering. Maybe it is genetic, yes? I wanted to know everything about building rockets and spacecraft. I studied hard and was accepted as a cosmonaut candidate

… but this was difficult for me as well. Always I would hear, perhaps in whispers and on occasion quite loudly, that the only reason I had been accepted was that my father was Dmitry Polyakov. It was sometimes very hurtful. I made my first flight into space to resupply the International Space Station. That was just before Russia again flexed its might toward the former Baltic Republics. They threatened military action against Estonia. That was when I was introduced to the Russians for Democracy movement. There are many, many of us who would not keep silent and watch our country once again be a bully toward smaller nations. We took to the streets, we marched, we lectured, we went on television, and my reward was to be grounded. I never again was permitted to fly in space, and I was removed from our Olympic Biathlon team for my activities and then …"

McGovern could see tears begin to well up in her eyes.

"And then, they killed my fiancée, Misha. He was so brave, refusing to back down. He was to speak at a rally in Red Square the next morning. He died that night, and I knew it was no accident. But … we did achieve small victories. Victor Simonov is now president. As soon as he took office, the confrontations between Russia and the West ended. We became a valued partner once again and no longer an adversary. We worry, though. There are many in the government who opposed Simonov, who want a return to the old days. Maybe not communism but to an Imperial Russia, out to reclaim what they believe is lost territory. I, like many others, fear for Simonov's life. If he is killed, everything we have worked so hard for and have suffered for will be for nothing. The men who killed my Misha will have won. It was a double blow for me. Shortly after Misha's death, my mother was diagnosed with terminal cancer. She fought hard to live … but in only a few months, she was gone."

John McGovern just sat there, studying Natasha. She was a kindred soul. Someone with real principles who wouldn't back down. He considered this as he thought to himself, *Yeah, I was wrong about her. She's no lightweight; she deserves a spot on this mission. She's earned it.*

"Listen, we've both taken our hits for what we believe in, you far more than me," he said. "At least they didn't kill my wife. Let's try to put this aside for a while. The band's almost ready; let's stay for a while and do some dancing. It'll do you good … me too for that matter."

It was well past midnight when the couple returned to the Space Center. John opened the door for Natasha and walked her to the front of her residence at the Cape. They stood there under the front light, and McGovern leaned forward as if to kiss her. Natasha looked as if she would return the gesture but then turned her head away.

"No, John. I do not feel this is right. Yes, you are a very attractive man, but we have the mission … and Misha is still in my heart along with the pain of his loss. His memory lives beside the hatred I hold for the men who killed him. He cannot rest and neither can I until they pay for what they have done, not just to Misha but so many others in Russia."

McGovern reluctantly pulled back. "It's okay, Natasha. I understand. I shouldn't have even made the first move. I'll see you in the morning. We're getting together with the rest of the crew and then there's an *Atlas* launch in the late afternoon. We're going to put a replacement satellite up for the Pan-African Federation. So, good night."

"*Spakoinoy nochee*, John."

* * * *

Captain Tso made a quick visual inspection of the device before returning to the bridge of the Jin Class Type 094 ballistic missile submarine. Every test of the device, including its first actual use to down a rocket in flight, had been a success. Yet, the strain that the massive high-energy laser's output put upon the electrical system and the nuclear reactor of his ship was substantial. Another worry was on Tso's mind as well: In the undersea world of combat, hunter and hunted glided through the depths of the sea in near total silence. The preheat phase to power up the banks of the laser's discharge type capacitors was noisy – noisy enough to give away his position to any

American Navy attack sub in the area. Fortunately, there were none on patrol here, of which Tso was thankful. That information could have only come from a source in the American Navy so he was doubly happy at the effectiveness his country employed to turn Americans to the service of China. Whoever this individual was, he would be rewarded for his assistance.

Captain Tso had read his orders and reconfirmed them. Now all he had to do was wait 15 meters below the surface of the Atlantic Ocean, until early evening. Then he could fulfill his task and report, once again, on a successful mission.

Kennedy Space Center, 0700 Hours

Anyone entering the mission planning room at KSC would be struck by its similarity to a college classroom. Individual desks with LCD computer monitors were arranged in the same manner as they would be for students. The front of the room was dominated by a 72-inch flat display monitor connected to the computer graphics systems to display mission simulations and profiles so realistically that it was hard to distinguish between them and actual images obtained in space.

Six of the desks had monitors turned on, and the six crew members of the *Alliance* were seated, notebooks and pens out. John McGovern sat between Natasha Polyakova and Remmy LaCasse. Next to the Frenchman was Jack Griffin from the Canadian Space Agency and McGovern's two fellow American astronauts – Tom Garcia, a payload specialist from New Mexico, and Lieutenant William Curtis from Fresno, California.

Garcia was a first generation American born to Mexican parents. He overcame a lot of peer pressure as a young man with the help of a very dedicated high school science teacher who took Tom under his wing and lit the fires of curiosity about space exploration. From that day on, Tom Garcia traded his nights of hell-raising with young men who were destined to go nowhere to nights spent glued to a telescope eyepiece.

Lieutenant Bill Curtis was a Air Force officer, following his father's footsteps. His dad, Captain Walter Curtis, was supposed to have been the first African American rotational commander of the International Space Station. He had already flown several shuttle missions, but one week before liftoff, in late 1999, Walter Curtis was coming in for a landing at the Cape in very bad weather, flying a T-38 trainer. No one was exactly sure what happened, since Curtis was a very experienced pilot, but he missed his approach, powered up to come around again and lost control of the jet, slamming into the tarmac area, cart-wheeling into a massive fireball. His son, Bill, was just thirteen at the time and mourned the loss of his father, a man he admired. As a young man, Bill Curtis swore he would see to it that his father's dreams of space travel would come true through him. At just eighteen years of age, Bill Curtis, a straight "A" student, became one of the youngest individuals accepted at the U.S. Air Force Academy in Colorado Springs. This would only be his second mission into space.

When Director Norman Taggert entered the training room followed by an Air Force officer, he paused at John McGovern's desk to give him a smile as well as a raised eyebrow. "Late night, John?" Then he proceeded to the front of the room. "Okay then gentlemen and lady," tilting his head in the direction of Natasha Polyakova, "this is the first time you've all sat down together, excluding breakfast that is, so we'll discuss the mission profile. I'll be giving the overview, and then Colonel McGovern and Captain Polyakova will brief you on their respective parts of the mission. Lieutenant General Christopher is here to discuss the aspects of incorporating defensive and offensive weapons and electronic countermeasures into the Salyut as well as the two lunar landers. So class, get out your number two pencils and crack open your notebooks, because there will be a quiz on this."

Only Natasha, looking confused, didn't get the joke. McGovern leaned over to her. "Don't worry; I'll explain it to you later."

Norm Taggert cleared his throat. "Okay then, I'm not going to sugarcoat this or give you the kind of optimistic spin on this that I'm sure some in NASA will be spouting. This is a risky and dangerous mission. We're just at the beginning of this process, so right now I want you to all give this some serious thought. Anyone who wants to opt out of this mission can do so. There's time to get replacements. No one will think any less of you if you choose not to go."

Taggert gave the assembled crewmembers a few moments. When no hands went up, he continued. "Now, I'm sure that you all have a pretty good idea on how this is going to go, but I'd like to bring you all up to speed. The plan is to get the six of you to the Moon, deploy the Bigelow Habitat, and set the two LEMs down on the surface. In addition to the habitat, you will also deploy from orbit a compact drilling and ice to water conversion system. To get it to the surface, a descent capsule will retrofire and set down on the Moon, and then the habitat will be deployed. We can't risk having the driller/converter damage the habitat when it sets down. This device is designed to dig down three feet or so until it hits the buried ice beneath the lunar surface. The tip of the drill has heating coils that will melt the ice and pump the water into a valve that leads to the habitat. You'll have one additional piece of equipment – a compact oxygen generator. This device is a mini version of the kind of equipment we'd eventually like to have in place on the Moon. This will split the water you'll collect into oxygen and hydrogen. Right now, the hydrogen will just be waste gas, but in the future, if we're successful in our quest for our own moon base, this will be used for rocket fuel. Hopefully this will give you all what you'll require for survival in the most hostile environment human beings have ever tried to live in. The new administration in Washington intends to go full speed ahead with the *Altair* landers and the *Ares V* rocket, but the best we can do is get them to the Moon along with more equipment and a replacement crew some ten months from now, at the earliest."

Canadian astronaut Jack Griffin raised his hand. Griffin was a veteran of two space station shifts and was known to many as a practical joker. Jack once smuggled a device on board the space station that he put to good use during the dinner shift. While eating with the other five members of the ISS, he suddenly doubled over in pain. When his fellow crewmembers rushed to his aide, Jack pulled open the front of his flight suit and, to everyone's horror, a huge rubber worm with a gaping spike-toothed mouth, sprung out from the device that Griffin had taped to his stomach. A few of the crew were in momentary shock, but Jack Griffin was laughing so hard he bounced of the compartment's walls several time in zero gee. However, today, he was dead serious as he digested the material about this mission.

"Yes Jack, you have a question?"

"Yes, sir. What's the story about food, I mean solid food, if we're expecting to be on the Moon for almost a year?"

Taggert nodded his head in agreement. "I'm glad that you asked that question because that's the very next item I'm going to cover. A human being can only last two to three days without water and just a couple of minutes without oxygen but we can go for weeks, sometimes months without food, although I don't know about you, Captain Polyakova with that ballerina's figure of yours. We're going to be supplying you with some very boring but high calorie energy bars. The mission will carry enough in the landers and on the Salyut to keep you all going for eleven months. They're very small and produce very little in the way of bodily waste, for obvious reasons. You'll also have a supply of tablets designed to disrupt certain hormones produced in your bodies to slow down your metabolisms. Lastly, you all have the most efficient food storage system available, courtesy of Mother Nature. Our ancestors would often have to go for weeks or even months without food 50,000 years ago during the Ice Age. Our bodies today still possess the internal mechanisms to preserve us in this manner. So, I expect between now and the launch date that you will all add at least ten pounds of body fat, just in case we wind up taking longer than planned to get your replacements to the Moon. Oh, and in your case, Captain Polyakova, you'd better make that 15 pounds. You may not like how you look in a bikini for a while but trust me, if you run out of food; you won't starve to death either. Now, if there are no further questions, I will turn this meeting over to the two mission commanders, Colonel McGovern and Captain Polyakova, and the ESA representative, Major Remmy LaCasse."

Natasha walked to the front of the room first. At five-foot-seven, she had a petite figure that even in her NASA-issued slacks and shirt displayed all the right parts in all the right places. This was certainly not lost on the male contingent of the crew and in particular John McGovern. Natasha's English was very good and her accent was lyrical and pleasing to the ears. Behind her on the six-foot-wide screen was a computer-generated representation of each phase of the mission that looked real enough to require the use of a spacesuit in the briefing room.

"So then, my fellow crewmembers, our launch schedule will be in six steps. The first will be the launching of the reconditioned Salyut core from Baikonur Comsodrom. Once the Salyut is confirmed to have achieved a stable orbit, Colonel McGovern and I will launch from Baikonur in a Soyuz to rendezvous and dock with the Salyut. We will be maintaining a 290 kilometer orbit and deploy the Salyut's solar panels for power. Next, Astronaut LaCasse, along with Lieutenant Curtis, will launch from here along with the ESA multi-port docking block."

Remmy LaCasse came forward to the front of the room, joining Natasha. He was slim with true Gallic French features and almost jet black hair.

"Lieutenant Curtis and I," LaCasse began, "will arrive in the Orion Capsule to install the ESA module. We will then mate the module to the aft section of the Salyut and come aboard."

John McGovern then joined the presentation at the front of the room. "A second launch, using a modified Titan IV-B, will place the two reconditioned LEMs into orbit, followed by a third launch of another *Ares I* with Astronauts Garcia and Griffin aboard. It will be their job to deploy the landers and join them to the ESA docking module, and then they'll come on board the Salyut. Their *Ares I* will be extensively modified. We are adding two of the same solid rocket fueled boosters from the Space Shuttle program to the *Ares I*. That's because their rocket also will carry the Earth Departure Stage into orbit. Now, we have only one complete Earth Departure Stage, so this had better work or we're not going anywhere. Natasha and I will maneuver the *Alliance* – what we are calling our collection of international space hardware – to rendezvous with the EDS. Major LaCasse and payload specialist Garcia will EVA to actually attach the EDS to the French docking module."

LaCasse turned to John McGovern. "Please, *mon amie*, be assured I shall be *very* careful of my tether this time, eh?"

McGovern chuckled. "Yeah, I guess one brush with death is quite enough. Lastly, the Russians will launch a Progress cargo ship that will carry the habitat along with some additional supplies as well as the driller/converter for getting to and using the lunar permafrost. The Progress is programmed to dock with the French module. Once we're sure that all components are in place and operational, we light up the EDS and head for the Moon. Captain Polyakova will command the flight from Earth orbit to lunar orbit, and I'll be flying the first LEM down to the surface and will be in command of the landing mission. Lieutenant Curtis and Major LaCasse will be flying the second LEM. It's our plan to have the second lander deploy 24 hours after we land and activate the habitat and the driller/converter. Jack Griffin and Tom Garcia will be in charge of the Salyut. They'll be relieved at some point in the future by a second crew that will be deployed on another Soyuz. If the worst does happen to our landing mission, both Griffin and Garcia can use the Soyuz that Captain Polyakova and I flew up in to return to Earth orbit and dock with the ISS. Now, I'll turn this meeting over to Lieutenant General Christopher."

McGovern snapped the general a salute, which was quickly returned.

Lieutenant General Paul Christopher was a tall man with short-cropped silver hair in an immaculate and highly decorated blue Air Force uniform.

"First, let me say I don't have words to express to all of you just how highly I regard you for undertaking this very hazardous mission." His eyes focused on John McGovern. "Perhaps, if we had listened to *some* of the voices warning us of the true intentions of the Chinese, this mission would not be necessary. But, such as it is, we intend to give you enough defensive as well as offensive firepower to stay alive and to hold our claim to the lunar ice fields. I'll discuss the landing mission first, since this phase is the most critical and it presents the greatest danger of attack. Each LEM will be fitted with four scaled down versions of our PAC-4 Patriot missiles. In addition, you will also have an ECM pod, electronic counter measures, grafted on to the LEM. We've also provided a limited number of decoys, so that if you are fired upon by more missiles than the Patriots can handle, the decoys should draw off some of their attacking weapons. Once you're on the ground, you will have the use of specially modified combat firearms to defend yourselves. Before you leave for Russia for the second phase of your training, you'll be fully experienced on these rifles.

Our second concern is the main body of the *Alliance*. We feel the ship is vulnerable in the same manner the first mission was. Again, we will be equipping the Salyut in Russia with their R-77 air-to-air offensive missiles, modified for use in a vacuum and our own mini-Patriots for defense. In addition, we are, at this moment, working with the Russian Energia Design Bureau to find a way to incorporate a downsized version of the Navy's AEGIS point defense system. Instead of twin .30-millimeter Gatling guns, your version will use a single .20-millimeter six-barrel Gatling with a four-thousand-rounds per minute rate of fire. This should be more than adequate against anything the Chinese may throw at you. It is my sincere hope that the use of these weapons will be unnecessary, however if history has taught us anything, it's that more than likely you will have to engage the Chinese at some point. To this end, we will begin active training on these weapons systems, both offensive and defensive, to all personnel."

Norman Taggert again took center stage. "Okay then, we have a great deal to do and not much time to do it in, so I want Major Remmy LaCasse and Lieutenant Curtis on LEM simulator one. I also want Tom Garcia on the simulator as well, to be able to do a lunar landing as a backup in case anyone is incapacitated. I want you, John, and Captain Polyakova, on simulator two, and I want Jack Griffin in the tank to begin practicing the hook up procedure for the EDS rocket with the French docking module. They'll be an Atlas launch at 1820 hours, so we can all take a break at that time and watch the lift off."

CHAPTER NINE

Washington, the Pentagon, Department of the Navy

Lieutenant J.G. Richard Underwood had just completed his assigned task of reviewing satellite images off the North Korean coast. He checked his watch for a second time and then went down to air surveillance to see his buddy, Marine Second Lieutenant Jeff Murphy. Murphy was just going over his air search schedules.

"Hey, Jeff, how's it going? What's up for today?"

"Ah, not much, Rick, just going over the routing for the Orion sub hunters out of Jacksonville NAS."

"Gee, could I see that? I've always loved those old four motors, and I have a buddy up there at Mayport. Maybe he's on one of the flights."

Underwood studied the flight path charts for that day's surveillance overflights. Orions were used for everything from stopping drug trafficking to locating and potentially destroying enemy submarines. One flight in particular caught his attention, going about seventy miles off the Florida coast, passing in a diagonal line off Cape Canaveral in less than an hour.

Hey Murph, I … ah … gotta go but let's get together tonight over at Ballentine's for some beers and nachos. The female selection over there is pretty decent I hear, what do you say?"

"Aw, that's okay … maybe another night. I've got a serious date with a good looking blonde ensign."

"Hey, don't do anything I wouldn't do. Catch ya later, bud."

Lieutenant Underwood walked quickly down the hall to a vacant storage area and placed a call with the special cell phone he always carried. Looking like a standard Nokia, the guts of the phone were anything but, holding high tech miniaturized encryption software.

* * * *

"A Message is coming in, Captain Tso. The American Navy will be flying a search pattern in this area in about 20 minutes. They are on a drug interdiction mission, but still we should proceed with caution. If they spot anything unusual, we will miss our interception window and may face the unpleasant task of having to avoid American hunter/killer submarines."

Tso looked at the print out. "Ah, very good." Then he snapped out a command. "First Officer Jiang, take us down to 180 meters, all silent."

Tso then thought, *Once the Orion has passed us by, we can be back on station. It is good to have friends in high positions who value our money more than their birth nation.*

* * * *

John McGovern stood next to Remmy LaCasse on the lower balcony of the administration offices. Natasha Polyakova was with the rest of the crew on the upper one with their cameras at the ready, all eyes fixed on the Atlas launch pad four miles away.

Hughes Corporation had a replacement satellite for the one lost over the continent of Africa nearly complete when the destruction of the Pan-African bird was announced. Had they not been so fortunate in this, it might have been another four months before a second satellite could have been ready. Even so, the Pan-African nations whose digital based economies depended upon this vital communications link to integrate into the world economy had to pony up another $2.8 billion. The bird would be hurled into space on a NASA Atlas-5-400 rocket. Over the years, the Atlas had become the most reliable launch vehicle in the NASA family of rockets. Conceived in the early 1950s during the escalating tensions of the Cold War, the Atlas that sat on Pad 14 today ironically was powered by Russian designed motors built under license in the United States.

It was down to T-minus five seconds. As hundreds at the Cape watched, the powerful rocket engines ignited in gouts of yellow and white flames. The gantry supports released, and the Atlas cut loose from her Earth-bound chains, climbing for the freedom of space. Everyone was cheering with Natasha Polyakova recording the spectacle on her video camera while narrating the event for her father. Cheers and whoops could be heard over the roar of lift off.

The late March sun had nearly slipped below the horizon, turning the sky toward the east a deep shade of indigo. The exhaust of the Atlas was bright enough to cast shadows on the ground at the Space Center as it continued to climb, its fiery tail seeming to stretch across the sky. All eyes followed it as it passed the one-minute mark into its flight. As it did, everyone on the ground at first thought the lower stage was separating according to the rocket's flight plan, but this was twenty seconds early. A bright spot on the Atlas seemed to grow and then swallow the rocket. In an instant, it turned the receding long tailed point of light into a huge fireball of angry reds and oranges. The Atlas was now nothing more than bits of shredded and charred aluminum and titanium, plummeting toward the Atlantic Ocean along with nearly 3billion dollars worth of replacement satellite.

Below the surface of that same ocean, seventy miles out to sea, an encrypted radio message reached out into space was captured by a communications satellite and relayed directly to the waiting director of space intelligence, Sung Zhao. The message brought a smile to the undamaged half of Zhao's face. *1821 hours: The target is destroyed.*

Hours later, Sung Zhao sat outside the chamber of the Vice Premier. On his way to the Party leadership hall in Beijing, Zhao couldn't help but notice the signs of spring. The first green buds, the early flowers poking their colorful heads up from underground. *Ah, a good omen*, he thought. *The world awakens from the grip of winter, just as China awakes to take her rightful place as master, no longer servant.*

Zhao's musings were cut short as a young military officer approached him and then bowed. "Sir, the Vice Premier will see you now."

Sung Zhao entered the office of the Vice Premier. The room was quite stark and functional, without the trappings and displays of overt power. Vice Premier Gao Xi was a man who knew how to exercise his control, knew he had power, and did not need overt displays to dazzle his subordinates. He held the fate of billions in his hands. Above his desk was the portrait of current Premier Feng Qu and on the opposite wall, the image of the great founder, Chairman Mao. Gao Li however was a man of psychology. His desk was quite large and placed in such a manner that whomever entered his chamber had to walk an uncomfortable distance under the glare of the lights mounted in the high ceiling, and then, sit in chairs that were slightly lower than standard, forcing that individual to look up toward the Vice Premier.

"So, Sung Zhao, I understand your plan is moving ahead like the powerful current of the Yangtze River."

Zhao could sense it was more of a statement than a question. "Yes, honorable sir. Our PLA-Navy submarine has successfully destroyed the replacement Pan-African satellite, and now it is time for the next phase of my master plan that will elevate China to the pinnacle of world power."

The Vice Premier studied Zhao thoughtfully. "I trust that you are correct, Zhao. A powerful current also may drown the most expert of swimmers. We have already gone to enormous expense to implement your plan. A plan that many in the politburo fear carries far too great a risk. If your plan fails, China is exposed for violations of treaties we had signed over 50 years ago along with our destruction of spacecraft and deaths of NASA and Russian personnel. However, I am of a mind to be more certain of its success. You have served China well. Even as a young man, your plan to obtain the American's missile guidance technology was a master stroke."

"Thank you, Vice Premier Gao. We have had much help with shaping the public opinion of the West. Those who depend on China for their economic survival have been of valuable assistance in helping to mold a positive view of our nation in America and the West, as well as providing us with an interesting intelligence source for information. We do not need to dirty our hands with the placement of espionage agents and the turning of their military officers. Corporate leaders in America, who flood their banks with Chinese money and their mega-stores with our products, have agreed to do this for us. It is fortunate for China that they value their positions and wealth above the security of their country."

The Vice Premier smiled and nodded in agreement. "Ah, yes. What was it that Lenin said – the capitalists shall sell us the ropes with which we shall hang them from?" Laughing loudly, Gao added, "They are handing us the keys to the world's economy on a silver tray. We have funded our entire military space program upon our sales of plastic dolls, cheap furniture, and bicycles to the foolish Americans. Very well done, Zhao. Now, what is the next step?"

"The replacement for the Pan-African satellite has been destroyed. It will take the Americans months to fabricate a new one, along with much of that time consumed by the investigation of the, ah, *accident* that destroyed it. China will respond to the plight of the Pan-African nations by offering to replace the satellite at no cost with one of our own in a matter of days from now, not launched from Earth but deployed from our moon base. We will not only capture the imagination of the world with our generosity but we shall dazzle the world's nations with our technological brilliance and achievement. We shall convince the world that China can even manufacture satellites on the Moon. Clearly, this will ensure China's exemption from the 1967 treaty and give us sole ownership of the lunar ice fields and lunar resources. Then our true plan can emerge and there will be nothing the Western nations or their Russian partners can do to stop us."

Vice Premier Gao again nodded his head in thoughtful agreement but added. "What about this second mission by the West? I have read the intelligence reports that indicate they are moving ahead with their mission to obtain their own claim to our resources."

"Fear not, Vice Premier Gao. The seeds of their destruction have already been sown. I can assure you they will never even reach Earth orbit, no less set foot upon the Moon … *our* Moon."

* * * *

"Damn it, Norm! That's just one too many coincidences for me. In fact, this should be way too many for anybody. Listen, I *do not* believe that explosion was an accident. This has China written all over it!"

John McGovern stood there, inches from Norman Taggert's desk, arms crossed in front of his chest, looking like he could bite through steel plates.

Norman Taggert replayed the video image of the explosion, frame by frame, while looking over the temerity printout from the on-board sensors just prior to the loss of the Atlas. He'd been at it now for over five hours since the evening sky over the Cape filled with the fireball that marked the destruction of the Pan-African satellite.

"Cool your jets, John. You look like *you're* the next thing to explode around here. I happen to agree with you, but before I kick this thing upstairs, I need a smoking gun … and I think I may have found it. Look at the telemetry data just prior to the explosion … right here." Taggert circled the numbers on his hard copy. "And look at this video frame less than a second later. You see that bulge begin to form on the first stage of the rocket body? This looks nearly identical to the explosion of the Falcon cargo launch. Now, here you have two entirely different classes of rockets with exactly the same catastrophic failure. I 100 percent agree with you, this was no accident, but how the hell was it done?"

McGovern, his pressure valve finally released, pulled up a chair and sat down with Norman Taggert. "I'm sorry, Norm, habit I guess. I've spent so long defending my theories against people who considered me a conspiracy nut that I kind of lost my cool. Walk me through the last few seconds of the, eh … *accident*."

"Okay, right here the fuel tank's sensors show a spike in RP-1 fuel temperature on the down range side of the rocket. Now … look here, the internal tank pressure starts to climb right off the charts because the

RP-1 is starting to boil. Here, about a tenth of a second later, the tank ruptures but just before that, the flight sensors gimbal the main engines to try and correct the lateral thrust from where the superheated fuel breaks through the rocket's casing in a plume. As this is happening, the tank finally ruptures, causing it to slice open the liquid oxygen tank and once these combine … *Boom!*"

McGovern leaned across the director's desk to watch the frame-by-frame replay of the explosion. "Norm, no bomb could have done that. The source of the explosion came from the outside. Now, we have no radar or tracking data to indicate anything was fired at the rocket, like some sort of interceptor missile and at the speed and altitude of the Atlas, nothing short of a hypersonic weapon could have caught up with it and that would be pretty obvious but there is one thing it might be. Norm, can you please pull all of this and send it on a secure link to Groom Lake in Nevada? They've got all the past data on the SDI tests over the last twenty years or so. Three weeks ago if I'd a said this, the jokes about the men in white coats would be flying, but I'm 100 percent sure that bird was taken out by a laser. A big one, like the first airborne lasers we had on the 747s and 777s."

Norman Taggert nodded his head in agreement. "Yeah, it sure looks like it, but radar showed nothing in flight anywhere near the missiles trajectory."

"What about some kind of ship, Norm. Something fired from the water?"

"Yeah, I suppose that could be it. I can ask the Department of Defense to review all the satellite images of that area of the ocean for any surface vessels. That *is* a possibility, and I agree with you. I'm going to get all this data off to Groom Lake within the hour. Man, this has been one hell of a night. Oh, and speaking of nights, what was yours like? I understand that you and Cosmonaut Polyakova checked into gate security around 12:45 a.m. Are you hoping to improve international relations or what?"

This was the first time Norman Taggert had ever seen his friend turn red.

"No, nothing like that, Norm. I came down on her like a 900-pound gorilla the first day because I was the one pissed off over the way they swapped her out for Kutuzov, but I was 100 percent wrong. Look, I know that either the Chinese or the American corporate interests who're feeding at China's trough did their best to shut me up and nearly killed me back in October. Well, if the Chinese have their hooks into us, they sure as hell have their hooks into the Russians, too. Natasha said the director of the FSB had told her the loss of the first mission was an accident. He must have known it wasn't. I swear this Golovko set her up to fail. After what she told me last night, Natasha and I are in the same boat … maybe for different reasons, but there are some very high profile people, both in Russia and in the States, that would be very happy to see our mission end like Roy Jackson's."

"So, are you interested in this woman? I mean more than just a professional interest?"

"Hey, Norm, I'm not going to lie to you. Since my divorce, the total number of women I've dated is zero. I just didn't want to go down that road again, but Natasha? We're more alike than you could imagine. The problem is she's just not interested or ready for any kind of relationship right now, and, yeah, I know it's not a good thing either to have to make a life and death decision about anyone you have an emotional relationship with. So don't worry. We're working together on a strictly professional basis … *damn it.*"

* * * *

The pulsing buzz of John McGovern's alarm refused to grant him any further rest. He reached over to shut it off, his body demanding more sleep. At 6:20 AM, he'd only had a little over five hours of sleep, sitting up with Norman Taggert, going over the loss of the Atlas. *Yeah,* he thought, *sure as hell the Chinese had shot down the bird but for what possible reason? Some test of a weapon? Doesn't make any sense.*

He picked up the remote and switched on CNN. As he was about to head into the bathroom for a shave, he froze. Grabbing the remote,

McGovern turned up the volume.

"After the spectacular explosion of the Atlas rocket carrying the replacement for the Pan-African communications satellite yesterday evening, experts at the Kennedy Space Center still have no clues as to the cause of the accident. This has created deep concern among the Pan-African member nations whose economies have been adversely affected by this loss. However, in a stunning move, China announced early this morning it would modify an existing satellite under construction and replace the lost communications satellite at no cost to the Pan-African nations. The Chinese Vice Premier also added that this satellite, unlike every satellite ever placed in orbit since the dawn of the Space Age, will not be launched from the Earth. Instead, it will be placed into orbit from the Chinese moon base, using a magnetic acceleration track as opposed to the use of a rocket motor. Chinese Vice Premier Gao Xi added that this demonstrates to the world the superiority of Chinese technology in the field of space exploration. Many here in Washington are in agreement that this spectacular demonstration of generosity, coupled with their amazing technological achievement, will almost guarantee that China will be granted an exemption by the United Nations to the 1967 Treaty of Outer Space and be given sole control of the Moon's South Polar resources which they seek."

McGovern stood staring at the screen as the broadcast went to a commercial break and spoke aloud, "Son of a bitch …"

* * * *

Lieutenant Richard Underwood was driving his new BMW-Z10 convertible north on I-395 toward the Pentagon. He'd been warned to keep a low profile, but this was one desire he had to fulfill. He hadn't been asked too many nosey questions about the car that he couldn't weave a good BS story about, but still, it was pushing the envelope. *Well, maybe my car and my computer system are just a bit out of the price range for Junior Grade Lieutenant,* he thought. "Yeah," he shouted over the wind that poured into the topless cockpit of the BWM. "This is more like Donald Trump's price range, *ha!*"

Underwood entered his assigned work area at 0750 hours and took his seat in front of a high-definition computer display screen to begin his day's work. Just as he opened the imaging program, his commanding officer, Captain Delgado, came up behind him and asked Underwood to step into his office. A chill, like an electric shock, raced from his chest and down his arms. He'd had a lot of them lately when his mind formed the kinds of unpleasant questions he'd imagine his superiors might ask him. But, he considered it a price he had to pay for his growing bank accounts and collection of big boy's toys.

He stood in front of Captain Delgado's desk, hoping the man wouldn't notice the beads of sweet that were starting to form on his forehead as the captain addressed him.

"Lieutenant Underwood, I have a project for you. Please pull up and review all the satellite sweeps from latitude twenty-seven and longitude seventy-eight."

Underwood realized someone was putting the pieces together and did his best to try and draw more information from his superior officer. "Sir, that's off Cape Canaveral … does this have anything to do with the rocket that exploded yesterday?"

"Lieutenant, that's not really your business to know, but okay, since you're working on the satellite images, maybe it'll help if you did know a bit more. What you're supposed to be looking for is anything out of the ordinary and certainly any activity involving a surface vessel, like a tanker or a freighter. Check out every image we have for that area for say from 1730 hours to about 1930 hours and in particular 1820 hours, okay?"

"Gosh, sir, do they think maybe someone shot the rocket down?"

"That's the scuttlebutt, son, but you didn't hear that from me. Now dismissed."

On his way back to his workstation, Lieutenant Underwood made a quick detour to see his friend, Marine Second Lieutenant Jeff Murphy. "Hey, Murph, what's up with all the activity this morning?" he asked with all innocence.

"Hey Rick, I'm really busy, but I ... ah … I can't say."

"Come on, Murph, we're all on the same team. Anyway, who's going to hear you? Besides, I'll tell you if you tell me. I'm supposed to be looking for some kind of ship that might have had something to do with yesterday's launch accident at the Cape."

Jeff Murphy's eyes got wider. "*Really Rick?* Well then, that explains why I'm supposed to route three Orions out over the ocean off Canaveral. And … don't tell anyone this Rick, but I heard it through the grapevine that we're dispatching a *Seawolf* attack sub from Kings Bay to go check out the area."

Now Underwood tried to hide his nervousness. "Gosh, they think a sub might be involved?"

"Hey, Rick, like I said, that's just the rumor. You didn't hear this from me, but two of the Orions are equipped with deep probe radar – you know, sub hunters."

Underwood needed to dig for one more piece of information. "So when do the Orions head out to snoop around?"

"Man, they're gone already, left about half an hour ago out of JAX NAS. Hey, Rick, you're sure interested in this, how come?"

"Ah … like I said, I've got a buddy up in Jacksonville. Just curious I guess. And thanks again. I've got to get back to my station. Maybe we'll get together for some brews tonight?"

"Yeah, Rick, that'll be cool. Just remember, I didn't say anything about a sub, okay?"

Underwood walked quickly down the hall as he thought, *That was a masterstroke, making friends with that moron Murphy in aerial surveillance. Good, we'll get together tonight and after I pour a few beers into him, he'll be a fountain of information.*

He knew he had plenty of time to review the satellite images because he knew exactly what he was looking for and if anything did show up, he could easily delete those few frames with no one the wiser.

Lieutenant Richard Underwood reached the office supplies room. Quickly checking that no one was inside, he pulled his heavily modified Nokia out and dialed a code on his phone.

* * * *

The board meeting was about to start. The executive conference room that overlooked New York City had a spectacular view of the East River from the top of the sixty-fourth floor. The East Wind Investments and Securities corporate headquarters was a magnificent creation of glass and steel built in 2011 with money from the soaring profits made in Chinese investments.

The president and CEO of East Wind, looking every bit the Hollywood image of a top corporate executive – tall with silver hair at the temples and attired in a $4,000 light gray suit – had just walked to the front of the conference room to take his seat to preside over the meeting. As he sat down, he noticed a light blinking on the communications console in front of him.

He suddenly rose. "Please excuse me, I'll just be a minute and I'll be right back." Quickly, he returned to his office and picked up the private line. "Yes, what is it? Oh … I see, yes, you were absolutely correct to call me. Yes, it will be taken care of immediately. And … you can expect another payment along with a nice bonus for this very timely information at the usual location next week."

He looked at his watch, a $30,000 Omega, and quickly dialed the number to the Chinese Consulate's office at the UN. Asking to speak with the Chinese trade representative, he relayed the vital information and then hung up, before returning to his meeting.

* * * *

Captain Tso looked at the message he'd just been handed. Maybe it was too late already; certainly there was precious little time left.

"Dive the boat; take us down 300 meters and ahead full. Get us out of the area immediately. Once we are clear, put us on the bottom. We must sit and wait in silence."

* * * *

At first, Ensign Shanna Watts thought it was a dream until she heard the metal supply room door shut. The voice on the other side of the storage room woke her up. *Last night was just a bit over the top at the Club Manhattan in Alexandria,* she thought. Out dancing until 2 a.m. was not conducive to her early morning Navy career.

Shanna had ducked into the large office supplies storage room, pulled out a couple of surplus cushions and fell asleep for twenty minutes. The sound of someone speaking on a cell phone slowly pried her from the arms of Morpheus. What she caught of the conversation seemed more like a dream as she replayed the words in her mind. Unbelievably as it sounded, someone had been talking on a cell phone warning someone about an active air-sea search. *Real spy sounding stuff,* she thought. For a while, she debated going to her superior officer about the incident, as she wasn't quite sure she dreamt it or not and how would she explain that she'd been sleeping while on duty? And, she only heard the last bits of the conversation without actually seeing who was talking … still … maybe this was something serious. She decided to speak to her superior officer about it at the end of her shift.

* * * *

Lieutenant Underwood sat reviewing the satellite images that he had compiled in his computer cache. He found it difficult to concentrate. Instead of counting frames and time intervals, he found himself mentally counting money. *If that's what I'm getting as a regular payoff,* he thought, *I can't wait to see what the bonus is like. I've got ten days of leave coming up next month. I can see spending it in San Tropez in a five-star hotel, that's for damn sure.*

The frames came up for 1818 hours, and he zoomed the magnification to what appeared to be a slight disturbance just below the surface of the ocean. The next image in the series showed that something was causing movement in the surrounding water, indicating that an object had broken the surface. The next few frames showed the object had retracted and vanished along with any underwater movements. Since the image was purely optical, it did not record the invisible laser pulse in the infrared range of the spectrum. Underwood bracketed the frames in the computer and deleted them. Quickly inserting a CD with the program his contacts had given him, he renumbered the images to eliminate any gap in the sequence. He could breathe easy now. His real work for the week was done, and no one was the wiser.

* * * *

It was 1315 hours and Ensign Watts stood very uncomfortably in front of her commanding officer Captain Janice Whetstone.

"I ought to place a reprimand for this on your record but … you did come to me and you were honest about falling asleep, no BS story about how you heard this conversation. Do you have any idea who it was or whom he was speaking with?

Ensign Watts, a young twenty-three-year-old African American naval officer shook her head. "No, Ma'am. He said they were sending search planes and an attack sub to *the area.* That's all I heard. But he was white … I mean I could hear it in his voice, his accent you know. Being black, I do notice these things. You'd notice, too, if it were the opposite and you were the one listening to a black man. And another thing, his voice was young. He'd have to be a young man I'd say."

"Are you sure no one saw you go into the storage room and decided to play a little practical joke on you?'

"No, Ma'am. No one saw me. I made sure of that. I was behind a big pile of boxes. I ah … didn't want to get into any trouble because I needed some more sleep."

"Okay, then. Thank you for the information as well as your honesty. I think this warrants a call to security … although I don't know how anyone could make a cell call especially from here without Echelon being able to track and record it. Doesn't make any sense, unless this guy had some pretty high-tech encryption software in that phone of his. Okay, Ensign, you're dismissed and do not repeat any of this to anyone. That's an order, and … try not to stay out so late with your friends."

After Ensign Shanna Watts closed her commanding officers door, Captain Whetstone picked up the telephone. "Get me Commander Burton in security. I may have something very important to tell him." *Interesting,* she thought, *Security might have to track down a young white male … That ought to be easy. After all, there are only about a few thousand people that fit that description working here.*

Kennedy Space Center, the LEM Simulator

Natasha Polyakova had her eyes fixed on the LED display screen mounted between the two triangular view ports as she called out the values. Her accented lyrical, almost musical voice read off altitude and distance to the Salyut.

"Climbing to 20 kilometers fifty down range. Rolling the ascent stage."

Out the triangle shaped view port, the lunar landscape slid out of view to present the star-studded black void of space.

"Fuel is nominal, range 100 kilometers and sixty up. John I have radar contact with Alliance. Eighty-five kilometers altitude and 130 down range … I see it!"

McGovern turned his head and looked over toward Natasha. "I see it, too. I've got us lined up for docking. I'm firing the forward thrusters."

He was concentrating on the head up display, lining up the a series of concentric circles that appeared to be floating just in front of his face with the docking target on the French module.

Natasha continued the readouts. "Forward at 25 meters per minute, now 10 per minute, slow … slow, you are 30 centimeters from the connection…"

McGovern's touch barely caressed the joystick to fire the aft thrusters, nudging the return stage of the LEM into the docking collar.

"… and contact. Docking clamps are locked and pressure is equalizing. Oh, John, you fly this craft like it was built just for you!"

McGovern laughed. "That would be a neat trick because the lander we're taking down the surface of the Moon was built nine years before I was a twinkle in my dad's eye. Don't forget, we're going to be flying a machine that was a museum display just a few weeks ago."

Just as they finished the return simulation, the lights came on with Norman Taggert standing in the observation area, clapping and smiling. "Bravo, John, and to you as well, Captain Polyakova. That was real teamwork and one of the smoothest dockings I've ever seen. Why don't you take a break Natasha and grab us a table for lunch. John and I will be over to join you in just a minute."

McGovern looked at his friend. "So this is just between us then?"

"Yeah, no sense giving the rest of the crew anything more to worry about right now. They all have to concentrate. The touchdown times on the second lander are not up to snuff yet. Curtis and LaCasse need a lot more practice."

"Okay, Norm, I know who needs work and who doesn't, but I'm sure that's not why you stopped by to see Natasha and I dock the upper half of the LEM. What's the real scoop on the loss of the rocket? What did Dreamland say?"

"You were right, John. I had the boys at Groom Lake run the data from both the Ares and the Atlas launches, and they came up with a perfect match to the DOD's tests in the late 90s of a carbon dioxide laser. An explosion due to superheating the rocket body is consistent with a series one high-energy laser. Now, what we're currently flying in our modified 747 and 777 is a little more potent and consumes a lot less power. The series one laser needed its own nuclear reactor to power it. Only trouble with this is no surface ships or any subs showed up on any of the defense department's satellite sweeps of that part of the ocean. The Navy dispatched several flights of Orion sub hunters to the area along with a *Seawolf* attack sub, but everything turned up negative."

McGovern shook his head. "Jeez, I do not like this one bit. We've got someone sitting off our coast able to take out any of our launches during the boost phase. If they want to stop us, they can, any time they want to."

"Yeah, but the Navy's working on it, and they have everything out there: satellites, over-flights and two attack subs looking for this bastard."

"It's got to be a Chinese nuclear sub, Norm. No doubt about it. Listen, I'm not going to soft peddle this, I have to discuss this with Natasha, my, ah … co-commander and then we have to speak to the crew. It's not fair to keep anyone in the dark about this."

John McGovern joined Natasha and the others at an outdoor table. She could see in his eyes something had changed between the time they left the simulator and now.

"Ah, Natasha, we have to talk. It's about the mission and the two launch explosions we've had …."

* * * *

John McGovern concluded the impromptu crew meeting. "… and so, that's what we're up against. Someone is sitting out there in the Atlantic with the ability to take us out on lift off. Now, Captain Polyakova and I will launch from Kazakhstan, so this doesn't affect us, but the four of you could be sitting ducks. Now, on the plus side, I've been told that the Navy will be putting a couple of hunter-killer subs as well as a destroyer group in the area along with sub killer F-18s to watch over things during the launches. Again, if anyone wants out, now's the time to speak up."

The other four astronauts formed a huddle among themselves. Lieutenant Bill Curtis spoke for the group. "Okay, you two," looking at Natasha Polyakova and John McGovern, "while the both of you are living it up on Borscht and Blini in Russia all safe and sound, and launching from the middle of Asia, we're all suffering here in this palm tree-filled paradise. Look, we all know just how dangerous this mission is going to be. If the Chinese have anti-satellite weapons on the Moon, more than likely they'll use them. I've got to put my faith in the U.S. Navy and their ability to find this SOB and blow him out of the water before he takes a crack at us. I speak for everyone on the mission; and we are a go for lift off!"

CHAPTER TEN

The Lunar South Pole

The lunar hopper had just passed over the near side-facing wall of the Crater Scott. This was the demarcation line between the area of the Moon visible from the Earth and the far side, hidden from view until October 1959 when Luna Three, launched by the Soviet Union, returned a grainy image of the mysterious and unknown land forever hidden from the eyes of man. As the hopper continued on its ballistic trajectory, the incredible site of humanity's home, painted a dazzling blue and white, crept above the horizon. The hopper could hardly be called a spacecraft, more a collection of aluminum tubes, fuel tanks and several small rocket motors. The hopper lived up to its name. Rather than actually flying above the Moon or achieving orbit, the skeletal framework was launched on a trajectory by a small rocket motor to travel a ballistic course, bringing it back to the surface a hundred or so kilometers away. To travel further, the engine would fire again sending the craft on another jump, hopping across the Moon.

The hopper had no cabin or pressurized environment. Rather, its pilot and passengers sat strapped into wire mesh seats with their spacesuits hooked into the life support system, providing oxygen and heat through flexible hoses. On this flight, General Wang, the base's commander, sat watching the tortured gray landscape flow beneath the hopper. In the pilot's seat was Major Yuan Xho. His display screen indicated they would shortly reach their landing zone between the craters Schomberger D and Manzinus C. It was in this location, clearly visible to observers on the Earth, that China had built a magnetic accelerator. The phased array of electromagnets along a four-kilometer track was designed to draw all the electricity required to power its 128 mega-joule magnetic track from a compact nuclear reactor. At the starting point of the track, a payload destined for Earth orbit would be affixed to a sled. The sled would then be accelerated along the track until a speed of two and half kilometers per second was reached. Once the sled reaches this speed, it flies off, into space, to arrive in Earth orbit, three days later. That was how China had begun to supply the nations of the Third World with nearly pure ingots of titanium and that was how the communications satellite, designed to replace the one destroyed by the very same Chinese would be placed into Earth orbit.

Major Yuan, seated next to his commanding officer, was thankful they were separated by the hard vacuum of space and enclosed in spacesuits. This way, Yuan's look of despair and frustration was hidden from Wang's eyes. As a young boy, Yuan Xho dreamed of traveling through space, of walking on the Moon or standing upon the red sands of the planet Mars, but always his dreams were of a community of nations, working for the benefit of all mankind. Here, China was creating a huge deception to convince the world to grant his country sole rights to the resources of the Moon and of space. Instead of cooperation between China, Europe, Russia and America, his government was planting the seeds of war. Already China had fired the first shot, killing two men. To Yuan, these men were fellow space travelers, brothers, taking humanity's first tentative steps toward the stars. He was heart sick at the waste of their lives and the incredible expense his nation was spending to promote this deception. Yuan thought that if the wealth of space were shared between all nations, there would be no limit to what humanity could achieve. It made him almost physically ill.

Worse yet was the thought of the second magnetic accelerator, the one hidden from view, beyond the terminator line that marked the boundary of the near side of the Moon. This accelerator would not carry the wealth of the Moon back to Earth but instead hurl terror and death. Already, with each supply ship from Earth, the stockpile of nuclear weapons continued to grow. Major Yuan knew these were not for defense, mining or any of the other myriad of justifications for bringing these perversions of technology to the pristine untouched realm of the stars. Yuan knew the truth. These weapons would be launched from the Moon undetected to achieve low Earth orbit and give China the ability to strike at will at any target on the globe without warning.

General Wang, his commander, boasted of this masterstroke and of the cunning of this plan. Major Yuan listened to how this plot for nuclear blackmail would bring the West to its knees and ensure China would take its rightful place as the dominant world power, no longer considered less than equal to the effete Europeans and the truculent Americans. But to Yuan Xho, was also a student of history, the hubris of China in this adventure echoed down the corridors of time to another era and another great Asian power whose military leaders truly believed their cunning plan of attack would also ensure them world domination. Yet, the results were millions dead, cities in ruins and two great metropolises all but vaporized by the first use of nuclear weapons in warfare.

Major Yuan sat in his quarters each night, consumed in frustration and dread of the path his country was walking upon. While his superiors saw glory at the end of this path, Yuan saw only death among the twisted and melted ruins of China's great cities once those nations that his country sought to subjugate struck back with all their might.

In his dreams Yuan Xho stood in his home city of Kunming. It was early morning. The streets are filled with men and women heading to work. Children, six and seven years old, in their dark blue uniforms walked, sometimes hand in hand into their schoolyards… and in front of him, his beautiful wife stood smiling, looking at him with deep affection, their young son in her arms and then …

The deafening sirens begin to blare and the peace of the morning was shattered. Without warning, the gentle blue morning sky turned an impossible all consuming white. Light and heat beyond imagination enveloped the city. The men and women going to work, the young children just reaching the steps of their school all turned to face him as if to ask, *Why Yuan, did not stop this?* just as an all-devouring heat boiled the flesh from their bones. For just a moment, their naked skeletons stand erect and then the shockwave from the blast pulverizes their remains, spreading them as ash on the radioactive wind. He reaches out for his wife and son only to see them evaporate before his eyes, leaving just an adult skeleton holding the bones of a child before being crushed and blasted into nothing. And … Yuan would awake, sometimes screaming, sometimes weeping but always terrified. *Was he the only one who saw this?* Major Yuan thought. *Could he muster the courage and the means to stop this madness?*

His dark musings were interrupted by General Wang speaking to him over his headset. "Major Yuan, behold our great achievement. You will set the hopper down within twenty meters of those men with the magnetic accelerator behind us. They are recording our arrival and my speech, dedicating the new replacement satellite that China has so graciously proved to the Pan-African nations."

To replace the one that we secretly destroyed, thought Yuan.

"We shall then send these images along with my speech to news organizations around the world, demonstrating the superiority of Chinese technology and our commitment to world peace."

Major Yuan could muster no enthusiasm for his commander's words. Again, he considered his nation's course of action and the road they were traveling. Despite the fact his suit heater was functioning correctly, chills shot through his body. The images from his dreams kept forcing their way into his thoughts. Last night was worse as the blackened skull of his child turned to him with empty eye sockets and asked, "Why did you let me die, Daddy?"

Yuan Xho felt he must say something. He switched his transmitter to the private channel. His commander did the same.

"You have something you wish to speak to me about, Major?"

"Yes, sir, I do. Look at the magnificent achievements we have accomplished already on the Moon. We have built the accelerator; we have extracted everything we need to begin humanity's march to the stars, yet how much more could have been gained by cooperation with the other space faring nations of the world instead of confrontation?"

General Wang, so focused on the deceptive plan of Sung Zhao, could not see the logic in Yuan's words but instead thought his subordinate was dismayed by the pace of China's progress. "*Ha,* do not worry, Yuan. Once we put the West and the Russians in their place, we will surge ahead. The flag of our nation shall fly proudly on the Moon and next upon Mars. There is no stopping us."

"No, sir that is not what I meant. How will the Americans and the others react to us once they learn this has all been a deception, a trick to gain domination over them?"

"Are you serious, Yuan? The self-absorbed West and the plodding Russians will yield to the superiority of the Peoples Republic of China!"

"Sir, do you know who Admiral Isoroku Yamamoto was?"

"I do not, Major. I was never that fond of history. Japanese, though I am certain, yes?"

Ignorant fool, Yuan thought, *of course you don't know your history. You rose through the ranks because of your political connections, not your military ability. I fear I'm simply wasting my breath.* "Yes, sir. It was Admiral Yamamoto who carried out Japan's bold plan to force the Americans from the Pacific by attacking and sinking their fleet at Pearl Harbor. When his commanders and pilots returned to their aircraft carriers flushed with victory, he turned to General Genda, who led the raid against the Americans and said, "I fear all we have done is to awaken a sleeping giant and fill him with a terrible resolve."

"So, what is your point, Major Yuan?"

"Sir, I fear that if we try to impose our will upon the West, particularly the Americans, China – as Japan once did – will pay a terrible price for our course of action."

General Wang turned to face his subordinate. Although the reflective coating of his visor hid his face, Yuan could imagine the expression it held from the anger in the General's voice.

"Major Yuan, keep your damned opinions to yourself. The war fought between America and Japan is ancient history. China holds the high ground and will be victorious. Do not speak another word of this to me or I shall report your comments to our political officer. That will end your military career. Do you understand me? Now, get out of my way. I have a speech to give before we launch our magnanimous gift to the African nations toward the Earth!"

As General Wang turned and walked off toward the magnetic accelerator track scattering the dust of four billion years, Major Yuan stared at the desolate lunar landscape but in his mind's eye, all he could see were burning cities littered with the dead and the dying.

* * * *

The NASA-registered 757 descended toward a thick white cloud deck. John McGovern was seated next to Natasha Polyakova who had the window seat. As they broke through the gray fog that had enveloped the aircraft, Natasha's home city of Moscow came into view. McGovern looked out the window with her, hoping to pick out a famous landmark such as the Saint Basil's or the Kremlin wall, but all he could see were row upon row of nearly identical apartment buildings. Natasha's perfume invaded his senses and his lips brushed against her hair as he moved closer to her, sharing the view from the small aircraft window. John felt a rise in his pulse rate and a tingling that spoke to him about just how attracted he was to this woman.

On the long flight from KSC, they talked for hours about growing up, their parents and family, and what fired their desires to leave the bonds of Earth for space. For Natasha, it was following in her father's footsteps. For John McGovern, it was just the opposite. His father was an insurance actuarial, a fancy name for an accountant. He was a man that always played it safe, never took a risk and never tasted the fullness of life. A vacation to the tropics, skiing in the mountains, buying that red convertible – these would always wait until "someday." Well, someday came all right but along with it was a diagnosis of terminal pancreatic cancer. John loved his dad but he saw in him a man that postponed the joy of living until it was too late and his time had run out. He lost his father at just age fifteen. He vowed he would not venture down that same road of a safe but boring life. That was one aspect of his teenage years he left out of the conversation with Natasha.

John was a risk-taker, racing motorcycles by age sixteen, diving on coral reefs, and taking to the air as a student pilot before he even had a license to drive a car. His craving for speed was unquenchable, leading him to the Air Force and the cockpit of a Mach 2.5 jet and then strapped to several million pounds of thrust in the form of a rocket and launched in to space.

McGovern's personal life was another matter. He had met Cheryl while at the Air Force Academy in Colorado. They dated for a few years and then married before John was sent to Iraq. He had thought his marriage to her was strong and they would wind up an old couple someday. Children were not in the cards due to a genetic condition Cheryl discovered she had about two years after they were married. But still, life was good, until McGovern's suspicions about the true nature of the Chinese space program began to surface and he made those views known to every news organization and every group he could. The results were a measurable fall of about 8 percent of Chinese products bought by Americans and one or two investment deals that went south. Eight percent may not sound like much, but when billions of dollars are involved, it was substantial. Many individuals, with vested interests in maintaining a trade relationship that enriched their companies and their personal accounts, found John McGovern a little too vocal and a little too influential for their tastes. One man in particular had made it a point to do something about it. That's when McGovern's life went to hell and that was when Cheryl walked out.

Looking over at Natasha this close, her powerful feminine attraction was making him seriously reconsider his silent vow not to become too involved with a woman again, at least for a long time. In truth, he saw Natasha as being very much like him – a space pilot as well as a strong personality who did not compromise when it came to what was the right thing to do. *If only I can break through that wall she's erected*, he thought, *she's the kind of woman I could easily see myself falling in love with.*

During the flight, they had both dozed off. He awoke once to find Natasha's head nestled against his shoulder, her thoughts far off in her dreams. McGovern found it extremely pleasurable and imagined just how complete he would feel to find her next to him after a long night of making love.

The sound of the landing gear locking into place brought McGovern's thoughts back to the reality of the task at hand. Outside the jet's window, objects on the ground zoomed from a child's toys to full size as the 757's wheels made contact with the ground. The NASA jet rolled to a stop at Russia's Zhukovski Air Force Base. Norman Taggert was first off the plane. Waiting for him at the bottom of the old style rollaway exit stairs was his Russian counterpart, Yuri Zhdanov, with a friendly smile lighting up his face, helping to dispel the damp chill that hung in the March air.

The two old friends embraced at the bottom of the stairs.

"Yuri! *Kak Dilah*! It's good to see you again!"

"*Da!* I will say the same. You are to have dinner with my family and I tonight. I will not hear any excuse for you not to come. Ludmila is making a feast for us!"

Taggert, slapping his old Mir crewmate on the back answered, "Of course I'll come. Just let me get the *Alliance* crew settled in over at Star City. They're pretty jet lagged so I hope you don't have anything too demanding on the schedule for them today."

"No, of course not, Norman, their training and simulations in the water tanks can begin tomorrow."

"Dinner sounds great but not too much *celebration* tonight. I have to leave for the Cape tomorrow evening."

As the *Alliance* crew descended the jet stairs and walked toward the waiting van, Zhdanov couldn't help but notice the interplay of body language between Natasha Polyakova and John McGovern. Yuri wondered if it was his imagination or not, but then thought better of pursuing it. They were both adults, and as long as it didn't affect the mission, Zhdanov didn't consider it any of his business.

* * * *

At that very moment, 3,000 kilometers to the east, in Alma-Ata, Kazakhstan, a meeting of a different kind was taking place.

The sprawling bazaar near the outskirts of the city held everything imaginable, from bootlegged copies of the new Windows Magnum-10 operating system, perfume from France to local fruits, vegetables and chickens. Embedded in the swarming mass of shoppers, was a man dressed in a knee length brown leather coat. His face was clearly Asian but easily blended in with the majority of Kazakhs, many of whose heritages included Mongol ancestry. The man looked again at the sketch indicating where to find the particular merchant he sought. After about 10 minutes of searching the myriad of stalls, he saw him, standing among dozens of small polished brass tables and copper cooking pots, hawking his wares. He could see by the way the merchant was dressed – a long robe and head covering, with a thick black beard upon his face –he was the Muslim that he sought.

The robed merchant fixed his eyes upon the Asian with a penetrating stare and bade him to come closer with the flourish of his hand. "I am Nadar, the one you seek. Let us retire within my tent to discuss your proposal."

The Asian looked nervous as he ducked below the tent's overhang, pressing his hand against the left side of his coat to feel the reassuring security of his semi-automatic pistol. Both men eyed each other warily for any sign of deception. Finally, the Asian spoke. "I am Chang. I understand that you are the Chechen."

The bearded man fixed his brooding dark brown eyes upon the Chinese agent. "I am Muslim first, then I am Chechen."

Chang nodded as he considered his answer. "Then I am certain you have no love for the Russians."

The banked fires behind those brooding dark eyes suddenly began to flare. "The Russian infidels have cost the lives of many in our towns and villages. Many of my fighters have died in their prisons or at the hands of their soldiers. I would seek to avenge the slaughter of my Islamic brothers over the broken bodies of the Russian dogs!"

"Then may I propose we offer you assistance in avenging your people's misery and deaths at the hands of the Russians. We will help you strike a blow against the bear that will reverberate around the world. The Russians will be seen as weak and foolish. Your people will laud over them as they crawl about in the dirt."

A look of suspicion flashed in the Chechen's eyes. "Tell me, why do you seek to aide us in our Jihad?"

"You have an expression, do you not? The enemy of my enemy is my friend."

Beneath the man's beard, a smile began to form on his face. "Tell me more of your plan … Chinese …"

* * * *

"Papa!" Natasha Polyakova burst from the transport van and into the arms of her father, Dmitry Polyakov, before the driver even pulled to a stop in front of the Star City administration building.

She rushed into his arms as he picked her up and swung her around, just like he did when she was a small girl. Natasha hugged him and kissed his cheek.

"So then, how is my *solniska*? Have they been treating you well in Florida?" Dmitry Polyakov observed the paleness of her skin. You do not look like a tourist returning from the tropics, eh?"

Natasha laughed. "No, Papa. With all I have had to learn and all of my training, the only sun I saw was the rising of it in the morning and the setting of it at night. Oh, please, let me introduce you to the crew of the Alliance."

Each crewmember shook hands with the legendary Dmitry Polyakov, the man who flew the longest mission in space. For the amount of time he had spent aboard Mir after the Soviet collapse, Dmitry could have almost flown to Mars and back. The experience resulted in a very prolonged recovery time from weightlessness and some permanent bone loss. Still, her father had a strong handshake and straight posture that spoke of his military career. Last to shake his hand was John McGovern. Natasha's introduction of him to her father was on a deeper level.

She spoke to her father in English so that John would know what they were discussing. "Papa, this is Colonel John McGovern, my co-commander for the mission. He will be flying the lander down to *Luna*, and I will serve as co-pilot. He is amazing at the controls of that craft!"

"Doctor Polyakov, it's an honor to meet you, sir," McGovern said. "I want you to know that I am very proud to share my command duties with your daughter. She's a fast learner and an excellent pilot herself. She's mastered the LEM, and she can fly it as well as any of the guys did back in the Apollo program."

Polyakov looked into John McGovern's eyes searching for disingenuous flattery about his comments. Seeing none, he still felt he had to ask the question. "So, you feel no reduction of your manhood, sharing your command duties with a woman?"

"No, sir, I do not. Natasha is not just any woman, although you should know that as her father. She's intelligent, brave and determined to succeed. I'd rather have her in a joint command position than a lot of men I know."

Polyakov considered this as well as the manner that Colonel McGovern's eyes seemed to light up while counting off his daughter's virtues. Perhaps there was more here to this relationship than just fellow space travelers. "Natasha, will you be able to have dinner with me tonight? I have a lot to discuss with you."

"Yes, Papa, let me get settled into my quarters and I shall meet you in one hour."

The sun had already set over the Moscow skyline as the astronauts entered the building to retreat from the chilled breeze that whipped about them. Spring was coming late this year to Russia, as winter would not relinquish its grip. But, the chill of the air was nothing compared to the icy grip of defeat upon the soul that the rising of the morning sun would bring to all involved in the mission.

* * * *

Natasha's father looked across the table at his daughter. "Yulia's *Solyanka* is excellent, yes?"

"Yes it was; she seems to be a very good cook, and she has returned the smile to your face."

Yulia had good intuition and got up from the table, saying she needed to straighten up in the kitchen, giving Dmitry and his daughter some private time to speak.

"I … was not certain how you would feel about another woman in my home after the loss of your mother. Believe me, *solnishka*, I loved her very much, and when she died, I felt my world was ending."

Natasha leaned over to stroke her father's hair. "Please, Papa, I will never reproach you for wanting to find some companionship and some happiness after Mama died. Everyone needs to feel loved and to have a chance to live again in the sunlight."

"And what of you, Natasha? You seem to have buried your heart along with Misha after his death. All I've seen in your life is constant work and dedication to your career, a career I might add that certain individuals have made extremely difficult for you to maintain. Yet, today, if I'm not mistaken, I saw something in your eyes when you introduced me to Colonel McGovern. It was more than just admiration. I saw real affection in your eyes, and in those of Colonel McGovern's when he spoke of your accomplishments, did I not?"

Natasha looked down at her hands, clenching them together, gathering her thoughts, now at war with her emotions. "Yes. Papa, perhaps you did. He is the first man that I have met since I lost Misha who has the soul of a warrior. Not in the sense of a soldier, but a man who sees no compromise between right and wrong, no areas of gray. There are individuals in America as well who fear the truth, and John was nearly killed for speaking out publicly about the danger China poses. I want to say he is a man I could fall in love with – perhaps I'm already in love with him – but between us stands Misha's ghost. How can he rest if the people who murdered him walk about as if they were untouchable by justice?"

"Yes, yes, I understand how you must feel but tell me of the mission. Before this, you made just a single Soyuz flight and now you are a co-commander? I feel that certain forces are placing you in this position to fail."

"You are correct, Papa. In fact, this is what John McGovern suspects as well, but we have trained every day, 10 hours a day, seven days a week until we know our jobs perfectly. I have more simulator experience on the LEM than any of the original Apollo astronauts. If I have to, I can fight on the surface of the Moon as well. We have received training with the Colt vacuum rifles. I was with John at the firing range when we were shooting these weapons at targets. John thought I had missed all but one shot until the instructor showed him the flower petal pattern in the target. All my shots hit the exact center of the target."

Dmitry just nodded his head. "Too bad they dismissed you from the biathlon team. Russia would have certainly earned the gold medal. But tell me; are you not afraid if you must go into combat? You are … my daughter … I love you."

"I love you, too, Papa, but I have my duty to my country. I must tell you that Colonel Nikolai Schevyenskey's death was no accident. I have learned that the first moon station was destroyed deliberately by a Chinese missile."

Polyakov nodded grimly. "Yes, I suspected as much but this gives me even greater concern for your life."

"Papa, how can I be any less of a patriot to my nation than Zoya Kosmodemyanskya when she faced down the Nazis behind their lines or Marina Raskova when she and our heroic women pilots took to the air to sweep the Germans from our skies? And … I feel secure and have confidence in my crew … especially when I am next to John. Perhaps … I should open my heart to him once we have completed our mission … perhaps …"

****

The driver of the KAMAZ tanker truck had been driving the long dusty and deserted roads that crisscrossed Kazakhstan since just after midnight. This was not a job he relished but one that paid him triple his usual wages for hauling what amounted to a huge bomb behind him. The tanker he was pulling from the JSC Khimprom chemical plant was filled with a deadly mix of hydrazine and methanol – highly explosive rocket fuel.

Konstantin had maneuvered his truck through the outskirts of Zhalagash and turned onto the main road, leading to the Baikonur Spaceport 70 kilometers distant. It struck him as odd to have received a call so late in the evening asking him if he wanted to drive this load of fuel to the launch complex. Usually shipments of this nature were contracted for weeks in advance.

Maybe they broke another toilet on the space station, he thought. *They'll be holding it all in until a replacement can be sent … or else they'll have to go outside, ha!*

Konstantin came to a sharp bend in the roadway, slowing his truck so as not to jostle the volatile liquid riding just a few meters behind him. There in front of him, a Volga sedan had overturned and was burning. A man and two women sprawled face down on the road were nearby. The man was bent over one of them, and appeared in anguish. Konstantin slammed on the brakes to keep from running into them, grabbed his first-aid kit and dropped down from the cab of the KAMAZ. As he walked toward the victims of the crash, one of the women suddenly stood up pointing an automatic pistol at him. Before his lips could even form a question, the woman pulled the trigger, blasting a hole in the man's chest. The shot was well aimed, and Konstantin was dead before he hit the roadway.

The man who had seemed to be in anguish then stood up and removed his long robe, revealing a set of coveralls identical to those of the Khimprom employee.

The man, with jet-black hair and somber eyes, said nothing to the women. To them he was simply the driver. It was not good to know his name or become familiar with a man who, in a matter of hours, would leave the world of the living.

The day before, the driver had spoken with Nadar. He then returned to his small apartment to shave his body and ritually bathe himself. He ate a final mean and kneeled down upon his prayer rug to prepare himself to enter paradise. The following morning, Nadar met him and provided the stolen Volga sedan to set up the ambush. Nadar handed him convincing documents that would allow him access to the launch complex along with two bricks of plastic explosives. These he would affix to the tank carrying the rocket fuel. In his hand, Nadar placed a black detonator, kissed him on both cheeks and said, "Go with Allah."

* * * *

John McGovern looked over at the alarm clock next to his bed for the fifth time. *Yep*, he thought, *the time's advanced all the way from 5:45 to 5:55.*

He swung out of bed, grabbed his jeans and pulled on a sweatshirt then opened his dorm room door into the hall. There was a large window at the end of it that faced east. He could see the first brushstrokes of salmon begin to color the sky over Moscow. Here and there people were walking, bundled against the chill of March, on their way to work. Cars and buses spat plums of white condensation from their exhausts into the damp chilled air.

As McGovern watched the pink band of sky push higher, he felt a light touch on his shoulder and turned to face Natasha. Even in gray sweat pants and a T-shirt, she looked beautiful. She smiled up at him. "I can't sleep either," she said. "I'm off my time from training in Florida for the past weeks."

"According to my internal clock, it's just a little before ten at night. I'm ready to go dancing, want to come?"

Natasha laughed. "You have a good sense of humor. I really like that in you … among other things."

That, thought McGovern, *was an interesting comment from her.* "So how was dinner with your father?'

"Very nice. He has a girlfriend now. I think that is good for him. He should not be alone, though I suppose I felt disappointed that he chose to replace Mama, but … he was so lost for a time."

"Your mom, can you talk about it?"

Natasha nodded her head but looked toward the floor before speaking. "Three years ago, Mama found a lump. It was a rare form of breast cancer with little chance of survival. She fought bravely but we lost her nine months later. I still miss her very much."

"I lost my dad like that when I was fifteen. When it happened, I couldn't believe he'd die, but he did, just six months later."

Natasha looked deeply into his eyes. "You never told me. I did not know that we shared the same pain. So, you know a part of my soul as well, yes?

"It's not the kind of knowledge I'd wish on anyone. Even now, it's hard to speak about it. So, what did you and your dad talk about?"

"You mostly, John."

"Oh what? How I was an absolute jerk, making your first two days at the Cape miserable?"

Natasha laughed. "No, of course not. I told him how much I admired your courage and your strength to stand firm for what you believe in. I told him that you were the kind of man I could fall in love with … someday after my heart has healed from my loss of Misha. I ... perhaps I should not say any more."

John McGovern had to fight the urge to take her in his arms right there. Yes, he was falling for her but now was not the time for anything but getting ready for the mission and she had said herself that she was not ready to unchain her heart.

"Yeah, I think you're the kind of woman I could fall in love with as well. You have the strength and courage of a lioness and beauty that men usually find only in their dreams … I ah, hope you don't mind that I said that. Let's get dressed and grab something to eat. I'm not tired, and I want some simulator time with you in a Soyuz. Just don't beat me up too badly if I screw up the first time, okay?"

Natasha fixed him with a devious smile. "Perhaps I shall compliment you on how brilliantly you managed to get us both killed."

"Ah, I guess I'll never live down those remarks I made to you."

"Well, only if you promise to join me for breakfast."

* * * *

The driver downshifted the KAMAZ tanker loaded with rocket fuel and approached the front gate of the Baikonur launch complex. By now, the sun had climbed much higher in the blue cloudless sky of central Asia. As he pulled abreast of the security office, a guard, dressed in the olive green of a Russian military uniform, walked up to the cab of his truck.

"We were not expecting a delivery this morning," the guard said. "Let me see your paperwork and identification."

The driver handed the man his ID badge. The security guard, a corporal, studied it closely, looking at the name, Igor Lutov. It was an ethnic Russian name, but the face of the man sitting in the truck was swarthy with black hair and deep set dark brown eyes. The officer apprised the driver with a good deal of suspicion. "I know most of the drivers for Khimprom. I've never seen you before."

Keeping his answers short to hide his Chechen accent the driver spoke. "I am new with the company."

The corporal, still cautious, replied, "I see. Your accent, it is not one I am familiar with. Are you from Dagestan, perhaps?"

The driver showed no emotion. He was completely calm, as he knew his fate had already been sealed. His mission of glory would soon be fulfilled. "No, my father was from Kazan. I was born just across the border in Orsk."

The guard looked over the truck and the 17-meter long tank of rocket fuel it carried.

"Perhaps I should call the offices of Khimprom as to why we were not made aware of your delivery this morning."

The driver reached for a clipboard with his documents held in place. "This is a military delivery, see here." He handed the paperwork out of the cab's window.

The young corporal immediately saw the seal of the Russian armed forces along with the name and signature of General Karpov, commander of the strategic missile forces.

As the guard studied the document, the driver again spoke. "I was told this delivery was urgent, ordered at the highest level of the military and cannot be delayed."

The guard handed the driver his clipboard then yelled, "Open the gate, let him through." Then he yelled up to the man behind the wheel. "Are you certain you know where to go?"

Fixing the soldier with a grim look of finality he answered, "Yes, I do. I know exactly where to go."

The driver pulled ahead shifting the gears of the KAMAZ as he headed toward the forest of pipes and silvery spheres that held rocket fuel and oxidizer. At the last moment, he turned the wheel of the truck and instead of going straight to the fuel storage area, he drove up to a large brick and metal storage building, parking his truck as close to the massive entrance doors a he possibly could.

An officer, looking through a pair of binoculars, yelled over to his companion. "Where the hell does that idiot think he's going? He's parked in front of the storage building. Radio a guard to tell him to get out of there and get back to the fuel depot!"

The private pulled his UAZ jeep up to the tanker and hopped out, staring at the driver in the cab. At first, he thought the man was ill, as he rocked back and forth and was speaking to himself. The soldier grabbed the cab's handhold and climbed up to order the man to move. Then to his horror, he heard what the man was chanting: "*Allah Akbar, Allah Akbar*" (God is great). He held a small back box in his right hand with a blinking red diode on it. The private leaped off the side of the truck, running for his life as the driver's thumb closed on the device's switch.

A minute radio impulse reached the two detonators at the speed of light, and electric current triggered the initial explosion. In a heartbeat, it propagated into the plastic explosives, releasing two huge blasts that shredded the tanker, causing the rocket fuel inside to erupt into a massive all consuming fireball. The blast reached out and took the young private then ravenously spread, enveloping the storage facility, turning steel and brick into flying shrapnel. In a matter of only 45 seconds, the fireball had completely gutted the storage building and everything inside of it with a heat of thousands of degrees. Fire crews raced to the epicenter of the devastation, but there was nothing left to salvage; they could only attempt to contain the blaze and prevent other buildings from falling victim to the flames.

* * * *

John McGovern and Natasha Polyakova had just finished their breakfast and were heading over to the Soyuz simulator when they ran into RSA Director Yuri Zhdanov. The color had drained from his face. He was nearly in shock and shaking. Natasha twice asked what had happened and then, his voice coming in short gulps, his eyes refusing to focus on either Natasha or McGovern, Zhdanov replied, "They're gone! The three Salyuts in storage are gone. There has been a massive explosion at the launch center. We no longer have any means of reaching the Moon."

Jack Griffin had just gotten off the elevator with astronaut Bill Curtis when he spotted RSA Director Zhdanov along with John and Natasha. All three looked as if they were in shock.

"Hey, what's going on … somebody die or something?"

John McGovern turned to the Canadian and answered, "Not somebody, some thing. The mission's dead. The Salyuts are gone. An explosion at the storage area in Kazakhstan destroyed the building they were in along with everything inside of it."

Tom Garcia and LaCasse were the next ones down from their dormitory floor, both hungry and eager for breakfast. However, the terrible news they were delivered killed their appetites. Tom Garcia, sitting in a chair, his elbows braced on his knees, his hands cupping his face, was a man in despair. "I can't believe it! I can't believe we've come this far, this fast only to have *this* happen? How?"

Natasha spoke with a dejected voice. "Another *accident* it seems: This time at Baikonur. Somehow, a fuel truck drove up to the building that the three Salyuts were stored in and exploded. Although I am certain this was no accident!"

Director Zhdanov, shaking his head, finished his conversation and hung up the telephone. "Cosmonaut Polyakova is correct. The body of the real driver of the fuel truck was found just outside of Zhalagash, about 70 kilometers from Baikonur. This was some kind of suicide attack. The gate guards are being questioned, but apparently the driver had what appeared to be genuine military paperwork signed by the commander of the strategic rocket forces himself. This was no ordinary terrorist attack. This was a very well planned operation by people who knew exactly where to hit us and how to stop us from reaching the Moon."

By then, many in the engineering and flight simulation departments, looking for the *Alliance* crew, had wandered into the hallway leading to the cafeteria. Anton Kovalchuk, the usually affable simulator technician, stood next to Natasha, his head bent in a posture of defeat.

John McGovern looked about to boil over with rage. Finally, he could no longer hold it in. *"Son of a bitch!* If you ever catch the bastards who were behind this you ought to lop off their heads and put them on display!"

Suddenly Natasha's eyes went wide, and she put her hand to her mouth, not daring to hope what she just realized might be true. "John … did you say *display?* Oh my, God ... Anton, your keys! Your keys to your car! Please … give them to me and quickly!"

"All right, Natasha, but please don't damage it. I just bought it."

"Anton, if I can pilot a Soyuz, I can certainly drive your car … John, *poshlee* … quick, quick, let's go and pray, pray the swine that destroyed the Salyuts do not realize the error they have made!"

McGovern was running along with Natasha into the parking lot of Star City. They jumped into Anton's new Skoda sport coupe and tore out of the exit and onto the main Moscow ring road.

"Hey, Natasha! What the hell is going on? Where are we going?"

"To the Hotel Kosmos. We'll be there in just a few minutes, but we must hurry!"

Natasha was pushing the 1.5-liter coupe for all it was worth, screeching through traffic and weaving from lane to lane. Somehow, they managed to escape being noticed by the Moscow traffic police. She downshifted the car and sped down Mira Prospect, past the huge U-shaped Hotel Kosmos. As she rounded the corner just opposite the hotel, Natasha jammed on the brakes and pulled to the curb.

"Natasha! Is that what I think it is? I mean is it *real* or just a model?"

Natasha, at last daring to hope that the mission had not been terminated by their enemies replied, "No, it's real. My father used to bring me here as a small child to look at it and play beside it. I liked to pretend I was a cosmonaut and I was outside, in space looking at my ship. It's real all right! Those stupid bastards never realized it was here. John, I must call Yuri Zhdanov and tell him to send the army. We need soldiers to protect it."

While Natasha placed her call to the RSA director, John McGovern just stood on the sidewalk gazing up at it. An actual Salyut space station with a Soyuz mounted to it, on display next to the Hotel Kosmos. Somehow, if this craft had not seen too much damage from sitting outdoors for so many years, then maybe, just maybe, the mission could be salvaged.

About 15 minutes after Natasha called the director, the first truckload of soldiers with Kalashnikovs arrived at the display. The people behind the destruction of the Salyuts in Kazakhstan had failed to stop McGovern's and Natasha's mission, and even if they realized one more of the space stations was still in existence, they would never be able to get near it now, not with armed troops guarding the Salyut.

By late afternoon, as if echoing the mood of those inspecting and readying the Salyut to be moved, the sun shone down brilliantly from a deep blue sky. The crew of the *Alliance* mission, along with an engineering team, as well as RSA Director Zhdanov and Dmitry Polyakov, Natasha's father, walked around it. The entire block about the Salyut, including Mira Prospect, was cordoned off by the military with a flat bed truck waiting to receive the Salyut. A crane gently lowered the space station onto a series of padded supports.

John McGovern had his arms crossed watching the operation when he felt someone step up beside him.

Dmitry Polyakov turned to McGovern. "They will be taking the Salyut from here to the Korolev-Energia space facility for testing and reconditioning. If everything is satisfactory, they will complete all upgrades and fly it to Baikonur for launching."

McGovern nodded his head in agreement. "Your daughter is a very quick thinker. While just about everyone at the training facility was crying in their coffee, she remembered this place. She said you used to take her here as a child, and she would pretend she was in outer space."

Polyakov laughed. "Ah, yes, when Natasha was only seven or eight, her mother and I would stop here sometimes. She liked this place better than the playgrounds near our home. Unbelievable, that if this craft is capable of space flight, she will actually travel to the Moon in it."

"Doctor Polyakov, Natasha told me about your wife. You have my deepest sympathies. I lost my father like that before I was sixteen."

"Yes, yes … and that is perhaps the real reason I wished to speak with you. I hope that I betray no secrets, but I am Natasha's father and I seek only her happiness. She told me that you are the kind of man she could fall in love with, but I have to know for myself if her intuition is correct. She has lost much – her fiancée, then her mother. She is a strong and dedicated woman, but she is also my child, and her soul is not made of iron. I have to know if you feel this way as well. Also, there is the mission. She will not back down, and as we have just learned, those who would seek to stop you will go to any lengths to do so."

John McGovern realized this was going to be a turning point in his life. *A heart-to-heart talk with the father of a woman that I am falling in love with?* "Dmitry, you and I are part of a very small and very special community of human beings. We're space travelers. I believe that we have a bond between us, not shared by those who have never looked down upon our world from the blackness of space, so I'll speak to you with truth ... ah ... *pravda.* You say that Natasha believes she is falling in love with me, and I have to tell you, I feel the same way. Your daughter is unique. I've never met a woman with such life in her soul, such a brave spirit and such remarkable intelligence as your daughter, not to mention I find her to be one of the most beautiful women I've ever met. I know about her loss, and I hold her in my highest respect. If she feels this way about me as I feel about her, then what is destined to happen will happen. And, believe me, I will take care of your daughter on this mission and bring her back safely to you. After that, if she feels the same way, I'll take care of her for the rest of our lives. That's a promise."

With that, Dmitry Polyakov embraced John McGovern as the whine of the crane's hydraulic motor echoed across the plaza. Slowly the Salyut settled down onto the padded supports and the driver of the flatbed pulled away, heading off to the Energia facility, under the watchful eyes of a military convoy.

CHAPTER ELEVEN

China, the Headquarters of Space Intelligence

It was before seven in the morning, Beijing time, when Space Intelligence Director Sung Zhao's three subordinates nervously filed into his office. All had heard the rumors and knew to expect a very unpleasant meeting. Zhao had his back to them, reading the hard copy of an intelligence report. His anger boiled to such a point that he picked up a ceramic cup from his desk and hurled it to the floor, smashing it to pieces. Then he turned to face his men. The look of anger on his face was even more terrifying by the fact it only registered on the undamaged side. The other half of his face was a blank emotionless mask save for the hideous scar that ran from his eye to his chin.

Zhao fixed his gaze on the Russian sector intelligence officer. "I want the bungling idiot who was responsible for this debacle in my office in 24 hours. How could you possibly not know about another Salyut, especially if it has been sitting out in plain sight for years? *How is that possible*?!"

Yang, the sector chief, shifted uncomfortably in his seat. "Sir, we did not realize this was an actual spacecraft. We assumed it to be a model. In fact, none of my men gave it any thought at all."

Sung Zhao was seething. "Yes, I can see just how much *thought* your men are capable of! We went to considerable expense, as well as risk, to ensure the destruction of the three remaining Russian Salyuts *and now this?!"*

His second subordinate, a technical expert, then spoke up. "Perhaps ... perhaps this space station has been too long in the elements and cannot be made flight ready, honorable director."

Zhao glowered at the man. "And perhaps flowers shall bloom in the dead of winter. Anything is possible, but we cannot count on *perhaps!* I must devise an alternative solution for preventing the launch of this mission! In less than an hour I must answer to the Vice Premier himself about our failure. I *must* have concrete answers as to how to proceed." He looked at his personal assistant. Chung! Place a call to the Admiralty immediately. We must keep our submarine on station off Florida. Yang, see if your idiots can redeem themselves in Moscow. Make certain that our contact there is aware of what he must do."

Yang cleared his throat. "And if he feels your plan risks his exposure and he refuses?"

"Then promise him Euros, two or three million, I don't care! I am certain with his tastes and ambitions, that will light a fire under him. Yang, report back to me as soon as he has been contacted. Do you understand? Remember, if any of you fail again, I'll have someone's head for this. Now, dismissed!"

Washington, DC, the Pentagon, Commander Burton's Office

Commander Chris Burton continued to review the information brought to him by Captain Janice Whetstone. She reported the incident involving her subordinate, Ensign Shanna Watts. Burton reread the report, thinking that perhaps someone was pulling a joke on the young woman, but as a naval security officer at the Pentagon, he had to consider this a serious matter and had called in the National Security Agency to review the information. The two lift-off explosions of the Cape certainly had all the earmarks of an SDI-type weapon. Burton had a copy of the data that compared the telemetry of the doomed rockets to data gathered in tests of a carbon dioxide laser. The resulting destruction of the NASA rockets and the SDI test rocket were almost identical. Captain Burton read further down the report about the limitations of the first generation high-energy lasers. The most obvious was the power needed to charge and fire the laser, over a hundred million electron volts fed into banks of high discharge capacitors. The power for such a device could only be a nuclear reactor. The only possible candidates for firing such a weapon would be a surface ship or just maybe a nuclear submarine.

Following the second loss, the destruction of the Pan-African satellite, the Department of Defense received the reports from NASA, along with the SDI tests results from Area 51. Early the next morning, a sweep of the area was completed by three Orion sub-hunting aircraft, but they came up empty and nothing had shown up on any of the surveillance satellite images of that area of ocean taken close to the time of the explosion. Something didn't pass the smell test.

Chris Burton was still trying to put the pieces together when his intercom buzzed, announcing the arrival of NSA agent Jack Gaffney. Commander Burton rose to open his office door.

"Good afternoon, Agent Gaffney. It seems we may have a mystery here."

The NSA agent was a tall man with an athletic build and a strong handshake. "Please, Commander, call me Jack. Believe me, we're as concerned about this as you are, maybe more so. NASA's getting ready to launch men and components for the *Alliance* mission in a few weeks. I'm sure you're already aware of the terrorist attack in Kazakhstan that destroyed the last three Russian Salyut space stations in storage. It was only by the failure of the people behind the attack to realize another Salyut was sitting almost in the center of Moscow that we even have a mission. We're convinced that China was behind the attack, although it appears they used Chechen terrorists as surrogates. If there is a Chinese surface ship or sub off our coast, capable of downing the next launch, we need to find it fast, along with anyone who might be tipping them off. Anyway, let's see what you've got, and we can compare notes."

"Okay, Jack. Captain Whetstone reported that one of her eh … young officers had been out very late the prior evening with friends and snuck into one of the office supply storage rooms to catch a little shut eye."

Gaffney looked up from taking notes. "Ah, where and what time was this?"

"About 0850 hours and over in the "D" ring, south side, down the corridor from the satellite imaging department, as well as one of the offices that's responsible for routing Orion surveillance flights."

Jack Gaffney's eyebrows rose. "That's pretty interesting. Someone having access to the Orion schedules could easily tip off a ship or a sub that we were looking for them. Did this ensign see or notice anything about who made the call?"

"No, as I understand it, she was sleeping. The man's voice woke her up and obviously didn't see her, but she heard him warning someone about a surveillance flight and whoever he was, he gave the grid coordinates of the sweep to whoever he was talking to. Ensign Watts said she could tell he was young and white. Watts is black, so she said it was noticeable to her."

Jack Gaffney opened his brief case and pulled out a computer printout of what appeared to be a series of red lines in peaks and valleys.

"You can have a look at this. It's from Echelon. As you know, Echelon was developed to pick out terrorists and anyone else plotting attacks against the United States. It grabs and analyzes signals for content. However, over the last fifteen years, since we've been using Echelon, we've added encryption detection. Now, most of the new encryption software is pretty sophisticated and nearly impossible to break, so we can't actually tell what a suspect is saying, but our detection equipment can show if a call was made using this kind of software.

"Here Commander, look at this. You can see the spike of a cell phone transmission that started at 0849 the day after the rocket explosion and the time the ensign heard this man's voice. GPS pinpoints the location to this general area, right here, the "D" ring of the Pentagon. Your leak is here, right here under your nose. Now all we have to do is find him and here's how we'll do it. We'll be using some new software called Omni-Probe. Basically, it sifts through data concerning bank deposits, credit card purchases, cash purchases and other things like that and compares this to the known income of a sample of individual subjects to find inconsistencies. Things like someone with a $40,000 income buying a half-million dollar vacation home in Florida or purchasing a Ferrari, that sort of thing."

"So, what do you need from us?"

"Get me all the personnel information on all white males, say between the ages of 21 and 40, working in the south side "D" ring. Don't worry, if he's there, we'll find him."

* * * *

Major Yuan Xho stood looking through the reinforced polycarbonate observation blister. The moon base, cloaked in the perpetual night of the cratered lunar South Pole, presented an unmatched view of the southern sky. Stars, undiluted in their glory by an ocean of air, blazed down unblinking from an absolute black sky. The Milky Way, that great band of stars that remained almost invisible through the light-polluted skies of Earth shined brightly along with the twin patches of light, the Magellanic Clouds, tiny dwarf galaxies that orbit our own. Only the brilliantly lit walls of the far side Crater Planck in the distance broke the even blackness of the alien sky.

Yuan's mind was in torment. He was a loyal citizen of China. He should be bursting with pride at this great accomplishment. *To achieve a human presence on the Moon, to prepare to challenge the depths of space*, he thought, yet his government had turned this achievement into a perversion designed only to gain power and dominance over the other nations of Earth. Major Yuan looked over at the enlisted men at the far side of the dome. Working in the Moon's one-sixth gravity, they easily hefted the stainless steel encased cylinders into their stealth housings. The housings were coated with anti-radar absorbent material. Once the cylinders were secured inside their housings, they would be mated to a collection of small fuel tanks and tiny maneuvering thrusters then brought to the magnetic acceleration track, the one China had built on the far side of the Moon, unobservable from the Earth. The weapons would be placed into an acceleration sled to send the packages hurtling down the magnetic track at over two kilometers per second and send them secretly on their way to take up low orbits that crisscrossed the major population centers of Europe, North America, Asia and Russia. These were the tools that China would use to enforce its quarantine of space of other nations and ensure Chinese dominance, for each package sent Earthward would be a 500 kiloton nuclear weapon, capable of striking virtually any target with little or no warning. For the first time since the advent of the Cold War and the doctrine of MAD – Mutually Assured Destruction - a nation could carry out a first strike, devastating its enemies without fear of detection. Those leading his nation saw this as a brilliant strategy to propel China to leading a true world empire, but Major Yuan saw it as a terrible error in judgment that could only result in a global nuclear war.

Sergeant Zhang K'un, a man who Yuan had personally promoted, was connecting the detonator system to the core of one of the weapons. Major Yuan called over to him. "Sergeant Zhang, you may take a few minutes rest. Please go over this schedule with me. I must make certain we are not falling behind."

The man bounded over due to the effects of the low gravity, nearly colliding with his commanding officer. "I am sorry, sir. I suppose I am still getting used to working and living on the Moon."

"Please Sergeant, think nothing of it. It will take us all some time to adapt to the challenges of other worlds. How is your timetable coming with the weapons?"

Zhang nodded his head in the affirmative. "On schedule, Major. We have eighteen completed so far, and I see no delay for the rest, once the other 20 warheads are delivered to us."

At that, the major looked as if he was about to be sick.

"Major Yuan, sir … are you not well? Perhaps you should go to the infirmary?"

Yuan could stand it no more. Even if he might face retribution for turning his words into thoughts, he had to say something to someone. The sergeant was not just his subordinate, but also a man he trusted and who he had a responsibility to watch over. He was Yuan's own nephew.

Yuan spoke to him in a whisper. "Nephew, my illness is not of the physical body but of my soul." The major shifted his eyes, scanning the enclosure, making certain his words could not be overheard. "In speaking to you of this, I risk everything, but I will trust you shall not betray me. What we are doing here is … wrong. This is a dangerous road we have chosen to travel. How do you think the West and Russia will react to being dictated to, to discovering armed nuclear weapons in orbit above their cities? Do you *really* think they will surrender their sovereignty to China? Do our leaders not read history? The Americans all but destroyed the Empire of Japan for such a plan. The Russians will never surrender. When Germany invaded their lands, they moved entire factories east of the Urals in a matter of weeks to begin the production of weapons to smash the Germans. Their soldiers died by the hundreds of thousands to repel the invaders. I greatly fear we are lighting the match to a war that will devastate the world."

His nephew was shocked. Had it been anyone but his uncle, he would have suspected he was being tricked into speaking his thoughts, only to be arrested and interrogated by a political officer.

"Major … uh … Uncle, I cannot believe what you have said about our country's present course of action. I cannot believe it because … I, too, have these thoughts. Uncle, can our leaders not see from the perspective of another? If it were China under subjugation, would we lay down our arms and raise the white flag of surrender? Did we just give up when the Empire of Japan invaded our homeland?"

"Nephew, are there others who share this opinion here on the Moon?"

"I do not know, Uncle. All are afraid of the wrath of our political officer. Any man may be an informer but … I have seen in some of the men's body language their unspoken words that they feel we are about to step over the edge of an abyss."

"Thank you, my nephew. Please, keep this to yourself. Do not share your thoughts with anyone but me."

"Uncle, are you considering somehow stopping this? If so, you may count upon me to be of help. I love my country too much to see it destroyed."

"No, no, I am not considering any such plan … I just wanted to share my feelings with you. Now you had better return to your task."

However, Major Yuan lied. *There must be a way to stop this madness*, he thought. *I must make a choice, to march my family and my nation to the slaughter or risk my life to stop it. I must think …*

Moscow, Gagarin Training Center

Natasha's voice was almost a whisper. She was trying not to break John McGovern's concentration. "Easy, John, just a very light touch on the thrusters, the Soyuz reacts best to a gentle hand."

McGovern cracked a smile. "You mean like a beautiful woman?"

Natasha, looking perplexed, asked, "Just what beautiful woman do you mean?"

"I guess I mean the one sitting next to me in the number two seat."

"Hmm, very amusing, now please try and concentrate on lining up the probe on the docking sleeve so that it gently slides into the Salyut's receptacle."

"Natasha, you have to stop talking like that. You're getting me very excited."

She leaned over and gently punched him on the shoulder. "John. I am *serious* here. You need to be perfect on the docking … just in case something … happens to me."

McGovern turned to her, breaking his concentration. Just her words, "*in case something happens to me*," were upsetting to him. "Natasha, *nothing* is going to happen to you. At least not while I'm around."

Suddenly the simulator gave a lurch, and alarms began going off.

"Something already has John. You just crashed our ship into the docking port. Now shall we try again?"

* * * *

The sun had set two hours earlier, but still he was working on files, comparing them against a small notebook filled with names. Some with stars next to them indicated very urgent action was required while those crossed out told him the problem had been eliminated. He finished with five files, carefully replacing them, and closed the notebook, planting it securely inside his jacket pocket.

Heavy set and in his sixties, he pushed his bulk up from the chair and was about to turn off his office lights when the telephone rang. It was not his main phone, with half a dozen extensions, but the solitary one of an older Soviet design he kept on the credenza. Most visitors to his office assumed it was an inoperative decoration. He pulled his hand back from the light switch and returned to his desk. This had to concern yesterday's debacle. He considered not answering it but after the sixth ring picked up the receiver.

"Hello," he said. "Yes, I thought it might be you. This is not a prudent time to contact me … you know why, your people bungled the operation very badly. If you had bothered to coordinate your plans with *my* agents, then you might have known of the existence of the fourth Salyut. You failed to destroy it. All your efforts went for nothing! Now I'm left to cover up your mess …. no, I do not like that option at all … not now. This isn't the old days anymore. Too many people can ask questions now … *How much?* Two *million? Hmm … let me think* …. No I can't be … umm *three* million, you say? All right … but as soon as the operation is carried out, I want it transferred to a Swiss account. I'll provide you with the number once I know the operation has been concluded. Do not call me again; I shall call you. *Dazvedanya.*"

Three million, he thought, *I can do a great deal with that.* He turned and placed another call. "Just observe but when the opportunity presents itself, conclude the matter; understood?" Then he stood up, shut off the light and locked his office door.

* * * *

Colonel McGovern stood on a metal platform overlooking the huge water-filled tank. In size, it rivaled almost any aquarium in the world, but this tank wasn't for fish, it was simulating weightlessness. Inside, was a mock-up of a Salyut space station and the French docking module, designed with multiple ports. For the past week, French astronaut Remmy LaCasse and Lieutenant William Curtis had been running seemingly endless simulations and were just finishing their last run through, practicing the manual connections that would mate the multi-port docking module to the Salyut. After another twenty minutes, both men finally came to the surface. Curtis was helped out of his spacesuit first. McGovern lent a hand with his helmet.

"How's it going, Bill. You two ready yet?"

"Well, *Jacques Cousteau* over there and I have spent so damn many hours in this tank, that I'm starting to grow gills … but, yeah, we're ready. I think I could join the multi-port to the station in my sleep. Tom and Jack checked out back at the Cape on the setting the two LEMs in place. The only thing left now is to make sure Jack, Remmy and me are proficient on mating the EDS to the collar. That's why we're leaving for the Cape tonight. This will give us five days to practice and that's it. After that, it's show time. Ah, how's our Cosmo-*nette* doing? Think she can hold the station steady while we line things up?"

"Yeah, she's ready. We've been running simulations, and every time she's nailed it. She's a good pilot."

Bill Curtis gave McGovern that look of his with one raised eyebrow. "Ah, John, that's the *only thing* you've been running with her … simulations I mean?"

"Hey, Bill, please don't even go there. This is strictly business, but I wouldn't mind getting to know that woman much better once the mission's over."

Curtis chuckled. "She is a looker, isn't she?"

"Yeah, and a damn good pilot. She's better on a LEM than I am on a Soyuz. I have a huge amount of respect for her. Say, what time are you and the rest of the crew heading out?"

"Right after dinner, about eight o'clock, why?"

"I thought Natasha and I might take a ride over to Zhukovski with you to see you off."

Curtis chuckled. "Ah … John, you wouldn't be thinking about pulling any of your old tricks from your academy days, would you? Man, you were a legend for going MIA out to the clubs in Colorado Springs from what I hear."

"Hey, Bill, that was quite a while ago. I'm not so much of a wild man anymore"

Curtis just shook his head. "You know what they say, a leopard don't change its spots … just don't get your *you know what* caught in the wringer, okay?"

The evening turned into a real Russian send-off with a banquet feast, as well as music and dancing. Jack Griffin entertained everyone by joining in with some traditional Slavic dances, nearly breaking an ankle. However, the best news of the evening came from RSA Director Zhdanov. The work on the Salyut that had stood for years opposite the Kosmos Hotel had been completed. The engineers at the Korolev-Energia complex had gutted and reconditioned the space station. They had even called in a few vintage aircraft restoration specialists from England, men who had made 80-year-old Spitfires from the Second World War airworthy again. The completed Salyut would be loaded on a flatbed, taken to the air base, and loaded onto a huge Antonov cargo plane to be delivered to the Baikonur launch facility in Kazakhstan. Considering the threat the mission was under, the Antonov would have two MiG-29s for an escort.

When the farewell party was over, everyone piled into the van and headed back to Zhukovski Air Force Base for a flight back to Kennedy Space Center. John and Natasha came along to see them off. They would all meet up again, in low Earth orbit, one week from then. Natasha, however, suspected something was up when John told her to put on her "out for the evening clothes." Jack Griffin noticed both she and McGovern were just a tad overdressed for a send off, but when he began to open his mouth, Bill Curtis gave him a nudge and put his finger up to his lips whispering, "Keep it on the QT."

With more than a few hugs, handshakes and pats on the back from Natasha and John, the four astronauts who would launch from Kennedy climbed aboard the NASA-registered 757. John and Natasha walked back to the van.

"So John, why did you ask me to wear my evening clothes just to see the crew off? What is in that devious mind of yours?"

McGovern chuckled. "Ah, yeah … say, what's a good Moscow dance club?"

"There are quite a few you know. I used to go to the Karma Bar, but I haven't been in a long time."

McGovern pulled out his wallet. "Sounds like a plan to me. Here, give our driver this fifty and have him drop us off at the … eh Karma Bar."

"Oh John, I don't know … we could face a reprimand."

"Come on, Natasha. We're going to fly off into space in a few days and then head for the Moon. Do you *really* think anyone would say anything to us, assuming that we got caught, which I'm pretty sure we won't? You know, I used to be a master at sneaking out. I had a perfect record … well almost perfect until I managed to run smack into my commanding officer while trying to climb back through a window. I almost got launched to the Moon right then … without a rocket!"

Natasha burst out laughing and then said, "All right, but let's not stay out too late. I'm looking forward to seeing you dance to something a little more modern than in Cocoa Beach; Somehow I can't imagine it."

"Hey, Natasha, I've still got the moves. Come on, let's go."

Boris, their driver, was very happy with the fifty and instead of heading northwest, out of the city, turned onto the ring road that led to the center of Moscow. Boris dropped them off at the corner of Kuznetski Street. The air was chilly but the nightlife in the city was going full blast with the streets filled with people out for the evening.

As John and Natasha exited the van, neither of them noticed the two cars that followed them back from the air base had also stopped one block down the street.

* * * *

The ringing of the telephone next to Sung Zhao's bed jolted him awake. He had only fallen asleep a few hours earlier, and now it was four o'clock in the morning. The intense scrutiny he had been put under by the senior director of intelligence operations for the failure to end the West's moon mission was a severe blow to his reputation as well as putting his bold plan in jeopardy. Fortunately, by using a certain contact in Russia, it seemed likely that he could redeem himself.

Zhao picked up the telephone. It was the agent in charge of the Russian sector.

"Comrade Zhao. I am sorry for this call at such late an hour, but I wanted to inform you right away that your problem will soon be just a memory."

Sung Zhao unconsciously breathed a sigh of relief. "Thank you, I appreciate this news."

Zhao hung up the phone and settled down to a restful sleep, believing that the problem that had dogged him of late was finally solved.

CHAPTER TWELVE

The Karma Bar: Moscow, Russia

The mid-April night air held a damp chill to it. Moscow was certainly giving New York, the original "city that never sleeps," a run for its money as even at that hour, as the city was alive with partiers, couples and groups of young men and women just hanging out. The streets reflected the overhead lights in the condensation formed by the cold late night air. With the temperature hovering at a chilly 3 degrees centigrade, John McGovern was glad he chose his U.S. Navy flight jacket, a Christmas gift from Norm Taggert, instead of the sport coat hanging in his closet. As he and Natasha exited the Karma Bar dance club, she took his arm and snuggled close to him against the chilly dampness. *Wow*, he thought, *this is a first. I think she's finally letting her guard down at last.*

He gave her a wide smile. "How's your hearing? That music was so loud I think I lost the upper frequency range of mine."

Natasha returned the smile and then added "What is your expression in America? If the music is too loud then you are too old?" She burst out laughing.

"Well, I'm not too old to play hooky. Maybe we'd better get back to Star City before they send the troops after us. I feel like I'm back at the Air Force Academy again, sneaking out for a little fun at one of the nightclubs in Colorado Springs. That almost got me tossed out of the Academy. Only my grades and my piloting skills saved my tail."

When she turned toward him, this close, John was struck by just how beautiful she was. Not just her drop dead figure in the body-hugging pantsuit she wore but her beautiful eyes, long lashes, and smooth ivory skin.

"John, I believe that you are a rebellious soul, yes? Remmy told me how you saved his life on the ISS. I can't believe you went after him without a thruster pack, just throwing tools and parts to propel you both back to the space station."

"Yeah, after I got back I told Houston my radio earpiece went out that and I never heard them tell me not to go after him. Sometimes I have a really bad time following orders, but if I'd waited for a solution from the ground, LaCasse would have been a dead man. I couldn't live with myself if I didn't try to save him."

"You are the kind of man who has a strong soul as well. Maybe you have a heroic soul, yes? You always feel you must do what is correct no matter what the personal danger or consequences are. I also know about your disobeying orders to save a fellow pilot's life in Iraq."

"Yeah, guilty as charged. My … ah radio must have gone out then as well. I guess I have really bad luck with radios. Anyway, this is the best evening I've had in a very long time."

"Even better than the meal we shared in Cocoa Beach?"

"Absolutely. Now I feel like I'm finally getting to know you. Back then I'd just come off like a real jerk, the way I treated you the first day."

Natasha pulled gently on his arm bringing them to a halt.

"John, I have to say something ... I loved Misha, and I have never had real closure because I know his death was no accident. They killed him for what he believed in. He was a brave young man who stood up when it was far safer to sit down. I had never met another man with his courage and principles before … that is until I met you. Yes, we launch in four days, and yes, I am frightened, but there is no one in the world I would rather fly this mission with than you. I … I want to say, I think I'm falling in love with you and I want us to come back alive. And … if we do not, at least I will face my fate with a man who I can truly believe in."

John held her and kissed her mouth deeply and long. It was a spontaneous thing and the first woman he had kissed since his divorce from Cheryl.

"Natasha, I … yeah. I feel it, too. I want to say … I love you. I was attracted to you the first time we met, even though I was acting like a little kid that didn't get his own way. I feel it in my heart that we can survive and can make this mission a success. We've beaten the odds so far, and every time the Chinese have tried to throw a monkey wrench into the works, they've been stopped. And … when we get back to Earth … I want you to come with me, to my home in the Berkshires and stay for a while; let me treat you like the princess you are. But right now, we have to stay focused on the mission. I know how I'd like this night to end … with you waking up next to me in the morning but not now. I don't want anything to distract us. We have a very dangerous mission ahead of us … But ... when it's over, I'd like us to share the sunrise together."

John and Natasha turned down Pushechnaya Ooletsa toward the metro station and continued to talk, unaware that two men in three quarter-length leather coats had come abreast on either side of them until one spoke in reasonably good English.

"Good evening Colonel McGovern and … Cosmonaut Polyakova. The center is aware of your absence, and we have been sent to retrieve you. The car is parked just a few dozen meters ahead. My associate and I will drive you back."

John McGovern had a sort of sixth sense and it was screaming to him that if he and Natasha got into that car, it would be the last ride they ever took. His suspicions were confirmed when, as they approached, the doors of a second car, a black Mercedes, opened and two more men got out. Natasha could see that the Lada sedan held yet another two men in the backseat, and she shot John a frightened look.

McGovern turned to the burly dark haired man escorting them to the car. "Excuse me, I forgot my watch. Do you have the time?"

His escort, not wishing to arouse McGovern's suspicion, decided to acquiesce to his request. When the man monetarily broke his concentration to look at his wristwatch, McGovern spun around in a half turn, using the heel of his hand to drive it into the bridge of the man's nose. It was a move he'd been taught in the Air Force Academy for use in hand-to-hand combat, and it was devastating, fracturing the delicate bones just under the nose, driving them up into the sinus cavity and creating a drenching torrent of blood. The man screamed and grabbed for his face. Natasha turned to the man escorting her only to see him pull the distinctive black barrel of a gun from under his coat. Realizing she had to act without hesitation she raised her right knee as high as she could and came down with all the force that she could muster, driving the stiletto spike of her Italian leather shoe deep into the man's calf muscle. She pushed down with all her might and felt the heel of her shoe dig deeper, ripping through muscle and tendon. The assassin howled with pain and dropped the automatic pistol, trying to staunch the blood. Natasha's well-aimed thrust had grazed an artery.

For the briefest of moments, McGovern stared down at the wounded man, Italian high heel embedded to the hilt in his calf. "Remind me never to criticize your choice in shoes ever again!" he said.

She and John turned to run, toward the metro station at the corner of Lubyanka Street only to see two more men in front of them blocking their path and about to draw weapons. Natasha spun around and looked behind her only to see the four men from the second car were now running toward them.

John McGovern's mind was adrenalin-charged as he looked about for a means of escape and then saw it. A Russian biker, looking not all that different from his American counterparts, had stopped his machine across the street near the Lubyanka Metro Station to talk to a couple of young girls. McGovern said a silent prayer that the leather clad young man had left the key in his motorcycle. As he and Natasha closed the distance, he could see the key gleaming under the street lights in the ignition switch of a Ural Night Wolf 750, a low slung BMW-like twin cylinder chopper.

Grabbing Natasha's arm, he flung her onto the back of the bike and fired up the twin cylinder motor, gunned it and took off down Nikolskya Street at full throttle, with the biker cursing and screaming at the top of his lungs for them to stop. Accelerating down the street at full speed, the bike's mirror suddenly exploded, spraying glass in a trail behind them. He could see the bullet hole in what remained of the mirror's housing. *No doubt about it*, he thought, *If I can't get to safety with Natasha, we'll both be dead.*

Racing away from their pursuers, McGovern made a quick assessment of the purloined bike. It was not an ideal machine for the task of making a getaway from whoever was trying to kill them. Snapping his head around quickly, he could see the Lada tearing after them at full speed followed by another car, the Mercedes. The Ural he and Natasha were on was a cruiser. The raked front end and extended forks combined with the fat rear tire and low center of gravity made for slow handing: Definitely not a sport-bike. The underpowered and clunky Lada would be easy to lose, but the Mercedes was fast and agile, like a shark in the water. Had they been on a long stretch of highway, they'd be dead meat in short order as the Mercedes easily had a 50 mile per hour speed advantage over the bike he and Natasha were on. But, this was not an open road, this was the busy center of Moscow, and the streets were turning into a deadly obstacle course as late night and early morning trucks were beginning to make their deliveries. Unlike most Western cities, there were no prescribed unloading zones. Russian truck drivers parked wherever they felt like to begin off-loading their cargo, sometime in the middle of the street. Crates of everything from vodka to vegetables turned the wide Moscow avenues into a lethal slalom course at the speed they were moving.

McGovern was at another disadvantage. He was in an unfamiliar city with pursuers who knew the streets. However, Natasha was with him, and she was screaming in his ear. "Quickly, turn here, at Novaya Square, we can cut up the pedestrian paths."

John leaned the bike over hard and the Ural left the road, scattering lovers and groups of youths as they raced up the walkway between park benches and memorial statues. One of their pursuers, however, realized the trick and was waiting for them as they exited onto Cherkaski lane. Blasting back onto the street at full throttle, the Lada with the four men inside raced after them. In the distance a second rapidly moving set of blue-white headlights had to be the Mercedes. John weaved through the myriad of boxes and crates that workers brought into the businesses lining Cherkaski lane.

McGovern made a tight turn around a parked truck, and then he saw it: tanks of liquid propane that had been unloaded and stacked in the road. He leaned the bike over at such a sharp angle to cut between the propane tanks, and the truck he thought for sure the right cylinder of the opposed twin would scrape the pavement, then he accelerated away with everything the Ural had. The driver of the Lada also screamed the car around the parked truck. As he did, to his horror, the stacked cylinders of propane loomed up in front of him. The Lada slammed into the tanks, jamming one up under the car's front end and snapping off the valve. In the instant, the sparks from the pavement reached the escaping gas, the tank erupted into a fireball, blasting the Lada a good 15 feet into the air before coming down on its side, enveloped in an all-consuming fireball, roasting its occupants like slabs of meat.

McGovern yelled back, "One down and one to go!"

Once they passed Ilyinka Street, the maze of trucks, crates and workmen thinned to nothing but a broad straight road. John had the Ural topped out at just under 90, but the blue white headlights of the Mercedes were closing the gap at a vicious rate of speed. He kept weaving the bike to throw off the shooter's aim. The near freezing night air tore at his and Natasha's faces as she leaned closer to his ear, screaming, "*Turn!* Turn here, turn here, it's our only chance!"

John strained to make the turn on the low-slung cruiser, nearly laying the bike down to do so. The Mercedes slid sideways but recovered and was again right behind them, accelerating full out down Varvarka Street. Ahead of him, John could see the brilliantly lit towers of Saint Basil's Cathedral and the Kremlin walls.

Natasha was pounding on his back. "Turn right, turn right!"

Again, McGovern leaned the bike over and was now racing toward Red Square. Natasha saw them. A group of soldiers standing guard near the entrance of the Kremlin. She reached into her jacket pocket and retrieved her identity packet, about the size of a man's billfold, and threw it with all her might at the soldiers as they passed. Momentarily distracted by the spectacle of a motorcycle and a car racing at full speed by the Kremlin walls, a corporal retrieved the packet and handed it to his commander, a tall slim major, who opened it and studied the contents intently. The packet was in two parts: half in Russian, half in English, with Natasha's photograph, the letters RKA and NASA along with her name: Cosmonaut Natasha Dmitrievna Polyakova and the symbols of both the American and the Russian space agencies.

The major stared incredulously as he watched the couple on the Ural make an impossibly tight turn just before the Nikolskya Street intersection and double back toward the Kremlin entrance. The Mercedes that was following them, instead of missing and overshooting the intersection, made a 180 degree handbrake turn, pivoting the car around the front wheels. The major shook his head in disbelief, thinking to himself, *Whoever was driving that car is either a professional or a madman.*

McGovern with Natasha wrapped around his back like a python slowed just a bit to aim for the middle of the group of soldiers when the bike felt as if it was sliding across slick ice. The shooter in the Mercedes had hit the fat rear tire of the Ural, blowing it out. John was losing control, sliding. He had just enough time to get his arms under Natasha's legs and launch them off the doomed bike as it crashed in the street, sending up a torrent of sparks. They hit the pavement hard, but John's motorcycle racing experience had taught him how to tuck and roll without getting hurt; only this time he had to think of Natasha's safety as well as his own. McGovern took the brunt of the impact on his left shoulder and side, shredding the Navy-issue flight jacket along with his pants' leg.

Natasha was unhurt and pulled McGovern to his feet. "Run John, run to the soldiers!"

Ignoring the pain in his shoulder and leg, McGovern and Natasha sprinted the last 10 meters or so toward the open mouthed group of men, one officer and four of lower rank. Stunned, the major helped McGovern over to the sidewalk. John reached into what was left of his leather jacket and handed the man his dark blue U.S. Passport as he did, the Mercedes screeched to a stop in front of the group and two men in black pants and heavy jackets exited the car.

"We are State Security, FSB, these two are under arrest. You will turn them over to us immediately!"

The major could speak some English but had difficulty reading it. However, he could read the word "Colonel" in McGovern's passport and all of the Cyrillic documentation in Natasha's identification packet. He eyed the two security men coldly, and then answered. "I rather think not. I must call my superior officer on this matter."

The bigger of the two security men stepped closer to the major. "*I* am your superior officer! You will hand them over *immediately!*"

The major could see both men start to reach for what could only be weapons under their jackets, and he shrugged and as if in agreement, made a move to pull Natasha over toward the two security men. As he did so, he barked a quick order, and his squad's four AK-47 automatic rifles came up to their shoulders. "Hmm. I'm afraid my four Kalashnikovs outrank your two pop guns."

The standoff lasted about five minutes until Colonel Makarov, of the President's personal Kremlin guard, arrived with an additional six men.

He first questioned the security men and then went over to John and Natasha. Makarov saluted McGovern then bowed toward Natasha. "Colonel McGovern, Cosmonaut Polyakova. I am deeply sorry about what has just happened, but I can assure you that you are in safe hands now. These men won't talk but eventually they will … when we are finished with them."

Both security men were close enough to Makarov as well as Natasha and John to hear every word. Mararov spoke. "Colonel McGovern, I would invite you to attend these men's interrogations, but I'm afraid that as an American you would not approve of our techniques."

"Are you kidding? After what these two just did, I'd like to rip their collective balls off and stuff them down their throats!"

"Ah, so you *are* familiar with our methods. Come then, I shall provide you with some ice tongs so you won't bloody your hands."

The younger of the two security agents began to look green as he stared down at the front of his pants. This did not go unnoticed, and Colonel Makarov looked him in the eye. "Ah yes, I see you *do* understand English, so I will ask you this question in English. The soldiers in my company do not need to understand our conversation. Who ordered this and why?"

The young security man was visibly shaking and stammered out, "I was told they were assassins, imposters sent to kill Marshal –"

Makarov stepped closer to the terrified man, grabbing his shirt just under his neck, "You've told me why … *now tell me who!* Tell me now, or may God have mercy on you because I shall not!"

The man stammered out one name. In an instant Makarov was on his radio in deep conversation. Then he turned to John McGovern and Natasha Polyakova. "You will both come with me please. President Simonov would like to speak to both of you. His personal physician has been called in to attend to your injuries Colonel."

* * * *

Hammering, hammering, yes, the finishing touches on my new dacha are wonderful … again the hammering. Director of the FSB Yevghenny Golovko sat up in his bed. He had been dreaming, but now he was awake and the pounding would not stop. He realized it was his front door, and he got up from his ornate gold and mahogany bed, put on his robe, and walked toward his front door mumbling under his breath. "Idiots … idiots; still I told them to notify me as soon as those two had been eliminated, just not at my home and not at this hour." Then he thought,

Perhaps not such idiots after all. It's morning in Beijing, and once they know this has been accomplished my 3 million Euros will be in my Swiss account. By this time tomorrow I shall be a much, much richer man.

As Golovko's hand reached to unlock his door, the voice on the other side shouted, "Director Yevghenny Pavlovitch Golovko, this is Colonel Makarov, commanding the Presidential Guard. *Open this door immediately!* You are under arrest for treason against the Motherland!"

Golovko stood there uncomprehending, the doorknob in his hand, his visions of wealth and power crumbling to dust before his eyes.

Makarov could hear the director's footsteps receding on the other side of the door, and yelled, "You men, break it down!"

The Colonel's two largest men slammed their shoulders into the director's door. On the fourth try, the wood split open, to the second sound of the crack of a pistol shot in another room. Makarov and his men raced toward the sound of the gunshot, only to find Yevghenny Golovko laying face down on his ornate dark wooden desk in a spreading pool of blood and brains, his pistol still tightly gripped in his right hand.

* * * *

President Simonov's personal physician, Doctor Budarin, had just finished applying a bandage to John McGovern's knee. "Remarkable that you are unbroken, falling at such a speed. Even more so that your companion is uninjured."

McGovern winced just a bit as he took his leg off the chair it had been propped up on. "I've had much worse crashes when I was racing motorcycles on the track but … I'll admit, that's the first time I've ever bailed off a bike with a passenger."

Just as he had finished his comment to the doctor; Russian President Victor Simonov entered the room. John, caught by surprise, tried his best to quickly stand up.

"Please, please Colonel McGovern and Cosmonaut Polyakova,

please remain seated. After your miraculous escape tonight, you should be resting. Doctor Budarin says you are not badly hurt."

"Just my jacket and pants along with a few scrapes and bruises."

The President turned to Natasha, "You are unhurt as well?

"Just my wits and my nerves."

John smiled over to her, relieved that they were both alive and in one piece. "See, I told you I'd take you for a motorcycle ride … but this wasn't exactly what I had in mind."

The president could see she was still shaking. "Please, join me in a late night or shall I say early morning toast with a small glass of vodka. It will help to calm your nerves.

McGovern answered him. "Normally when I'm in flight training, I don't drink, but after what just happened, I'll take you up on your offer. Thank you very much."

An attendant brought a silver tray with a bottle and three glasses. Simonov held his glass high. "To your good fortune and to your successful mission to the Moon." After all three downed the burning liquid, President Simonov spoke again. "Ah, the Moon: To travel in space. Something I had always dreamt of as a boy."

McGovern smiled at him. "Once we secure our own base, maybe you could join President Price and inaugurate it from the surface of the Moon."

Simonov looked deep in thought and nodded his head. "Perhaps so, Colonel, if all is successful that is."

"It will be, sir. We have the right people and the right equipment. My fellow crew member, Natasha Polyakova, can certainly fly a Soyuz and she can pilot the LEM like a pro now. Everyone is 100 percent positive about the mission, and we're not going unarmed this time either."

Just as Simonov was about to answer, a military officer interrupted him and took him aside to converse privately. A concerned look crossed the President's face, and he slowly shook his head. "I'm afraid FSB Director Yevghenny Golovko will not be joining us for your send-off into space. He has apparently met with an accident with his own pistol. I'm very, very sorry to say that apparently it was Golovko who had ordered you both to be killed. On his desk were some of his papers. One held a Swiss bank account number and the notation, 3 million Euros next to it. The second item was a small note book containing your name, Cosmonaut Polyakova's name, along with many of those in the Russians for Democracy movement. Many names, such as yours, were marked with a star and some were crossed out. Those which were crossed out included your late fiancée, Cosmonaut Polyakova, who I understand died under mysterious circumstances.

Natasha brought her hand to her face, wiping away a tear that formed in her eye and then the briefest of smiles crossed her face. "Thank God. Now he can rest. That evil man, Golovko, has died like the filthy coward he was."

The President reached over to comfort Natasha and then spoke. "Now that the lead rat has been exposed, it will be a small matter to hunt down and clean out the minor vermin that have infested the FSB. By morning, many of them will be receiving unexpected and very unpleasant visits at their homes and offices."

McGovern could imagine just how unpleasant those visits might be. "Thank you for your hospitality, Mister President, but we must be getting back to Star City."

"Nonsense, you and Cosmonaut Polyakova will stay here the rest of the night as my guests. I have already contacted the space center to inform them, as well as your ambassador. He said that if there is anything you want, just to ask him. The lieutenant will show you to your rooms."

"There is one thing Mister President. I'd like to call my embassy. There's a very angry biker who just had his motorcycle trashed outside of the Kremlin. Once the police calm him down, I'd like him sent over to the U.S. Embassy to pick up a blank voucher and go to the Moscow Harley Davidson dealer. The U.S. Embassy can let him know he can pick out any bike he wants, no charge: Complements of the United States Government."

* * * *

Natasha Polyakova and John McGovern stood facing each other in the hallway of the President's Kremlin residence, their rooms on opposite sides of the corridor. They were both thinking the same thing, but a young guard was stationed at the end of the hallway. The guard could see them looking at each other, their deep gaze and that they held hands. In an exaggerated movement, he stood up yawning loudly, "*Oy … ya hachoo spat'! Mne nozhna koffe!* (I want to sleep! I need some coffee!) and walked off down the corridor, leaving the couple alone.

McGovern looked deeply into Natasha's blue green eyes. "Are you *sure* you want to do this?"

"Yes John, with all my heart. Tonight I have closure. I know those who were responsible for Misha's death will meet their own terrible fate. Their vile leader is dead already. Now, quickly before the guard returns let us prepare to watch the sunrise together … from our bed."

John McGovern washed the road grime from his face and hands and exited the bathroom of their guest quarters. The lamp was off, but the silvery light of the nearly full moon bathed the room, pouring its luminescence through the tall courtyard window. Natasha stood before him, awash in a glow of silver gray, like a vision in the mist. Her head was titled slightly to one side accentuating the graceful line of her neck, her body was draped in moonlight and she wore only a smile. John drank in her features like a man thirsting in the desert. Her small but firm upturned breasts, the narrowness of her waist and that mysterious patch of darkness where her thighs joined her hips, holding the promise of infinite pleasures and delights. He took her in his arms, and she returned his passion, full and strong. Morning would come, the sun would rise and duty would call but for now … time was standing still.

Morning did come and too soon. With new clothing provided for him, John McGovern and Natasha joined President Victor Simonov for a breakfast fit for the Czar. Over coffee and thick slices of bread topped with black caviar, the President spoke to both of them, a slight smile crossing his face.

"I hope that you enjoyed your rooms … or was it *room* … last night. Your privacy is safe with me. I wish to say that Russia owes you both a debt of gratitude for helping to expose the evil plans of Yevghenny Golovko, but it is I who owe you far more. I am leaving tonight for New York to join President Price for a series of meetings and to prepare for our joint speech at the United Nations. Our men have been working all night and this morning on the files and the computer records of the deceased director of the FSB. His tentacles have run deep indeed and his comrades are men that I have unfortunately placed my trust in. Had it not been for your escape, I would be dead by tonight. My plane would have exploded somewhere over the Atlantic Ocean. Due to the nature of your mission and the secrets that must be kept, I cannot present these to you in a formal ceremony, however, please accept these decorations with my sincere gratitude for what you have helped accomplish: Hero of the Russian Federation, my nation's highest honor. When you have finished eating, my personal driver will return you to the Gagarin Space Center at Star City."

Then the President turned to John McGovern. "I had read your file, and I had insisted you be place in a position of command for this very dangerous mission. I can see I made the correct choice. Cosmonaut Polyakova, if you choose to excuse yourself from this mission, I will understand. It was Golovko that insisted on your replacing Major Kutuzov. It was his intention to see to it that the mission would fail."

Natasha looked over at John McGovern first.

"It's okay Natasha, if you want to opt out, that's fine with me," McGovern said. "You shouldn't be forced to put your life on the line."

She smiled at John and shook her head in the negative, then turned to President Simonov. "Sir, I have trained for this mission, and I am the best person for the task. Also … there is no other place in the universe I would prefer to be than beside Colonel McGovern."

President Simonov smiled deeply and put his arms around both of them.

"May God hold you both in the palm of his hand."

* * * *

Pyotr Kampov had thought he was the butt of a practical joke at the police station that morning. He had come in to report his motorcycle had been stolen by a crazed looking man and a woman with no shoes on her feet just outside of the Lubyanka metro station. Instead of having him fill out the usual unending forms, the officer on duty made a quick telephone call and then told the young man to go immediately to the American Embassy. Once there, he was brought inside and given a piece of paper, a blank voucher, and directed to proceed to one of Moscow's three Harley Davidson dealerships.

The biker, still clad in his leather jacket and pants, entered the shop. Seeing the piece of paper in his hand with the U.S. Embassy seal on it, the owner of the dealership approached him. "Ah, you must be Pyotr Kampov, I've been expecting you. Please look around. You may choose any motorcycle you wish."

Kampov stopped to inspect two 1200 cc Sportsters, one in Harley orange and black livery and the other in dark metallic blue. He then paused to look over a black and chrome Fat Boy. Finally his eyes locked upon the centerpiece of the showroom: a highly polished, chrome draped Soft Tail with a gleaming springer front end in dark red and gold metallic paint. Then his eyes fell upon the price tag: 1,300,000 rubles! Over 30,000 Euros! His eyes nearly popped from his head. He looked at the voucher and then again at the owner of the dealership questioningly and asked, "Any motorcycle?"

"Yes Pyotr, any motorcycle you would like. Have a seat on that one you've been admiring and I'll bring you your paperwork. Georgi! Bring a can of benzene for this man's bike. This fellow has places to go to today."

* * * *

Sung Zhao stood unmoving before the senior director of Chinese Intelligence. Zhao tried to maintain some sense of inner calm and to compose himself after having been assaulted by Fong Kim Hua's verbal blows. Fong was livid about his section's latest failure to derail the

West's moon mission. After receiving the call from the head of the Russian sector, Zhao had slept his first peaceful sleep since learning of the fourth Salyut that had been sitting for years as a static display, nearly in the center of Moscow. If Sung Zhao thought that error had caused him great discomfort before his superiors, it was nothing compared to what he was receiving now.

Earlier that day, Zhao sat in pleasant contemplation at his desk. Then at 11:10 that morning his telephone rang. On other end of the line, in Moscow it was just after four in the morning. Zhao knew immediately from the man's tone of voice on the other end that all had not gone according to plan, but as his Russian sector agent unfolded the events of the early hour, Zhao became increasingly agitated, feeling physically ill. Not only had their contact, Russian Intelligence Chief Yevghenny Golovko, failed to have his men dispose of the two mission commanders, but Golovko himself was dead by his own hand. Still, that piece of news was the one ray of light in the sea of blackness that Sung Zhao now found himself drowning in. Had Golovko been taken into custody, he would have certainly cracked under the Russians' interrogation techniques. In fact, Golovko's intimate knowledge of those techniques was probably why he chose to end his own life rather than face interrogation.

Good, thought Zhao, *at least the knowledge of Golovko's connections to China died along with him.* This information however, did not mitigate the wrath he was facing from his superior. Fong had spent most of his rage earlier in the meeting. Now it was time to limit the damage and devise solutions.

"Sung Zhao, I cannot fathom how badly the direction of your plan has turned. There are those in the politburo, many of influence, that have the ear of the Premier himself who feel we must cut our losses and abandon this quest for sole domination of the Moon. Vice Premier Gao is still confident of your success, but I must warn you, there can no longer be room for error. This incident in Moscow defies logic that eight trained FSB agents were defeated by one man and a *woman.* How is that possible?!"

Zhao steadied himself. He was after all Sung Zhao, the youngest intelligence director in the history of the People's Republic of China. He did not intend to be bullied.

"This was the fault of the Russians and in particular Golovko. He had always misjudged the abilities of the Americans and of us as well. His head was so full of Russian superiority and his nose held so high in the clouds, he believed no one could possibly escape his agents. He should have realized this man, McGovern, is a trained military officer and astronaut and very resourceful. However, had it not been for his luck to escape by motorcycle, then perhaps we would not be having this discussion."

Fong pulled another report from his desk draw as Zhao stood at attention before him.

"I see in this report from our American sources that he escaped death once before while on a motorcycle. Did you not read these reports?"

"Yes I did sir but …"

"*But what?!* Do you share the late Golovko's nationalistic hubris that our enemies are inferior to mighty China?! That is a delusion. You are beginning to believe your own propaganda. Read *The Art of War* and then read it again! You must never, never underestimate the skill or resourcefulness of your enemies. To do so is to invite disaster. Now, how can we make this the best of a bad situation?"

Good, Zhao thought to himself, *the typhoon has finally blown itself out.* Zhao's body relaxed, and he pulled a chair forward to sit.

"Director Fong, six days from now, our ambassador will go before the United Nations to formally request that China be granted an early exemption under Article 16 of the Treaty of Outer Space, granting us sole sovereignty over the lunar ice fields. We have the support of the entire group of non-aligned nations of the Third World plus the Western media and the support of millions, even within the United States. The Pan-African nations regard China as their savior for immediately replacing their primary communications satellite. Our war of propaganda has succeeded beyond our wildest expectations. The stockpile of stealth nuclear weapons continues to grow on the Moon. Very shortly, we will have everything we want, and it will be China who dictates the terms to the rest of the world, not the other way around. We cannot stop the launch of the Salyut from Kazakhstan, but we can make certain that the Americans never reach orbit from their Florida launch site. Captain Tso's submarine must remain on station to shoot down the launch vehicle that will carry the critical EDS stage. Once their opportunity to reach the Moon is gone and our petition is approved by the United Nations, we shall set the world's agenda and conclude our unfinished business."

Fong Kim Hua, now far more relaxed added, "Yes, and that first order of business is to take back our province of Taiwan from the Nationalist dogs. Then we shall grind the face of that *Negro woman* that sits in the American White House in the dirt. China will have its revenge for her insolence." Fong smiled and nodded to himself, his sense confidence restored. "Very well Zhao, I shall inform Admiral Shen that our submarine will again be needed. However, I do not expect any more failures. Do you understand, Sung Zhao?"

"No sir, there shall be none. I assure you."

* * * *

John McGovern sat looking out the window of the Antonov 148 jet. Its overhead wings gave him an unobstructed view the steppe: that enormous area of grasslands rolling endlessly beneath the aircraft. Natasha Polyakova was beside him sleeping with her seat reclined. Toward the front of the plane were about a dozen technicians. Some were reading or listening to MP3 players while others sat with laptops open, reviewing vital information for the next day's launch.

The huge Antonov 124 that carried the Salyut space station from the Korolev-Energia complex had touched down at the Yubilinly Airfield four days earlier. The Salyut had then been brought to Building 92-50 to be mated to a mighty Proton Rocket. The Proton with the Salyut atop it would be rolled out to its launch site later this evening to be fired into space at 0630 the following morning. If all went well with the launch and the Salyut was injected into a stable orbit, John McGovern and Natasha Polyakova would lift off and pilot their Soyuz to a rendezvous with the space station twelve hours later. Once the Salyut was powered up and checked over for any potential problems, an *Ares I* then would launch from the Kennedy Space Center with French Major Remmy LaCasse and American Lieutenant Bill Curtis aboard. Their ship would be carrying the French-built docking module. Once in orbit, the two men would have to EVA and manually attach the module to the aft end of the Salyut. At this point, it would no longer be the Salyut but the *Alliance*, the ship that would take the crew to the Moon. One of the critical components of the moon ship would be the defensive and offensive weapons systems that had been added. The Salyut now sported a rotating turret that housed a six barrel twenty millimeter Gatling gun, a mini version of the U.S. Navy's AEGIS defense system along with launch racks for both defensive American mini-PAC-4 Patriot missiles and Russian R-77 offensive rockets. The *Alliance* was voyaging to hostile territory, and unlike the first mission her crew would be well armed.

The Antonov carrying them was not alone in the sky. Because of the attempt on both their lives that had exposed Golovko as a traitor, their jet was being escorted by two armed SU-35 Super Flanker fighters. The more President Simonov's personal security people dug into Golovko's files, the worse the news became. Golovko, as well as the Minister of the Interior, and several high ranking military officers had been identified as the ones who had hatched a plot to kill the president. A bomb had been set to explode five hours into his flight to join American President Cordelier Price for their joint speech to the United Nations. The plotters had decided not to repeat the error of 1991 when General Secretary Gorbachev was briefly overthrown. This time there would be no president left alive to be rescued and to re-establish his power. More traitors were still being ferreted out, but being prudent,

Simonov assigned two loyal pilots to fly the escort mission to Baikonur.

McGovern had a lot on his mind. Each launch had to go perfectly and on schedule to make this work. He took his gaze away from the window to look again at Natasha Polyakova. The night they had spent together was etched in his memory. She had been the perfect lover for him as he was to her. They seemed to move together in an erotic ballet, with each caress, each kiss and embrace choreographed on a deep intuitive level, bringing unbelievable mutual pleasures to them both. John felt something else as well. The deep sense of contentment that he knew was love. Yes, he loved this woman, and she had returned love to him. This made everything far more complicated for him. In a combat situation he would be thinking of her safety and protection before his own. The problem was changing Natasha out for another cosmonaut was simply not an option as this late date.

She finally began to stir in her seat. "Hi there sleeping beauty. How are you feeling?"

"*Horosho* … ah good John. I am well rested. Where are we?"

"We should be landing at Baikonur in about 30 minutes or so. You looked beautiful while you slept, like an angel."

Natasha leaned over and kissed him, their seats blocking the view of the engineers in the front of the plane.

"Natasha, this … this changes everything. In a way it makes our jobs far more difficult. We're going into a potential combat situation, and I want to make sure we both come out of this alive. I want what we started together to continue to grow. We complete each other. You're my missing half. You're my soul mate. Wow, I don't usually go on like this …"

Natasha smiled at him and gently stroked his cheek. "John, I feel this way as well. I once thought I could never love again … never love another man after I lost Mikhail, but I was wrong. We are one, as if God had destined us to find each other. And … I want to say, we will be strong in battle if necessary. We are the powerful together. You are the lion and I the lioness. We are as one."

As John McGovern kissed her again they both felt the jet begin to slow for its descent into the Krainiy airfield. The two fighters would land ahead of their aircraft and they would begin their pre-launch preparations for the following day. That night they would be in separate quarters, but one day, John McGovern vowed, he would have Natasha beside him every night. All they had to do was stay alive and complete the mission, but that was looking like a very tall order.

Washington: Office of Commander Christopher Burton

When the telephone rang, Commander Chris Burton was just heading out the door, but with the series of American launches coming up in just days, he decided to take the call as it could be important. It was very important. On the other end was the voice of NSA Agent Jack Gaffney.

"Hello Commander, we got him. Omni-Probe sifted through about 2,700 names, everyone who fit the profile of the caller with access to that storage room in the "D" ring. His name is Underwood, Lieutenant JG Richard Underwood. We've come up with the following. He has accounts in eight separate banks here in the States and one off-shore account in the Bahamas. He keeps the amounts in the accounts fairly small, under $10,000 so as not to trip any bank or IRS protocols, but that is a lot of money for a junior grade officer. We found that he recently bought a BMW-Z10 with the top-of-the-line performance package. Now he's making payments on it, so he's trying to keep a low profile, but when you add up his car payment, the tax and insurance, it comes to around 1,270 a month, plus he just moved into a pretty nice two bedroom condo just outside of Manassas. The rent on that is over 3,000 a month, and he always pays cash. No way he's doing this on a JG's pay."

Chris Burton's anger began to boil over. He had a singular loathing for any American-born man or woman wearing the uniform of the armed forces who would sell out their country.

"So, do I bring this little weasel in for questioning?"

"Not just yet, Commander. We think he's small potatoes. He made that call to someone, and while we want Underwood arrested, we're far more interested in who his contact is. That should provide us with some concrete answers. I'll be in to meet with you tomorrow at 0800, and we can figure out the best way to keep tabs on him. That way we can identify mister big."

Chris Burton was trying to hold his temper in check but it was a losing battle. "Don't wait too long. NASA's launching three rockets from the Cape to complete the moon ship. This little bastard is going to get these people killed if we don't grab him before then. Once we do, I'd like to twist his head off like a bottle cap."

"Commander, I feel the same way as you do, but the NSA will twist him constructively. Underwood's just a cog; we want the main spring of this operation."

* * * *

The sun had barely begun its climb above the mountains to the East when the skies above Launch Pad 200 flared with the brilliance of high noon. The mighty Proton rocket with its six RD-253 rocket motors roared into the sky in an eastern arc, breaking through the few low hanging clouds that glided above the launch site.

Natasha Polyakova and John McGovern, along with the entire team of engineers – both at Baikonur and in Houston – kept their fingers crossed as well as saying silent prayers. The Protons had a 96 percent success rate, but if this one was unlucky, that would be the end of the only remaining Salyut space station in the world as well as the mission. However, their luck was holding, and each stage fired on cue to hurl the space station into orbit. It only took a few minutes to confirm that the orbit was stable and the space station would not begin a fatal fiery descent back to Earth.

Once the exhaust gasses from the lift off had cleared, both John and Natasha stepped out onto the observation deck of the launch control building to view their ship, a Soyuz –TMA-6 atop its CVEL launch rocket, cradled upon a massive transporter, moving slowly to its launch pad.

McGovern turned to her. "What do you think? Are you ready to fly?"

She reached over and gave his hand a squeeze. "Yes, I'm ready. I would be ready to cross the universe with you … John."

* * * *

The mystery of the two launch accidents from the Cape continued to deepen as no sign that indicated either a surface craft or a submarine had shown up on the DOD satellite images, the ones that were compiled by Lieutenant Richard Underwood.

First was the explosion of the fuel tank of an unmanned Falcon-9 re-supply rocket bound for the International Space Station, followed by the destruction of an Atlas rocket carrying the replacement communications satellite that was destined for a spot in geosynchronous orbit over the African continent. The Pan-African Congress had been screaming for a replacement since without it, telephone service, financial data, and fast links to the World Wide Web were severely compromised. In addition, the participating African nations were at a loss to predict the next year's agricultural yields. Their existing satellite suddenly stopped functioning a month earlier. China, in a gracious move, offered to replace the African satellite at no charge, and instead of placing it in orbit from Earth, they had assembled and launched it from their moon base. This dramatic and unselfish gesture clearly had a global impact on their standing in the propaganda war, impressing even Sara DelGenio a young and idealistic college graduate, now working in the imagining section of the Geo-Sat Corporation, a private environmental firm. Geo-Sat used satellite imaging to monitor ocean water temperatures for evidence of global warming, as well as fishing resource management and prediction of potential hurricanes. Sara was just completing a second batch of images, but she was still puzzled over the one from six weeks earlier. It was a vexing problem to a young woman who prided herself on always having all the right answers.

It was a little after 6 p.m., and she was still trying to understand the problem with digital image on her screen. In frustration, she called over David Greenberg, her boss. "Sir, I have no idea what this is. It's been bothering me for the last four weeks. At first, it I thought it was a malfunction in the program or maybe just some noise that didn't get filtered out. I ran several clean-up programs to try and eliminate it but it's still there."

David Greenberg put on his reading glasses and stared intently at the screen. "Where was this image recorded from?"

"Oh, just about latitude 27 and longitude 78, about 70 miles off the Florida Atlantic coast. You can see it's part of the infrared imaging for water temperatures. It really messed up my calculations, sir."

Greenberg continued to stare at the bright white steak that traced back to a point in the ocean and then a suspicion began to grow in his mind. "What was the date and time that the satellite caught this image?"

"Oh, here it is, March 21st at about 6:21 in the evening. Why, is that important?"

The puzzle pieces suddenly came together for David Greenberg and in a flash of insight he erupted, startling the young imaging specialist."Good God! This was taken about 60 seconds after the launch of the African satellite. Please don't say anything about this to anyone. I'm going to call a friend of mine at the Pentagon. I have a feeling that the destruction of that rocket was no accident."

"How is that possible sir? No one could have possibly destroyed that rocket with a missile. Someone would have recorded it on radar."

Greenberg putting his glasses back into his jacket pocket replied to her, "No, not a missile. An infrared laser fired from a submarine, and I have a damn good idea just whose submarine it was."

"You mean the Chinese don't you …. Oh … oh, oh my gosh, Mr. Greenberg, There's a launch just three days from now. The crew for the second moon mission is going up on Thursday! They ... *they'll be killed!* You have to call now! Call the Navy or the CIA or whoever … *Please, Mr. Greenberg!*"

David looked at his employee; she seemed terribly distressed maybe not just from the discovery that some kind of laser weapon had been used to down the rocket but perhaps from coming to terms with her view of the world. "Don't worry Sara, I'll call right now. The people I know in the military will know how to handle this. Listen, I know that you and I are on opposite sides of the political fence, and that's okay. Everyone in America is free to express their own opinion but … tell me, do you still think it's America's fault that we and the Chinese just can't seem to get along?"

"No sir, I guess not. I guess we're not the bad guys after all."

While her boss dialed the number to Admiral Stanton's office at the Pentagon, Sara DelGenio sat back down feeling just a bit confused as well as embarrassed that she, along with millions of others, had believed China's lies.

* * * *

"John, you did not christen the tires of the transporter van. It is supposed to be tradition."

"I thought it was supposed to be that both cosmonauts have to take aim and hose down the tires. That would prove a bit difficult for you, don't you think?"

McGovern opened the Velcro pocket on the leg of his flight suit and slid his hand down into the opening. It was there where he had put it while they were suiting up. It was an impulse. A young engineer named Arkady was eager to show off the rocket assembly building to John. On his tour, they passed bins of parts and electrical components. Then he saw something that caught his eye. Arkady told him it was a connector for part of the fiber optic system, and it was plated with pure gold. There were dozens of them in the parts bin, and he asked the engineer if he could keep it as a souvenir. Arkady shrugged and told him to take it. Now it was in the palm of his hand, a gold connecting ring, just the right size for a woman's finger. Sitting next to Natasha inside the Soyuz capsule he reached over to her.

"Natasha, I'd like to start a new tradition. This is just a gold electrical connector, but it'll have to do until we get back to Earth." McGovern then took her hand in his. "Natasha, when this mission is over, and we're back on Earth and one piece, I want us to have a life together with you as my wife."

Natasha looked down at her hand. After losing Misha, she believed a ring of commitment would never again grace her finger. *Yes,* she thought yes, *John was the kind of man that she could love and feel secure with. He was strong and brave and she knew he loved her as she did him.* "Oh, yes John, yes … you have made me very happy, and I am filled with the strength I need for this mission. I love you. When we return, I will gladly have you for my husband."

The sound of applause suddenly filled their headphones followed by the voice of Yuri Zhdanov at mission control in Moscow. "I believe Captain Polyakova and Colonel McGovern that you may have neglected to check the operation of your onboard microphone and camera. However, it seems as if they are working. Your father is here to the center. I think he would like to speak with you."

Dmitry Polyakov wiped a tear from his eye and smiled broadly. "Natasha, my *solnishka*, you have made an excellent choice. I am very happy for you. John, you will be my new son; take care of her and bring her back to me."

McGovern keyed his throat mike, "I will Dmitry, I promise."

At 1834 hours, the motors of the Soyuz rocket came alive with the heat and flames of a controlled explosion. The support scaffolding fell away and the restraining clamps retracted, freeing the craft to soar out of the Earth's gravity well. It was Natasha's ship under her control leaving Central Asia far below them, climbing out of the dark blue of the upper atmosphere and into the black vacuum of outer space.

The Soyuz was now in an orbital chase that would bring it into range of the Salyut for docking. Half a world away, other activates were moving toward a point of finality as well. At the Kennedy Space Center, two *Ares I* rockets and one Titan IV-B stood on their launch pads ready to be sent into space the following day. The Titan would carry the two reconditioned lunar landers into orbit. This would be followed the launch of the first *Ares* with Remmy LaCasse and William Curtis carrying the French docking module into orbit. Finally, Tom Garcia and Jack Griffin would ride atop the second modified *Ares* that would carry both men into orbit along with the EDS to send the *Alliance* to the Moon. .

In New York, Russian President Simonov and American President Price huddled with their advisors for the next day's UN address. The Chinese were to state their case for being granted sole control of the resources of the Moon. Price and Simonov would speak just following the address by the Chinese Foreign Ambassador. How those speeches would play out was totally dependent upon the success of the launches from Florida and the link-up with the Salyut in orbit.

Cruising below the depths of the Atlantic Ocean, the Chinese nuclear submarine commanded by Captain Tso awaited his orders to fire upon the American rockets.

* * * *

At 20 minutes after midnight, the darkness blanketing the central east coast of Florida was split by the roar and flames of a Titan IV-B climbing into the star filed sky. At three minutes into its flight, the two solid fuel rocket boosters, having exhausting their fuel supply, fell away toward the Ocean below. The main stage continuing to burn through its supply of propellants and was soon left behind with the second and finally the third stage firing and placing the cargo module, holding the two reconditioned lunar landers, into orbit. In 14 hours, the module's orbital track would cross that of the Salyut. At the same time, 300 kilometers above the Earth, the Soyuz piloted by Natasha Polyakova had just come within visual contact of the Salyut.

"I can see it Natasha, coming into range. The radar reads 20 kilometers and closing. We'll be on top of it in just a couple of minutes."

The Salyut continued to grow ever larger as the Soyuz closed the distance to the space station.

Natasha fired the front thrusters to kill the ship's forward motion, coming almost to a halt. She sat for a moment staring at the space station in deep thought, and then she spoke. "I can't believe it. I'm actually docking a Soyuz to my space station … *my* space station, the very same one I used to pretend I was floating outside of as a child."

McGovern smiled at her with a contentment he thought would never be a part of his life again. Natasha was like a small girl staring in awe at her childhood playground floating before them in orbit. He reached over and gave her hand a gentle squeeze. "Well then, just line up the docking probe, and we'll link up and you can finally go inside."

Then John gazed at the Earth below. "Hey look at that, dawn's just breaking over the East Coast of the United States."

* * * *

A brilliant April sunrise bathed the city of Washington in a golden light. The cherry trees along the Potomac were in full bloom and the city was coming alive, having discarded the blanket of night. It was going to be one of those spectacular spring days in the nation's capital. However, for Lieutenant Richard Underwood this morning was about to become his worst nightmare coming to fruition. In the office of Commander Burton, a meeting that started before 0600 was nearly concluded once the satellite downloads of March 21st had been retrieved.

Admiral Walter Stanton held the photo images that his friend David Greenburg had provided to him.

"Thank God for private satellite imaging firms. Without this, we may have been too late to do anything. Here, this is the Geo-Sat image in infrared and here on the monitor are the unaltered images that we re-accessed from the surveillance satellite. As you can see, the heat trace from the Geo-Sat image corresponds to this disturbance in the water at exactly the same moment and location."

The admiral then adjusted the magnification on the computer screen. "You can see here, this object in the water is just about at the limit of resolution of our imaging technology, but if I add some compensation so the computer sharpens the fuzziness, we get this."

Jack Gaffney looked closely at the image. "Damn, that's the business end of a high-energy laser poking out of the water. There's a Chinese nuclear sub out there that can blow our rockets out of the sky. That's a pretty sophisticated software program Underwood has. He deleted these images with it and it reprogrammed the sequence so no one would know they're missing."

Commander Burton leaned forward in his chair. "Lieutenant Underwood should be arriving in that 65,000 dollar car of his any moment. I have two non-coms keeping an unobtrusive eye out for him. I want to see how he's getting his information out and who's he going to call."

Jack Gaffney added, "Did you tell his buddy over in flight surveillance to be generous with information?"

"I sure did. But, I told him to play it cool. Let Underwood think he's drawing out the information from Lieutenant Murphy."

Just then Commander Burton's earpiece peeped. "Okay, as Sherlock Holmes would say, the game is afoot. Underwood just entered the building."

About 10 minutes later, Captain Delgado, Underwood's commanding officer called to Chris Burton. "Yeah, he just stopped by my office. Said he's going to grab a coffee and then get to work on his image downloads."

Lieutenant JG Richard Underwood walked past the coffee machine and straight into Jeff Murphy's cubical. Murphy would be playing along, feeding him enough disturbing information to hopefully trigger a phone call to his contact.

"Hey Murph, what's up this morning? You look pretty busy."

Jeff Murphy looked up from his LCD screen, still playing the part of Underwood's pigeon, "Yeah I sure am. We just put eight Orion sub hunters in the air heading for a spot off Cape Canaveral."

"*Really?* What's up with that Murph?"

"I shouldn't say anything about this but … the scoop is there's a

Chinese missile sub out there with some kind of laser planning to knock down one of our manned rockets. They launch today. In just a couple of hours."

Underwood tried his best to hide his nervousness and kept digging for information. "*Jeez!* I can't believe that! That's pretty serious! But that's all we sent? Just sub hunters?"

"Ah come on Rick, you know I can't tell you anything else, you don't have clearance for this."

"Hey Murph, I just want to know, okay. Tell you what; you can borrow my Beemer next time you're taking that blonde ensign out. What do you say?"

"Aw shit, okay, but you didn't hear it from me. We've got two attack boats out there as well: the *Connecticut* and the *Virginia* looking for a Chinese sub. They've been ordered to sink her on contact. No warnings."

"Hey, thanks a lot. Really, I was just curious you know. I have to get back to my station."

"See ya Rick – and don't forget that I'll need your car Saturday night, okay?"

Underwood's heart was racing as he headed for the supply room. The work at his station would have to wait until after he made the call. He'd tell Delgado that Mother Nature called and he was in the head or something.

Underwood glanced up and down the hallway. Seeing no one, he ducked into the supply room and pulled out his encrypted cell phone, punching in the code to his contact and then raising the phone to his ear. Instead of the telephone on the opposite end ringing, all he heard was a terrible squeal through the earpiece and he checked his phone again. Underwood was about to hit redial when the door to the supply room burst open and two marines with AR-15 rifles along with Captain Delgado, Commander Burton, and the NSA agent flew into the room. Commander Burton was holding a small black box in his hand. "Having trouble placing your call Mr. Underwood? Perhaps this jammer's the reason. I'll just turn it off. By the way, this is Special Agent Jack Gaffney of the NSA. We'd like to know who you're calling."

Underwood was almost in shock and breathing hard. "I … I've got nothing to say to you. I have rights under military law, you know."

Commander Burton grabbed the man by the neck and shoved him against a wall. "You don't have shit, you little twerp! Now, it was up to me, I'd twist your damn head off right at the neck right this second, but instead I'm going to give you a chance to save your ass. *You* are a piece of garbage fouling the uniform of a U.S. Navy officer! You're a spy and a traitor! I can have you shot on the spot, and I can order these marines to do it *right now*!"

Both marines brought their rifles up to their shoulders, aiming dead center at Underwood's chest.

"Or … I can give you a chance to cooperate and let you live. Which would you prefer, *Lieutenant*?"

Underwood was shaking very badly, and the yellow stain that formed on the front of his uniform pants did not go unnoticed. "Okay, okay, what do you want me to do?"

"Hand over your cell phone to Agent Gaffney."

Underwood did as he was told, and the NSA man clipped a wire to the antenna that led to a small device about the size of a TV remote. Gaffney chuckled. "This will pinpoint his contact. Give us everything: name, location, the whole enchilada. Now go ahead, Underwood, place your call. Only here's what you're going to tell your contact."

* * * *

The morning sun was shining into the offices on the 64th floor of the East Wind Securities building. Below, New York City was still in shadow with the tall buildings, blocking the sun from illuminating the city streets. The ringing of the special line tore him away from his view. On the other end was his contact. The man listened carefully.

"They called off the search of the Cape waters. The *Seawolf* sub we put out there has reactor troubles. They're heading back to Kings Bay in Georgia for repairs."

"Thanks. I'll make sure there's something extra for you next week at the usual location."

He hung up the phone. Glancing at his gold Rolex watch, he decided to call the Chinese Consulate right away. *Ha,* he thought to himself, *reactor problems? They must build those subs like crap in Groton these days,* and picked up the telephone to make his call.

* * * *

Jack Gaffney turned to Commander Burton, "Got him! This will transmit to NSA headquarters. I'll have an answer back just about … now."

The tiny LCD screen on the device that Jack Gaffney was holding came alive with the name and address of the person the call was placed to. Gaffney had to look at it twice as he thought his eyes were playing tricks on him. "Holy shit! You are *not* going to believe who was on the other end of that call …"

Kennedy Space Center 0710

"T-minus five, four, three, umbilicals are free, two: start is positive! One …. *Ignition!*

The first *Ares I* rocket with Major Remmy LaCasse and Lieutenant William Curtis on board roared skyward from the launch pad. At the controls of the Orion Constellation vehicle was astronaut Susan Mulholland. She was a veteran pilot on the space shuttles before they were retired in 2011 and had already flown the *Ares-Orion* into space and back three times. The Orion, unlike the space shuttle, harkened back more to the days of the old Apollo capsules of 50 years earlier. However, the Orion was larger, capable of carrying a crew of four plus a pilot to the International Space Station. The Orion would have been a key component of America's return to the Moon two years in the future until the Chinese beat everyone to the punch. Now the craft was ferrying two of the *Alliance* crew along with the French docking module to the growing collection of space hardware that was called the *Alliance,* the core of this craft being the Salyut space station that had sat for over three decades outside of the Kosmos Hotel in Moscow.

F-18s armed with air to surface torpedoes along with the electronic eyes of sub chasers prowled the skies, scanning the waters of the Cape for any disturbance. Below the surface, two *Seawolf* class hunter-killer submarines patrolled the depths, like great predatory sharks. However, there was nothing to be seen or heard from the enemy submarine.

Sitting on the bottom, 200 meters down, Captain Tso reviewed his orders. He was to fire only upon the third and final launch from the Cape. This would be the rocket that carried the critical Earth Departure Stage. Without this powerful rocket, the *Alliance* spacecraft would never leave Earth orbit. There was another reason for not firing on either the first or the second launch. The final rocket would lift off at 1500 hours, just after the Chinese Foreign Minister would make his case at the United Nations for sole rights to the Moon's resources. With the support of the Western media and virtually every government in the Third World and developing nations, China felt the approval was a foregone conclusion.

For now, Captain Tso had to keep totally silent. Modern nuclear submarines were so quiet, that sonar operators in hunter-killer subs had to listen not so much for the noise of an enemy boat but the lack of it. The operator was basically looking for an acoustic dead zone, a hole in the ocean devoid of sound. This troubled Tso. The laser that had been installed on his submarine made it extremely noisy when in operation. The reactor had to be run up to full power with the cooling pumps running at maximum RPMs, sending the super heated coolant into the sub's heat exchangers. The laser itself generated tremendous heat that was cooled by circulating liquid sodium around the capacitor banks and into auxiliary heat exchanges that had been grafted onto the submarine. These creaked and popped like old steam radiators when the superheated cooling medium came into contact with the cold seawater surrounding the heat exchangers. Fortunately, Caption Tso thought, this cacophony only persisted for about 45 seconds. The only other presence of the Chinese submarine was the radio intercept antenna, on its retractable tether, just a few meters below the surface of the water.

* * * *

"Are you *sure* you got the right guy?" Commander Burton was incredulous at seeing the name on Agent Gaffney's portable device.

Gaffney then noticed the red LED on the device begin to blink. "Hold on. He's making a call. Now that we're liked up with his phone, we become the ultimate flies on the wall."

The three men gathered around the device with Underwood sitting dejectedly on the floor in handcuffs. The male voice on the telephone call was familiar. They'd heard him often enough giving TV interviews. "Ah, Minister Chu. I have good news to report. The search for your submarine has been called off. The American attack boat had some sort of accident on board and was recalled."

* * * *

A few minutes later, the submerged antenna of the Type 094 missile submarine captured an encrypted transmission. Captain Tso was in his cabin reading a book when the young officer knocked and opened. "Message sir. From central command, sir."

Tso unfolded the paper and a smile broke across his face. He immediate walked to the control room and spoke to his second in command. "Excellent news, Bao! The Americans have withdrawn their *Seawolf*. We can perform our duty without risk of reprisal."

* * * *

Captain Delgado turned to the NSA agent. "So what are you going to do now?'

"I'm going to make a call to the NSA office in New York City and have two agents arrest Mr. Crowley, just like they would arrest any other stinking traitor who was selling out the United States. *That* son of a bitch is history!"

Nathan Crowley was the President and CEO of the East Wind Securities and Investment Corporation. The sprawling multinational firm handling billions of dollars of Chinese money and had offices in several countries as well as in San Francisco and Dallas. Crowley, the former head of one of the largest investment banks in the United States, was instrumental after the economic upheavals of 2010 and 2011 in bringing a flood of Chinese investment money into the country to shore up the economy. Crowley also was instrumental in making certain the flow of Chinese-made products into the country was unimpeded by those with nationalist agendas. In the process, he had become very, very rich, and was counted among the world's 50 wealthiest individuals. All in the room except Underwood were incredulous that this man who gave America such incredible opportunities would turn around and put a knife into the back of his own country.

President Cordelier Price received the call on her way to the United Nations. She and the Russian President were in separate motorcades, heading to address the Security Council and the entire array of member nations. On her way to the UN, Price could see the sidewalks lined with demonstrators protesting America's refusal to go along with the Chinese in its bid for sole ownership of the lunar ice fields. There were effigies of her with exaggerated racial features on display and signs decrying her and America as obstructionist. The "Greens" were out in force, as well, having bought into China's promise of developing huge orbiting solar collectors once they had unimpeded access to the Moon. The voice on the other end was the director of the National Security Agency.

"Yes director, I'm surprised but perhaps … I'm not a way … I'm just extremely disappointed and angry," Price said. "Mister Crowley was my guest last year at the White House. I suppose I should have counted the silverware when he left. Fine, you can arrest him in about 30 minutes. I'll be inside the UN by then and … this helps our case tremendously. Make certain that I get a copy of Nathan Crowley's call to the Chinese Embassy before I speak."

* * * *

Agents Gunther and Mosley were known as New York's salt and pepper team back at NSA headquarters, with Mosley being African

American and Gunther a tall blond of German extraction. Both men were well dressed in dark suits that did little to disguise their athletic frames.

Exiting the elevator at the penthouse offices of the East Wind Corporation both men stopped at the receptionist's desk. Mosley spoke first. "We're here to see Mr. Crowley. I assume that door leads to his office?"

The receptionist's eyes flashed with annoyance. "I have *no idea* who you men are! Do you have an appointment? Mr. Crowley is not to be disturbed."

Agent Gunther then produced his NSA badge, "Oh, I think Mr. Crowley is going to be *very* disturbed once we talk to him."

Nathan Crowley had just signed on to his computer to review an investment deal between Shanghi Steel and what was left of the Bethel Steel Corporation in a final buyout when his office doors bust open. Two men entered the room with guns drawn. Mosley made the introductions.

"Mr. Nathan Crowley, you're under arrest. The charge is treason against the United States of America."

Both agents had pulled their badges out, but Crowley didn't look carefully at their designations. Crowley's face took on a dark shade of red and his lips blanched white with anger. "You two *idiots* are going to wish the hell you never set foot inside my office! I have a lot of highly placed friends in the FBI, you know!"

Agent Gunther just smiled and answered. "That's very nice Mr. Crowley, but we're *not* FBI. We're NSA, and we'd like to know *all* about your … *friends* in the FBI. Now, come along with us and don't make a scene. You sold out your country and put the lives of a lot of good Americans in jeopardy.

Nathan Crowley stood up from his chair and with all the anger he could muster replied to the agents. "I know my rights! I'm calling my attorney!"

As his hand reached for the phone Agent Mosley grabbed his arm and forcibly pushed him back into his chair. "Mr. Crowley, you no longer have any *rights*. You abdicated them when you became an agent of the Chinese Government. At this point, I'd have very little regret about shooting you. Oh, certainly not to kill you – we need to talk to you first – but I can promise you I can place a shot so you'll never have the use of one of your legs again. Either that or you'll never have the use for a woman again; take your pick ... Or, you can come along with us quietly and tell us what we want to know. Your choice ... which will it be?"

Crowley nodded his head nervously in the affirmative and let the two agents lead him out of the building and into a waiting, nondescript black Ford Taurus.

* * * *

President Cordelier Price sat in the special section of the General Assembly next to Russian President Simonov awaiting the pivotal speech by the Chinese Foreign Minister. The Russian President spoke to her. "By the look of all those Americans supporting the position of China, I would have to say, my predecessors would have been quite impressed. We did not succeed nearly so well in converting useful idiots to join our cause."

Price, fluent in four languages that included Russian answered in Simonov's native tongue. "If you mean using propaganda to turn young and idealistic people against their country, I guess you could say the Chinese did your old Communist Party one better. Although, I believe there are a lot of college professors and journalists in this country who are quite enamored by Karl Marx. Once we put the evidence we have before the UN, they may start singing a different tune."

"So why then did you agree to allow the Chinese to present their petition first?"

Cordelier Price gave the Russian President a sly smile, like a poker player about to reveal a winning hand. "We have an expression in this country: Give a man enough rope and he'll hang himself. I want China to boast about all their achievements and their technological prowess as well as their generosity toward the developing nations of the world. Let them build a towering house of cards, and then we'll knock it over with the truth."

Just as Price finished her last sentence a secret service agent handed her an encrypted mobile phone. "Yes, this is President Price … I see. That's excellent. Make sure you get him to Washington without any incidents that might wind up in the press. I see; have NSA transmit the recording. Yes, I will be using it."

Simonov turned to the American President. "Was that something I should know about?"

Now she had more than just a sly smile, it was a broad one of triumph. "What we just got will help put the nail in the collective coffin of the Chinese drive to have sole control of the Moon. On the other hand, I'm quite distressed that people who owe their very success to the freedoms and opportunities they've been born into in America have sold their nation down the river for personal gain. I'm also waiting for another call. It may come any minute. If I have this news before we finish our speeches, the Chinese Foreign Minister will be running out of here, propelled by a chorus of boos … or at least I hope so. China will be seen as nothing more than an aggressor nation built on lies and deceit. I'll let you in on a little secret happening right now off the coast of Florida."

Simonov gave Cordelier Price the raised eyebrow, of his well know cynical look. "Don't be too disappointed if our presentation does not bring down the house as you say. Illusions, particularly the ones that these nations and individuals have invested heavily in, often die hard."

* * * *

Sonar operator Mat Jablonski on board the *USS Connecticut* watched his display screen intently as well as using the old sonar man's standby, listening to his headphones. Both the *Connecticut* Seawolf class submarine and the smaller *Virginia* were running silently in hunter killer mode, 70 meters below the waters off of Cape Canaveral, looking for the Chinese Type 094 ballistic missile boat that had been reconfigured into an offensive laser platform. The captains of both American ships had been apprised that information had been fed to the Chinese to assure them they had nothing to fear from the American Navy. The crew on the *Connecticut* had been informed of this as well. Torpedo man Dennis Constantine, overseeing the loading of four MK 48 torpedoes into their firing tubes, said to another sailor on duty, "Nothing for the Chinese to fear, eh? Well, *fear this!*"

* * * *

Sitting on the bottom of the Atlantic, Captain Tso carefully watched his clock. When the digital readout marked 1435 hours, he picked up his microphone and ordered the sub up to just 15 meters below the surface and to run the reactor up to full power to begin charging the laser's capacitors.

* * * *

"Got him!" It was Matt Jablonsky's voice. He quickly fed the coordinates to his captain indicating they could be on top of the Chinese boat in less than 10 minutes. The *Connecticut's* Captain, William Jonas, ordered his ship ahead full speed, then smiling to himself, thought, *Ah ha, David and the Virginia are out of range. Dinner will be on him when we get back to port.* Then Jonas also considered the deadly seriousness of the mission. The Chinese missile boat would be in a position to fire on the *Ares III-A* carrying three astronauts and the EDS stage in less than 20 minutes. The Chinese captain, whoever he was, would be ready to fire with the *Connecticut* arriving with less than 10 minutes to spare. This was going to be a very close call. If both subs had been out of range, it held the potential for a disaster. Even though F-18s were in flight with air to surface torpedoes, it was a mighty big ocean to cover completely. Captain Jonas checked his weapons' status: *Four fish in the forward tubes and two in the rear. Time to go hunting,* he thought. Then quietly under his breath he said, "That Chinese captain is about to get a *really* nasty surprise."

Over the intercom Captain Jonas issued another order. "We have very good water transparency. When we close to 500 yards, let Snoopy out of his doghouse."

"Snoopy" was the name submariners had given to their latest secret weapon in the shadowy blue-green world of undersea combat. Snoopy was a surveillance device for covertly gathering data and video images of enemy submarines. About the size and shape of a large tuna, Snoopy was in truth a mechanical fish, complete with fins and tail. Other attempts at building an undetectable surveillance probe failed due to the ever increasing sophistication of sonar and underwater listening technology. The probe that was about to be released from the *Connecticut* would image the sub in the visual spectrum as well as the infrared to see how efficient the heat exchangers were on the Chinese boat. It would make a close investigation of the Chinese 094 submarine, and it was completely undetectable, just simply another fish in an immense ocean. The probe could also swim up to an enemy sub and attach itself like a remora to a shark. Once in place, it could monitor speech and other activities right through the hull, using the acoustic properties of the sub's metal structure and the surrounding sea water. Snoopy even could send a homing signal that would attract torpedoes that had been fired like flies to honey. An enemy submarine's countermeasures would be useless.

That day, the job of Snoopy was to obtain as many detailed images of the modified Chinese sub as possible for a slam dunk indictment of their aggression and deliberate downing of American rockets. If they were lucky, Snoopy also would record the kill of the Type 094 boat.

CHAPTER THIRTEEN

New York, the United Nations General Assembly, 1420 hours

Smiling with self-confidence, Chinese Foreign Minister Shang Lu ascended to the main podium to address the 190-plus nations represented in the UN. The Chinese Foreign Minister, dressed in a dark gray business suit, had a lightness to his step, like that of a man assured of victory. He had considered that the presidents of Russia and the United States would follow his speech and attempt to dissuade the granting of exclusive development rights to the Moon's resources, but their voices would be nothing more than bluster and wind against the march of history. China already had the votes, as well as the good will and enthusiasm of millions around the world for their achievements. China's unselfish acts in providing refined ore to the world's developing nations were working better than anyone had anticipated in gaining supporters.

The ruse involving the destruction and then the replacement of the Pan-African satellite was a stroke of genius, but then it came from the master of deception himself, Sung Zhao. Shang smiled inwardly with overwhelming smugness. This was going to be the easiest victory in history. In just 20 more minutes, China would gain control over not only the resources of the Moon and space but the entire world's economy as well, and it would be achieved without armies or battles. Like an expert pickpocket that could relieve a man of his wallet by stealth, the world's nations would surrender their freedom to China without even realizing they had done so … until it would be far too late. *Even if the Russian/American/European coalition attempts to fly in the face of the UN and send their mission to the Moon,* he thought, *in 25 more minutes their opportunity to do so will be blown out of the sky.*

* * * *

"Up 15 degrees on the dive planes. Bring us level at seventeen meters." Captain Tso then turned to his second in command. "Start the charging procedure and prepare to open the laser access doors."

* * * *

Jablonsky called over his headset to the captain. "Sir, he's coming up. Can't miss him, he's bubbling and popping like a shook-up bottle of Pepsi! I … I'm getting a sound I'm not familiar with, sir. It's not missile hatches opening, sounds more like … doors."

Bill Jonas called back over his own headset. "Don't worry about it, Jabber; their sub had to have been modified to incorporate an anti-missile laser. They must have replaced the launch tube hatches with some sort of access doors."

"Sure is noisy, sir."

Jonas chuckled. "Ah, the better to hear you my dear and then kill you."

Over his earpiece, the boson's mate called out. "Sir, Snoopy is within range. I have images coming in … *Wow*, what the hell *is* that?!"

Gliding like some great gray prehistoric beast, silently stalking its prey, the *Connecticut* would be within torpedo range of Tso's submarine in slightly more than three minutes. Captain William Jonas considered the action he would take as a commander in the next few minutes. This was not a drill or another exercise between submarines of his navy. This was the real thing; it was his responsibility and his alone to give the order that would, in all likelihood, send every man on the Chinese missile sub to his death. He also considered the fact that if he did not act, in less than 10 minutes an American rocket carrying three men and his country's last desperate chance of heading off Chinese domination of the Moon would come crashing down into the sea in a shower of flaming debris.

* * * *

Thoughts of a different sort were running through the minds of those three men atop the modified *Ares I* watching the countdown clock in their capsule steadily running backward and down to zero.

The *Ares V* would have been the space transport system to carry the Earth Departure Stage into orbit. The EDS would provide the thrust necessary to carry the Constellation, America's return to the Moon in 2020. Only it was 2018 and the *Ares V* did not yet exist, other than on paper and as a computer graphic. The *Ares I* was never intended to carry the EDS into orbit. The rocket was simply not powerful enough on its own to do so and required extensive modifications.

On the launch pad sat the sum total of the Herculean engineering effort – the *Ares III–A*. By grafting on two additional solid rocket boosters, the same type used on the now retired space shuttle, the *Ares* had sufficient power to send three men plus the EDS stage into Earth orbit. Once that was accomplished, the pilot would begin an orbital chase of the Salyut station that had already been added to with the French docking module. If all went well, in another seven hours they would close the distance to the Salyut and begin the difficult and dangerous task of mating the Earth Departure Stage to the French docking collar. The two lunar landers then would be coupled to the docking module and, if all went as planned, a Progress cargo rocket launched from Northern Russia, carrying the inflatable Bigelow Habitat, would be carefully attached and later deployed on the Moon. There were so many opportunities for disaster that the entire cobbled up project named the *Alliance* seemed destined for failure.

Sitting in their seats, all three men knew that more than likely someone 70 miles out in the Atlantic Ocean would be trying to kill them, blasting their rocket out of the sky with an invisible beam of infrared energy.

Air Force Major Vernon LaBelle sat in the number one seat of the Orion capsule, feeling the adrenalin-fueled tension in his body rise as the launch clock spiraled down to zero. LaBelle had volunteered for this mission, one that he knew he had a significant chance of not coming home from. He, along with astronauts Garcia and Griffin, now strapped into two of the seats further back in the capsule, had met with NASA Director Norman Taggert as he explained the dangers of this particular mission; Taggert's briefing was replayed in Vernon LaBelle's thoughts:

"Okay then men, I'm not going to give you any spin on this or try and minimize the risks. That's not my style. I'm not some government hack painting a pretty picture for you. The Ares I was never designed or intended to carry the Orion plus the EDS stage. As you are well aware, just from looking out at the launch pad, we've added two AKT solid rocket boosters to the vehicle to give it more than enough thrust to get you and the EDS into orbit. Now, the only tests of this system have been computer simulations, and, believe me we've used the best, most powerful linked mainframes available to run the simulations. According to the data, everything should go as planned, but this is the real world and according to the old expression, you know what happens. Well, we're 98 percent sure that it'll work but I want Major LaBelle over here to be ready to engage the abort/escape system if everything starts going south in a hurry on you.

"Now, here comes the more difficult part. We had suspected someone was out in the Atlantic is picking off our rockets with an SDI type laser weapon. Now we've confirmed it. It seems that a modified Chinese ballistic missile sub has been sitting off our coast using a high-energy laser. We're pretty sure her captain believes he's home free. In reality, we have two hunter-killer subs within range of him and just before launch, the skies above that area will be thick with sub hunters and Navy F-18s armed with anti-submarine missiles. I can't say don't worry and that everything is under control. But, we're confident about nailing this bastard before he can shoot. Still, Major LaBelle, keep an eye on the abort system. If this son of bitch does fire, you'll know it. Your sensor panel will be lighting up like a Christmas tree. You'll only have a matter of seconds to engage the abort system and get the hell out of there. Now, any questions?"

Jack Griffin sat strapped into his acceleration couch on top of enough explosive propellant to equal a one-half kiloton tactical nuke shared LaBelle's same thoughts. *Did I have any questions?* he thought to himself. *Yeah maybe, like what the hell am I doing here? Aw crap, if the mission's a success, they'll be naming Canadian universities and public schools after me in 50 years. If we all get killed, they'll start naming them next week.*

Vernon LaBelle's eyes were locked on the countdown timer. *Fifteen minutes to go,* he was thinking. *In 18 minutes, we'll either be above the atmosphere or parachuting down to the ocean … if we're lucky. If not, we'll all be heading straight down at 200 miles per hour, whole or in pieces, and I'll be the little pile of black pieces they can ship home in a shoebox.*

* * * *

The thunderous applause that erupted for the Chinese Foreign Minister when he walked to the General Assembly podium lasted for almost five minutes. Without exception, the representatives of the developing nations of the Third World were on their feet for this man, with many actually yelling, "China! China!" At the same time, most in the Western delegations remained seated, offering only polite applause. Presidents Price and Simonov sat silently, hands folded in their laps, awaiting their turns to speak.

Finally, as the din receded, Shang Lu adjusted his microphone and began his show, complete with a powerful visual display on the two huge projection screens above the main platform of the General Assembly. "Fellow citizens of the world! Fellow human beings who struggle to rise up from the chains of oppression to claim your place in the sun, China is with you!"

Shang paused for a moment to let the cheering subside then began again. "Today is a great day for you, for your nations and for your people. Today, China is lifting the twin boots of capitalism and imperialism from your backs. Today, you will no longer beg for scraps from the Western powers. Your nations will no longer be commodities to be bought and sold on the international markets. Today, your voices will be the ones to shout aloud that China is your friend and your benefactor and that China shall cut through the chains that bind your people to lives of poverty and subsistence. Today, China comes before you as a nation that will use her technological prowess and her greatness not to oppress you, but to uplift you, making all equal among the community of nations!"

Again, the din of applause continued for over a minute, followed again by the chant, "China! China!" Then the two huge video displays flanking the central podium came to life with a computer-generated presentation to rival any big budget special effects blockbuster from Hollywood. As the Chinese Foreign Minister continued his speech to the gathered delegates, the images of a vast lunar mining and processing complex, showing detail so realistic, it would have been nearly impossible to determine if this was actual footage or not. From there, the images and the narration showed dozens of magnetic accelerators sending refined ore back to low Earth orbit, to be packaged and delivered to resource-poor nations with the use of re-entry shields. The scenes then switched to a huge orbital construction project of five-mile wide solar collectors in geosynchronous orbit to beam nearly unlimited and nearly free electricity to the nations of Africa, Asia and South America. Futuristic scenes of metal rich asteroids being moved into Earth orbit for mining and processing were the next images to spellbind Shang's audience. Finally, images of Third World slums with desperate poverty encumbered inhabitants magically morphed and transformed into gleaming cities and clean towns populated by healthy, prosperous and smiling people.

"And this is the promise of China to you, the formally oppressed nations of the world. I say again *formally oppressed* because as of today, once you grant China exclusive ownership and rights to her claim of the Moon's resources, your shackles shall be removed, and your people will begin their journey to a new destiny, standing proudly, no longer at the back but now at the front of the community of nations. From China, according to her great technological abilities to the nations of the developing world, according to your needs, shall flow the fruits of our great leap forward for all mankind!"

Again, the roar of the gathered international delegates persisted for over a minute, further delaying the Foreign Minister's speech.

"I also say to America and the nations of the developed world," he continued, "do not block our path, for this great change is about to transform the world like a powerful river. Do not stand immobile before the great flood of history or you shall be swept aside. Instead, join us! Give China what is rightfully hers by her accomplishments. Grant us our legitimate and rightful claim to what is ours. Grant China our rights through our legal petition to our claim of the Moon for China and for all humanity!"

The applause within the chamber of the General Assembly was deafening.

* * * *

Below the surface of the Atlantic Ocean, calm and placid as a picture, the brilliant Florida sun shined down into the depths, painting the undersea world in undulating shades of blues and deep greens, illuminating the Chinese ballistic missile submarine just 55 feet below the surface. As the sub slowly crept closer toward that surface, the doors replacing the missile hatches began to open and the business end of the high-energy laser slowly began to rise upward, breaking the surface of the water.

Captain Jonas stared at the display screen, watching the images from the *Connecticut's* remote probe. "Are we getting all this?"

The answer came back immediately through the captain's earpiece. "Yes, sir. We have everything so far and we can transmit on your order."

"Okay ensign, zoom the camera in on the head of that device. I want solid evidence with no room for deception on the part of the Chinese that what we're looking at is an offensive laser weapon, and then pull Snoopy back before we shoot. I'd like to get our little $10 million fish home in one piece."

* * * *

On board the Chinese Type 094-missile boat, Captain Tso's eyes focused on his display screen. The image it showed through the wide-angled lens was of the smooth ocean surface as the camera, mounted on the laser projector, sat six feet above that surface.

Tso called out over the ships intercom. "Complete the charge to the capacitors and route the waste heat to the exchangers. Stand by to fire in three minutes."

* * * *

Sitting 220 feet up, on top of several million pounds of explosive chemicals, Major Vernon LaBelle watched his launch clock register three minutes to lift-off with still no word on the deadly submarine waiting to smite them from the sky.

* * * *

"Captain! The Chinese boat must be charging their weapon. It's noisy as hell. With that thing sticking up out of the water, they're sitting ducks."

Jonas looked down at his weapons panel, fighting back the intruding images of the carnage he was about to unleash. "Stand by tubes one and three. Ready … on my mark … fire!"

The two Mark 48 torpedoes left their tubes with their propulsors pushing the deadly weapons through the water, racing away from the *Connecticut* at over 50 knots. At this range, the two explosive tipped instruments of death would close the distance to the enemy sub in less than 30 seconds.

* * * *

On board the Chinese sub, all hands were awaiting the launch of the *Ares* from KSC, 70 miles distant – almost all hands. The ship's sonar operator was glued to his screen with the external hull sensors converting sonic wave patterns into visual images. The bubbling and popping from his ship's heat exchangers was masking all other sounds in the water, but as the capacitors finished charging, like a curtain being pulled away to reveal the outside world, the sounds of the ocean began to once again filter back in. Except the sound was wrong … very wrong!

"*Captain*! I have two torpedoes in the water! *Fifty meters*!"

Tso stared at his countermeasures screen in shock and horror. Nothing could save him or his ship. Still he gave the order, "*Dive!* Dive the boat! *Take us dow–*"

With almost simultaneous impacts, the two Mark 48 torpedoes, homing in on the metallic mass of the sub, slammed into her hull, releasing the tremendous explosive force of two 650-pound warheads. The first explosion ripped through the double pressure hull followed in a near instant by the second detonation that split the Chinese sub in two. White hot flames and superheated compressed air raced through the entire length of the boat, screaming down passage ways, blasting open water tight doors and ripping heads, arms and flesh from the doomed sailors, bringing instant death. To any of the Chinese crew still left alive at the extreme ends of the sub, the inrushing water with the force of hundreds of tons per square inch instantly snuffed out their lives.

* * * *

Captain William Jonas watched stunned, as the images from Snoopy continued to pour in, only momentarily disrupted by the concussion wave propagating through the water.

Jonas's fire control office was standing next to him also looking at the display. "Holy crap, sir, looks like we nailed the son of a bitch but good!"

William Jonas, still looking at the video images of what was left of the Chinese boat descending to the bottom with the buoyant debris floating to the surface, finally broke his intense concentration. "Radio the Cape. Tell them we got the bastard. Tell them they can breathe easy … and upload these images immediately then transmit them to Washington. Helm, ahead slow, take us down 300 feet."

* * * *

The other alternative was to scrub the mission, but Major LaBelle, along with Garcia and Griffin, were adamant about not losing the launch opportunity. Launch, assembly of the components of the Alliance in orbit, and injection into a trans-lunar profile was precisely timed to correspond to Presidents Cordelier Price and Victor Simonov's addresses to the United Nations, where they planned to turn the tables on the Chinese.

LaBelle's heart rate continued to climb as the clock passed T-minus 90 seconds. He was taking deep breaths to try and remain calm. It was not the launch that drove his fight or flight response; he'd flown into orbit six times previously. He knew that his rocket might be blown out from under him moments after they began to streak skyward. At T-minus 82 seconds, over an encrypted channel, came the words that Vernon LaBelle had been silently praying for. "*Ares-Alliance Three*, you are a go for lift off, *they got the bastard!* I repeat, the Navy sunk the sub. You are clean and green to go."

Both Garcia and Griffin saw Major Labelle loudly clasped his hands together and raised them above his head in a gesture of thanks, then he yelled back to the crew. "Just got the news. The Navy got 'em. Gentlemen, we are good to go!"

Both Tom Garcia and Jack Griffin exhaled loudly, neither realizing they had been holding their breath. Monitors in mission control saw all three men's heart rate drop steeply.

"*Ares-Alliance Three*, don't go to sleep on us now, you still have to get into orbit. Sixty seconds and counting."

* * * *

The applause within the huge expanse of the UN General Assembly finally began to subside. Russian President Simonov then turned to Cordelier Price. "His speech was very convincing, but we have an expression in Russia: It was nothing more than cheese for the mouse."

Before she could answer him, a Secret Service agent brought over a secure encrypted telephone to the American president. Simonov watched her expression go from one of concern to almost elation. She quickly hung up and turned to the Russian President. "Cheese for the mouse is right! Except, we're the ones who are about to spring the trap!"

Presidents Price and Simonov walked quickly to the podium, earning glares and whispered comments of the gathered delegates of the world's developing nations.

Cordelier Price glanced at her watch and moved to the podium just ahead of the Russian president. "Ladies and gentlemen, honored representatives of your nations. We in the West and Russia do not wish to control your economies nor deny you the riches that can be obtained from space. Rather we wish to promote honest cooperation without sinister hidden agendas."

To that comment, there was an increase of murmuring among the audience, accompanied by a few scattered "boos." President Price ignored them and continued. "Today, our international coalition, with representatives from the United States, Russia, France, and Canada, will complete the final assembly of our spacecraft, the *Alliance,* and begin our voyage to the Moon in the spirit of the 1967 Treaty of Outer Space to exploit and develop our own resources, which will benefit all of mankind. In fact, I would like to direct your attention to the live video feed on the two main screens from the Kennedy Space Center. In less than 30 seconds, the third and final launch from the United States will occur, placing the final stage into orbit for link-up to the core of our moon ship, formed by the Russian Salyut space station. Please keep your eyes on the screens as this is not a clever video simulation of what might be possible in another 10 to 20 years in the future, but the reality of what is possible today."

Both presidents locked their eyes on the Chinese Foreign Minister who seemed oblivious to their observations: His eyes were glued to the nearer of the two screens, his body pushed forward with an intense look of anticipation on his face, waiting for something to happen. As the powerful solid rocket boosters ignited, the *Ares* slowly climbed from her launch pad, shrugging off the binds of the Earth's gravity. Within a few seconds, the rocket had cleared the tower and climbed on triple tails of fire into the blue black of the upper stratosphere. A minute into the flight, Shang broke his concentration on the screen, glanced at his watch, and kept doing so every few seconds, shifting his gaze back and forth from his wrist to the main screen so often it seemed as if he was keeping time to some unheard music. After another minute came, the announcement that the separation of the boosters was successful.

Another 60 seconds passed, and the audio from the Kennedy Space Center spoke the words that drove the Chinese Foreign Minister into a frenzy: "The *Ares III-A* has achieved Earth orbit."

He stopped in mid-sentence and could see Simonov and Price's eyes boring into him. In a flash of insight, he knew that they knew the truth. Cordelier Price wanted to look Shang in the eye and ask him, "Why all the disappointment on your face? Did you expect a different outcome for the launch?" Of course, she knew he did, and now the man seemed to squirm uncomfortably in his seat. *Not as uncomfortable as he will be when Simonov and I get finished up here*, she thought. However, neither president was going for the kill immediately. Both had carefully considered their strategy for dealing with the Chinese Foreign Minister. Rather than dispatching his pack of lies in one quick blow, instead it would be a death by a thousand cuts in front of his rapt audience, turning him as well as China from a giant and their perceived savior to small nauseating crawling things beneath their feet.

President Price continued. "As you all can clearly see, the United States and our coalition partners have successfully placed the final component of the *Alliance* lunar mission into orbit, save for the launch of a cargo rocket from northern Russia." Looking directly at the Chinese Foreign Minister, President Price continued. "NASA was aware of only one potential problem that threatened the launch; however, this was eliminated just prior to lift-off."

Both presidents watched as Minister Shang cast his eyes about, looking anywhere but at the podium. He then grabbed an aide, his hands shaking with barely controlled rage, and sent the man off to make contact with Beijing, no doubt.

Price continued. "Our mission is not to dominate the resources of space but to develop those resources for the good of all people. If a nation or nations are pledged to increasing the wealth of the Earth in such a way that all people benefit and all nations, both developed and developing, climb to higher levels of prosperity, this makes the world a safer place for all. For if all nations prosper, there is no longer a need for wars over territory and resources. We become a global integrated economy. If this is truly the goal of China, they should welcome our efforts to develop the resources from the most unforgiving environment known to man, the hard vacuum of outer space. If China *really* has the interests of the developing world as their goal, they, and you, should welcome the participation of even more nations in harnessing and exploiting these resources for the good of all. To oppose international development, China must have an agenda in hiding beyond the horizon marking the lunar far side. This could be the only reason for China's opposition to sharing these resources with the other space faring nations of the planet. Why do they fear our mission? Let both China and our coalition have competition as well as cooperation to propel all of us, as human beings, to even greater heights. America and our partners have no wish to dominate the heavens. When stepping off from the Earth to reap the riches of space, we should put aside our national pride, for we are infinitesimal in comparison to the vastness we seek to harvest."

Cordelier Price's speech was beginning to chip away at the unified consensus by the delegates of the developing nations to grant China sole ownership of the lunar ice fields. Still, it was just the first hairline crack. Now it was Russian President Victor Simonov's turn to begin to split it wide open. Cordelier Price left the podium to polite applause, replaced by the elegantly dressed Simonov.

Victor Simonov, tall, silver-haired with piecing gray eyes, the color of a Saint Petersburg winter sky, surveyed his audience, pausing on the Chinese Foreign Minister who was beginning to look as if he wanted to be anywhere but in the seat he currently occupied. As the subdued applause ceased, he began speaking.

Cordelier Price, as well as the gathered delegates, listened to the translation of Simonov's Russian into more than 40 languages. "Fellow members of the human family. Fifty-seven years ago, Russia placed the first man into orbit about the Earth. For political reasons that existed at that time, it sent the Americans and ourselves on a quest for the domination in space that mirrored the intense and dangerous competition between our two militaries on Earth. Instead of enriching our two nations, we both became the poorer for it. While not all of our differences are behind us, we realize that cooperation, rather than conflict, are what is necessary to enrich both our nations. We do not seek the militarization of space along with the potential for warfare in realm of the heavens. Yet, if we must, Russia shall engage any enemy that threatens our sovereignty. As signatories to the 1967 Treaty of Outer Space, Russia, as well as America, and in particular China, renounced any claims to any celestial body and we have pledged to ban the use of weapons in space. China has come before you in a petition to be permitted an exception in that treaty, granting her exclusive claim to the Moon's resources. Yet, how can such a petition be granted to a nation who has already violated one of the key provisions of the 1967 treaty?"

With that, Simonov paused as the two huge theater-sized screens above the stage of the General Assembly came to life. On one was a montage of American Major Roy Jackson, his wife, and their life together in Arizona. On the other, the poignant and touching scenes of the life of Russian Cosmonaut Nicolai Schevyenskey, his wife and two young daughters playing together in the Russian winter and on summer holiday at the Black Sea.

President Simonov continued his speech. "Above you are small glimpses of family and happiness of the two brave explorers whose lives were cut short during our joint attempt to place a space station in orbit about the Moon. I'm certain that you have all heard the official explanation by the People's Republic of China as to the cause of the … eh … *accident*, for it happened beyond the side of the Moon that faces away from our world. You no doubt accept the explanation that a meteor, a piece of orbiting rock, ended the lives of these brave men. However, I think now is the time to reveal that the occupants of the Chinese moon base were not the sole witnesses to this … *deliberate act of aggression!"*

A low murmur from the delegates rose to a level that coincided with the Russian President's dramatic pause. Simonov could see Shang looking increasingly agitated with a stain of purple seeming to rise from his neck and spread across his face.

"Thanks to the fortunate orbital placement of an American surveillance satellite, both of our nations have known the truth for some time."

The images of the two lost men and their families were quickly replaced by a background of stars and the magnified cratered rim of the Moon.

"Please direct your attention to the lower third of the image. This is a part of the Moon that is forever hidden from our view but observable from a satellite that was at an extreme angle."

From the edge of the Moon came a bright orange streak, climbing away from its battered surface. In a matter of seconds, a bright white dot appeared against the backdrop of stars. It bloomed and then, turning a dull orange, faded away. The audience sat in rapt attention, watching the image.

Again Simonov spoke. "But this was not the only evidence captured by the satellite, for as you may know, not only can we not see the far hemisphere of the Moon, we also cannot detect any radio transmission from behind it. In this case, not only did the American's satellite capture these images but this final radio transmission as well."

On cue, the transmission played over the headphones and loudspeakers:

"Jackson, I show a launch from South Pole! It is a missile; it has radar lock on our ship!"

"Damn it! I can't shake it! Hang on Colonel, I'm going to try and outrun it! Come on, baby! Come on … I … aaahh…"

Minister Shang sat stunned. He had no idea that the Americans had this evidence of the destruction of the space station. As he looked about the cavernous room, he could see all eyes boring into him. When he looked back to the podium, he saw that the American president had joined her Russian counterpart. He quickly realized he had blundered into a well-laid trap that had been set for him, turning his glowing promises of shared wealth to the men and women representing the world's developing nations into a festering pool of lies.

Cordelier Price then joined in. "China, like a malignant tumor, has inserted its tendrils into both our nations. Here in America, one of her strongest proponents, Nathan Crowley, made this call to the Chinese Minister of Trade just one hour ago.

That phone message then played as well over the headphones and loudspeakers:

"*Ah, Minister Chu. I have good news to report. The search for your submarine has been called off. The American attack boat had some sort of accident on board and was recalled.*"

"And who was that message intended for?" Price said. "This submarine 70 miles off the Florida coast!"

The screens again came alive with an underwater image of a Type 094 Chinese ballistic missile submarine. The image was dazzlingly clear in the warm blue-green ocean water. As the audience watched, two large doors on the upper hull opened and a device emerged and unfolded, breaking the surface. Quickly the image spun as whatever underwater device was recording it, retreated to a more remote distance. Just as the image of the submarine, now much further away refocused, two massive explosions could be seen on the hull, slicing the underwater craft into two halves that trailed debris as they headed for the ocean floor.

"I mentioned just after the launch that a problem for the lift-off of the *Ares* spacecraft had been eliminated," Price said. "The United States Navy had two hunter-killer submarines waiting for that vessel whose captain had been ordered to shoot down our rocket. Not only this, but in reviewing the evidence of the loss of the rocket that carried the replacement Pan-African satellite, we see exactly the kind of explosion caused by an antimissile laser, the type carried onboard the now destroyed Chinese submarine.

"While we cannot prove it, we also suspect that it was China, not another *meteor* or some other *accident,* destroyed the first Pan-African satellite in Earth orbit. Then China destroyed its replacement, launched from Cape Canaveral, in order to convince you of the nonaligned and developing nations as to China's technological prowess and generosity toward your countries. All of this is nothing more than a sham, a means to trick you, and to deceive you into granting what China wants – a quarantine of the Moon, preventing other space-faring nations from landing and making use of those resources.

"While the true scope of China's motives have yet to be uncovered, rest assured they will be. Their contacts and agents in both the United States and Russia have been discovered and many are already in custody, including Mr. Nathan Crowley. We are certain of obtaining the information we need to expose the true depth of China's sinister plans. We suspect those plans are for the domination and control of the space between the Earth and the Moon along with economic control of the world's economy. Acts of war, as well as sabotage and espionage, have been committed against the United States and Russia by the Chinese. Both President Simonov and I urge the government of China to renounce these acts before it's too late, to renounce their claim to the Moon and end this threat to world peace immediately. China has ventured down a very dangerous road that only can lead to global conflict. Both the United States, Russia, and our allies are prepared to issue a declaration of war against the People's Republic of China unless they cease all hostile actions immediately and permit unfettered access by our expedition to the lunar ice fields."

The assembled delegates sat stunned, eyes riveted upon either the two presidents or the Chinese delegation. All had realized they had been tricked and lied to on a monstrous scale. Some members were so angry they physically tried to restrain the Chinese delegation as they hurried to exit the building with at least one punch thrown that connected solidly with one of Minster Shang's aides.

CHAPTER FOURTEEN

Earth orbit

The link-up between the Russian Salyut and the French docking module had gone flawlessly. Both French Major LaCasse and American Lieutenant William Curtis had spent nearly two hours on an EVA to secure all the necessary fittings and electrical connections between the Russian space station and the docking module. The orbital container holding the two lunar landers was in a matching orbit and sitting just a few dozen meters away, waiting for another EVA to remove and help guide the two LEMs into position to be docked with the French module. Already coming into visual range, was the Orion capsule that had been mated to the powerful Earth Departure Stage.

Lieutenant Curtis and Remmy LaCasse had finished the installation of the docking module four hours earlier. Now, Bill Curtis had suited up again and had exited the Salyut in order to lend an extra hand with the installation of the EDS stage. This would be attached to the specially modified collar which had been added to the French component of the *Alliance*. John McGovern and Natasha Polyakova were just finishing the final power ups of the new computer systems when the radio message came in from the Johnson Space Center in Houston. It was not in the clear, but rather it used an encrypted series of frequencies that the onboard computer in the Salyut had to decode and reconstruct. Still, the time lag was only a second or two. It was for McGovern, and there was no mistaking the voice of Norm Taggert on the other end.

"John, the *you-know-what* has really hit the fan. Both Presidents Price and Simonov ripped the Chinese to shreds in front of the entire UN

General Assembly, as well as showing the actual sinking of their ballistic missile sub off the coast of Florida. Both had said that if China does not back down and open up the lunar ice fields to our mission, then the U.S., the Russians and the EU will seek a declaration of war against the PRC. I want you all to be on your toes. Right now, I want your number one priority to be getting your weapons systems online and functioning for defense. While the crew is assembling the components and mounting the EDS, you're sitting ducks up there."

* * * *

The presidential motorcade left the United Nations building at high speed, flanked by secret service SUVs and New York City Police on motorcycles. President Price's limo and her attending group of vehicles were parked in front of the Russian president's car and entourage so in a departure from standard protocol, she had him join her in her limo. Both sat with their military aides, both of whom carried the American and Russian "footballs," the special cases holding the nuclear codes with the capability of unleashing thousands of atomic weapons. Cordelier Price was on an encrypted telephone to the Chairman of the Joint Chiefs in Washington as they raced to JFK airport. As Price listened, a look of grave concern came over her face. She turned to President Simonov, addressing him in Russian. "Victor Andreavich, our global reconnaissance satellites, as well as NORAD, have detected unusual and increased activity within and beyond the borders of the PRC. I concurred with the military's decision to put airborne laser platforms in flight to intercept any ICBM or anti-satellite launches. I would like to ask you to do the same."

"*Da.* Of course, I agree with you. I will make that call at once, and I am also prepared to bring our strategic missile forces to a status of high alert. I assume you will be doing the same?"

Cordelier Price placed her hand to her forehead for just a moment, trying to focus and remain calm. "I'm not prepared to move our current level of alert up to anything higher than DEFCON 3. I do not want to start down a road we cannot turn back from. Certainly now that the entire ruse of the Chinese bid to obtain exclusive rights to the Moon has been blown wide open, someone in the Chinese government has to come to their senses. This is madness, and if we do not contain this, we face the very real possibility of a global nuclear war. We don't want them to react like cornered animals, striking out. We have to show we're serious without closing off an exit for the Chinese to back down without losing face."

President Simonov then reached into his briefcase and handed Price a document. Her spoken Russian was flawless but reading the correspondence in Cyrillic took her a bit longer than if it had been in English.

"Victor, are you sure of this? There's no mistake?"

"No, I received this document just prior to our address before the General Assembly. I had considered using it but I felt it might have been too inflammatory. Our security service, or should I say our new security service, now free of Golovko's tentacles, found this information in the former director's computer records. Golovko had known about this for some time, but it seems his loyalties were to the funds Beijing was placing in his Swiss account rather than that of the *Rodina*."

Price reread the document just to make certain she did not misunderstand the words. "*Good God!* The Chinese have brought up dozens of nuclear weapons into orbit? Are they already on the Moon?"

"We are not certain, but if they have been taken to the Moon, there could be more than 50 nuclear bombs."

As President Price handed the paper back to Simonov, the motorcade, having driven directly onto the aircraft apron, pulled alongside President Simonov's jet, an IL-96, the equivalent of Air Force One. Sitting off to one side of the silver and sky blue four-engine jet were three U.S. Air Force F-22 Raptors and a two-seater F-15B.

As soon as President Price's car pulled to a stop, she exited and engaged in an animated conversation with a high-ranking air force officer. The officer, a lieutenant general, quickly ducked into the president's car to speak with Simonov. "Your flight's been cleared for immediate take off. We're giving you three armed F-22s as a fighter escort. They'll stick with you until you're over Nova Scotia and there, four Canadian F-18s will escort you as far as Iceland. Your flight will then be met by NATO Typhoon fighters who will hand you off to the Russian Air Force, once you're over Eastern Europe. We have no idea what the Chinese may try, but I can assure you, we *will* get you safely back to Moscow."

Cordelier Price had already unbuttoned her jacket and was carrying a standard issue flight suit. She took Simonov's hand in both of hers. "Good luck. I want us to stay in communication on this matter at all times. We have to head this off before it gets out of control. Our mission will leave from orbit, God willing, in another eight hours. I just pray we're not sending those people to their deaths."

Simonov could only nod in agreement as he climbed the steps to his aircraft. Cordelier Price, instead of boarding Air Force One, stepped inside a military van to change out of her light gray business suit and into an olive green flight suit, complete with a helmet. Speed was of the essence, and the lieutenant general who had been directing air support for the Russian President would shortly be flying the American President back to Andrews Air Force Base in Maryland, as the rear seat passenger in the F-15B waiting on the apron.

CHAPTER FIFTEEN

The People's Republic of China

Sung Zhao sat in the red leather clad central seat, facing Premier Feng Qu, head of the Communist leadership of China. To his left sat the Vice Premier and opposite him, General Peng Li, head of the People's Liberation Army, Supreme Commander of the Chinese military. Flanking Zhao was Fong Kim Hua, Director of Chinese Intelligence, and seated in the room were a dozen various ministers of the Communist politburo.

It had been a little more than five hours since what everyone in the room believed was a foregone conclusion – that China would be granted sole guardianship of the Moon's resources –
had crumbled to dust before the eyes of those seated in the General Assembly in New York. During that time, Sung Zhao had exercised his connections within the Party and the military to insulate himself from the wrath and fury of Premier Feng Qu and his supporters. Not only to insulate, but to triumph. For a man who was about to receive the fiery blast of an angry dragon, Zhao seemed unusually clam. This puzzled his superior, Fong, director of all Chinese intelligence. Many days earlier, he had warned Sung Zhao that any more blunders would not be tolerated. Here there were blunders on a colossal scale. The destruction of the first Russian-American mission had been revealed before the United Nations by the president of Russia, as an attack by China. The American president had shown to the world that a Chinese submarine had destroyed the rocket that carried the replacement Pan-African satellite, and the American Navy had sunk Tso's $2 billion modified ballistic missile submarine. Fong was certain that this meeting could

only end in the dismissal and disgrace of Sung Zhao, and a very uncomfortable admission of guilt by China to the American and Russian governments. However, as certain as Fong Kim Hua was of the outcome, he had greatly underestimated Sung Zhao's persuasiveness and connections within the military and he would soon be proven wrong in his assumptions.

The Premier of the Peoples Republic of China was a departure from his predecessors. While most of the Chinese leadership had traditionally been composed of men well past the age of seventy, Feng Qu had just turned sixty. His hair was still full but turning silver at the temples. Feng wore a conservative Western-style dark blue business suit. His face, usually calm and placid, had flushed red with his lips blanching white with barely controlled rage. Feng was from an economics background and not a military one. He was a man who delegated, preferring to leave his Vice Premier, Gao Xi, in charge of such matters. While focusing his attention on the Chinese economy, he was only peripherally aware of the details of the Chinese moon base and Sung Zhao's plans.

The reports he had received from his vice premier had given him little reason for concern until he was awakened from his sleep by the telephone call bearing the news of the disastrous United Nations meeting in New York. Now he would have to put the pieces together and quite possibly issue dramatic apologies to the West and Russia, as well as provide massive compensation for the actions of his subordinates. Most disturbing were the documents concerning the placement of nuclear weapons on the Moon that were to be deployed against targets on the Earth. This was not just a violation of the Treaty of Outer Space and international law but an act of war. This action had been taken without his consent or his knowledge.

Already he had been given the reports showing that Russian strategic missile forces had gone to a high level of alert. British and French nuclear missile submarines had been disbursed, and the Americans had moved their alert status on their nuclear missiles and nuclear-armed bombers up to DEFCON 3. Mao had boasted that nuclear bombs were paper tigers, that even if the West killed three quarters of the population of China they would still have more people left alive than in any Western nation. This kind of twisted logic and complete disregard for human life sent a chill through Feng Qu, as well as ratcheting up his anger that his trusted subordinates had placed his nation in this precarious position.

Premier Feng's eyes narrowed, boring into the Director of Space Intelligence. "*Sung Zhao*! Your plans, your actions and your provocations have placed our country in the utmost jeopardy! How *could you* have let this happen?! I had been assured by my own vice premier that your entire plan was flawless and moving forward like a well-oiled machine! I was assured that this was to be a *political operation* and not a *military* one! This was to be an effortless means of gaining control over the valuable lunar resources, not provoking a war! Until just a few hours ago, I had no idea of the scope of your operation or of your stupidity and recklessness! *Who in the name of heaven authorized the shipment of nuclear weapons to the Moon?! Who* authorized placing a modified ballistic missile submarine off the coast of the United States?! Yes, I knew some of the details but I had no idea how this operation of yours was being carried out! You are a rogue, a loose cannon, and a danger to the future of your own country! You are dismissed as of this moment, and you are to consider yourself under arrest!"

Feng then turned to his vice premier. "*Gao Xi! You are insane*, and you are a *liar*! You have provided me with reports of Sung Zhao's plans but only those for which I would have agreed to! You seemed to have neglected ever informing me of placing nuclear weapons in space and the use of one of our submarines to shoot down American rockets! You also *claimed* the destruction of the Russian-American moon mission an accident! I believed your reports that said their craft was struck by a meteor as it approached our base. *You* stood there in front of me, feeding me lie after lie! You are dismissed as well and I shall seek prosecution of your actions under the Chinese Constitution!

"And, *you,* General Peng! Who authorized *you* to begin mobilizing our forces? Now I must crawl to the West after what you fools have done! Do not provoke Russia and the West any further!"

Premier Feng, still boiling with anger, stared at the Director of Space Intelligence's disturbing half-animated face. The reaction he had expected to see was the man hanging his head in shame. Instead, he saw a smile begin to form on the undamaged side of his face. He could see Zhao was looking at Vice Premier Gao Xi, and instead of having the look of a man condemned by his own actions, was grinning. Feng began to have a very disquieting sense that he was the condemned man, not his subordinates.

Quickly, the premier addressed his director of intelligence. "Fong Kim Hua! Summon the guards! Place these men under arrest!"

As Fong began to rise up from his seat, an army officer in the Premier's conference chamber stood in front of the director and forced him back into his chair. The Vice Premier quickly made a gesture, and the guard at the chamber door opened it to a squad of soldiers. The Chinese commanding general, Peng Li, ordered the men in, leveling their weapons at Premier Feng and half of the politburo.

Sung Zhao rose from his seat and strode about the chamber with a deliberate cockiness to his step. A sneer appeared upon the animated half of his face. "I'm afraid it is *you*, Premier Feng Qu, who is about to be placed under arrest, *not me*! You seem … overly disturbed, and … mentally exhausted, incapable of rational decisions concerning the responsibilities of your office. You wish to *crawl* to the West? *To beg their forgiveness?!* You have already done this in your retreat from taking what is rightfully ours – the lost province of Taiwan, held by the Nationalist pirates! You *crawled* like a cowardly slug to the *Negro whore* who the Americans refer to as their president! You *disgraced China* in the eyes of the world and caused her military to lose face! We lost over 2,000 men in our quest to claim what is rightfully ours. You caved to the Russian dogs as well, while our pilots were being shot out of the skies over Vladivostok! You retreated! *You sued for peace!* Oh, how the military despises you for what you did! *You* are without courage, without honor and, as of this very minute, you are hereby removed from office! *Premier* Gao is now in command, and I am his vice premier. This time, we will *not* back down! *Do I make myself clear?!*"

As the soldiers dragged the premier from the room, he yelled back, "Zhao! *Think* what you are about to do! You place billions of lives in peril! *You are insane!* You must stop …"

Premier Feng's words were silenced by the impact of a rifle butt against the back of his head, and the guards carried his limp body to a waiting car and then a detention cell.

* * * *

"Madam President, I have some very serious news." Admiral Warner, Chairman of the Joint Chiefs, had just entered the White House's situation room. It was now past ten at night, with a meeting that looked as if it would not be ending any time soon.

President Price, usually smiling and animated, was beginning to show the intense strain of a day that started at six that morning for her joint presentation with Russian President Simonov to rebut the Chinese petition at the UN and included a mach two flight in the back seat of an F-15B to Andrews Air Force Base. Now she was huddled with her cabinet, as well as Vice President Adler, four floors below the White House in the secure situation room.

Joseph Adler, the former speaker of the house was a surprise pick for V.P. coming from the academic field, but it was her firm belief that the man's credentials as an expert in foreign policy at this dangerous time when facing a new Cold War with China was essential in her administration.

Cordelier Price rubbed the tiredness from her eyes and prepared to hear more bad news. "Okay Admiral, give it to me straight and without any sugar coating."

James Warner cleared his throat. "There has been a sudden increase in military activity in the People's Republic of China. Our surveillance satellites indicate they're arming their bomber fleet with nuclear ordinance and have brought their ICBM forces up to a state of full readiness. There are also indications of massive concentrations of ground units and tanks moving toward the Russian border. May I suggest we move our state of readiness up to DEFCON 2?"

Cordelier Price clasped her hands together almost in prayer and shook her head from side to side. Warner for a moment thought she would not agree to his suggestion on readiness, but then she turned toward him with a sense of great sadness. "Go ahead, on my order. Bring our missile forces up to DEFCON 2 and get our bombers in the air and to their holding points. I want any ballistic missile submarines still in port dispatched immediately, and please make certain we have our airborne laser platforms flying just outside of Chinese airspace. I … I feel like we may be leading the entire human race to the slaughterhouse, but I have no choice. What is *wrong* with Feng Qu? Can't he see this is madness?"

The president's Secretary of State, Gloria Austin, entered the conference room but chose not to interrupt her president as she finished her comments. Once the president did, Austin said, "Madam President, Premiere Qui Feng is no longer in control or in power. He's been deposed in a coup that happened less than two hours ago. This information was just obtained from Nationalist Chinese sources. His former vice premier, Gao Xi, has assumed leadership and a man named Sung Zhao is calling the shots. Zhao is brilliant, but the man is certifiable. Apparently, this entire deception about their moon base, the shooting down of our rockets and placing nuclear weapons into space was all his doing with assistance from Gao. Premiere Feng may not have known much or for that matter anything about the true nature of his plans. You are dealing with a very dangerous fanatic obsessed with Chinese nationalism – not a rational man – and he's armed to the teeth with nuclear weapons."

Price was about to respond when the red telephone in front of the Admiral buzzed loudly. Quickly his hand shot out and grabbed it. As he listened, a deep look of concern appeared upon his face. Everyone in the room could hear him utter, "*Good Lord.*" Then he held the phone away and addressed the president. "NORAD has confirmed six A-SAT launches from central China. I need authority, Ma'am, to shoot them down. The probable target is the *Alliance* in orbit."

"Yes, yes do it! Shoot them down!"

As the Admiral gave the order, he began to shake his head. "We can't get them all. We can see a Russian Antonov on the big board with a laser platform is within range as well, but at least one will get through."

Cordelier Price immediately stood up. "Warn them, warn the crew to take whatever action they deem necessary to save the ship. If nothing can be done, tell them to save themselves."

* * * *

Natasha Polyakova floated effortlessly in the Salyut, having completed the integration of the computer systems, linking the docking sensors on the French module. She had been toiling for hours and had taken a moment to gaze out the circular view port at the spectacle of the incredible panorama of the Earth turning below them. At that moment, the station was over the dazzling blue of the Pacific Ocean. Natasha could see the cargo module that was sent aloft by the Titan IV-B hours earlier, so clear and so close it seemed as if she could reach out and touch it. The bang of the EVA spacesuit storage locker brought her attention from the view port.

"John! What are you doing? You are not supposed to EVA."

McGovern was just starting to pull on the lower half of his spacesuit. "Natasha, I'm going out to help Garcia and Griffin with the EDS module and then we can get the two LEMs mounted to the docking collar. Things are getting pretty shaky down there, and I want us to get the hell out of Earth orbit as quickly as possible. Has Lieutenant Curtis got the weapons systems on line yet?"

Natasha now had a real look of concern on her face. "Yes they are, John. AEGIS is ready but we have only half of the Patriot missiles on line at the moment. We have not completed the connections to the starboard bank. But … John, you have not taken a rest period yet. You've been up for over twenty hours."

"Yeah, I know that… believe me I know that, but we've got to pick up the pace. And besides I …" McGovern stopped in mid-sentence as his earpiece came alive. It was not the Johnson Space Center or Mission Control in Moscow, but a transmission from the North American Aerospace Defense Command with a chilling message. Natasha could see a look of shock cross the face of her fiancée, as he quickly pulled off the lower half of his spacesuit, pushing himself toward the docking tunnel that led to the Soyuz at the far end of the station.

* * * *

The two Air Force Boeing 777s, out of Osan Airbase in South Korea turned eastward off the coast of Yancheng China. The flight had just been joined by five F-22 Raptors when the radio call came in to track and destroy as many of the Han anti-satellite launch vehicles as possible. Six were climbing into orbit and on a course for the *Alliance*. The two Boeing wide-body jets were at 42,000 thousand feet, well above 80 percent of the Earth's atmosphere in the thin air that would allow for maximum effect of their onboard lasers. The radar systems on both aircraft were clearly reading the six rockets that had just been launched out of Jiuquan, the Chinese military missile complex. This data was augmented by a live feed from a Pegasus military satellite that showed their plumes in infrared on the Boeing's threat display screens.

The blister domes that housed the optical systems of the lasers, on both jets, swiveled under the direction of the two planes' computers and tracked the flight of destructive weapons as they crossed the threshold of space at one hundred kilometers altitude. When the optimum angle was reached, both lasers fired in unison, each blasting a Han missile out of the sky. Quickly, the weapons' techs on both planes set the recharge on their lasers and continued to track the flight of the remaining four rockets.

Several hundred miles to the north, a Russian Antonov 124 was tracking the Chinese rockets as well. The Antonov, using nearly identical SDI technology as the Americans, was also in a position to fire, and as the four Han missiles continued to accelerate into orbit, the turret on the Russian plane locked onto one of the targets and fired, disintegrating it. The weapons' technicians on both American flights retargeted the three satellite killers, streaking into orbit. They were at the extreme range of the Boeing's weapons but the shots were accurate, firing a beam of intense coherent energy at the speed of light. Now only one Han A-SAT remained, but it was well out of range of both the Russian and American laser platforms. The final stage of the rocket fired, as it moved along an orbital track at seventeen thousand five hundred miles per hour to intersect with the *Alliance*, was being assembled in low Earth orbit.

* * * *

"John, what are you doing?"

McGovern turned back to look at Natasha. "I'm going to undock the Soyuz and intercept the last Chinese missile. We have men outside, the LEMs are vulnerable, and the EDS is not attached. We're sitting ducks. Even if we hit it with our weapons, the pieces will continue on their same track and slam into us. Doesn't matter if they detonate their warhead or if we blast it to pieces. Those fragments will still kill us all."

"Wait, John! The Soyuz is a two-man ship. I'll go with you."

"*No way, Natasha!* I'm going to ram that thing … knock it off course. I might detonate it. If that happens, you have to fly the LEM to the surface, understand? Besides, I can't allow you to put yourself in danger like this."

Natasha began to look panicked at the thought of losing John and blurted out, "I'm supposed to be in command of the outbound mission. I *order* you to wait for me! Is that agreed?"

McGovern shrugged. "Okay … okay, I'll get the Soyuz prepped and you grab the suits, just in case."

As Natasha Polyakova headed toward the suit lockers, McGovern pushed ahead and down the connecting tunnel to Soyuz, slamming the airlock hatch shut behind him and depressurizing the tunnel.

Open–mouthed Natasha continued to drift toward the rear of the station. Then over her earpiece, she heard John's voice: "Sorry, 'Tasha. You know I have a problem following orders. Listen, get everyone back inside the Salyut. I'm going to have the Orion dock with you and take everybody off. The French module is ready. I'm going to radio the pilot to take everyone off the station and get out of range. If I fail, at least you and the rest of crew will be safe."

Anger first masked cosmonaut Polyakova's angelic face then fear, fear for the life of the man she had fallen in love with. "*John!*" she blurted out angrily. Then softly, "John … yes, I will do this but … please, please … be careful … come back to me."

McGovern was at the controls of the Soyuz. Having retracted the docking clamps, he fired the thrusters in the nose of the ship and backed away from the Salyut space station. Once he was clear of the station, the two lunar landers and the EDS stage that the crew was still working on, he engaged the main engine and flipped on the target acquisition radar to locate the oncoming Chinese weapon.

The Soyuz TMA-6 spacecraft could hardly be called graceful. With its spherical forward section, cylindrical middle followed by the large housing for fuel and a rocket motor; it took on the look of a huge insect with a head, thorax and abdomen. Once green paint was added and outstretched wings made of solar panels, the entire spacecraft looked like an enormous dragonfly.

McGovern hit transmit. "Soyuz TMA to Orion, please come in. This is Colonel McGovern to Orion, come in, over."

There was dead air for just a moment and then, "Roger, Soyuz, this is Major LaBelle commanding the Orion capsule. What are your orders, sir?"

"Major, I want you to dock with the Salyut, using the French docking collar. Get everyone off, understand? I don't care if it's like a sardine can in there, get everyone onboard and get out of range. If I can't stop that Chinese A-SAT, then all that'll be left of the *Alliance* will be an orbiting pile of scrap."

LaBelle radioed back. “Affirmative, sir, but … how do you plan on stopping it? I thought the Soyuz didn’t have any onboard weapons.”

“The Soyuz doesn’t Major, but I got an ’A’ in military aviation history at the academy. Back near the close of World War II, the Germans sent hundreds of their V-1 flying bombs against England. They were unguided cruise missiles. The Brits figured out they could keep up with them in their twin engine Mosquitoes and early jets. They’d fly alongside them and use their wings to tip them over, making them crash before they could strike London. That’s what I’m going to do, bump the A-SAT or ram it, knock it off course. Now get moving and get everyone off.”

Natasha heard the conversation between her fiancée and the man commanding the Orion, and a chill ran shot through her body. She pressed her hand to her head to steady herself. *John was right,* she thought. *He wanted to wait until after the mission for our time together. I didn’t listen to him. I wanted him so much … I can’t lose him. I can’t face that again.* Then she thought about his rescue of LaCasse. Against all odds, he brought him back to the ISS. Then there was his rescue of the doomed A-10 pilot in Iraq and their own miraculous escape in Moscow. Her John would not fail. Suddenly, she felt courage enter her soul. She was in command, and she would get her crew to safety.

She keyed her microphone. “Major LaCasse, Lieutenant Curtis. This is Captain Polyakova. Get back to the Salyut immediately and prepare to evacuate to the Orion. Right now, do you understand?”

Natasha could see both men replace their tools into their suit pouches and begin moving toward the Salyut airlock, using their thruster packs. The airlock on the Salyut was not designed to let two cosmonauts enter at the same time. She saw the pressurization system begin to cycle in the air as the first man had entered the spacecraft. Natasha’s attention was then riveted on the Orion crew capsule, making a visual approach to dock with the station using the newly fitted French module. As she watched the craft swell on her screen from the video transmission, her earpiece came alive with the disembodied voice of a military officer at NORAD.

"*Alliance*, this is NORAD. Repeat, *Alliance*, this is NORAD. We show the Chinese A-SAT on course to intercept you in 11 minutes. You *must* evacuate the station. Do you understand?"

Natasha tore her vision away from the docking maneuver by Vernon LaBelle. Remmy or Bill Curtis, she had no idea who had gotten in first, was not out of the airlock yet. Could the pilot of the Orion dock in time? Could both astronauts get back into the Salyut and then everyone squeeze into the Orion in just eleven minutes?

Natasha called out over the radio. "Orion, line up on my signal. I will pulse the laser. Lock your receptor onto it and come in for docking. We are running out of time."

She looked at the red LED display now showing nine minutes until impact from the Chinese weapon. Again, Natasha turned back to the docking display and saw that LaBelle had the capsule just a few meters from the docking clamp, but his was moving with aching slowness, trying to line up the nose of the Orion with the clamp. Too slow and the mechanism would not engage. Too fast and he risked a collision that would damage both the Orion and the docking tunnel. With incredible relief, Natasha saw the inner airlock door open and Remmy LaCasse pull himself in, quickly pulling off his spacesuit. Now Bill Curtis would have to follow the same routine. But, with just seven minutes remaining could he get inside, and could she get everyone off and into the Orion? Her Salyut, the two LEMs, the entire mission all would be destroyed unless the anti-satellite missile was stopped. The only man who could stop it was at the controls of the Soyuz TM with its search radar on, sweeping the void in front of him. John McGovern was also on an encrypted radio link to NORAD.

"Colonel McGovern, we show you and the Chi-Com A-SAT on an intercept course, but you need to pitch your ship three degrees and roll starboard five. Do you copy?"

"Ah, roger, NORAD. Where's the bastard now?"

"The A-SAT is 52 miles down range of you and moving at 300

MPH relative to your orbital velocity. Do you intend to bump it?"

"That's my plan. Bump it or ram it. The Soyuz is a pretty tough bird, you know."

For a moment, there was silence on the other end of the transmission, and then, "Colonel McGovern, this is Major Gustav, weapons evaluation. We're tracking you, but I'm sure the Chinese have you on their boards as well. The Han anti-satellite interceptor missile has three ways of finding its target: radar, infrared and a photo proximity sensor. The Han has a 120 degree field of vision with its sensors. If you're going after it, you have to approach from behind it, either above or below the target. Get into its sensor's field of view, and the son of a bitch will turn on you and detonate its warhead. Do you understand?"

"Yeah, got it. Thanks for the info … hey, I see it. I have it in the periscope. I wish to hell the Russians gave this thing some decent forward vision instead of having to use this viewport."

Gustav's voice came again over his earpiece. "We can see you both. Fire your thrusters and swing wide of him."

McGovern, concentrating on the rapidly approaching A-SAT, suddenly saw it fire a thruster in the rocket body's mid-point. "Uh oh, I think it's trying to line up on me. Hold on, I'm going to give the main engine a bust."

The rocket motor on the Soyuz flared momentarily. It was like slamming on the brakes, and the A-SAT raced by him. Quickly, John McGovern fired his thrusters and again engaged the main engine. He was now closing in on the weapon from below it, relative to the position of the Earth.

Onboard the Salyut, Lieutenant Bill Curtis had finally opened the inner airlock. He tore off his EVA suit and, wearing just his standard issue long underwear, pushed through to the docking collar tube and got ready to enter the Orion capsule.

Vernon Labelle knew he was running out of time, and in his haste applied too much forward thrust. The nose of the Orion slammed into the docking collar, sending vibrations through the Salyut as the *Alliance* crew, less John McGovern, squeezed into the capsule. Nothing on the ship seemed damaged, and he called out to all aboard. "Okay, we're getting out of here!"

LaBelle reached up, throwing a switch to retract the docking clamps, and … nothing happened. Again, he tried and still nothing. Franticly, he opened a panel marked "manual override" and pulled the lever. Still nothing! He looked at the time: 120 seconds until impact. LaBelle tried firing his thrusters, desperately attempting to shake the Orion loose from the clamps, but the capsule would not budge. He turned to the Alliance crew with a deep look of sadness in his eyes and shook his head. "I … I'm sorry."

* * * *

SLAM! The sound of metal on metal reverberated throughout the Soyuz. McGovern had given the Chinese missile a solid hit, but it automatically fired its thrusters and corrected its course. The missile had a lock on the *Alliance*. He could see the Salyut and the Orion that was still docked to it. The warhead would detonate in less than 30 seconds.

"Line it up line it up, baby …" McGovern was talking to himself as he aimed the long docking probe of the Soyuz directly at the bell-shaped rocket nozzle of the A-SAT. He engaged the main engine, slamming the nose of the Soyuz into the motor of the Chinese missile. The docking probe sliced through the exhaust bell, rupturing the weapon's fuel lines. McGovern applied full starboard and port thrusters, pin wheeling the Soyuz with the A-SAT jammed onto its nose. He again fired the main engine. He was looking straight down at the cloud-streaked globe below him. Engaging the rocket motor for ten seconds, he put the two vehicles into a death spiral that would lead to a 10,000 degree atmospheric reentry. McGovern fired his forward thrusters to disengage but the A-SAT was stuck tight to the nose of the Soyuz. In desperation, he tried a very dangerous maneuver. Firing thrusters on opposite sides of the Soyuz, he put it into a rapid spin along its center of gravity and felt his weight returning from the effect of centrifugal force. Finally, with a screech of metal transmitted through the body of the Soyuz, the doomed A-SAT slid off the docking probe, tumbling end-over-end on a fatal descent into the upper atmosphere. McGovern, however, was also on that same deadly descent. While many men would panic, overcorrect, and fail to bring the craft under control, John McGovern cleared his mind and breathed deeply, searching for that calm center, the eye of the hurricane in a storm of emotions. He replayed the simulations at Star City in his mind and could see himself as if standing outside his body, coaching the John McGovern doppelganger sitting strapped into the Soyuz's seat, directing him through the correct sequence of thruster activations to regain control of the craft.

Slowly, he killed the spin and brought the craft back into a stable orbit, although much lower than he would have liked. McGovern checked his fuel reserves, as well as his vector back to the *Alliance*. He'd make it but there would be precious little fuel left in case they needed the use of the Soyuz again in lunar orbit.

Taking a final deep breath, he keyed his microphone. "McGovern to Orion. I just splashed the A-SAT. I'm okay. Let's get everyone back inside *Alliance*."

With emotions flooding her mind and body, Natasha Polyakova grabbed the transmitter with tears forming in her eyes. "Oh John, I thought you'd been killed. We are all safe … but, the Orion capsule, it's jammed in the docking collar. We must decide what to do … and John, please … hurry back to me. I must see your face before I can truly believe you are still with me."

CHAPTER SIXTEEN

Washington, DC

The president and her cabinet had been watching the events 200 miles up and 8,000 miles to the west over the Pacific unfold on the large flat panel display screens mounted above the conference table. With simultaneous sighs of relief, everyone could see that by the quick thinking and actions of John McGovern, disaster had been averted. Just as the tension was beginning to drain from the individuals in the room, Admiral James Warner was on the phone, staring intently at the big screens. Streaking over the water from the Chinese coast were 12 pinpoints of light with vector angles pointing directly at the two Boeings and their escort jets. Admiral Warner called out to the president. "NORAD shows twelve Chinese J-10 fighters in bound to intercept the flight in about eight minutes!"

Cordelier Price responded. "Can we get our flight clear?"

"I'm afraid not, Ma'am; the two Boeings could never outrun them."

Price turned to look at the board then, with a tone of resignation in her voice, spoke, "Tell them to engage the fighters. Protect our assets and then pull them back, out of fighter range. I don't want to cost the lives of our pilots or have this situation blow up any worse than it already has. What's the status of our SDI assets on Guam and Alaska?"

Warner tapped his fingers on the table, considering the implications of revealing the very existence of these weapons, but he finally spoke. "Both Sky Striker weapons are operational as well as the third one on Kwajalein. You know that putting these into action takes the wind out of our sails with regard to China violating treaties?"

Price turned to Vice President Adler. "What's your thoughts on this?"

"I think we have no choice here, Cordelier. China has upped the stakes by launching anti-satellite weapons and engaging our defensive forces over international water. But … I would place a call to Simonov right now and tell him you're about to use weapons that, while not banned in the anti-missile treaty, certainly stretch the interpretation of that treaty we signed decades ago."

"Those were my exact thoughts. I just wanted to bounce them off of you. If the Chinese see we can shoot down anything they send up, and we can do it unmolested from U.S. territory, just maybe they'll think twice about upping the stakes."

Warner interrupted. "The F22s have engaged the Chinese fighters … eight J-10s were blown out of the sky. The remaining four are running for home. No losses to our planes, and we're withdrawing our flight. Let's see what they do once they see we no longer have any air assets nearby."

Cordelier Price placed a quick call to Victor Simonov. Without the need for a translator, she engaged him in Russian. "He understands. He's withdrawing the Antonov and … I suppose we should have guessed – apparently Russia has two similar long-range particle beam weapons at secure sites. They're getting them prepared as we speak."

Warner, Price and her cabinet didn't have to wait long. Almost as soon as the Boeing laser platforms were out of range, NORAD detected another launch. The admiral listened carefully and then spoke to the president. "This is serious. It's a DF-31A long-range ICBM, but it's not on a ballistic trajectory. It's on an orbital track to intersect the Alliance … and ... *damn it* … excuse me, Ma'am … NORAD confirms there's a high probability the missile is armed with a nuke."

Price shook her head in disgust. "They've really upped the ante now. Go ahead and shoot it down. But for God's sake, don't miss."

"The Guam site is closest and primary, but the Kwajalein weapon will be ready to fire as a back-up in case we miss."

* * * *

The Ordinance Annex, located on the south central area of the Island of Guam, was comprised of nearly 9,000 acres of hilly uplands, which used to be known as the Naval Magazine. It was remote as well as off limits to the civilian population of the island. In 1998, intelligence sources revealed that China had a significant number of long-range ICBMs targeting the United States. By 2002, the new administration began a secret program for building powerful high-energy particle beam weapons powered by five 100-megawatt nuclear reactors. This was a "black program" where funding was diverted from other military budgeted programs and covered up by cost overruns, such as the development of the Osprey vertical takeoff and landing assault aircraft. The materials and personnel for the covert project known as Sky Striker were brought in over a period of 18 months through Andersen Air Force Base, with construction beginning in earnest in 2004.

The highly complex weapon required enough electrical power to light up a small city, as well as considerable volumes of liquid nitrogen to cool the components of the device and enhance its efficiency by creating superconducting surfaces and conduits for the zero resistance flow of the electrical currents. These currents were then fed into massive banks of capacitors that would hold a charge of several hundred million electron volts. In principal, the weapon worked like a cyclotron, an atom smasher. Except in this case, the stripped electrons were fired from the rubidium-beryllium snout of a particle beam cannon. With a bank of radars powerful enough to sterilize birds in flight that flew over the installation, the electronic eyes of the weapon swept the sky for the Chinese DF-31A. It only took a matter of moments for the target acquisition computers to locate and track the missile as it continued to accelerate into low Earth orbit.

Sitting at a console, surrounded by computer displays showing the track of the target, the intercept point and the charging status of the weapon, was a young air force lieutenant. Although the system was designed to be fully automatic, the human element was added against the very remote potential that the weapon had tracked a manned or commercial space launch. However, in this case, there was no mistaking the nuclear-armed ICBM on a direct line to the coalition's spacecraft.

The officer watched his screen as the missile tracked to the center to the firing reticle. Under his breath, he exclaimed, "Time to reach out and touch someone!" and hit the firing button. Instantly, the 200 million electron volts, held at bay in the capacitors, gave up their charge. It propagated through the conduits of the magnetic containment fields of the weapon, racing at light speed into the firing chamber. From the camouflaged retractable dome, the blunt barrel of the weapon discharged the electron punch of atomic particle moving at just below the velocity of light with a tremendous thunderclap that reverberated across the island. The Chinese missile, having just engaged its third and final stage, was still accelerating the warhead into orbit when it was struck by the beam, vaporizing the entire upper stage, turning it into spherical blobs of aluminum and titanium. The 50-kiloton nuclear warhead, blasted free of its rocket, began to tumble wildly and begun a descent back into the Earth's atmosphere, superheating and breaking apart at an altitude of 80 kilometers, spreading radioactivity as the plutonium core, now exposed to the heat of re-entry, began to disintegrate.

* * * *

Sung Zhao, now the acting Vice Premier of the Peoples Republic of China, watched the display screen in the central command bunker with satisfaction. The anger that filled him earlier with the destruction of the six anti-satellite weapons had vanished, as he, General Peng Li, and his staff viewed the progress of a nuclear-armed ICBM on course to its target, the international collation's spacecraft, *Alliance.* The 50-kiloton warhead it carried, four times more powerful than the bomb that leveled Hiroshima, would vanquish this thorn in his side with a fireball half a mile wide. Nothing but disassociated atoms would be left of the West's attempt to reach the lunar ice fields.

It happened just as the rocket passed 100 kilometers in altitude and fired its third stage to insert the nuclear warhead into orbit. Suddenly, the radar image on the screen broke apart as the incredible power of the American's particle beam weapon vaporized the upper stage, sending the warhead tumbling out of orbit.

"*What was that?!* What just happened to our missile?!" Sung Zhao was livid. The military and Party members in attendance were at a loss as to what destroyed the missile.

Finally a young weapons expert, who had been intently reviewing data on his computer screen, spoke up. "It was either a very powerful laser or, more likely, a particle beam weapon fired from Guam. The Americans may not be as unprepared as we have believed. Perhaps our intelligence sources should have anticipated that they possessed such a weapon. They appear to have placed this and, most likely, other long-range weapons that can shoot down our ICBMs while they are still in their boost phase."

Sung Zhao walked over to the young officer and clasped his shoulder in what was at first a gesture of thanks for identifying the weapon, and then he closed his hand like a vice on the man's shoulder causing him great pain.

"Your *duty* is to analyze and report on the enemy's weapons systems, *not* to offer your personal opinions. *Do you understand*?" Zhao then turned to General Peng. "If this is correct and the Americans are using such a weapon, then we must consider an alternate plan."

Turning to a communications officer, Zhao ordered him to send an encrypted transmission to General Wang, commander of the Chinese Moon Base. Then, Sung Zhao spoke aloud, to no one in particular, within the control room. "So, the Americans and their running dog coalition believe they have neutralized our ability to strike. They will soon find out it is a very big mistake to underestimate China."

* * * *

It was another six long grueling hours of work outside the *Alliance* that first involved mating the potent Earth Departure Stage to the reinforced collar of the docking module. This required connecting fat ropes of insulated cables to electrical stub-up points that were grafted onto the EDS during the rushed modification process. These connections would allow Natasha Polyakova to control the rocket motor on the departure stage from her command seat inside the Salyut. The mounting of this piece of NASA hardware was comparatively simple compared to joining the two lunar landers. This involved unpacking the LEMs from the cargo container that was sent aloft by the Titan rocket, and then placing thruster packs to guide them into a position for docking. The addition of the Orion capsule, still jammed into the docking clamps of the French module, was making the job far more complicated do to its extra mass.

Natasha Polyakova was working two joysticks, doing her best to line up the Salyut with the EDS stage firmly attached – one stick-controlled thrusters on the old Soviet space station, the other on the NASA departure stage. At last, after an exhausting hour and a half of intense concentration, both of the 50-year-old Lunar Modules were joined into place, secured on the docking rings of the French mission component.

Bill Curtis was in the seat behind Natasha in a section of the space station that had been converted into a weapons control center. Curtis was glued to his console, watching the search radar and listening for any alerts from NORAD, eyeing the controls for the ship's defensive weapons. The very fact that the Chinese had tried again to destroy the ship, this time with a nuclear weapon, had everyone on edge and working double time to complete the assembly of the *Alliance*. Finally, the indicators on the airlock hatch showed the first of the four astronauts, which had been working feverishly outside, was coming back in.

Lieutenant William Curtis relaxed for a few moments and turned to Natasha. "Say, we've been so busy working straight out that I didn't even have time to congratulate you on your engagement to John. He's a good man you know. In fact, we probably wouldn't be here at all if he didn't take your Soyuz out and headed off that A-SAT."

Natasha tried to put on her most serious face. "Lieutenant Curtis, if this is your way of trying to excuse Colonel McGovern's deliberately disobeying my orders…then you have an excellent point. Yes, John is … I don't know the word for him in English; perhaps *Superman* would be the best description. And … the engagement really isn't official until we return to Earth, after we finish our mission."

Curtis shook his head in the negative. "Let's hope we actually have an Earth to return to and we don't get blown out of the sky … that is if you can even use the word sky to describe the space around the Moon. Things are getting completely nuts down below. Believe me, I know what it's like for those men and women who are sitting in those silos right now in America, probably in Russia, too, holding their launch keys and wondering if the world is going to end in a matter of hours. Now it's up to us, I suppose, to try and force the issue. God, I hope we're doing the right thing. My wife and little girl are down there, just outside of Atlanta. I'm pretty certain my city has a bulls eye drawn around it on some Chinese attack program."

The inner airlock completed its cycle with the first man in. It was Remmy LaCasse. He pulled off his helmet, his hair drenched with sweat, and took a long drink of water from the plastic squeeze bottle. "Oh, *mon dur* … if it were not for zero gravity, I would collapse like a pile of rags!"

Within the next 20 minutes, all were back on board the *Alliance*, floating about the Salyut, the largest component of the ship. Finally, after a quick meal squeezed out of plastic zero gee tubes and hot coffee, Captain Polyakova and Colonel McGovern huddled with the crew for a conference.

Natasha spoke first. "We have completed the final assembly of the *Alliance* six hours ahead of schedule. The Russian Space Agency has assured us that the Progress cargo rocket will launch in a little over one hour from Plesetsk, in Northern Russia. This is fortunate, as I doubt the Chinese have any capability of destroying the rocket from this location. It is carrying both the inflatable habitat from Bigelow Aerospace and the drilling device that will be used to extract water under the surface of *Luna.* Once we secure the Progress to the final open docking port, we leave Earth to arrive in lunar orbit three days from now. I want all of you, especially you, John, to get some rest starting now. You all are exhausted."

Vernon LaBelle cleared his throat. "Ah, what exactly is my status? I'm supposed to be returning back to Earth."

John McGovern spoke directly to the man. "Major LaBelle, we don't have a lot of options here. Your capsule is jammed solid to the docking collar. We're too beat, and we don't have enough time or the tools to try and manually free the clamps, although I'm sure we can try during the outbound leg of our mission. So, you've been officially Shanghaied and pressed into service as the seventh member of the crew. Besides, we may very well need the Orion once we get into lunar orbit, especially if things get hairy with the Chinese. I just about ran the tanks on the Soyuz dry taking out that A-SAT, and I think I shorted out one of the solar wings when I smashed into the missile. Major LaBelle, grab a bunk, or rather, a sleeping bag, and consider yourself one of the crew. I think you and the rest of us are in for one hell of a ride."

Four hours later, after an orbital chase, the Russian Progress module docked with the *Alliance* and its cargo placed aboard inside the Salyut. Then 56 minutes later, over the night sky of North America, Natasha Polyakova ran through the countdown to launch.

Anyone on the ground with a small telescope or binoculars could see the craft's ignition as the quick moving point of light grew a long and fiery tail. The EDS stage of the *Alliance* fired on schedule, accelerating the craft to just over 25,000 miles per hour, sending her crew off into trans-lunar space. Most of those citizens on the ground were only peripherally aware of the fact that the world was creeping ever closer to the edge of the abyss, leading to global nuclear war.

CHAPTER SEVENTEEN

The Chinese Moon Base

Yuan Xho, along with his nephew, Zhang K'un, and sixteen other Chinese garrisoned at the lunar South Pole, stood in the moon base's storage and assembly area, the largest open area within the structure. The men stood at attention in front of their commanding officer, General Wang. The general surveyed his troops comprised of young officers and enlisted men. Major Yuan was his second in command, but the general was still feeling irritation toward the man for his earlier questions about his nation's course of action. He had stern words for his subordinate officer on the journey back after completing his tour of the first magnetic accelerator. Major Yuan, on the other hand, was aware of the rumors, as well as reports of an increased military alert in China and the report that America had used some sort of directed energy weapon to smite a long-range missile from the edge of space. Again, the dreams came to him and his fear for his family and his country continued to multiply with each passing hour. The very fact the General Wang had called all the men to order, and at this late hour of the night, could only mean the crisis had deepened.

Wang, ramrod straight in a deep green jumpsuit-styled uniform complete with red epaulettes, regarded his men with a stone-faced look of determination. "Men, soldiers, heroes of the People's Republic of China! Today your nation is again threatened by the forces of imperialism! But … unlike before, China will not back down. We will not turn away from or surrender our true destiny. A destiny that has been denied to us for centuries. China, not the West or Russia, is the future of civilization. The old has been swept away. The cowardliness of former Premier Feng has been excised, like an infection from the body. In his place stand men of courage, vision and determination. Our new leader is Gao Xi, and at his side stands the military genius of Sung Zhao! The forces of counter-revolution believe they have placed China in a box. They believe that we will again acquiesce to their demands, but they are *very* much mistaken! My orders come directly from Vice Premier Sung Zhao. Immediately we are to complete the second far side magnetic accelerator. You men in ordinance are to assemble the final components and arm our nuclear strike packages. They will be fired earthward from the accelerator to take up orbits over the major population centers of the West and Russia. Those who seek to oppress us will be watching our missile sites on Earth while we shall fill the skies above their nations with nuclear weapons launched from the Moon. Then, when it is too late for them to react, we shall *demand* their surrender and our recognition as the powerful and rightful nation to dictate the future course of human history!"

General Wang marched back and forth as he spoke, bouncing slightly higher with each step in the low lunar gravity. If the deadliness of the situation hadn't been so obvious, he would have appeared almost comical. "Your second task," he continued, "is to take our two stealth excursion ships to locate and destroy this insolent imperialist coalition and their collection of antique garbage which is on its way to our Moon. Those are your orders. You are to carry them out immediately. Is that understood?"

Everyone replied, "Yes, sir!" – even Major Yuan. He did so mechanically, without thinking for if he did stop to think he might have spoken, spoken aloud about the terrible visions of global war running through his mind.

General Wang paused directly in front of him. "Major Yuan, I am placing you in charge of completing the magnetic accelerator. I want the device ready to deliver the nuclear strike packages into Earth orbit no later than three days from now. Work your crew 24 hours. Have them use their stimulant packs. I don't care if they are on their feet for the next three days. I want the accelerator ready to fire. Do I make myself clear?"

"Yes, sir, understood. And … sir, may I enlist the assistance of Sergeant Zhang? I find his work exceptional."

The general nodded in agreement. "Very well, but be certain he has installed all the triggers for the plutonium cores on the ordinance before joining you at the accelerator site. Now, you are dismissed. Begin your task as of now, Major."

After the general left the ordinance storage and assembly facility, Sergeant Zhang tuned to the Major. "Uncle, why did you ask this of me? Are you planning to stop this madness? Because if you are …"

"Shh, quiet, nephew. We must speak softly about this. I shall help you with the triggers, and you and I shall speak as we work."

"Uncle, I must tell you that there are three more men who will support you in this, maybe more."

"Do you trust these men? I mean, trust them with your life? Because if you are mistaken, we will both face immediate execution for even thinking about such actions."

The sergeant rubbed his chin, deep in thought. "Yes, yes I do, Uncle. I am sure of these men but not of the others. I have not spoken aloud to anyone else, I just keep my eyes and ears open. I know what some are thinking, but they may be too fearful to act."

"Listen to me. Because of my rank, I have been privileged to much classified information. Our government tried, at first, to destroy the coalition's spacecraft with conventional anti-satellite weapons. When that failed, the vice premier ordered the launch of a nuclear-armed rocket far beyond the range of the American and Russian flying lasers. The rocket was destroyed by some kind of energy weapon fired from an American base in the Pacific. It had to be either a huge laser or a particle beam. This idea of placing nuclear weapons in Earth orbit is madness! Once they are discovered, and they will be, the nations we seek to threaten will unleash their entire nuclear forces upon our land. Hundreds of millions will die, and for what?"

The young man nodded in agreement. "But, Uncle, what are you going to do to stop this?"

"I … I don't know yet. I must think, but somehow … I must prevent the launching of the nuclear strike packages. Nephew, do what you can to slow down the assembly and installation of the triggers. I must have time to form a plan … and yet … I feel I am a traitor to my nation."

"Uncle, it is not so. If the driver of a bus is about to go off the side of a mountain, is it not your duty as a passenger to stop him and save the lives of everyone on board? Think of our country and our families. This Sung Zhao is leading them like sheep to the slaughter."

Major Yuan rubbed his forehead, as if his very thoughts were creating great pain. He was in turmoil between logic and emotion. "Yes, Nephew … you are correct. Now, I will prepare a hopper to journey to the accelerator, and I need to choose a crew. I want the names of those three men. I'll take two of them with me. You will meet me there as soon as you are able to with the third. Understand?"

"Yes uncle. Do not fear. We act to save our nation, not to destroy her."

* * * *

The pleasant days that heralded spring just a week earlier had retreated before a return engagement of winter. The morning had dawned cold and gray, with a dampness that seemed to cut through even the warmest jackets and raincoats the citizens of Washington D.C. were wearing that day. The depressing chill mirrored that of the soul of Cordelier Price. The entire fate of the world was in her hands. She began her day kneeling in prayer, asking for strength, guidance and wisdom to bring the world back from the brink.

President Price sat drinking coffee in the Oval Office, not bothering with the egg and cinnamon toast the White House chef had prepared for her. It was just after 6:30 in the morning when Jeffery Palmer, Director of the National Security Agency, and Admiral James Warner, Chairman of the Joint Chiefs, joined her.

Price first spoke to Admiral Warner. "Jim, what's the situation as of this morning?"

For James Warner, it had been a very late night and an even earlier morning. His uniform, usually crisp with razor sharp creases, looked rumpled, a clear sign he had slept in it for the few hours of rest he could find during the crisis. "There was only one incident involving a missile launch, and that happened at around 4 AM local time. If it had been anything of a more serious nature, you would have been awakened. The Chinese launched an intermediate range missile from their base at Delingha, in Central China. The missile was heading for a predicted impact on Perm, Russia, although it did not appear to be carrying a nuclear weapon. The Russians put their own particle beam weapon, housed near Novosibrisk, into action and took it out at just under one hundred kilometers altitude. We, as well as the Russian military, believe it was a test to determine if Russia had the same shoot down capability as we have. Since then, things have been uncharacteristically quiet. Too quiet. Nothing has been pulled back. In fact, massive amounts of Chinese armor and infantry have been moving across Mongolia and approaching the Russian border, but they've stopped, and it looks as if they are just waiting for something. The Russians have placed all their nuclear forces on first alert – you know, launch on warning. The air is filled with nuclear-armed bombers and strike aircraft. We have our entire bomber fleet airborne and at their holding points just outside Chinese airspace. The way things are looking, if someone even sneezes at the wrong moment, World War III is going to start."

President Price rubbed her arms as if a sudden chill had invaded the room. She had made history as the first woman to hold the office of president. If she could not bring this crisis to a successful conclusion, she might very well be the last American president in history as well. "So what's your assessment, Jim?"

"They're planning something, but we have no idea what that might be. However, we're reading a lot of encrypted chatter between Beijing and their moon base. If something's going to happen, it may very well be coming from there."

"What about our mission? When do they arrive in lunar orbit?"

"Two more days. Although, I don't have a lot of hope for their chances. I think they're going to be in for the fight of their lives but … our mission may be the key to ending this thing if McGovern and his crew can stop whatever the Chinese are planning up there."

The President then turned to her national security director. "Jeffery, are you having any luck running down the Chinese infiltration here?"

No, Ma'am, it seems that their agents and contacts are keeping one-step ahead of us. I hate to say this, but I believe that individuals in the FBI have been compromised. We saw it in Russia. China bought its way into the heart of their security apparatus and may have done the same here as well. Nathan Crowley, backed with billions of dollars from China, had a lot to do with that as well as … this."

NSA Director Palmer handed the president a document. As she scanned it, a look of shock came across her face, and a single tear welled in her eye. She bowed her head briefly had wiped it away. "Are you sure of this information?"

"Yes, Ma'am. Our agents culled it from Mr. Crowley's computer records. It was very well hidden. I'm certain he thought he deleted it some time ago, but we have the means of finding a data trace even if the user thinks he's gotten rid of it."

Cordelier Price stood up from her desk. "Is he being held at NSA headquarters?"

"Yes, Ma'am, he is."

"Then I want to see him *right now*, understand?"

"Are you sure you want to speak with him?"

"Yes I do, immediately!"

* * * *

Nathan Crowley sat looking dejected and disheveled despite the elegantly tailored dark blue Versace suit he was wearing. Crowley scanned his stark surroundings: harsh overhead lighting, gray cinderblock walls, a simple metal table and two chairs made of tan metal with black vinyl upholstery. His thin padded chair was made even more uncomfortable by the fact his wrists were handcuffed behind his back. The only movement in the room was the analog clock, ticking off the minutes and the occasional sound of the two ceiling mounted security cameras that faced him, refocusing their lenses.

He had been quickly hustled out of New York by helicopter and flown in a government registered Gulfstream jet to National Security Agency headquarters in Washington D.C. No phone call, no Miranda Rights and no access to his lawyers. For the first time in his life, Nathan Crowley, billionaire and CEO of East Wind Investment and Securities Corporation, finally began to realize he was in deep shit.

As he contemplated his predicament, he could hear the sound of a key being inserted into the door. It swung open to reveal two marine guards armed with AR-15s. They were quickly followed by two well-built secret service men in black suits who entered the room and made a quick inspection of Crowley's handcuffs. This piqued Crowley's curiosity as to who would be entering next. Certainly that much muscle and firepower meant the next person in the room had to be someone pretty important. When she entered the room, it took a moment for just who he was looking at to register on his consciousness: President Cordelier Price.

Crowley made a move as if to stand but Cordelier Price fixed him with a glare that could have done real physical damage, it was so powerful. Her voice dripping with sarcasm, she addressed the billionaire CEO. "Oh, please … don't get up. Standing would be a sign of respect, and you certainly have no respect for me, the Office of the President, and absolutely none for your country. The NSA has been sifting through your files and your computers since yesterday. You'd be just amazed at what they found … or then again, maybe not, since you put it there."

Nathan Crowley, shifting in his seat, blurted out, "I have rights! I demand to speak with my attorney!"

President Price walked over to Crowley, regarding him like some kind of unpleasant garden slug, and then she smiled, chuckled and shook her head at the absurdity of his statement. "Mr. Crowley, you have *rights*? You *demand* to speak to your attorney? You're sitting in underground level number four, 300 feet below the National Security Agency building, being held on the charge of treason, as well as murder. You may as well be on the far side of the Moon, which is what this is about after all: the Moon and China's attempt to gain control not only of space but the world's economy. Since you've been held incommunicado, you don't know it yet, but very shortly, a state of war may exist between the United States and the Peoples Republic of China."

Crowley looked as if someone had just punched him in the gut.

"Yes, Mr. Crowley, war, possibly nuclear war, after what we've learned about China's real intentions. Because of what you've done, the blood of hundreds of millions will be on your hands and those of your cohorts. Oh, and while we were digging in your papers and computer files, we found your connection to the assassination of President Richmond. John Richmond was not only my president, he was also my friend, and I swore on his death when I took the Oath of Office, he would be avenged."

Cordelier Price turned and spoke to her secret service agents and the two marines. "Please, unlock his handcuffs and wait outside. Mr. Crowley is not a violent man. He pays people to do his dirty work for him. Now please excuse us … and switch off the cameras and the audio. What I have to say to this man is between the two of us."

Nathan Crowley rubbed his wrists, finally free of the handcuffs, and watched the four men leave the room. Cordelier Price noticed his watch; this time he was wearing a gold Rolex.

"Nice watch. How much in blood money did that cost you, or was it a bargain at 30 pieces of silver?"

Crowley tried to straighten his tie and regain some semblance of control over his destiny. "What do you want from me? I'm *Nathan*

Crowley, and I don't have to answer *anything* to *anyone*, not even to you!"

Cordelier Price's almond eyes flashed a warning, and with just her look he began to stammer thinking better of his blustery comments. Letting his predicament sink in, he realized she could have him shot with a snap of her fingers.

"Ah … okay, maybe we *can* talk," He said.

"*Talk*? Believe me, Mr. Crowley, the last place on Earth I want to be is in this room, talking with you. You disgust me. My fondest wish is to see you dead. If I open my mouth and scream, those men will be in here so fast with guns blazing that you'd be dead before you hit the floor, and if I had my way, I'd kill you myself! But, I have to think about the lives of the crew on their way to confront the Chinese on the Moon and those men and women sitting in their launch silos as we go to DEFCON 1, staring at their unopened codebooks and holding their launch keys, ready to open the door to nuclear Armageddon. We are talking about ending the lives of millions, maybe billions, of human beings if that happens. So, for that reason alone I *have* to keep you alive. You don't say another damn word to me until I *say* you can speak! I talk and you listen! This is between you and me, there are no cameras and there is no audio recording. Because we have more than enough to convict you for treason, as well as the murder of President Richmond, I'll tell you right now, you *will* be tried by a military court, and the sentence *will* be death This won't be the kind of quiet death where you're strapped to a gurney and put to sleep before you're injected with lethal drugs. Your death will be far more violent. You'll be strapped to a chair in front of a padded cinderblock wall, looking down the barrels of a dozen high powered rifles, crapping in your pants as you watch twelve soldiers' fingers slowly squeeze the triggers of their weapons. I want your last moments on Earth to be filled with terror and pain. Or … I can invite the secret service agents back in, along with an NSA interrogator, and you can tell him everything, and I mean *everything,* that you know. Every contact, every mole in our military or the FBI and every last bit of information you know or even suspect about what the

Chinese are planning. You do that, and as distasteful as it is to me, I'll commute your sentence to life in prison."

Nathan Crowley, once a VIP, one of the most powerful men in the world of international finance, was reduced to a puddle of quaking fear, tears actually welling in his eyes. He shook so violently, he could hardly get his words out.

"O … okay, okay … I'll tell them everything, everything you want to know, I swear it! I'll give you everything …"

President Price just stared at him. "That is the smartest business decision you've ever made, Mr. Crowley, but I'm warning you, after the NSA is finished with your interrogation, you'll be put on a plane and flown to the military prison at Fort Leavenworth, Kansas, to await your trial. If any of your information proves false – and I mean *any of it,* just one lie or just one missing fact – a door will open on that jet, and you, sir, will find yourself exiting the aircraft at twenty thousand feet. *Do I make myself clear*?"

Nathan Crowley sat in his chair, breathing hard and unable to speak, just nodding his head in agreement. He looked as if he was going to hyperventilate.

President Cordelier Price stood over him, regarding him like a cockroach. "Very good, Mr. Crowley. I'll have the NSA interrogator speak with you. I'm heading back to the White House to attend to the crisis at hand, but first I need a good hot shower to wash the slime off of me from being in the same room with you."

CHAPTER EIGHTEEN

Trans-Lunar Space

The stars shone brilliantly and unblinking through the view port. The contrast between the dazzling pinpoints of light and the absolute blackness of space was profound, far greater than even then sky as seen from the mountaintops of Earth. Natasha had only the red emergency lights on inside the Salyut to allow the exhausted crew to sleep and recover their stamina from the Herculean task of mounting the various components to the core of the *Alliance*, a 44-year-old Soviet built space station. Natasha so intently gazed at the Milky Way as it weaved a star-strewn ribbon through the constellations of Perseus and Cassiopeia, that she didn't even notice the rustle of fabric until John McGovern joined her in the second seat. Startled for just a moment, she jumped.

"Don't worry. I'm not a bloodthirsty alien that stowed away on board the ship."

Natasha pressed her hand to her chest in mock terror. "You scared me, and I hated that movie. It gave me nightmares as a child. You are supposed to be sleeping! You are not on duty for another hour."

McGovern turned his gaze away from Natasha and out the viewport, captivated by the cold hard beauty of space. "I couldn't sleep any longer, thinking about what's happening down on Earth. Those stars that we see, suddenly flaring and dying, random gamma ray busts that can't quite be accounted for. Are those the remnants of the death throes of technological civilizations as they destroy themselves in some all-consuming war? I don't know, to have come this far this fast. One hundred years ago we were flying cloth-covered wooden airplanes that could barely reach a hundred miles an hour, and now we stand on the threshold of claiming the stars. It's us, you know. War, it's in our genes. Our technology races ahead, but our emotions are still back there in the stone age when we were beating each other to death with clubs and rocks."

Natasha reached over and took his hand. "John, I never saw this side of you before, so thoughtful and introspective. Is this the other side of the warrior?"

"Warrior? Yeah, I suppose if having a career in the military classifies me as a warrior, then I guess I am. I've killed men in battle. I took out that carload of security thugs in Moscow without any regrets, but being in space changes a man. It changes the way you see your planet and your fellow human beings. I wonder about them, the enemy. Those Chinese soldiers on the Moon right now. Do any of them have doubts? Are any of them appalled at the road their country has chosen? I don't know, but if I have to, I'll take them out. I just hope to God we're not lighting a match to something that can't be stopped."

Natasha glanced around to see if anyone else was awake. Seeing no one, she leaned over and kissed McGovern deeply. "John, I'm going to try and rest for a few hours, and then we must wake the crew. We are two days from lunar orbit. I love you."

Slowly McGovern released her from his arms. "Yeah, go ahead and get some sleep. Meanwhile, I'll be using my 21st century logic instead of my 50,000-year-old emotions to try and devise the best way for us to come out of this alive and victorious. I want us to share a long life together, with some kids, I hope, if that fits with your plans."

Natasha again leaned over and kissed him. "Oh yes, John, that will be our plan."

* * * *

The lunar hopper had lifted off from a leveled and graded launch area eight minutes earlier. The assent was smooth, clearing the crater walls and putting the small six-person craft on a ballistic trajectory to the nearly complete far side magnetic accelerator. The hopper would reach an altitude of 20 kilometers and then begin its gravity-assisted fall back to the lunar surface. Major Yuan again checked the control panel, which showed everything was functioning within programmed limits, and that the craft was on course to arrive in 20 minutes. Major Yuan was most definitely not functioning within his normal limits, however. His heart raced, and sweat continued to bead on his forehead. His gloved hands shook so badly that the first man in the forward seat, a young private, even noticed. He considered asking the major if he was ill but thought better of addressing a superior officer about his health.

The two men seated in the hopper with Major Yuan were the friends of his nephew, Zhang. They were young men, but well educated, conscripted out of technical and engineering universities for duty on the Moon in China's clandestine bid to control the resources of space. Major Yuan again eyed the men. The feeling in his gut was almost making him sick, and he could feel his chest tighten. He felt as if he were about to step in front of an oncoming train. *Is my nephew correct? Can I trust these men? If not, I'd rather crash the hopper now than face an execution squad.* Finally, he could wait no longer. They would be at the accelerator site to carry out the work for launching the nuclear strike packages. Yuan considered this and decided it was now or never. If his nephew were wrong, he'd be a dead man within 24 hours. Yuan spoke over the men's private suit radios. "Do you men know that I am Sergeant Zhang's uncle?"

The reaction was interesting. Only one man, a corporal, was aware of this.

"How do you men feel about our mission?" Yuan said.

The answers Major Yuan received at first were full of patriotic fervor, the men all speaking the party line.

Yuan now took a great risk. "Is that really so? Because I believe China is on a course to disaster. I believe our actions will lead to global nuclear war. I believe our true duty to our country is to stop this madness before it is too late."

Yuan's relief at finally speaking his mind was like a great stone lifted from his chest; still he had now placed himself in mortal jeopardy with his statements.

The two men were silent and looking at each other as if in shock. Was this some kind of loyalty test? Was it some kind of trick? Had their friend, Sergeant Zhang, betrayed them?

Finally, the private, not older than twenty-three, spoke up with caution and hesitation. "Major … you could be shot for speaking such words, but I sense this is not a test of our loyalty. You have spoken about this to Sergeant Zhang, am I correct?"

"Yes, private, you are correct, and what I speak are my true thoughts. I speak them with as much unease as you can imagine, for if my nephew has misjudged you, then I am a dead man."

The young corporal then spoke. "Major, we not common soldiers. We are all educated in the finest technical universities in China. We are not ignorant of the world. We, as well as your nephew, agree with you. This is a terrible mistake. I am sick at the thought of arming nuclear weapons to place into Earth orbit. It can only lead to disaster. The pages of history are drenched in blood with misjudgments such as this. It can only cause the annihilation of millions of innocent people."

Yuan finally realized, to his great relief, that his nephew had great insight and chose his friends correctly. "Then I must tell you, men, we cannot allow the launching of the nuclear strike packages from the accelerator. I have a plan but we must all work together. We will arrive in just a few more minutes. Time is short, so listen to me carefully and do as I say when we begin work on the magnetic sequencer …."

* * * *

"So, what were you able to discover from Mr. Crowley's information?" Cordelier Price, now well into the second day of the crisis with China, addressed CIA Director Roger Blackwell. They were meeting at 7 AM to discuss the flood of revelations divulged by the CEO of the giant Chinese-American investment firm, East Wind Securities. Crowley, realizing that his life hung in the balance, gave up every last bit of information he had to the NSA officers that had interrogated him, including the very interesting fact that once China had achieved domination over the world's resources, he would be set up as a provisional governor to rule over a portion of the United States, after it came under the control of the PRC.

Roger Blackwell, a man in his late fifties, had retained a deceptively boyish face. He held a pleasant smile and the kind of quick wit and Texas humor that afforded him not only quick confirmation as director in his congressional hearing but intense loyalty from his agents. This morning, however, the sparkle in his light blue eyes had been replaced with a look of deep concern.

"President Price, we've been reviewing the information from the NSA, and it's really taken me aback. I've seen the list of FBI higher ups Crowley turned, and it makes me physically sick. I know some of these men. I've had one of them and his wife over to my home, played tennis with him … I almost can't believe what I read, but when we sent our agents to check out the eight Crowley told the interrogators about, we knew he wasn't lying. Three of them committed suicide before we arrested them. Three are in custody and two have vanished, making a run for it out of the country. That includes my friend, Assistant FBI Director Henry Snow. And … there's more. You have two congressmen whose campaigns were secretly financed by East Wind with Chinese money. They happened to be the two on the committee that vetoed the plan to place defensive weapons on the first moon mission."

Cordelier Price was seething. Her almond-shaped dark hazel eyes flared with anger. "I want those two arrested. I want them led out of Congress in handcuffs for all to see. They're traitors in the service of a foreign government, and they cost the lives of those two astronauts. I want every single one of their colleagues to witness their arrest. I'll have the attorney general see to it this morning, but I want your men to carry it out. I don't want either of them to meet with an *accident* at the hands of the FBI, just in case we haven't dug out all the vermin who have infested our nation's national law enforcement agencies. Okay, what else?"

"Crowley spoke of a plan to quarantine us, as well as Russia and Europe, from space. To somehow dictate terms through ironclad intimidation. However, he said he wasn't told exactly how this would be done."

As Director Blackwell finished his statement, a marine guard announced that the other two men the president was expecting had arrived.

Entering the Oval Office was Major General Walter Cronin, an authority on space-based weapons, and with him Colonel Pavel Buryak of the Russian Federal Security Bureau.

Roger Blackwell stood up to shake their hands. "General, very nice to meet you and Colonel Buryak … nice to be working on the same side for a change."

Buryak gave the CIA director a firm handshake. "Many of the issues you may have had with my government in the past were the fault of the late Yevghenny Golovko. Although he is no longer here to provide us with information on his traitorous relationship with China, his computer records have been a treasure trove of information. I am here because his files indicate that every supply launch from China to their moon base carried nuclear weapons. To our best estimation, the Chinese have amassed perhaps 80 nuclear devices in the 500-kiloton range on the Moon."

General Cronin added, "We have a very good idea of how the Chinese may intend to use these weapons, but I wanted to ask NASA Director Taggert to join us in the conversation. He's standing by in Houston."

Cordelier Price flipped a switch on her desk as a panel on the office wall slid away, revealing a large LCD screen. "Okay, General, place the call."

It only took a few moments to connect, with the image of Norman Taggert appearing on the screen. Cronin then spoke to him. "Norm, good to see you this morning. I think I know the answer to this, but I'd like to run this by you, just for confirmation. If you had nukes on the Moon, how would you deploy them for use against the Earth?"

Taggert didn't hesitate for a moment. "I'd use the same method the Chinese used for delivering those refined ore packages to Earth orbit; same as they did with their dog and pony show for the Third World. I'd use a magnetic accelerator and fire the nukes toward Earth. If they were coated with radar absorbing materials, we'd never see them coming. They could decelerate using small retrorockets and take up orbital positions over the Earth. They could de-orbit any one of those weapons over a city with absolutely no warning at all. They'd have us by the bal- ... oh excuse me, Madam President … they'd have us cornered, and there's not a thing we could do about it."

Cronin then asked his next question but he already suspected the answer. "Wouldn't we see them being launched from their accelerator?"

"Sure we would, General … if they used the one on the Moon's near side. I'd bet my life there's another one, just beyond the far side horizon – one we can't see."

Cronin nodded in agreement. "Thanks Norm. You confirmed my suspicions. Madam President, the *Alliance's* task must be to locate and destroy that magnetic accelerator. If this wasn't a combat mission before, it certainly is now."

President Price regarded the three men from behind her desk. "So … is there any *good* news coming out from all of this?"

Blackwell pulled a report from his briefcase. "If there is a bright spot to any of this, it's the Chinese people themselves. This isn't 1989 anymore, when the Chinese government rounded up thousands of students during the Tiananmen Square demonstrations. Now we have the Web, Internet, Vid-Net, Twitter, camera phones, every form of instant communication you can imagine. The Chinese people, as well as their military, are getting quite a lot of news filtering in from the West and over the Net, and they don't like what they're hearing. Look at the reports coming in. We're seeing some significant student demonstrations around the country. In Shantung Province, the governor addressed a sea of protestors. They even stopped a tank column, handing out flowers to the soldiers. Maybe there's a way we can turn up the heat on this."

Price drummed her fingers on her desk and considered what the CIA director had told her. This was the Cuban Missile Crisis times ten, but with the World Wide Web there was a way to reach out to the people of China in ways that John Kennedy could never have done with the people of the Soviet Union.

"Okay. I'm calling a press conference for tonight, but before I go on the air I will personally speak to the heads of every major network and news organization at the White House by this afternoon. I'll send planes for them if I have to. While we can't reveal our knowledge about the Chinese nukes on the Moon to the public, we can fill in the media heads in confidence and we can wage an aggressive information war directed at the Chinese people. It worked for Boris Yeltsin during the Soviet coup of 1991 and in Libya in 2011. Maybe it'll work here as well … God, I hope so for the sake of our nation and our planet."

* * * *

"The electromagnets must fire in a precise sequence, one right after the other, to continue to accelerate the sled that will carry the strike packages," Major Yuan said. "The far side accelerator is not complete. Thirty more electromagnets are required to complete the track. Each magnet has a polarity switch. We will reverse the magnetic field on the last thirty. Instead of accelerating the sled, these will act in the reverse, like putting on the brakes of an automobile. The sled will not be stopped but will be slowed down enough so that the strike packages will not leave lunar orbit. In fact, they may even fall back to the lunar surface several hundred kilometers from here."

Corporal Zho spoke up. "What if we are discovered? How can we explain this to the General?"

Major Yuan thought for a moment. "It can be explained as a production error on these units. They were all shipped together on the last supply rocket. This is my area of expertise. General Wang knows nothing about how the electromagnets function. I will claim that they cannot be repaired. With Russia and the Americans interdicting our launches from Earth, no replacements can be sent."

The private, a young engineering student, raised his voice. "Are you certain we do the right thing, Major? I … I feel I betray my country."

"Your country has betrayed the Chinese people. It has been seized by madmen. Did you study your history as well as your engineering?"

"Yes, sir, I was quite good at."

"Then put yourself in the shoes of a German in 1938. Suppose you could look ahead to 1945 and see millions of dead, your cities in ruins. Would you feel you were betraying your nation if you somehow were able to stop the madman Hitler? If history teaches us anything, it is that such threats and aggression will only bring misery and destruction upon the aggressor. Now quickly, as soon as we set down, I will show you where to find the access panels on the magnets. Reverse the polarity on each electromagnet before we move them to the installation area. Is that understood?"

The two men nodded in agreement but hidden behind the faceplate of one of them, his expression revealed his true thoughts and intentions.

* * * *

The ungainly collection of multinational space hardware known as the coalition spacecraft *Alliance* was within 5,000 miles of the Moon. That small silvery sphere that touched the night with a soft, almost mysterious illumination, now dominated the view ahead, filling the viewports with its cratered, asteroid blasted surface. The main control section of the Salyut had no direct frontal view, but when Cosmonaut Natasha Polyakova pivoted the craft, the surface of the Moon came into full view through the side port. There was something about this view, looking out and seeing it with your own eyes that was viscerally different from what could be seen on the main display screen. It was something akin to being at the Olympics as opposed to watching them on television.

Natasha was in position to retro fire the main rocket motor on the EDS when McGovern received an encrypted radio transmission. A look of concern crossed his face. "Natasha, we're supposed to look for a second magnetic accelerator beyond the near side demarcation line and if we find it, destroy it. I don't like it. I want to release an *Eye* and see if we can get a look at what the Chinese have for defenses before we go blundering in there."

The *Alliance* carried several Eyes. Each one was about the size of a beach ball and studded with cameras and other sensors. The *Eye* had a small rocket motor as well as attitude thrusters. The tiny probe could swoop down and determine what sort of fortifications had been put into place to defend the Chinese base from attack. The *Eye's* very size made it difficult to detect. It was a spy device designed to gather information then report it to the crew.

"Natasha, I don't want you to put us into a polar orbit until we know what's waiting for us down there. If we're in an equatorial orbit, we're out of range for any of their A-SATs. We have enough fuel in the EDS to change our orbital inclination."

I agree John. Let's ..."

The bleating of the microwave detectors signaled their ship was being scanned by a powerful search radar.

Bill Curtis called out from his weapons console. "I guess they know we're coming. Let's not make ourselves an easy target."

Curtis then hit a switch on his console and on the hull of the Salyut, the restraining clamps secured one of the three Eyes. It drifted out beyond the ship, and its tiny rocket motor ignited, sending on a course toward the lunar south pole.

When the *Alliance* had closed to within 2,000 miles of the Moon's surface, Natasha fired the EDS stage's rocket motor, slowing the ship down and taking up a nearly circular orbit 50 miles high. The *Eye*, released earlier, continued on its course, sweeping low over the lunar surface and flashing over the second accelerator site, unnoticed by either the base's radar or the three men working below.

The *Eye's* cameras recorded everything within range with both wide-angle and telephoto lenses, as well as seeing into the infrared range of the spectrum, detecting potently camouflaged weapons and structures by their heat signature. As it reached the bottom of its parabolic trajectory, the tiny motor fired, pushing its small mass upward against the one-sixth gravity of the Moon and back into a matching orbit with the *Alliance*.

Bill Curtis began receiving the telemetry from the *Eye*. "Heads up, pictures coming in … *Damn!* They were right! There *is* a second accelerator, but it's not completed yet. Look here, I can see three individuals at work on it."

McGovern floated over to Curtis's station. Ten long tubes on lattice-like frames caught his attention. "Are those A-SATs?"

"Yeah, sure looks like it and plenty, too. Good thing we didn't come in on a polar orbit, or we'd wind up like the first mission. Defensive weapons or not, they out gun us three to one."

"Okay, this is how we have to do it. I'll take the first LEM down to the surface in that crater about three kilometers from their accelerator. If I come in low and in a horizontal approach, the crater walls will block any radar as well as any visual observations. I'll set down and cover the distance on foot. Give me enough plastic explosives and detonators to take out its track. Natasha, I … want you to stay on board to take the second LEM to the surface after I've taken out the accelerator track."

Natasha Polyakova floated up to McGovern with fire in her eyes. "You expect to go *alone?! Down to the surface?!* Or perhaps you will choose Garcia or Remmy who have not trained with you?! I know your every move on the lander and how to complement your skills with mine. John, whatever your feelings are for me, you cannot change the mission. We have trained for this landing together and, what will happen once we get to the surface, answer me that? Do you plan to defend yourself and fire a gun while setting up explosive charges? I suppose you have eyes in the back of your head as well! I am one of the best marksmen in the world. In this low gravity, I can hit a target at three kilometers. You don't want to lose *me*? Well I *certainly* do not want to lose you! And the best way I can think of that not to happen is to have me right by your side, working together and watching out for each other. Do you agree?"

John McGovern took a hold of both of her hands. "Yes, you're right. But there is something that just goes against my grain to place the woman I love in harm's way." McGovern just shook his head. "Wow, I said one of the qualities I really love about you is your strength. I guess I really got what I asked for. Come on. We'll watch each other's backs. Let's get the LEM powered up. I want us to be ready to undock in an hour."

* * * *

"General Wang, the coalition spacecraft has entered lunar orbit."

Wang regarded the radar operator with an imperious look. "Then coordinate with our weapons' officer and shoot them down."

"We can't, sir. They have entered an equatorial orbit and are out of range from our anti-satellite weapons."

The Chinese general then considered the situation and made his decision. "Then we shall arm one of the Pods and send Lieutenant Tzen to attack their craft."

As Wang was about to order the placing of four small missiles into one of the Pod's weapon's racks, the base's communications officer bounded over to him, nearly overshooting the general in the low gravity.

"Sir? I apologize for this interruption, but one of the men at the second accelerator site, a Private Kuo, has an urgent message for you."

The general, visibly showing his annoyance, fixed the young officer with a glare. "What is it? What did this *private* say?"

"I am sorry, sir, he said he needs to speak with you himself and says it is an urgent matter and must talk directly with you before our relay satellite passes out of range. The man says that our entire mission is at stake."

Wang followed the officer back to his station, and picked up the man's headset. "Very well, put him through, but for his sake I hope his urgency is well founded."

* * * *

Major Yuan, busily opened the access panels on the electromagnets and scanned the desolate gray-brown surface, then turned to the man working with him.

"Where is Private Kuo? I see he has many more sequencers to disable."

The corporal stood up from the pile of large black rectangular devices he was sabotaging and also looked about for him. The Moon was an unforgiving environment, and if Kuo had injured himself or put a hole in his suit, chances are he was already dead. Then the corporal saw him, over by the hopper. He had paused for a moment and then came bounding back in kangaroo hops that sent clouds of pulverized basalt and microscopic glass flying each time his boots hit the lunar surface.

"I … I'm sorry, I needed a tool. I must have dropped it in the hopper earlier."

It was unfortunate that the gold reflective visor hid Kuo's face, for the lie that was written there would have been plainly visible for Major Yuan to see.

* * * *

Natasha spoke quietly as she ran down her checklist. In the lunar lander's tight confines, there was no need to shout. John McGovern stood shoulder to shoulder with her in his pilot's position and was aware of each word she said. Despite the seriousness of the mission, he marveled at the sweetness of her voice, her delicate lilting accent and her beauty. Her light brown hair drifting about her face in the zero gravity of space appeared as if a soft breeze was gently caressing it as it did the first evening they ate and danced together after a long day of training at the Cape. Now it seemed the blue skies and warm salt-tinged air of that evening had happened a lifetime ago. They were about to descend to the surface of the Moon in a 50-year-old museum exhibit. It was a mission that had become far more dangerous than before due to the discovery of a second magnetic accelerator, capable of firing undetectable nuclear-armed warheads into low Earth orbit.

"Docking clamps are retracted. The LEM is now clear. John, you can engage the thrusters and pull free of the docking module."

"Okay … we are good to go."

The rest of the *Alliance* crew, including Major LaBelle, watched from the Salyut's viewport as the LEM slid past and dwindled in size, drifting against the impossible star-strewn backdrop of space.

LEM – Lunar Excursion Module. These were the two-man bug-like landers that took the Apollo astronauts down to the surface of the Moon. This particular lander had sat in the Smithsonian Air and Space Museum for more than 40 years. The LM-2 was never destined to reach the Moon. Instead, it was supposed to be used as a test craft in Earth orbit, prior to an actual landing. However, the first test of such a craft, the LM-1, had been so successful that it relegated this lander to the quiet existence of a museum exhibit. Yet here it was, completely reengineered with modern electronics and a Russian rocket motor, gleaming in its coverings of gold foil, legs extended, like some enormous insect, silently tracing a path over the desolate surface of the Moon. The craft that had begun life 51 years earlier was at last in the environment it was created to fly in.

John McGovern and Natasha Polyakova were now a safe distance from the *Alliance* when they briefly fired the descent engine to scrub off speed and begin their gravity-assisted fall toward the mountainous regions of the Moon's South Pole. The *Alliance's* radar showed the LEM clearly, standing out against empty space. However, what the ship's electronic eyes failed to record was the rapidly approaching single seat craft, blanketed in stealth materials and wearing the color of night. The craft's pilot, Lieutenant Tzen, saw the LEM leaving orbit but could not radio this information back to the moon base for fear of giving away his position. His orders were to attack and destroy the coalition ship. General Wang would decide if and when a second Pod would be needed to deal with the lander that he could see falling toward the Moon.

U.S. Air Force Lieutenant William Curtis sat strapped into his seat at the improvised weapons console in the Salyut, the core of the ad hoc vessel know as the *Alliance*. He was concentrating on the receding image of the LEM as it dwindled to a tiny point of light, no longer distinguishable from the other thousands of stars visible in the lunar sky. His first hint of trouble came from his radar screen. As careful as the Chinese weapons' tech had been to coat the craft with radar absorbing materials, the Pod still had to have a view port for the pilot to see out of. This small rectangular window on the two-meter diameter sphere that held one man was reflecting just enough microwave radiation that it barely registered on Curtis's radar screen. He watched the trace – at first he thought, it might be a piece of debris from the earlier mission that was destroyed months ago – until he realized it was on a direct course for the *Alliance*. Bill Curtis had just enough time to call out to Remmy LaCasse to fire the forward thrusters, changing the position of the ship as a small but deadly missile streaked away from the invisible attacker.

"*Jesus*! We're going to take a hit!" Bill Curtis then flipped on radar acquisition for the AEGIS system and the mini-Patriot missiles cursing to himself, "Son of a bitch!" Curtis had assumed that with the ship in equatorial orbit, they were well out of range from any of the Chinese weapons. Sending a small manned interceptor after them came as a very nasty surprise.

A mini-Patriot PAC-4 streaked away from the external launch rack but the Chinese missile was too close and its vector angle too extreme. The interceptor missile missed its target. The AEGIS 20-millimeter gun tried to track the incoming missile, but its aim was blocked by Vernon LaBelle's capsule, still firmly wedged into the upper docking port. It was only by the greatest stroke of luck that French Astronaut Remmy LaCasse fired the thrusters at exactly the moment that he did or the meter-long Chinese missile would have slammed dead center into the Salyut. Instead, it missed the main body of the ship and plowed into the jammed Orion capsule.

The missile punched through the thin sidewall of the gumdrop-shaped craft and exploded inside, blasting the craft apart and into hundreds of pieces of flying shrapnel. The Orion's heat shield came away intact, propelled by the force of the explosion, and, like a machete, sliced off one of the Salyut's three extended solar wings. Tiny shards of razor edged metal flew away from the blast in a lethal cloud, smashing into the second LEM, punching holes through the outer skin. It was only by a miracle that none of the shards of aluminum penetrated the fuel and oxidizer tanks on the 50-year-old craft, or it would have caused a devastating second explosion.

Alarms were sounding inside the Salyut as several jagged daggers of metal punched holes into the exposed side of the Salyut, causing the atmosphere inside the craft to rush out. Quickly, the crew gathered up sealant kits and began patching the holes. The material in the kits was pliable for the first thirty seconds, but once exposed to the air inside the ship on one side, and the hard vacuum of space on the other, became a solid plug, strong as steel. While Lieutenant Curtis swept the space around the *Alliance* with his defensive radar, the other men raced weightlessly about the interior of the Salyut patching holes and trying to get a handle on the damage caused by the first missile.

The radar-absorbing stealth material that cloaked the tiny manned craft could not completely cover it. The exhaust bell of the Pod's rocket motor was exposed and reflected a tiny bit of microwave energy to be recorded on Curtis's screen. Still, it was not sufficient to get an automatic radar lock on such a small and fast moving target. The pilot of the Chinese Pod saw that his first shot did not destroy the spacecraft, and he fired his thrusters to pivot for another shot. Bill Curtis had to make a mental calculation as to where the antagonist would be, leading the almost invisible target on a path that was, at best, an educated guess. Curtis switched the AEGIS Gatling gun to manual and tracked what appeared to be empty space past the point where what was left of the Orion capsule no longer blocked the gun's path. He depressed the trigger, laying down a murderous barrage of fire from a weapon that could spew 4,000 rounds in a minute. The very force of the recoil was causing the *Alliance* to roll in the opposite direction of fire with the ship's automatic thrusters firing to maintain position. Curtis watched the shells vanish into empty space, cursing under his breath for his stupidity at letting the Chinese pilot get off the first shot that nearly killed them all. Finally, as his ammunition counter was nearing zero, the hail of 20-millimeter explosive rounds found their target. An enormous white flash followed by a bright orange fireball bloomed 200 yards off the ship's starboard side.

Lieutenant Curtis let out a whoop, realizing he had nailed his target, but his sense of euphoria evaporated as he looked around the inside of the Salyut at the chaos that the detonation of the Chinese missile had caused. Alarms were wailing, warning of the perilous drop in air pressure as the crew worked like madmen, rushing to each wound in the hull of the former Soviet space station, patching the air leaks with vacu-seal material. Then he fixed his eyes upon his fellow officer, Major Vernon LaBelle, floating motionless near the aft section of the ship, his life's blood forming crimson spheres in zero gravity, making a trail leading to yet another gash in the hull of the station and disappearing out into space.

Bill Curtis grabbed a vacu-seal patch, unbuckled himself, and pushed away with his legs, propelling himself to yet another wound in the Salyut that was open to the vacuum of space, sucking LaBelle's blood and the ship's atmosphere out and into the void. Quickly, he slapped a patch over the two-inch gash. Satisfied that the leak had been plugged, he turned to the severely wounded LaBelle.

"Major … Major LaBelle … Vernon!" Curtis turned the man over to see a deep bloody gash in LaBelle's chest, just below his collarbone.

The dagger-like piece of shrapnel, which had punctured through the hull of the station, was buried in Vernon LaBelle's upper body. As Bill Curtis inspected the wound, the major groaned and opened his eyes. His teeth were clenched, fighting back the pain of the injury.

"Take it easy, Major, you'll be all right. I just gotta stop the bleeding." Curtis looked around to see Jim Garcia closest to the first aid locker. "Garcia! Quick, bring the first aid kit. The major's been hit! We have to stop the bleeding … hurry up. I think he's going into shock!"

Thomas Garcia grabbed a large white box marked with a red cross from the cabinet and pushed off against the side of the station, coming to rest next to the two Air Force officers "How's it look?"

Curtis shook his head in the negative. "Bad … he's really bleeding. It may have hit an artery, I don't know yet but we have to pull the metal out of his chest … *Oh Jesus*, get me a long-nosed set of pliers from the tool kit, and I'll wipe them down with alcohol, then get ready to pack the wound with gauze. And toss me a morphine ampoule. He's in a lot of pain, and I gotta go digging in there for that shard."

"Here, Bill, I'll do it. I've had emergency para-med training."

Garcia grabbed the sterilized pliers while Curtis injected the small morphine cylinder into LaBelle's arm.

Curtis spoke quietly to Tom Garcia. "Do you think he'll live?"

Garcia probed with the long thin set of pliers into the ruined flesh of the major's chest then pulled them away with a three-inch long razor sharp splinter of metal between the blades. Instantly a blob of blood shot from the wound, forming bright red spheres that began drifting about the station. "Yeah, as long as I can stop his bleeding. Now, I'll start packing the wound, and then you can keep pressure on him just to the left of his sternum. If he'd been hit just a little lower, it would have taken out a lung or even his heart. If we can control the bleeding, he'll be okay."

Their breaths were now coming in short deep gasps. Curtis felt as if he was struggling up the side of a 15,000-foot mountain, as the air pressure alarms continued to blare fatal warnings. Garcia continued.

"But if we can't plug all the holes in this Russian tin can, we're all going to be real dead real soon."

With Tom Garcia packing and wrapping the injury, Lieutenant Curtis grabbed three more vacu-seal kits and began locating and patching more of the holes created by the explosion.

* * * *

In the LEM, John McGovern and Natasha Polyakova were already beyond the limb of the Moon, with all radio signals blocked by its curvature. They were both unaware of the drama taking place on the space station just as they were equally unaware of the second black cloaked excursion pod that was rapidly approaching the Lander from the their one o'clock position.

"Downrange 200 kilometers, dropping another ten K ..." Natasha was quietly calling off the figures as the Lander they had christened *Seagull,* flew on a descending course toward the southern lunar ice fields and the rock-strewn lading area just beyond the far side magnetic accelerator. Colonel John McGovern was concentrating on the heads-up display that was almost magically displaying computer graphics of the flight profile directly over the real view of the Moon's landscape seen out the triangular window of the lander.

* * * *

Lieutenant Bao had just turned 23 a day earlier. He was bound tightly to the thin metal seat of the excursion pod. His craft consisted of the forward spherical section, mounted to the fuel and oxidizer tanks that were surrounded by a lightweight aluminum lattice, leading to a small bell-shaped reaction nozzle. The entire craft was less than four meters long, about the size of a small car. Every external component was painted mat black, then sprayed with radar absorbing stealth material. For all intents and purposes, the tiny craft was invisible. This was an attack craft, for mounted to the outside of the sphere were four small, but deadly, one-meter long missiles with explosive tipped charges, powerful enough to turn the 50-year-old LEM into an orbiting cloud of scrap metal.

Bao was above the LEM, looking down on the ungainly "bug" with four outstretched legs covered in reflective gold foil. The lander stood out cleanly with razor sharp features, bathed in the undiluted sunlight of outer space. Lieutenant Bao matched the descending orbit of the LEM with his pod and, with only minor thrust corrections, was in position to fire. He lined up the center of the craft in his improvised sight and closed his finger on the firing button of his control stick.

Natasha Polyakova had been concentrating on the flat LCD display between the two view ports, but as the craft began its slow descent, she took her eyes off the screen for a moment to gaze out at the stars above the lunar horizon. Directly in front of the LEM was the constellation of Orion, one of the most noticeable star groups in the sky, but to Natasha's eyes something was very wrong with the configuration of the stars. Orion's belt and sword were missing as if something directly in front of the LEM was blocking her view. It was puzzling to her, seeing the incomplete constellation, and it reminded her of nights on Earth when an errant cloud would disrupt her view of the heavens, but in space, there were no clouds. So what was blocking the stars? And then it came to her in a flash of insight. "*Bozhye Moi!* John! Port thrusters *now!*"

Bao shielded his eyes from the glare of the missile ignition, but just as he had the lander in the center of his targeting array, it slewed wildly to one side. Cursing loudly, he watched his first shot race past the ungainly craft as a clean miss. He grabbed the stick, firing thrusters to pivot and follow the Lander on a spiral course.

"*Jesus Christ!*" McGovern had the joystick fully over to the right as the lunar surface and the star fields above slid wildly past his observation window. He tried putting some distance between their craft and the attacker. The small but deadly missile had missed the Lander by no more than two meters. "Natasha! You've got a good pair of eyes in that pretty head of yours! Hang on … I'm going to try and shake this bastard, then we're going to take him out!"

McGovern, using both hands to fire the thrusters and the main engine, sent the lander on a wildly gyrating course over the Moon's cratered surface.

"Tasha! Give me our fuel readouts! Let me know when I'm cutting into the reserves. I can't see the son of a bitch and I'm running blind!"

On April 26, 2018, the first dogfight in outer space was taking place. Unlike air-to-air combat in the skies over the Earth, there were no aerodynamic forces in play. Neither spacecraft could bank or turn in what would be seen in conventional flight; rather the LEM and its pursuer moved at sharply defined angles against a star-strewn black sky.

Natasha's eyes scanned the large LCD panel that had replaced the myriad of analog gauges between the two view ports, running her fingers over the touch screens below it, calling up fuel consumption data.

John McGovern again fired the thrusters, doubling back and at a right angle toward where he guessed the attacker was lurking. "Damn, he must be cloaked in stealth foam. I've got nothing on radar, and I can't get a missile lock on him – and I can't see him either. Brace yourself; I'm firing the main engine. I've got to get above him!"

The quick maneuvers caught the Chinese pilot by surprise. *Whoever was at the controls of the lander is a very good pilot,* he thought. Again Lieutenant Bao tried to place the lander in the center of his firing reticle. As before, when his finger hit the firing button, the lander seemed to jump just as his missile raced away to its target, only this time, the proximity-triggered warhead was close enough to the LEM to detonate.

There was no sound in the vacuum of space but the telltale flash reflected off the parts of the LEM visible from the view ports indicated that a missile had detonated very close by. This was followed almost immediately by the rattle of what sounded like hail hitting a tin roof as the exterior of the lander conducted the sounds of shrapnel impacting the underside of the craft. In a heartbeat, alarms inside the LEM began to sound. Before Natasha Polyakova's eyes, ominous red symbols began appearing on her display screen.

"John! We've been hit! I show fuel pressure is dropping in the two outboard tanks and one landing footpad is damaged. I have no idea how badly."

McGovern's mind was racing. If he couldn't get a clear shot at their attacker, the next missile would surely finish them. He had to get above his attacker. The only way to get a visual on his adversary was to climb above him. John fed more fuel and oxidizer into the reaction chamber of the main engine and the sensation of weight returned to both him and Natasha. The LEM shot upward, burning precious fuel, as it was leaked away from the holes the second missile had put into the tanks. With Natasha reading out the dwindling kilograms of fuel left in the tanks, McGovern finally got a visual on his attacker. The jet-black stealth clad pod stood out as a distinct silhouette against the brilliantly lit lunar landscape below. Incredibly, the enemy pod had been turning back toward the LEM in a classic Luffbery circle. While this maneuver was an excellent tactic in level flight, but it left an adversary highly vulnerable to a vertical diving attack.

McGovern killed the main engine and tilted the LEM forward to bring his four modified mini-Patriot missiles to bear on the distinct outline of the Chinese craft below him. Since the radar could not get a lock on his attacker, he had to lead the moving target with his heads-up display and fire a full deflection shot. McGovern's finger pulled twice on the firing button, loosening two missiles. Both closed the gap between the two craft at a vicious rate of speed. The first missile crossed in front of the pod, barely half a meter from its target, but the second projectile slammed into the fuel and oxidizer tanks just behind the main sphere containing the pilot. Instantly, the combined chemical components created a ravenous yellow and orange fireball that ripped apart the aluminum framework that held the craft together, sending the engine bell and the sphere containing the craft's pilot spinning away on a fatal descent to the lunar surface only twenty kilometers below.

"John! We're losing a lot of fuel. Our safety reserve will be gone in moments. You've got to get us down to the surface. *Hurry!*"

McGovern had no time to savor the victory that he had just scored against an enemy determined to kill them both. He had the LEM pitched over, looking straight down at the lunar surface that was mushrooming before his eyes, with Natasha calling out the decreasing fuel numbers. At one kilometer above the surface of the Aitkin Basin, the depression that marked the darkened southern polar area of the Moon, he brought the LEM vertical, flying low and fast toward the rim of a far side crater. McGovern hoped that the crater rim would conceal their descent from Chinese radar. Still, the low fuel alarms wailed.

McGovern had the craft just one hundred meters above the surface with zero linger time left to find a level landing spot. The ground below was strewn with car-sized boulders and deep pockmarks and then ... a disquietingly calm female voice began to speak. "Thirty seconds until engine shut down ... 21 seconds until engine shut down...nine seconds until engine shut down." The LEM was still some 80 feet above the surface when ... "Three, two, one ... engine shutdown."

The feeling of weightlessness again returned as the lander suddenly plummeted toward the surface. In desperation, McGovern fired the lander's thrusters, trying to lessen the impact of the fall. "*Tasha!* Brace yourself for impact!"

The LEM came down hard and at a slight angle, slamming into the lunar surface and destroying the descent engine bell on a large rounded boulder. The lander toppled backward with the damaged landing leg bending and then snapping off at the extension joint. Inside the craft, the sound of tortured metal screamed as the landing leg ripped away, and with Cosmonaut Polyakova and Colonel McGovern in their standing positions, they tumbling backward against the storage lockers and the circuit breaker panels. Natasha held her breath, waiting for the telltale whistling of their air rushing out a gash in the cabin. Hearing none, she turned to John McGovern, who had a cut on his forehead from striking the edge of a metal cabinet. The LEM was on its back within the deep black shadow cast by the crater wall. The only illumination inside the cabin was the emergency lights, bathing the two pilots in a lurid red glow.

McGovern pressed his hand against the side of his head. It came away wet, followed by a sharp pain. "Natasha, are you okay?"

"Yes, I am unhurt. I don't think we are losing cabin pressure, but I think I can smell burned insulation." She turned to look at McGovern and could see him holding his head. "Oh, John, you're hurt!"

"It's fine, Natasha. Just hand me a rag. I'll be okay. Let's get our helmets on and get the hell out of here. I know the Chinese didn't get an exact fix on us, but they must have a pretty good idea where we came down. This area is going to be crawling with them pretty soon. We'd better see if the hatch will open."

Natasha sat up and grabbed her excursion pack and helmet. At that moment, the shock at what had just transpired overcame her like a fast moving wave. She dropped her EVA pack and helmet and seemed to stare straight ahead into the darkness. John pulled himself up and put his arm around her shoulders as she began to shake, and then start to sob.

"John, we are going to die here, aren't we? Here on the far side of the Moon, in the freezing darkness. I can't … I can't … breathe. I wanted us to have a life together. Instead, everything ends here!"

John McGovern pulled Natasha closer to him. She was feather light in the one-sixth gravity of the Moon. He looked into her tear-streaked eyes, for a moment not seeing the trained space pilot but the small girl who had once played cosmonaut next to the very same Salyut space station that they had traveled to the Moon in – the one that once sat outside a Moscow Hotel. Even in the deep red glow of the emergency lighting, her features were beautiful. Her long hair falling to her shoulders, full and sensual lips, she was one of the most beautiful women McGovern had ever seen. However, now he had to bring her out of the grip of a growing sense of panic. He held her close to his body and gently kissed her, stroking her hair.

"Natasha, remember your Russian spirit. The father of your space program, Sergei Korolev, always said there's no such thing as an unsolvable problem. We survived an attack in Earth orbit. We made it to the Moon. Then we engaged an enemy ship and destroyed it. We put the lander down in pretty much one piece. At least we still have some power and life support left. We're not dead yet! We can make it to the accelerator, and if we have to, we'll shoot and kill those men there. I'm certain they must have supplies as well as extra air packs. I didn't come this far to die on the far side of the Moon and neither did you. We're going to get through this and get back to Earth alive. Do you believe me?"

Natasha looked up into John's eyes. They held courage as well as the truth. She should see and feel this was not bravado or some act for her benefit; he really did believe they would get out of this alive. She felt her sense of panic begin to ebb and a calmness start to fill her being.

"Oh John, I'm sorry. It was just so much, so fast. The attack, and our crash landing. Yes … I believe you. We will survive and we shall live for each other. I'll get out the rifles then I'll help you into your suit-pack. You need to close my seals and we will depressurize. I'll hurry and … I love you … very much"

"Not so fast, angel. We can't afford a suit failure. Once we're out, we only have about four hours of air, three if we're really exerting ourselves. I'm pretty sure we came down pretty close to the accelerator, maybe an hour's walk or less. We'll get going as soon as our suits check out green."

Natasha was looking up at the still functioning LCD display panel. "John, it appears as if we can re-pressurize the cabin, but only once. One of the reserve air tanks must have been damaged in the attack or when we crashed."

"Landed, Natasha, not crashed, because we have a saying; any landing you can walk away from is a good one. Listen, with the LEM in this position there's no way I can use the antenna to contact the *Alliance*. We can try with our suit radios, but I'm afraid we may be below the horizon in relation to their orbit."

With the lunar module lying on its back, John McGovern piled the lightweight aluminum cases containing food stores on top of each other then checked the exit hatch. According to the indicator lights, the hatch appeared to be undamaged and would open.

"Come on, Natasha, close my last suit seal and I'll start the depressurization, okay?"

CHAPTER NINETEEN

Beijing China, Vice Premier Sung Zhao's private chamber

"*Traitors!* It would seem, Fong, that we are surrounded by traitors! I have seen the reports from some of the demonstrations in the provinces as well as Beijing's own mayor standing in front of a tank column. And … I see from General Wang's transmission that those with treasonous goals are not limited just to the surface of the Earth."

It was a very disconcerting feeling, now to be addressing his former subordinate as his superior. Intelligence Director Fong Kim Hua began cautiously, suspecting that his former Director of Space Intelligence was beginning to lose his grip on the reality of the situation. He spoke carefully and deliberately, choosing his words to avoid a jail cell or worse, a nine-millimeter bullet to the back of his head if he were accused of treason.

"Vice Premier … Zhao, as Director of Intelligence, I am well aware of the situation in the provinces. The fact that these demonstrations are occurring points to the fact that information from the West about your and Vice Premier Gao's ascent to the leadership of China is not being greeted with absolute approval. This occurrence of disloyalty on the Moon is troubling as well. Major Yuan is a highly decorated officer and astronaut. It begs the question as to our course of action … *sir.*" The final word "sir" seemed to stick in the director's throat.

"Explain yourself, Fong, but be aware you are no longer *my* superior officer."

"Yes … ah, *sir.* We … chart a dangerous course. I recall our discussions when our positions were reversed. You had confidence that we could subjugate the West and the Russians before they were even aware of our actions. Now we have placed China at great risk." Director Fong was very careful not to say, "*you* have placed us at great risk," for fear of his life. He continued. "The Americans have their entire ICBM force at DEFCON 1, as do the Russians. Their missile firing submarines are deployed and hidden beneath the waves, and NATO, American and Russian nuclear armed bombers prowl the skies, just beyond our airspace."

Sung Zhao turned a cold eye toward his former superior. "I have ordered the moon base to commence launching the nuclear packages immediately, after the traitors have been rounded up. The devices will arrive in Earth orbit in a little over two days from now. Then we shall issue our ultimatum."

"But what if the Russians, the Europeans and the Americans retaliate or even attack us? What shall we do?"

"*Do,* Fong? *We shall do nothing!* We, and the entire Central Committee, are almost a kilometer below the ground. No matter what our enemies attack us with, we start with 1.5 billion Chinese! Even if they kill three quarters of our population, we will far outnumber their survivors. Our military has planned for this possibility for decades, as you well know. We have resources for the support and reindustrialization of a total population of 20 to 25 percent of those currently alive today. We will be in a far better position to rule the planet after an all-out war then even today. Most of our population is composed of ignorant, filthy peasants, either that or weak-minded businessmen, blinded by the lure of gold and profits from accommodating the West, bowing to them like servants, becoming their manufacturing shops. Their insignificant slanted-eyed slaves, scurrying about to please their Western masters. They disgust me! The new China will arise from the ashes with far more population than all the nations of the world combined once we unleash our devastating first strike! Then we shall retrain and re-educate our survivors. China will be the most powerful all-encompassing power on the face of the Earth.

Finally, we shall fulfill the destiny of the Chin, the Ming and the Han. China will rule the world!"

This was one of the very few times in his life that Fong Hua felt the cold dagger of fear penetrate his soul. Vice Premier Zhao had risen from his chair during his tirade and was now standing behind of his ornate ivory-adorned desk, pounding both his fists on the work surface in a fervent rage, his ruined face twisted into what could only be called a snarl. Fong realized for the first time that he was not confronting a Chinese zealot but a madman.

He had just finished bowing to Zhao and was about to walk to the operations section of the bunker when the vice premier's telephone rang. Fong Kim Hua watched cautiously from the exit as Sung Zhao's face contorted into paroxysm rage. He pulled the telephone away from his ear, slamming it with such force against his desk that the receiver broke in half. Then his eyes met those of the intelligence director. "Fong, get back in here, *damn you!* You must stop the American She-Devil's broadcast immediately! Do you hear me – *immediately!* Shut it down … *now!*"

Cordelier Price, America's first woman president, had met a day earlier with the owners and executives of almost every major media outlet in the United States to ask for their complete cooperation with the night's broadcast. At the emergency conference, it was requested that any dissenting views by commentators be held in check for a united effort to head off a potential catastrophe beyond imagination. While everyone in the White House conference room was well aware of the gravity of the crisis with China, none of the participants had any clue about China's intention to launch nuclear weapons toward the Earth from their lunar base. All sat listening to the president speak while the icy seeds of fear began to grow in the pits of their stomachs. The world was one-step away from a nuclear holocaust that had the possibility to consume billions of human beings with even the possibility of ending the reign of the humanity upon the planet … unless … unless the potential for dissent in China could be unleashed.

The plan was an address carried live on American television to coincide with addresses by Russia and the EU that would be not only for their home country's citizens but also translated into Mandarin Chinese then beamed with powerful transmitters, overwhelming and supplanting normal broadcasts in China. At the same time, the World Wide Web would carry the news and information directed at the citizens of China, telling them the leadership, which had removed their leader and replaced him with former Vice Premier Gao, was about to plunge the world into a nuclear war that would most certainly claim the lives of four out of every five Chinese, leaving their cities and their entire nation in ruins.

At that very moment, Vice Premier Sung Zhao was pounding his fists upon his desk, demanding the invading transmissions be silenced, President Price was nearly finished with her speech.

"… And today, at this very moment, the skies just beyond the borders of the People's Republic of China are filled with the aircraft of many nations, armed with nuclear weapons. The navies and strategic missile forces of five nations are holding at their final launch points to commence a war that will not only devastate China but many parts of the planet as well. And … where are the leaders of China? The ones who, three days ago, replaced the rational leadership of your nation with the unthinkable insanity of nuclear war? While, they are hiding deep below ground, prepared to live in luxury, awaiting the skies to clear and the radiation levels to drop, over a billion Chinese men, women and children will die on the surface. Oh yes, they will tell you they can win this war. They will restore and rebuild China when they are victorious, but how shall this be done? It will be done upon the blackened bones of your wives, of your husbands, of your parents, and of your children. Your so-called *leaders,* who have illegally seized power, will lead you all into the grave to achieve their twisted goals. We say in a collective voice, rise up! Rise up and save your nation and yourselves. Restore to power your rational leaders and stop these madmen's march to Armageddon. We speak as one voice – America, Russia and Europe.

We speak as one voice, the nations of Africa, Asia and South America. You, the Chinese people, have the power, have the strength in numbers, to rise up and turn your nation away from the abyss that those who seized power are about to hurl you into for their own selfish motives."

Fong Hua had switched on the nearly two-meter wide television screen in Sung Zhao's chamber. The American President's speech was on every channel. Her image was not entirely clear as it was overwhelming local and national Chinese broadcasts – still seen were the ghost images of the domestic broadcast signal in the background – but the translated speech of Cordelier Price was strong and audible over each channel. As she finished her words, her image was replaced by that of Russian President Victor Simonov, again repeating much of what Price had said and again translated into Chinese. Fong quickly placed a call to the Minister of Communication for the PRC. He picked up on the second ring, his voice was on the edge of panic for there was nothing he could do to stop the broadcasts. No, honorable director … I cannot stop it. We have tried to overwhelm and jam their transmission but they are using tremendous broadcast power. I believe that off the coasts, American, NATO and Russian ships are transmitting in the 500,000 watt rage as well as beaming their signals in from space. There is nothing, nothing in my power that can stop them, except for smashing every television in every home in China!"

Fong hung up the phone and turned his attention to the Russian's speech. Somewhere, perhaps deep within his subconscious mind, an idea began to stir. An inner voice that began as a whisper was building to a scream that he must choose to either stand with men of reason or be dragged down into the pit of hell with madmen who would consign more than a billion Chinese to their deaths to achieve their ends.

The thoughts that began to grow and take hold in Fong's mind vanished in an explosion of plastic and glass as the enraged Sung Zhao hurled a heavy brass paperweight through the plasma screen. With fury in his eyes, he addressed his intelligence director.

"*Get out!* Get out of my chambers now, Fong! Get on with your duty *now*! I *order* you to send in the army! Quell these growing demonstrations! I want tanks on the streets. I want my generals informed that they are to order their men to fire on any dissidents. No exceptions! Do you hear me? *Do you?!*"

As Fong Hua exited the Vice Premier's chambers, propelled out the door by the ranting and screams of a man on the edge of madness, the idea that had begun to bloom was still there in his thoughts and still growing. Somehow, Fong, a committed and loyal Chinese Intelligence Office, had to find a way to stop this headlong march into the jaws of the abyss.

* * * *

"All right! Everyone get into your O2 packs now! Suit up!" Lieutenant William Curtis's voice was becoming ever more attenuated in the rapidly thinning air.

Jack Griffin was still ripping off insulation and removing panels, searching for the additional wounds to the Salyut that were bleeding out precious breathable air. He turned and yelled back to Curtis, his own breathing becoming ever more difficult as the air pressure continued to drop. "The major's too badly hurt to get into a suit. Even if you have him on oxygen, if we're in a hard vacuum, he'll die anyway. His lungs will burst. We've got to try and find the last of the air leaks …" The Canadian stopped in mid–sentence, watching the trains of red globules, the blood trail from Vernon LaBelle's hemorrhaging wound floating past his face and down the leg of the centrally located table. "Hey ... Hey! I think I found it! I couldn't see it before. The table was blocking my line of sight. Quick Tom, get two packs of vacu-seal and we'll jam them in around the table leg!"

Tom Garcia pushed hard with his legs on against the rear bulkhead of the ship, nearly overshooting the table. He ripped open both packs and he and Jack Griffin began stuffing the putty-like material into the last of the leaks in the hull. The low air pressure alarms were still wailing but the needles that had indicated the fatal plunge in cabin pressure had finally stabilized.

Tom Garcia yelled over to Remmy LaCasse. "Okay, open the valves. We can re-pressurize the ship now. We've got all the holes plugged."

As the crisis ebbed, Tom Garcia and the others looked about the inside of the Salyut at the carnage inflicted by the Chinese missile. Panels and containers, insulation and wiring were floating everywhere. The lighting had been cut in half due to the drop in power caused by the loss of the upper solar panel and Major LeBelle, just regaining consciousness, was being wrapped like a mummy in bandages and placed into a webbed sleeping bag that was Velcroed to the wall of the space station. Jack Griffin shook his head, considering that all four of them had just narrowly escaped death, and then turned to Tom Garcia. "I sure as hell hope that John and Natasha are having an easier time down there we are right now."

* * * *

John McGovern had been very careful in exiting the ruined LEM in the dark, taking pains to push himself away from any of the sharp metal projections rising up at vertical angles from the lander. The last hurdle was a nine-foot drop over one of the holed fuel tanks and down to the surface. McGovern fell in slow motion, his treaded boots making deep groves in the lunar soil as he hit the surface. He turned to look up at the access hatch, now pointing to the stars instead of the horizon and at Natasha Polyakova pushing herself up to a sitting position atop the LEM.

"Here, John, take the rifles. I've loaded them with 30-round clips."

Next, she tossed a light gray shoulder bag down to him that contained several bricks of Semtex plastic explosive and detonator caps. Natasha, like Colonel McGovern, carefully picked her way down the outside of the lander with McGovern grabbing her legs, pulling her free of a jagged spar that had torn loose from one of the lander's legs.

Once Natasha was firmly down on the lunar surface, McGovern flashed his suit's light over the LEM. The rearmost landing leg had been twisted and was bent skyward; the support brace's completely torn away gold Mylar foil was lying about everywhere. One of the side fuel tanks for the descent engine was torn open, and the engine bell had been crushed after striking a bolder the size of a Volkswagen by the much higher than normal landing speed. He turned to Natasha, speaking over the short range suit radio. "What a mess! We've damn lucky the oxidizer tank didn't rupture as well, or we'd have been blown to bits."

Where the lander had toppled over on its back, an ascent stage fuel tank had a rip in the side of it that was boiling and bubbling rocket fuel that vaporized and disbursed in the hard vacuum of the Moon. Brilliant, unfiltered sunlight reflected off of the crater walls in the distance that climbed into the black star-studded sky. Some of that light helped dispel the pitch-blackness that blanketed the shallow crater where they had landed. One prominent feature in the sky was missing – the Earth. The LEM had passed beyond the horizon that divided the near and far side of the Moon. Now that brilliant white and blue bauble, home to over 7 billion human beings, was beyond reach. Unless Colonel John McGovern and Captain Natasha Polyakova could complete their mission and somehow return to the *Alliance* before their air supply was exhausted, they would both die on the barren boulder-strewn plains of the far side of the Moon. Their only hope lay with the second LEM that, unknown to both of them, had received major damage from the first missile attack.

Turning away from the wreckage of their landing craft, John and Natasha shouldered their rifles and began walking in short hops in the direction of the Chinese magnetic accelerator. Two hundred forty thousand miles from the pock marked lunar surface, other life and death dramas were beginning to play out.

* * * *

The telephone buzzed by her head on the nightstand next to her side of the bed. Cordelier Price had only gotten to bed two hours earlier. Now, as she looked over at the red LED numerals of her clock, she could see it was just –3:20 in the morning. She turned to her husband, Derek, who was also now awake. The "First Gentleman," Derek Price, was a brilliant neurosurgeon. However, with the crisis in full bloom and the ever-present possibility that his wife, the President of the United States, and her family, along with her cabinet and the Joint Chiefs, could be whisked away at any moment to a secure underground bunker meant that Dr. Derek Price was staying close to home. His wife sat up on the side of the bed, hesitating to reach for the telephone. "Derek, at this hour, it can't be good news."

He looked at his wife in the low lighting of their White House bedroom. The softness of her face that she awoke with was suddenly filled with tension. She quickly got out of bed and put on a long-sleeved sweater and a pair of dark blue slacks.

"Derek, I know this a stupid thing to say, but try and go back to sleep. I've got to go to the situation room."

"Bad news?"

"Not good, our spacecraft's been fired upon and nearly destroyed and we have reports of fighting on the border of China and Russia. Two B-52s have been shot down over international airspace as well. This is getting extremely dangerous. I'll see you when I can. Stay close with the kids and our grandchildren. They may evacuate us to the bunker at a moment's notice."

If Derek Price had any sleep left in his body, it was certainly gone now, as he watched his wife walk out of the bedroom and into the teeth of the growing maelstrom.

When President Price entered the situation room, all stood up as a sign of respect. She reached over for her coffee cup, full of the steaming caffeine rich liquid, before she spoke.

"Please, this is not the time for formalities. Everyone sit down and let's put our heads together on the information we're getting. I want to avoid any groupthink decision that could be disastrous. "Jim," she said, turning to Admiral Warner, "what's the situation? I understand that our Moon ship's been attacked. How bad is it?"

"We have radio contact with the crew. A small Chinese spacecraft attacked the *Alliance*, considerable damage and wounding one man. They destroyed the attacking craft, but the second lander was seriously damaged. The *Alliance* was hit pretty badly as well, but she's still flying, and the crew compartments are all intact.

Price nodded then asked, "How about the lander that left for the surface? The one Colonel McGovern was piloting, any news yet?"

"No, sorry, Ma'am. Once they passed beyond the far side horizon, nothing can be heard from them by Earth receivers, but what's troubling is that the *Alliance* can't pick them up either. They may have been shot down as well … We just don't know yet."

Cordelier Price rubbed her arms as if a sudden chill had overcome her. "What about our B-52s?"

"A flight off the coast of Ningbo, China, was jumped by their J-10 fighters. Two B-52s went down in the East China Sea. They were each carrying nuclear-armed cruise missiles. F-15s out of Okinawa engaged the Chinese fighters and shot down six of them. The other four B-52s are still on station. We did manage to pick up a few survivors."

As the admiral finished his last sentence, the red telephone in front of him buzzed. He picked it up and a look of concern followed by shock as the color drained from his face. "There's been a nuclear detonation. A small one, maybe two to three kilotons. A large Chinese force of tanks and infantry apparently made an advance across the border near Khabarovosk. Russian forces fired what we think was a nuclear artillery shell or perhaps a mortar shell at the advancing force. We know it wasn't a missile. Anyway, it detonated over the columns of tanks and troops. They report very heavy casualties with many Chinese soldiers dying in droves. The Russians haven't confirmed it, but we certainly suspect it was some kind of enhanced radiation weapon, like a neutron bomb."

Cordelier Price rested her elbows on the conference table and cupped her hands around her face, rubbing her temples. "Good Lord, Jim, a first use of a nuclear weapon since 1945? I've got to speak to Simonov right away. If we let this genie out of the bottle, we're never going to get it back in again, and then there'll be real hell to pay. Tell me, is there any good news coming from this? Did my speech have any impact or effect?"

"Sorry, Ma'am, I was just getting to that before this very serious piece of news came in. Yes, it is having some real effect and that sudden attack across the Russian border may be a part of it. We have reports of mass confusion and fighting breaking out within Chinese army divisions. Tanks firing on tanks, and there's general chaos taking place. In the cities, there are huge protests going on. In Shenyang, soldiers have joined the mass demonstration, using their tanks to protect the protesters instead of intimidating them. It's bad in Baotou, however. A crack PLA division fired on a crowd of about 200,000; a lot of innocent people died. We have reports in Beijing of their mayor and the province's governor standing together on a stalled tank addressing a crowd of close to a million people. The leadership that seized power, however, is not to be found. We're sure they're in a nuke-proof bunker directing operations. Our only hope is to keep up the pressure and pray that no one does anything really stupid. We also have to pray our Moon mission succeeds as well. If they can place nuclear strike packages over our major cities and we can't track them or even know if they're there or not … then we have big, big trouble. The Chinese could force us into a very unfavorable position of surrender."

"Well, Jim, at least that's some good news in all of this. If the Chinese people and segments of their army are rising up against the coup leaders, then we might have a chance."

Admiral Warner still looked very uneasy. "I have to tell you, Ma'am, that if the Chinese people cannot halt this march to Armageddon, then we have a very grave choice to make. Those nukes fired from the Moon are an unacceptable option. If they have been fired, they'll arrive in Earth orbit in a little more than two and half days. We may have to order an all-out first strike against China before that happens."

To Cordelier Price, it felt as if the temperature in the room had just dropped 20 degrees.

* * * *

Natasha Polyakova and John McGovern had been walking across the 4 billion-year-old boulder-strewn surface of the Moon for close to 45 minutes when they came to the demarcation line between light and shadow. Just beyond the next hill, they could see the unfiltered sunlight glinting off the track of the far side magnetic accelerator. Slowly they advanced, couching low to keep out of sight.

Unlike like the lunar exploration suits of the Apollo era, the ones they wore were light and form-fitting. They were also a mottled grayish tan camouflage to blend into the colors of the rock and lunar soil. These moon suits were for combat. Both pilots carried the special Colt vacuum rifles, and both were ready to fight and kill the enemy. This was now a matter of survival, not just for John and Natasha, but very possibly the entire human race.

McGovern crawled to the crest of the hill on his hands and knees, the sticky gray lunar dust coating parts of his suit. He activated the long-range camera built into his helmet. This projected an image on the inside of his faceplate, much in the manner of a virtual reality display. He lay motionless watching the scene in front of him unfold then, after about five minutes, he climbed back down and behind the boulder concealing Natasha. Once he was within 10 feet of her, he could communicate over the short-range radio transmitter.

"Tasha, I'm not sure I understand what's going on out there. I can see seven men all together, but they don't seem to be all playing on the same side. Two of them are being held at gunpoint. They appear to be prisoners. One of them looks like he's a high-ranking officer. There seems to be another officer and one enlisted man guarding them. The other three are loading the sleds for the magnetic accelerator."

"John, let me see for myself. Maybe we can figure out what is happening here." Then a thought came to her. "Do you suppose there is some sort of mutiny or rebellion within their ranks?"

"Maybe, it sure looks that way. Come on, let's get a better look. If that's what's happening, we just might stand a good chance of stopping this thing, but first we have to figure out who's who and what side they're on."

Kang Lu eyed his prisoners with contempt; however his disgust for Major Yuan was far greater than the corporal he held at gunpoint. In his mind, Yuan, who had risen through the ranks of the People's Liberation Army, had betrayed everything that the Chinese Communist Party stood for. Kang was a political officer. His duty, like those of his counterparts that severed aboard the submarines, fleet boats, army bases and air bases, consisted of constant reinforcement of the mission and goals of the Party and to keep political thought pure and uncorrupted from counterrevolutionary ideas. Major Yuan's motivations for his actions would mean nothing to this man. To Kang, Major Yuan and the corporal were vile cockroaches that had invaded the purity of correct political thought. The fact that China was about to throw perhaps 80 percent or more of the world's population into a nuclear grave meant nothing to him. Kang would be marching straight off that very abyss with banners flying and trumpets blaring.

Kang Lu activated his transmitter and spoke to Major Yuan. "Yuan, I would like you to know something before you die out here beneath the unforgiving stars. Your nephew's treasonous thoughts and deeds have been discovered thanks to Private Kuo. He has been placed under arrest at the base. His sentence, along with yours and Corporal Wu's, is death for treason against the government of the People's Republic of China. As soon as we have finished undoing your attempted sabotage, I will personally execute you."

Major Yuan's face was hidden by his helmet's visor so Kang Lu could not see him shaking his head in despair, but he felt that if he was a doomed man, at least he should finally speak his mind. "Kang, you are a fool, a puppet who dances at the will of insane masters. Do you actually think a single thought for yourself? Do you imagine, in your wildest fantasies, in that tiny brain of yours, that the West and the Russians will simply lay down their arms and bow like humble servants to the will of China? They will not! They will fight and lay waste to our nation and our people. Your so-called *leaders* are marching the world toward oblivion, and here you stand, like some sort of brainless robot, obeying their every word, never questioning the lies you have been fed. Kang Lu, you are a mindless idiot!"

Major Yuan and the corporal were on their knees. The political officer, enraged by the major's comments, leaned back and kicked him with all of his might. This action in the gravity field of Earth would have had the predictable effect of imparting a rib breaking impact to the major, but on the Moon in one-sixth gravity, the political officer only weighed 30 pounds and the force of his muscles resulted in an equal and opposite reaction, sending the man flying up and backwards for eight feet.

Laying motionless and unobserved 100 meters away, John McGovern and Natasha Polyakova observed the entire spectacle. The corporal, seizing his chance, kicked viciously at the other guard, knocking him down in the lunar dust. As he fought desperately for the man's rifle, Major Yuan lunged for the political officer, hitting him solidly in the chest but the man had obvious martial arts training and shot backwards and away from Yuan, scooping up the rifle he had dropped when the major lashed out at him. Yuan saw him bring the gun up to a firing position, but it was not aimed at him. Corporal Wu had managed to wrestle the rifle away from the second guard and swung about to bring it to bear on Kang but he was just not fast enough.

John and Natasha saw the flash of the rifle's discharge and at the same instant saw the second prisoner's faceplate explode outward with the force of a catastrophic decompression. He tumbled backwards, with his now lifeless arms flailing uselessly in the low gravity, a crimson fog along with bits of the ruined helmet sprayed out as he sailed over the surface, finally collapsing like a deflated balloon, a good 15 feet from where he was shot. The political officer then turned his rifle on the major.

"That is how traitors die! And now it's your turn!"

Kang Lu aimed his weapon at the crouching man. Yuan saw his pressure gloved finger begin to close on the over-sized trigger. Just as he was about to turn his head away, the political officer stopped and let go of the weapon. In the same instant, the man seemed to shoot sideways, and his suit exploded outward on one side as he was rocketed a short distance by the force of the impact of a high velocity bullet.

Natasha Polyakova lay quietly for a moment, the targeting reticle showing the cross hairs in her helmet display still aimed at where the political officer had stood. This was not a paper target. She had taken a life. She closed her eyes for a moment, fighting back feelings of nausea and then took a deep breath. John McGovern was staring at her.

"You were correct, John. I was monitoring their radio transmissions. I know a little Chinese. I could understand the worlds *die* and *traitor*. I had to act. If this man is on our side, we may have a chance."

McGovern pulled himself up and over the boulder that had concealed them. "Let's hurry. I can't see the others. They went behind the accelerator. Come on, let's go!"

Both of them pushed hard and shot over the boulder, arcing out nearly 20 feet in the low lunar gravity. They hit the ground running and hopping as fast as they could over to the stunned Chinese major. The guard, who had been knocked to the ground, quickly retrieved his weapon from the dead corporal's hands and swung it toward the two rapidly approaching figures. McGovern's boots dug into the lunar soil and he dropped to one knee, firing as he went down. The bullets ripped into the guard's body, shredding his spacesuit and knocking him backward a good 15 feet. Then both of them came to a halt directly in front of the stunned Chinese officer.

Major Yuan, having just been pulled back from the grasp of death, looked up at the two unfamiliar moon-suited individuals. He could see on one the flag of the United States and the other had the tri-color of the Russian Federation. He sat still while one of them quickly adjusted a radio frequency dial in the front of his moon suit. Yuan was surprised when the figure spoke to him in badly accented and halting Chinese and even more so to hear a woman's voice!

Yuan replied in English. "You are from the coalition, yes? I speak no Russian, but I can speak English. Thank you … for saving my life." Yuan looked over to the lifeless body of his corporal. "He was a good man. He died bravely."

Natasha reached over to John's transmitter and matched the frequency to that of the Chinese major. "I'm Colonel McGovern, United States Air Force. This is Captain Polyakova, Russian Aerospace Force. Where are the others?"

"They are at the accelerator launch controls. This is good. My transmitter is not short range, but the intense electromagnetic field of the accelerator is blocking my transmission. Quickly! They are preparing to launch stealth nuclear strike packages into Earth orbit!"

As Major Yuan finished his sentence, a flash of light caught the eyes of all three of them as the slanting rays of the sun reflected off the bright metal of the acceleration sleds as they shot down the metal track and began curving into space. Each sled held three beach ball-sized spheres with tiny rocket motors attached. The spherical devices were covered with inky black foam, radar-absorbing stealth material. In all, nine orbital nuclear weapons had been fired earthward.

The major turned to John and Natasha. "Quickly! We only have about a minute before they recharge the systems and dispatch more bombs. We have over 80 weapons at the site."

Then Yuan reached over to the body of the political officer and grabbed his rank insignia, pulling it free from the Velcro that held it to the dead man's suit. "I may have use for this. Come, let us go."

The three space-suited figures moved quickly, keeping within the shadow of the magnetic accelerator track. When they got within 50 meters from the power station, they could see that three more sleds had been loaded with cargos of death and one of the Chinese technicians was reaching for the launch switch. Quickly, Natasha checked her fiber optic cable connection from the rifle to her suit. She thumbed a switch and a virtual targeting reticle appeared to be floating in front of her faceplate. She put the launch panel in the center of her electronic cross hairs and fired.

Technician Chung's hand was less than an inch from the firing switch when the panel silently exploded in a shower of sparks. All three men turned, staring open-mouthed at the major and the two others in their dirty gray camouflaged moon suits. With the power shut down, the three could finally hear their former commanding officer's voice. "Drop your weapons and put your hands up. Do it right now!"

Two of them carefully removed their weapons from over their shoulders, but the political officer's security man pulled a small caliber pistol from a Velcro patch on the back of his suit and fired. Both McGovern and Yuan heard Natasha scream over her suit radio as she spun around, trying to maintain her balance. Horrified, McGovern brought the barrel of his vacuum rifle level and fired three times, hitting the security man directly in the chest. He looked like a deflating balloon, his pressure suit collapsing, spraying out a mist of blood that vaporized in the lunar vacuum. The impact of the bullets threw the man backward, and he somersaulted end over end before crumpling like a pile of rags in a shallow crater.

McGovern didn't even watch him long enough to hit the ground. Instead, he rushed over to Natasha's side, but the Chinese major had already wrapped his hands around the arm of her suit, trying to stem the air leak.

"Colonel, she appears to be unhurt, but the bullet pierced her suit," Yuan said. "Quickly, reach into that pouch on the thigh of my suit. I have a patch kit that will stop the leak."

While McGovern dug into the pouch and handed the major the kit, Private Kuo, who had betrayed Yuan and his nephew, sprinted like a madman for one of the two hoppers, a short distance away. The other man, a technician, stood still, rooted to the ground in fear. Yuan had just finished applying the sealant and the patch when the rocket motor of the hopper came to life, blasting Private Kuo into the black sky, heading back to the moon base.

Yuan screamed over his suit radio, "We must stop him. The relay satellite is out of range but if he gets above the mountains, he can transmit to the base."

Still shaken from being nearly killed, Natasha Polyakova sighted her rifle on the rapidly diminishing craft. Her target was the main turbo pump between the oxidizer and the fuel tanks. Natasha could shoot and kill the man but if Kuo had set the autopilot, the hopper would continue on, carrying his dead body, to finally touch down at the Chinese base. She squeezed off a shot, and the pump exploded in a shower of flames as the two hypergolic liquids reacted catastrophically. The hopper was nearly a kilometer high and the force of the explosion blew it in half. The forward section with Private Kuo at the controls tumbled end over end before smashing down onto the lunar surface in a huge cloud of dust. Even in the reduced gravity of the Moon, the fall from that altitude was not survivable.

Yuan turned to his two saviors. "Quickly, gather up the weapons. I have a plan, but you must promise me that you will help. My nephew is a prisoner on the base and set to be executed for treason. You must help me free him."

McGovern nodded his head. "Yes, of course, we'll help but what about this one? We can't really take him as a prisoner. We can't leave him here or radio your base once your relay satellite passes overhead again, and I'm sure as hell not going to execute an unarmed man."

Yuan thought for a moment. "Yes, I understand. That is not something an American would do. For us, it is far too easy to kill without remorse. Let me talk to this man. Perhaps I can persuade him to join us."

John and Natasha watched the two men in conversation. McGovern couldn't understand a thing.

"Colonel, he is not convinced," Yuan said. "This man believes the plan to subjugate yours and the Russian captain's countries will succeed."

McGovern walked over to the Major. "Translate this for me. I assume this man is not fluent in English?"

"You are correct Colonel, he is not."

"Okay then … Technician, why do you think we showed up at your magnetic accelerator? Because we know what your plans are. While you've been up here on the Moon, we and the Russians have been rounding up all of your agents and behind the scenes supporters and we know all about the orbital bombs. Our mission was to destroy the accelerator before the bombs could be launched, but we crash-landed and lost communication with the space station. Maybe they think we're dead. If that's the case, the USA and Russia and the EU cannot take a chance that you'll succeed. It takes a little over two days for your stealth bombs to reach Earth. Our governments will not take that risk. Before your bombs can reach orbit, an all-out first strike will be launched. The targets will be all military and command and control assets in China. Your country will be devastated. Your death toll will be in the hundreds of millions. Now, you can either believe me and help us stop this insanity or you consign millions of your countrymen and, yes, innocent women and children, to nuclear fire because of a few power-crazed men who are sitting safely hundreds of feet below ground, trying to enforce their warped will upon the world. Is that who your loyalty is to?"

Major Yuan paused in his translation and turned to look at McGovern. "This is true what you say? Are you being honest with me Colonel?"

"I'm afraid so. If I know my president as well as I think I do, and the military officers in charge, they'll wait as long as possible before issuing an order for a first strike but not beyond two days from now. However, I'm not so sure of the Russians. They may be pushing hard for an immediate attack. In case you haven't heard, broadcasts were made directly to the Chinese people about just how grave a danger the men who overthrew your government have placed them in. Just before we started our descent, we heard reports of considerable unrest in China. We're hoping that your people will force a halt to this insanity."

"Then, Colonel, we must hurry. I truly believe this young technician wants to return to his family and see them alive instead of numbered among the millions of the dead. Come, let us get aboard the other hopper. You will have to trust me. My plan requires that you give me your weapons. Is that agreed?"

McGovern spoke to Natasha on a private channel then switched back to the Chinese frequency. "All right, major. We'll trust you. Let's go."

As the major was walking over to the hopper, he reached across to his left shoulder and tore off his rank insignia, then quickly replaced it with the one he had taken off the dead political officer.

CHAPTER TWENTY

Beijing, China

Fong Kim Hua, director of Chinese Intelligence, sat at his desk debating the orders he had been given to turn the army loose on the growing sea of demonstrators. He checked again on his computer screen to review the images from China's surveillance satellites. The information was ominous. U.S. and Russian air force bases were empty of bombers; all were in the air, loaded with nuclear weapons. No ballistic missile submarines remained in Russian, European or American ports. They had been dispatched to their undersea firing positions and no surface activity could be seen in the American missile fields in Minot or Malmstrom, North Dakota. The sites were locked down with their missile crews ready to fire hundreds of ICBMs at his country.

Quickly, Fong called to his subordinate. "Get my car and have a driver take me to the prison, immediately."

* * * *

President Cordelier Price had managed to get a few hours of fitful sleep, but she was awakened by a nightmare vision of hundreds of nuclear detonations across the globe. She sat up in bed, heart racing and breathing heavily. Her husband, Derek, reached over to comfort her, but even his gentle touch failed to give her a sense of peace. She quickly reached for the telephone by her bed and called to her secretary of state. Then, she got up and hurriedly dressed.

Her husband looked over at her with anxious eyes. "Any news, Cordelier?"

"No, nothing that I can say that's positive … except my speech and

Simonov's seem to be having some effect in China. There are reports of massive demonstrations and entire army units laying down their weapons and joining the people. However, we're also getting reports of vicious attacks on demonstrators as well. And … there's been no communication from Colonel McGovern since he and the Russian cosmonaut undocked from the space station. Admiral Warner is pretty certain they're both dead. I'm going to the situation room and speak to President Simonov. I have to urge him to wait and give the Chinese people a chance to take their country back. I can't launch an attack. Not now, not without every option being tried. Oh, Derek, I want to scream and I want to cry, but I have to hold it all together and try not to start something that can't be stopped."

Derek Price put his arms around his wife. "You'll do it. I know you'll make the right decision. You're the strongest and the smartest woman I know. In fact, most men I know would have cracked under the strain a long time ago. Go on, get down to the situation room and try and hold this mess together. Just remember, Cordelier, I love you."

"I love you, too, Derek. I sure hope that our future isn't one of being crowded together in an underground bunker for the next six months, waiting for the radiation levels to drop. I cannot have the blood of over a billion people on my hands. This has got to stop before it comes to that. Before I go, kneel down with me, honey. Kneel down and let's pray. God, give me strength and please give me wisdom … please God …"

* * * *

The corridor was narrow and claustrophobic. The air held a fetid odor of mildew and stale urine. As Intelligence Director Fong walked down the gray cement pathway to the lower cells, the naked ceiling bulbs cast harsh shadows on the floor and walls. Finally, he came to the last sentry. "Guard, open the gate. I'm here to speak with our former premier."

The heavy steel-barred cell door swung open to reveal former Chinese Premier Feng seated on his cot dressed in a light gray prison uniform. His cramped compartment held a small writing table with an ancient wooden chair, an open toilet in the corner, and the narrow bed from which Feng Qu stood up from.

"Did you come to gloat, Fong … or is it my time to be taken out to the courtyard and shot? How are things in *your* world? From the rumors I hear, they are not so good. Riots in the streets, soldiers firing upon each other, and this speech by the American and Russian presidents … they are preparing to annihilate China. Is this not true?"

Fong pulled the wooden chair from the desk and sat down, his large frame and bulk causing the chair to creek and groan. "Yes, what you may have heard is true. I am not here to see you crawl in the dirt, nor am I here to order your execution. I am here to talk."

"Yes Fong … talk. I have been doing a lot of talking with the man in the next cell. How ironic that you have placed me next to dissident leader, Wan Bo, a man that I personally ordered arrested. How delicious it was for him to see me in the very same prison that he occupies. That is until we both heard our guards speaking. Some even asked me if this could be true, that we are perhaps hours away from nuclear war. Wan and I spoke together for many hours; I don't believe I have slept yet. The rats have a tendency to wake you up by chewing upon your hands and feet. It seems that I finally begin to appreciate Wan Bo's views. Our system is corrupt. We allow men like Sung Zhao to be placed in positions that threaten our very survival. I wish I had turned my ear to the views of the dissidents' years ago, instead of listening to you, urging me to arrest them. Go on … say what you came to say and then get out!"

"Feng Qu, I have made certain there are no active listening devices in this cell. I ordered them turned off. I … was aware of the plans of Vice Premier Gao and Sung Zhao. Yet, I did nothing to stop them. This is the doing of Zhao more than anyone. I believe he is … insane. We met often to discuss the progress of his plan. It was excellent, but the West knew far more than we had given them credit for. Once it was discovered, the operation should have ceased. Sung Zhao would have been demoted for his failure. Perhaps he understood well that all blame would fall to him and no one else. He has convinced Vice Premier Gao that subjugation of America, Russia and Europe by nuclear blackmail will succeed. By doing so, he has become the most powerful man in China. Even Gao Xi is under his spell. I truly believe his goal is for China to be the single nation with the most survivors after a nuclear war. With the number of weapons arrayed against us, I even feel this is doubtful. When I left my office, I had a report that the first group of nuclear strike packages had been fired from the Moon and will arrive in Earth orbit in two days or so. I have also seen the reports and images of nuclear-armed bombers in flight, submarines are ready, and nuclear tipped missiles armed and awaiting orders to fire upon us. I'm here, not as a traitor but as a patriot of China who will not let my former subordinate destroy her. Listen carefully to me, Feng. I will have you taken out of here. I will say you are being brought to Intelligence Headquarters for further questioning. Then we must formulate a plan to restore you to power."

The deposed premier thought for a moment. This was not something he would have ever expected from Fong, but then he did something completely unexpected as well, even to himself.

"I'm not leaving without Wan Bo in the next cell. In many ways over many hours, he has convinced me of his point of view. It is one that enhances not diminishes China. He must come with us. He has millions of followers and supporters. They will listen to him. I believe his help will be invaluable in saving our nation from these madmen."

* * * *

"Check the charge in the emergency batteries, Remmy. I'll go to work on the water recycling system. It's not as bad as I first thought; just needs a new connector hose. Tom, I have to talk to you about Major LaBelle."

Tom Garcia, the payload specialist, huddled with Lieutenant Curtis. Garcia was a sort of spaceflight jack-of-all-trades, well versed in astronomy as well as spacecraft electronics systems. He was also trained in paramedic level first aid and the closest thing to a real doctor for a quarter of a million miles.

"Tom, that's a really bad wound in the major's upper chest. He's still bleeding but you've slowed it down a lot. You're going to have to try and surgically repair it. Are you up to the task? Because if not, I'm afraid he'll die."

Tom Garcia looked down, gathering his thoughts. "With everything going on, we may all die up here. If war breaks out on Earth, I think sending a relief mission will be the last consideration on the list, but while we're alive I'm going to do all I can to keep every one of us that way. I'll need a spotlight and the med-kit. It has a few surgical scalpels and other instruments. Grab a few more morphine ampoules. That's the only anesthetic we've got. And … I'll need to cauterize those blood vessels to try and stop the bleeding. Get me the soldering gun out of the station's repair kit. I wish I knew what was going on with the colonel and Captain Polyakova. He told me that he'd found his true soul mate. I hope to God they're not buried together on the Moon in a pile of wreckage."

Remmy LaCasse had been half listening to the conversation while checking the status of the two remaining eyes, the small spy probes. Both were too badly damaged in the attack to be usable in trying to locate the missing Lander. He floated over to Garcia and Curtis.

"Not McGovern and not Natasha. This man saved my life against all odds. They're both alive, I can feel it."

Tom Garcia turned to the Frenchman. "I hope you're right." Then he spoke to Lieutenant Curtis. "Come on, Bill. Grab some alcohol and gauze and get the med-kit and the soldering gun. I'll sterilize my hands. Let's get the major prepped for surgery."

* * * *

Colonel John McGovern looked over the side of the hopper as the cratered and blasted surface rolled underneath them. The Chinese lunar hopper could hold six individuals, sitting inside an open lattice-like framework of aluminum tubes. The craft, if you could actually use that term, looked more like a collection of leftover parts from a wrecking yard. The hopper had six seats set in three rows of two. The young technician was piloting the craft with John and Natasha in the center two seats and Major Yuan, playing the part of the political officer, was in one of the rear seats with John and Natasha's weapons. Yuan felt that he trusted the young tech but only to a point and had removed the external transmitter controls from the man's suit radio.

Major Yuan felt the tension in the pit of his stomach. Four individuals were about to slip into the moon base and attempt to subdue three times that number of men on duty, as well as rescue his nephew. They would arrive in less than 20 minutes, and he convincingly had to play the part of Kang, the recently deceased political officer.

Major Yuan Xho mentally reviewed his story. *The Russian and the American were his prisoners. There had been a fight, and they had killed two of his men. He had, of course, shot and killed Major Yuan and Corporal Wu.*

Yuan was about the same height and weight as Kang Lu and with his helmet on, it would be impossible to tell the difference between the two men. Still, it would only give them one chance to attack by surprise then seize the base. He and McGovern had talked about their tactics. The American had divided a brick of Semtex plastic explosive into three five-ounce slices and inserted programmable detonators in each one. Yuan hoped they wouldn't require such drastic measures, but he felt better knowing they had the explosives in case they were needed. The major considered something else as well. Even in their lunar combat suits, he could detect the body language between the American and his female Russian partner. When he looked over the back of their seats, he could see their gloved hands were interlocked. There was a story here. He sincerely hoped both he and his two rescuers would still be alive in the coming hours to speak about it.

The hills and craters began to give way to the more mountainous uplands that marked the edge of the Aitkin Basin and the Moon's South Pole. Beyond the southern mountains were the high ridges forming a barrier to the sunlight, leaving the floor of the basin in total darkness. John McGovern nudged Natasha, pointing in the direction of the winking lights that signaled the hopper landing area for the moon base. Other than hand signals, they sat in silence with their transmitters off. Short range or not, if even a hint of this deception were detected by those on the base, they'd all be dead. McGovern's thoughts centered on what he would do in the next few minutes after they touched down. He said a silent prayer that they would not fail.

The main engine fired, gently lowering the hopper to the surface. A curtain of ancient lunar dust rose and then fell about the spindly transport as the landing pads touched the ground.

John and Natasha got out first with their arms raised above their heads. Yuan had his weapon trained on them and had given the accelerator technician the political officer's pistol minus its ammunition clip. He thought he could trust the technician, but because of the spacesuits they wore, Major Yuan could not see his eyes or his facial expression. He had to make a judgment on the man's voice alone. What would happen in the next few moments would test his loyalty to Yuan.

With both of their vacuum rifles swung over his shoulder, Major Yuan marched the two coalition pilots at gunpoint up to the airlock. The main floodlights came on, and a voice boomed over Yuan's headset.

"Political Officer Kang. Please report on your situation immediately. Who are those men? Why did you not report in earlier?"

Major Yuan realized the voice was that of General Wang. He cleared his throat and tried to recall Kang's exact tone and the inflection of his voice. He had to be convincing. His life and that of his nephew's depended on it. Yuan took a deep breath to calm himself as he realized his body was shaking inside of his pressure suit.

"General, sir. We were attacked by forces from the coalition spaceship. Two of my men are dead along with the two traitors. The technician and I managed to kill one of the attackers, and we took these two prisoner. I maintained radio silence as I had no idea if there were others waiting in ambush."

"Ah, Officer Kang, it is good that you are unharmed. You and your prisoners may enter the airlock. We shall interrogate them soon enough. So then, you have dispatched Corporal Wu and the traitor, Yuan?"

"Yes sir, I did."

"Good. Now you may dispose of his treasonous nephew as well."

Yuan wanted to shout with joy. His young nephew, the man he had promised to look after, was still alive. Again taking on the vocal persona of the political officer, Yuan answered, "It will be my pleasure, General, to execute the dog myself!"

The major hit the outer airlock button and slowly the door slid open, revealing a stark gray metal interior illuminated by the harsh green hues of the overhead mercury arc lamps. Trying to appear menacing for the surveillance cameras he pushed his two prisoners forward with the barrel of his rifle, but the young technician was acting more like a prisoner himself than a guard, looking about nervously and shifting from side to side, not even aiming the unloaded weapon in the direction of the two captives.

As the airlock chamber began to fill with oxygen and attain normal pressure, General Wang, watching the nervous tech on a monitor grew increasingly suspicious and called up two men to station themselves, rifles at the ready, behind the inner airlock door. The lights cycled from red through amber and finally to green and then the inner door began to slide open.

Wang, flanked by the two soldiers, first called out in English. "Prisoners, remove your helmets immediately!"

John and Natasha unsealed the neck rings to their helmets, twisted them and then pulled them away from their suits. The base commander seemed surprised that one of the two captives was a woman. Then he eyed his political officer suspiciously. "Now *your* helmet *Officer* Kang!" Wang yelled to the two-armed guards. "Rifles up!"

The accelerator technician still had his helmet on. Now on the verge of panic, he began shouting almost incoherently and began to run directly toward the general, trying to warn him of the ruse, but with his suit's transmitter disabled, all the guards could see was the pistol he was waving in his right hand. Unknown to them, the ammunition clip had been removed. Both soldiers took aim at the tech and fired bursts of automatic rounds, most of them hitting the man, tossing him through the air like a bloody rag doll in the low gravity, but a few bullets shot past him, punching holes through the lightweight aluminum airlock door. Instantly, alarms began to wail as the air inside the chamber screamed out through the bullet holes. Major Yuan tossed the two rifles he had been holding to Natasha Polyakova and Colonel McGovern. John grabbed his first and opened up on the two PLA men, blasting them back down the corridor with the force of the impact from his shots.

General Wang, having sensed that something was wrong, had pushed back hard with his legs and began running down a side corridor. Before Yuan could reach the opening, the airlock door's emergency activation system, sensing the drop in pressure, slammed the inner door across its track, sealing off the compartment.

Yuan cursed in Chinese then turned to McGovern. "My plan has failed. We're trapped in here!"

John McGovern reached into his thigh pack and pulled a one-third slice of Semtex out, wedging it against the edge of the inner airlock door and set the detonator for six seconds. "Get back and cover your ears!"

* * * *

"*Surgical strike?!* And who's the surgeon … *Jack the Ripper?!* President Cordelier Price was on her feet, temper flaring, leaning across the wide mahogany conference table in the White House's situation room, staring in disbelief at Air Force General Clayton Andresen. "General, we've all been on our feet for far too many hours, fueled with coffee and the anxiety of not knowing if in the next five minutes we'll all be herded onto a helicopter and evacuated to a fallout-proof bunker, but for God's sake, I will *not* authorize a nuclear first strike against the Peoples Republic of China at this time. The intelligence reports I've received from the CIA seem to indicate our broadcasts are working. In many areas of China, the people are rising up."

"Respectfully, Madam President, in many areas they are not or their protests have been forcibly put down by the army," the general countered. "We cannot take the chance of those nuclear strike packages arriving undetected into low Earth orbit and then dropping on our cities. I've been in communication with my Russian counterpart, Marshal Lyakov, and his missile forces of SS-24s and SS-18s are programmed for launch on command status. The Russians are one button away from striking the Chinese mainland and taking out a significant number of their command and control centers. We have to be prepared to act in concert. Anything less would be seen as ..."

"As what, general? *Unmanly?* Is that what you're trying to say? *Yes*, I am painfully aware of the danger of those strike packages arriving into orbit and being used, but we still have over a day before we act. If we strike now, hundreds of millions of innocent people will die!"

"Ma'am, our anti-missile weapons . . ."

"Will what, general? Stop *every* incoming Chinese warhead? How many U.S. cities and how many millions of American citizens will vanish inside million degree fireballs? How many Russian and European cities for that matter. *No!* You will not get an authorization from me to strike until *every* last option has been exhausted!"

President Price then turned to Assistant Secretary of State Goldman. "Get me President Simonov on the hotline. We all need to keep our heads and give the actions we started by our television broadcasts a chance to bear fruit. I have to convince Simonov that the military option is not on the table just yet. I only wish to God I knew what was happening on the Moon. If we can put a stop to this insanity there, maybe we'll avert a full-scale war. Now please, Jake, put that call through for me right now."

* * * *

Even with the palms of their hands pressed hard against their ears, the concussion wave in the confined space of the airlock left their heads ringing. McGovern jumped up from his crouching position where he had covered Natasha's body with his own to look at the damage. The inner airlock door had been blown off its track and was hanging open. The corridor was bathed in red and amber flashing lights and emergency alarms were going off all over the station.

When McGovern stood up, he winced in pain. A fragment of metal from the explosion had lodged in his upper back just above his shoulder blade. Natasha saw the blood starting to drip out the hole in his combat suit.

"*John!* Oh my God! You're hit!"

"I've had worse. Come on let's go!"

Major Yuan quickly pulled the automatic pistol from the dead technician's hand and slammed the nine round clip into it then helped pull Natasha to her feet. "We must hurry! I'll lead the way. If the pressure doors in the access passageway close, we'll be trapped again. This time, Wang will make certain we all die!"

McGovern picked up his rifle. "Where're we going?"

"To rescue my nephew. I know where he's being held. This will give us a fourth man for our cause. Quickly, before the pressure doors shut!"

The trio leaped over the sill of an emergency pressure door just before it sealed behind them, their momentum in the low gravity carrying them into the electronics and communications room. Two startled corporals spun around quickly with one falling out of his chair. Major Yuan had his pistol aimed at the two men and was shouting in Chinese. Immediately, both communications technicians put their hands in the air with one of them answering the Major's questions.

Major Yuan yelled over to John McGovern. "Get that white container in the first cabinet. It has large electrical securing straps. We can use them just as easily to secure these men." Turning to Natasha, Major Yuan shouted, "You must stay here and guard the communications room as well as these men. We must transmit to your governments that only nine nuclear strike packages have been sent Earthward, not all eighty-two. We must prevent this war from starting. You, colonel, come with me. I will take us to where my nephew is being held."

McGovern grabbed Yuan's arm. "Wait a minute. They must know it's you. Your face is all over the security monitors now. Don't you think they'll be waiting for us?"

Yuan thought for a moment. "Yes, you are correct. In my concern for my nephew I did not think with logic. Yes … I believe I know another way, but we must split up. Get that stool."

Major Yuan then aimed his pistol at the room's security camera and fired, preventing anyone from knowing their next move.

A purple stain that crawled up the neck of General Wang began to color his face, except for his lips, they were pressed together tightly with rage, forming a thin white line. "Damn that stinking scum of a traitor! He's enlisted the aid of the enemy! Tao! Open the arms locker and distribute weapons!"

Private Tao, looking about the room with resignation did not meet the General's eyes. "Sir … we did not unpack the new automatic rifles. They are … still in the storage area of the base. We have only two pistols in the locker … sir."

General Wang, boiling with rage, grabbed the private by the front of his uniform. He hauled him off of his feet, bringing the man's face within inches of Wang's. "Then get me those guns and all of the ammunition in the locker, you miserable toad! *You,* Corporal Liang, come with me!"

John McGovern was up inside one of the ventilation ducts slowly making his way toward the center of the complex where the Major said his nephew was being held. McGovern was grateful for the fact that in lunar gravity he only weighed 35 pounds or else he would have come crashing down through the flimsy, paper-thin air ventilation tube he was crawling through. He moved slowly, stopping when he heard voices. Once they diminished, he moved on. Major Yuan had said this main duct would take him directly to where the young man was being held under guard.

McGovern could hear more voices. Some were panicked while others shouted in anger. Through a grill slit, he could see a fight break out between four men. Obviously, there were others who shared the beliefs of the major and his nephew but he had no idea who thought what. John only hoped that the men who would follow Major Yuan would be victorious. If that were the case, then there would be fewer soldiers to deal with.

McGovern moved on. It took him almost five minutes of inching along to come within sight of the central complex module. The entire base had been laid out in the shape of a starfish with all main corridors leading to the central command and living compartments. It was here that Sergeant Zhang was being held. With the confusion of their attack on the complex, it appeared as if no one was guarding the man who had been locked inside a mesh cage designed for something the size of a large dog. McGovern considered this and the kind of sick minds who would order such a confinement device to be brought along to a base on the Moon. He was about to drop down out of the air duct when Major Yuan leaped into the confinement area, wearing his EVA long johns and carrying a rifle. Without hesitation, he aimed the gun at the cage's lock and shot it off.

The major and his nephew embraced but as they turned to head back down the corridor, a shot rang out. Yuan doubled over, clutching his shoulder and dropping his weapon. Then the base commander and two soldiers entered the hub. McGovern couldn't understand the language, but he could hear the menace in the general's voice.

"So, Major Yuan … the true nature of your traitorous actions are here before us for all to see!" Wang then gave the man a vicious kick to his injured shoulder with Yuan howling in agony. "I see you are in much pain. But in a moment you shall feel nothing. However, before you die, I shall execute your treasonous nephew before your eyes so that his death and your failure will be the last thing you ever experience. Corporal, kill Sergeant Zhang!"

The man, looking not older than twenty-five, placed the barrel of his M-77 automatic against Zhang K'un's temple. That's when McGovern smashed through the ductwork, firing on full automatic as he dropped to the floor. His 5.56 NATO rounds stitched a line from the midpoint of the Chinese corporal's chest, up his neck, ending just under his chin. But, as the man was hit, his arm jerked up, pulling the trigger on his pistol. Yuan's nephew fell back against the wall and slumped to the floor, his face covered in blood. Major Yuan, despite his wound, rushed to the young man's side in despair and grief, taking no notice of the general as he fled down another corridor.

Major Yuan, with tear-filled eyes, gently laid his nephew on his back and then … Zhang's eyes fluttered open. Wincing in pain, he brought his hand to the side of his head. A two-inch gash had been sliced open, exposing the white bone of the man's skull by the grazing bullet. He would live, although he had narrowly escaped death by less than a millimeter.

McGovern had his rifle trained on the private. Major Yuan grabbed the terrified man with his good arm and slammed him against the side of the corridor. "Where is the general going?! The private stood stone-faced and silent. Yuan took the pistol he had retrieved and pushed the barrel up under the man's chin. "One last time … *where* is the general going?!"

The private's eyes seemed to pop from his head with fear. "He … he goes to the storage compartment to get the automatic weapons!"

McGovern caught Yuan, helping him to a sitting position. "You're hurt pretty bad. Which way?"

"Down that one. The blue corridor. It leads directly to the storage area and another airlock. Hurry; if the general gets his hands on the automatic weapons, we'll be finished."

McGovern, grasping his automatic rifle, charged down the color-coded corridor in running leaps that carried him ten feet and further with each bounding step. He reached the storage and assembly area, piled high with lightweight containers and oxygen cylinders only to find it empty. Slowly he scanned the room. A flurry of motion caught his attention, but it was too late. As McGovern turned, a shot rang out. The bullet smashed into the magazine of his rifle, destroying the firing mechanism. John dropped the now useless weapon and dived behind a plastic crate.

Seeing McGovern's weapon fall to the floor, General Wang, armed with an SKS automatic rifle, strode menacingly toward Colonel McGovern. "Come out from there, American, with your hands high, or I will empty this ammunition clip right through that container you cower behind!"

In the moment before John McGovern stood up, he had just enough time to reach into the thigh compartment of his combat suit, pull out a lump of gum-like material and stick it to his suit, just below the back of his neck ring of his pressure suit. He rose with his hands in the air.

"So American … who are you? How many others are there?"

He had to keep the Chinese talking if his plan was going to work. "I'm Colonel John McGovern, United States Air Force. Under the rules of the Geneva Convention, I'm required only to give you my name, rank and serial number."

"Is that so … *Colonel* McGovern! We seem to be a very long way from Geneva and the so-called rules of warfare, don't you agree? Before I'm finished with you and your companion, you will tell me all I want to know. Now move toward the exit!"

McGovern now had his back to the exit with the general facing him. Wang had his back to the outer wall of the storage compartment. John was distracting the man while maneuvering him into just the right position.

As he spoke, McGovern moved ever so slightly to the left. "So, you're the commander that ordered the destruction of our first mission. Is that right?"

"Yes, what of it?"

"My friend, Major Roy Jackson, was on that ship. I made a vow that I'd kill the son of a bitch that ended his life. Now I intend to do just that."

Wang began to laugh. "That would be a very clever trick to accomplish, Colonel, considering that it is I who will shortly end *your* life after you tell me what I wish to know. *Now,* put your hands behind your head and turn around!"

As McGovern's hands went behind his neck he grabbed the sticky lump of putty that was stuck to his suit's neck ring and thumbed the detonator switch, hurling the object as hard as he could. The soft plastic lump stuck against the outer wall of the storage compartment as McGovern dived for the floor. General Wang, too stunned to fire, stared at the tan glob with the blinking LED glued to the wall. In an instant, and to his horror, he realized what the object was just as the detonator triggered the Semtex.

A deafening explosion filled the compartment, but just for a moment. The air inside the enclosed space was sucked out the opening that had been blasted in the wall with hurricane force, pulling crates of supplies along the floor out through the gaping maw into the vacuum of space. McGovern grabbed a support column and wrapped his arms around it tightly as he felt the air rush out of his lungs. Before he scrambled for the exit, he had just enough time to see General Wang, arms flailing wildly, being sucked out into the unforgiving airless vacuum of the Moon. His body contorted in the minus 300 degree blackness, as his lungs exploded from attempting to hold his breath. The searing pain in his chest and the feeling that his eyes were being forced from his skull were the last sensations the Chinese general felt as his life ended, with the cold grip of space turning him into a grotesque frozen statue in seconds.

The emergency door slid solidly across the exit as John McGovern scooped up an oxygen cylinder and threw it into the track of the airtight door, stopping its progress. With a pounding in his ears and the feeling of a million ants crawling across his body, John squeezed through the opening and kicked the oxygen tank back into the storage compartment as the emergency door slammed shut. Sounds returned with the roar of the air pumps in the corridor compensating for the loss of pressure. John McGovern took a deep breath. He had tasted the vacuum of space and lived to tell about it. Quickly he ran back down the corridor to where he had left Major Yuan and his nephew. But, as he did, two men confronted him. John was about to pull out his utility knife when one of them spoke in halting English. "Please, we are with you. We wish to help."

McGovern took his hand off the knife handle and replied to the men. "Your commander is dead. Come with me. Major Yuan's been wounded, and we need to secure the base before it's too late to stop a war between your country and mine."

Sitting against the corridor wall, with his nephew resting against him, Major Yuan was still keeping pressure on the bullet wound to his left shoulder. His nephew, Sergeant Zhang, had managed to staunch the blood from the nearly fatal wound to his head and was holding Yuan's pistol. He almost shot the two men that bounded into the central command area but released his aim when he saw John McGovern right behind them. One of the men rushed over to Yuan's and the sergeant's side and began tending to their injuries.

Yuan looked pale and close to shock, but he pulled himself together to speak to McGovern. "This man is a medical assistant. I am told both my nephew and I will live. The bullet passed out the back of my shoulder. Zhang K'un's head wound needs to be stitched but will heal. What happened to General Wang? Is he still alive?"

McGovern shook his head. "He decided to go moon walking … only he forgot to put on his spacesuit."

Yuan closed his eyes for a moment grimacing at the thought of death by vacuum and then he smiled. "I cannot think of any man who deserved such a fate more, except perhaps for Sung Zhao. Come, help me up and hand me the microphone. It is just behind you. I must address the base personnel immediately."

McGovern handed the Chinese major the transmitter, putting his arm around him to help steady him. Yuan keyed the mike. "Attention, attention all base personnel. This is Major Yuan, in command of the moon base. I repeat, this is Major Yuan, and I am in command. General Wang is dead. You are to follow my orders. Lay down your weapons and proceed to the communications room with your hands up. The base is under my command. You will surrender immediately to the Russian captain in the communications room. That is an order."

Putting the microphone down, he turned to Colonel McGovern. "We must get to the communications room at once."

"Fine with me, Major, but I don't want you bleeding to death on the way there."

The medical officer spoke up. "The bullet did not strike an artery, but it has broken Major Yuan's collar bone. He is in great pain, but he will not die."

Yuan was white with his teeth clenched together. "Come, we must make contact with the Earth before it is too late."

By the time McGovern, Yuan and the others reached the communications room, Natasha Polyakova had seven Chinese military men kneeling on the floor with their hands behind their head. When John entered the room, she nearly jumped eight feet into the air in the low gravity. Not looking very soldier-like, she wrapped her arms around her fiancée, holding him close to her body.

"John! Oh thank God you are alive! You've come back to me my love … I knew you would! Are you all right?"

McGovern returned the embrace. "Except for the pain in my head from being the founding member of the vacuum breathers club, I'm fine. I'll tell you all about it later." He looked at the men she'd been holding at gunpoint. "*You* certainly seem to have the situation in hand!"

Major Yuan smiled, despite the pain, while holding his pistol on the kneeling base personnel. He then addressed the men on the floor. "This base is now under my command. I have not surrendered it to the coalition; rather we have become allies in a race to stop the annihilation of our country and quite possibly the human race. As of right now, we are declaring our independence from the illegal government that has seized power in China. You will obey my orders and cooperate completely with the American and the Russian. Is that understood? You men are not traitors but will be known as heroes – but *only* if we can avert a full scale nuclear war on Earth."

Turning to the telecommunications tech, Yuan gave his order. "Turn on the main transmitter and get the camera on the two coalition astronauts and myself. Open the channel. Do it quickly!"

* * * *

"I've only bought us five more hours before a first strike. Simonov was adamant. A Russian armored division has been wiped out 150 miles south of Krasnoyarsk, near the Mongolian border. The Chinese hit a column of about thirty T-90 tanks and several thousand men with a tactical nuke, about ten kilotons. No survivors. The Russian military command wanted to launch an immediate strike that will take out vast areas of China. I've been pleading with President Simonov for a 24-hour delay but his generals are out for blood. Five hours is all that he could promise. Oh my God, we're going to need a miracle to stop this thing."

Cordelier Price, resting her elbows on the situation room's conference table, placed her head in her hand with tears filling her eyes. *My cabinet and the Joint Chiefs be dammed,* she thought. In five hours the end of the world would arrive and there was nothing she could do to stop it. Memories of her family, of being a small girl playing, of high school and then college, her marriage, the birth of her children, in a matter of hours the lives almost everyone she had ever known and the lives of the millions she did not would end, and for what? Because a madman sealed in a bunker nearly half a mile below the city of Beijing could not be stopped? *One man for the lives of millions or perhaps billions?*

President Price looked up at the men and women assembled in the situation room. All of them were in deep emotional pain. Wiping the tears away from her coffee-colored cheeks, she addressed everyone. "I want you to gather your families together quietly and have them report to Andrews Air Force Base to prepare to be evacuated. I'll inform the Speaker of the House to be ready as well and to inform the congress and the senate. This city … our beautiful city … it will be one of the first targets. General Andersen, you expect your SDI systems to be able to stop 70 percent of the incoming warheads?"

Andersen looked distraught. "Yes … yes, Ma'am, that's correct, maybe even 75 percent."

"And if the Chinese use their MIRVed ICBMs, that would be about 700 inbound warheads, is that correct?"

"Ah … yes, Ma'am, that is correct."

"General, what kind of casualties could the United States expect?"

General Andersen put his hand to his head, finding it difficult to think. "About 50-60 million, maybe a bit more depending on the targets. But … that's from the immediate strike. The radiation and the hard freeze that will follow will most likely kill that number again … and, that doesn't take into account their manned bombers and submarine launched missiles. The total number of dead could easily reach 200 million or more."

Cordelier Price put her hands to her face, rubbing her forehead. "All right, General. Prepare to transmit the launch codes on my command. I have no other alternative than to order a first strike and try to take out as many of China's missile sites as possible. God forgive me. I'm about to send hundreds of millions of innocent human beings to their deaths."

Then she addressed everyone in the situation room. "Please, right now, bow your heads. I will lead us … Our father, who art in Heaven … hallowed be thy name … thy kingdom …"

A Marine Corps major stormed in from the communications room. "Madam President … *everyone!* We have news … *news from the Moon!* They're patching it in now … audio and video!" It's Colonel McGovern … Ma'am! *He's alive!*"

President Price was on her feet. "Quickly! Get it on the screen!"

In moments the six-foot wide plasma screen came to life. "… am speaking to you from the Moon …. I repeat, this is Colonel John McGovern and Captain Natasha Polyakova speaking from the Chinese moon base. We are standing here with Major Yuan Xho, in command of the moon base. Major Yuan has declared the base's independence from the People's Republic of China. We are all working together to avert a catastrophe. We hope you can see and hear our transmission in America, Russia and Europe. Our transmission must be rebroadcast to the Chinese people as well. The launching of the Chinese stealth nuclear packages has been stopped although nine orbital weapons are on course for Earth."

The Chinese major stepped forward with McGovern helping to support him. His uniform was stained with blood, and his face showed the excruciating agony of his wound. "I am Major Yuan, in command of the liberated moon base. We will begin transmitting immediately the codes necessary to turn on the locator transponders inside of the nuclear strike packages. Once you have these, the devices should be easily located and destroyed. We did not launch any additional strike packages. I repeat, our base has declared independence from the criminals who have seized the government of China. We are ready and willing to cooperate with coalition forces."

Natasha Polyakova then stepped up to the front and began making the same address in Russian, hoping the signal was getting through to Moscow. In the situation room, men and women wept with joy. Others hugged and pounded each other on the backs. Cordelier Price wanted to rush into the arms of her husband, Derek, but she knew the crisis wasn't over yet. Not by a long shot … still, she looked over at Clayton Andersen, his macho persona giving way to tears that had formed in his eyes. Maybe, just maybe, God had heard those prayers and maybe He would give the human race one more chance.

"General! Send a transmission. Tell them we're getting all this! Jake, get every high-powered transmitter on every ship and plane and in every nation that borders China to rebroadcast everything from the Moon. Overpower their TV and radio channels! Make sure it's translated for the Chinese people to see and hear. Admiral Warner, locate and destroy those orbital weapons and then place us at DEFCON 2. Pull our bombers back to their second hold points. I don't want any accidents to start a war that we might be able to end without getting a lot of people killed. Get the communications staff in here as well. In case Moscow and the EU aren't getting this, make sure they do and get me Victor Simonov on the telephone immediately. Oh thank God, we have a chance."

It was as if a great crushing stone had been lifted from her chest. Suddenly, a lightness and a deep peace seemed to descend over President Price. Then quietly she spoke, "Thank you, Lord, for hearing our prayers and sparing us … thank you."

CHAPTER TWENTY-ONE

The Underground Bunker of Premier Gao Xi and Vice Premier Sung Zhao

The project had begun under the orders of Chairman Mao Tse Tung in 1972, during the reproach with the Soviet Union and their ideological split. In 1971, border incidents hostilities between Soviet Red Army troops and Chinese soldiers began to escalate at an alarming rate. By the early 1970s, China had begun a full-scale military production of high yield hydrogen bombs, but lacked an accurate long-range missile to deliver them. However, the weapons were capable of being carried by intermediate range missiles and manned bombers. The bunker was only half completed in 1973 when Soviet-Chinese tensions escalated to the point that war was imminent. While China could field an army of millions against the Soviets, the Russian military machine held the upper hand in technology and the sheer numbers of large accurate missile launched nuclear weapons. Sensing the futility of such an unequal conflict, the Chinese government backed off but vowed never to be placed in this position again and began an expensive modernization and upgrading of its nuclear war fighting ability that was paid for by cheap exports to the West.

By the late 1990s, the central command bunker had gone through numerous revisions and expansions to the point that it consisted of more than 12 miles of tunnels to house 3,000 people. The bunker was 700 meters underneath the Forbidden City or nearly half a mile below ground, tunneled through solid bedrock. Even a direct surface burst with anything less than a 20 megaton bomb would leave the complex virtually untouched. In their subterranean lair, Premier Gao and Sung Zhao awaited the arrival of more than 80 cloaked nuclear weapons to arrive in Earth orbit.

When Sung Zhao's first plan was discovered by the West, accused of failure and facing disgrace, he managed to convince Vice Premier Gao of a fall back plan. They would still use the stealth nuclear strike packages to succeed despite China's failure at the United Nations. These weapons, coated with thick radar absorbing black material, would arrive from the Moon, launched by the far side magnetic accelerator. Unlike a launch from Earth, the bombs would be undetectable and invisible. Eighty invisible and unstoppable nuclear weapons that could be de-orbited over any country in the world and strike with less than five minutes warning would give Zhao and China the power to dictate terms to the world.

Sung Zhao was obsessed with Chinese nationalism. He believed it was the destiny of China to rule over the other nations of the Earth. Soon it became Zhao's only passion and goal. China, denied her destiny by the round-eyed devils of the West, would at last stand above all others, even if three quarters of the Chinese population would have to be scarified to archive it. With China's nuclear war fighting technology coupled with 80 undetectable high yield orbital bombs, if the West did not bow down, then their nations would be turned into lifeless graves. China, by sheer weight of numbers with a population of more than 1.5 billion, would rise from the ashes and claim what was rightfully theirs. Using his persuasive arguments and decrying the failures of the Chinese premiere, he and Vice Premier Gao, along with many in the military took control of the government and arrested Premier Feng. Now Sung Zhao felt that victory was within his grasp.

Zhao's room within the underground complex was small, with just a desk holding a computer terminal, a nightstand with a lamp and his narrow bed. Space was at a premium, and only top ranking party officials and generals had their own quarters. All others slept dormitory style. The pounding on the door of his compartment brought Zhao fully awake. Glancing at the clock on the nightstand, he could see it was just past 5:30 in the morning. Zhao put his feet into his slippers to ward off the chill from the cement floor and opened the door. He was greeted by a flustered and nervous looking military officer.

"Yes? What is it you want at this time of the morning?"

The officer shifted his eyes, fearing Zhao's wrath if he stared too long at his disfigured face. "You must come to the communications room at once. Our television and radio channels are again being overpowered by transmissions from the West."

A look of disgust came over the undamaged half of Zhao's face. "Again they bombard us with their mindless propaganda? Order our jamming stations to block the signals!"

"We cannot, sir. They are far too strong and … there is a difference. This broadcast originated from our base upon the Moon. A Major Yuan is addressing the people of China and claims to have seized the base with members of the Western and Russian coalition."

A look of shock came over the half-mobile side of the vice premier's face. "Has this treasonous filth been heard inside of the bunker?"

"No, sir. It is confined to just a few men in the communications room."

Sung Zhao quickly threw on a sweater and a pair of black slacks. "Show me. I want to hear this for myself!"

The communications section of the bunker was a three-minute walk from the private officials quarters and by the time Zhao had arrived, the major's speech was close to being finished.

"… so I say, my fellow citizens of China, you have been deceived. The criminals, Sung Zhao and Gao Xi, are planning to lead you to your deaths. They will build a new China upon your ashes. But … their plans have failed. They are finished. All but nine of their orbital nuclear weapons still sit upon the Moon. I have already provided the codes to the Americans to disable those on their way to Earth. Sung Zhao and Gao Xi … if you are listening, surrender. Give China back to her people. To the army, navy and air forces of the People's Republic of China, lay down your weapons. Do not turn them against your own people, your mothers, your fathers, and your children. China will achieve greatness, but not by spilling the blood of millions. People of China, break free of your chains and take back what is yours!"

Zhao shook with rage. He picked up a chair and smashed the plasma display screen, littering the communication's room with shards of glass. He then called over the intercom. "General Shen, report to me immediately in the war room … do you hear me? *Immediately!*

When Sung Zhao entered the war room, the general, along with Premier Gao Xi, was waiting for him. Gao said nothing, seeming too stunned to speak, by the loss of the one advantage China held – the orbital nuclear weapons.

Zhao, however, paced about in an animated rage. "Seal the door right now!"

The door, with a design that looked like a heavier version of the entrance to a bank vault, slowly closed as the electric motors that controlled it whined. The door was over half a meter thick, composed of super hardened tungsten steel. It would take a small army hours to begin to cut through it with torches. Only powerful shaped explosive charges could blast it open.

Zhao was shouting in a rage. "Quickly, Shen, bring up all the ICBM launch sites on the main display board!"

Command and control for China was quite different than in Russia or the United States. From this room, one man with the missile launch codes could unleash a nuclear holocaust. The general hit a switch and the huge wall display came alive with winking amber lights that signified the locations of multiple warhead missiles lurking within underground silos, ready to launch. Suddenly, groups of lights began to wink out and go dark. Behind him, a television monitor had come to life. Someone in the communications room had activated it. The image that it conveyed first filled Sung Zhao with disbelief and then into a rage, roaring like animal. This was no longer the work of the West, using high-powered transmitters. Rather, it was Chinese broadcast television, live from the streets of Beijing. There, standing atop a tank with his arm around Wan Bo, one of China's leading dissidents, and flanked by members of the military, was Premier Feng, the same man that Zhao had personally ordered locked away in a prison cell. Also with him was his former superior officer, Fong Kim Hua, who vanished after Zhao had personally directed him to order military units to fire on the demonstrators. Feng Qu was speaking. The roar of a crowd that had to number in excess of 2 million intermittently drowned out his words.

"… of the People's Liberation Army to lay down their weapons and for all military units to stand down. All manned bombers and fighter aircraft are to return to their bases immediately. All missile forces are immediately ordered to deactivate their launch systems. All hostilities between the People's Republic of China and the Russian-American-European collation are to cease immediately. All orders and directives from the criminals, Gao Xi and Sung Zhao, and any of their henchmen, are to be ignored. The legitimate government of China has been restored, and I promise the people of China a more open and democratic government as well. We will step into the future in a new beginning with the other nations of the world. Not as adversaries but as partners in a great …"

Zhao turned to the general demanding answers. "What is happening? Where are the launch indicators for my weapons?"

General Shen was appalled. "Excuse me, sir … *your weapons?* It would seem they are being disabled and taken offline by their crews. It is apparent, is it not, that you are no longer in command here? They are obeying the orders of the legitimate government of China, not you or your so-called *Premier*, sitting in the corner like a terrified rabbit. I have just been ordered by *my* commander, Premier Feng Qu, to stand down and I intend to do just that. Now, unseal the access door!"

Sung Zhao turned on the general with an almost blinding fury, pulling an automatic pistol from his pocket and aiming at it at him. General Shen's eyes went wide. He realized he was dealing with a dangerous psychopath. Still, instead of trying to rush him and grab his weapon, Shen foolishly attempted to reason with him. "Just what do you intend to do? Your plan is finished. Surely you do not intend to provoke a nuclear war with the West if we have nothing to gain? Please, end this foolishness and hand me your weapon."

"Shut your damn mouth, General! I am *still* in command here. There … those missiles in the Oilian Mountains, they are launch ready?"

"I cannot permit this insanity to go any further!" The general reached for his own sidearm, but Sung Zhao was quicker, and pulled the trigger of his automatic pistol. General Shen stumbled backward, clutching at his chest as a dark red stain crept across his green uniform. Desperately, the man lunged for the fail-safe switch that would disable the war room's launch system, but Zhao fired again, this time hitting Shen just behind the right ear, blowing his brains all over of the launch console. Premier Gao stood up, his mouth open in shock and horror.

Zhao strode about the war room menacingly. "So, Gao, now it is just you and I. Let the West try and destroy us. We will rise like the Phoenix and claim our rightful place as the world's true rulers. They will launch a retaliatory strike as soon as the missiles I am about to fire hit their targets. Premier Feng and his adoring millions on the streets above us will be incinerated in less than an hour."

With that, Zhao's palm came down on the launch button to activate four DF-31 missiles, each armed with four independently targeted 250-kiloton nuclear warheads.

* * * *

The missile crews, deep in their hardened launch silos had just received orders to take the four long-range missiles off launch status when they felt the deep vibrations of the explosive charges blowing off the missile silo covers above them. In a heartbeat, the red launch warning lights came on, followed by the blaring of the alarm sirens. The technicians on duty tried to disable the controls, but the launch commands had already been uploaded into the onboard computers within the missiles. From that point on, launching was automatic. There was nothing the missile crews could do to stop it.

The silo control room shook and bounced on its internal system of dampeners from the shock waves, as the four long-range missiles climbed into the pre-dawn sky, breaking through a low cloud deck, on their way toward the North American continent.

* * * *

Cordelier Price was just beginning to relax. Deposed Premier Feng Qu had re-established his authority and Feng, along with former imprisoned dissident Wan Bo, now in control of most of China's military, and their moon base in coalition hands, it looked as if the crisis was finally over. She had been in communication with Norman Taggert concerning the fate of the *Alliance.* Despite taking damage from the Chinese attack, the craft was not in any further danger; although one of the crew had been badly wounded, it appeared he would survive. Taggert was busy arranging a relief mission with the Russian Space Agency to get the man back to Earth.

She had just gotten up from her seat, body aching with exhaustion, to head back to her bedroom to try and catch a few hours of sleep when Admiral Warner burst into the conference room with a look of anguish on his face. *"Cordelier!* NORAD shows four ICBM launches from the Chinese mainland. SATSCAN shows they're either modified DF-31s or DF-5s. Either way, we've got real trouble. Those are MIRVed warheads. Each missile carries four independently targeted 250 kiloton nukes."

Cordelier Price felt as if ice water had just been shot through her veins. She had to catch her breath. "Oh my God … how many other launches have been detected?"

"None, that's it, we believe it was either an accidental launch or someone figured on getting in one last shot at us. We have high confidence the targets are all in the western United States, most likely California."

"Can you stop them? What about our SDI assets?"

"Just a minute …" Warner put his hand up to his blue tooth earpiece, listening carefully, then he slammed his fist into the palm of his hand. A brief smile crossed his face. *"Yes … got 'em!* Sorry, Ma'am, but we have some good news. One of the Russian airborne lasers took out an inbound missile. Now we only have three to deal with. Alaska is tracking them, and we'll try to take the rest out with Sky Striker, our particle beam weapon … but that's 12 inbound warheads. With our rate of accuracy, I can pretty much say for certain two or three may get through … one will for sure."

The President clasped her hands together gripping them tightly. "Is there anything else we can do … should we try and warn the West Coast cities?"

"Ma'am, I'm not certain that would do any good. The warheads will reach their targets in twenty minutes, but we won't know for certain which cities they're aimed at until the warheads separate from their re-entry buses and begin their descent … although there might be something …" Admiral Warner called over his communicator. "General Andersen, please return to the situation room immediately."

* * * *

Once Clayton Andersen was told about the inbound nukes, he placed a call to the China Lake Weapons Center in the Mojave Desert. He quickly finished speaking and turned to the President. "Ma'am, China Lake has several active Sprint-2 interceptor missiles. It's a black program. You ah … have never been informed about it. The Sprint was developed in the 70s and then deactivated with the advent of the ABM treaty … except we kept a few secretly online, improving their range and accuracy. The Sprint carries its own nuclear warhead, designed to destroy incoming warheads by vaporizing them."

"Do it, Clay, do it … shoot them down and … whatever happens there will be no retaliatory strike, is that clear? This was either an accident or the work of the men who seized power as a last act of vengeance. Premier Feng is back in control of the Chinese government. I will not go to war when peace is within our grasp. Is that understood?"

"Yes, Madam President. I will personally order our missile crews to stand down, but my God, if even one nuke gets through, there could be a million casualties."

Cordelier Price took Clayton Andersen's hand in hers. "Then please … do everything you can to stop them."

The three remaining DF-31 missiles had dropped their first stage boosters over the Kamchatka Peninsula at an altitude of 80 kilometers. The upper stage rocket motors continued to push the missiles with their deadly cargo on a high ballistic arc that would take them just south of the Aleutian Island chain on their inexorable descent toward the West Coast of the United States. Powerful NORAD search radars swept the incoming missile bodies, feeding the information at the speed of light to U.S. Air Force Missile Command, then on to the Sky Striker installation sited on the barren highlands of Umnak Island in the Aleutian Island chain.

A dome, built to resemble an astronomical observatory, slid open to reveal the blunt crystalline barrel of one of the crowning achievements of SDI technology. The Strategic Defense Initiative, sometimes derogatorily known as "Star Wars" during the Cold War, was intended to shoot down incoming Soviet ICBMs. With the end of US/Soviet hostilities, the bulk of the projects under development were cancelled, but Sky Striker was much further along and using breakthrough particle beam technology. Three Sky Strikers were constructed, each with its own potent nuclear reactor to power the massive banks of capacitors designed to channel 200 million electron volts into what amounted to a powerful linear accelerator. The weapon packed an enormous punch of stripped electrons that could travel to the edge of space at the speed of light. The secret program had technically not been a violation of the Anti Ballistic Missile Treaty as it was an energy beam, not specifically referenced under the treaty. Now, in Washington prayers were being said that the device could take out the three Chinese rockets carrying a total of twelve 250-kiloton nuclear warheads.

The officer on duty had received the call from NORAD to power up and engage the missiles. Major Brice, commanding the installation, could see the incoming missiles both on radar and in infrared. He knew his weapon and was certain of hitting two of the targets, but the recharge time needed to rearm the device would allow one of the missiles to get through. Plans during the Cold War had been to build a series of twelve Sky Striker sites from Alaska to Mount Hood in the Cascades for redundant firepower. This would ensure the Sky Strikers could take out multiple targets, but only one site in the Pacific Northwest defense chain was ever built. Now it would receive its baptism of fire.

Major Brice's eyes were focused on the large display screen that produced a virtual image of the three Chinese missiles. He watched them come into range of the Sky Striker as his technicians called out the firing information.

"In bound at –122 miles altitude, speed 8,000 … range to intercept 90 miles. Radar has locked on target one and … fire!"

The deafening sound of an incredible thunderclap reverberated through the air as an invisible beam of charged particles shot skyward at the speed of light, hitting the first missile body just behind the nuclear strike packages. The beam punched a hole though the thin skin of the missile, super heating it and blasting it apart, causing the four nuclear warheads to tumble out of control and begin to burn up in the upper atmosphere.

Brice then called out, "Recharge, recharge and acquire a second target!"

With the reactor at full power, electricity flowed into the capacitors, but it took nearly 45 seconds to rearm the weapon. By that time, the second missile had passed beyond range of the Sky Striker but the third trailing rocket was still a target. Once again the mother of all thunderclaps rolled across the cold gray Bering Sea as 200 million volts of energy leapt skyward, smiting the third missile from the sky over the Northern Pacific. Still, missile two continued on, dropping in altitude on a direct course for the Southern California Coast. The last missile now empty of fuel, jettisoned the final stage from the ablative reentry shield that housed the four warheads. The nosecone glowed red as friction of the upper atmosphere superheated the re-entry shield. At 200,000 feet, the re-entry shield separated from the warhead bus and the computers onboard the four nuclear weapons acquired their targets. Three would fall on Los Angeles, and one was aimed directly at San Diego.

Three miles from the triangle pattern of aircraft runways that formed the main airbase at China Lake, the warning klaxons were wailing. Sector five was a classified installation for the enhanced Sprint-2 interceptor missiles. The Sprint was a point defense weapon designed to counter multiple incoming targets by destroying them with its own three-kiloton nuclear warhead. Although tested extensively at both Area 51 in Nevada as well as China Lake, the Sprint-2 had never tried to intercept and destroy live targets in flight with a nuclear weapon.

The three-story high pyramid shaped radar transceiver scanned the skies over the Pacific Ocean and located the four incoming targets, just minutes away from the city of Los Angeles. The ground crews had scrambled to activate the warheads in the interceptor missiles but after earlier orders to stand down, only one Sprint-2 was launch ready. One missile would have to take out all four Chinese warheads.

The system was completely automated for at the speeds both the targets and the Sprint-2 would travel, no human being could ever react fast enough. The cluster of incoming warheads had just crossed the coastline. The optimum target vector was plotted, and with a brilliant flash, the cone shaped Sprint-2's rocket motor ignited and tore free from its launch container. The interceptor missile accelerated to nearly 8,000 miles per hour in a matter of seconds. Radar operators both at China Lake and in the nerve center of the North American Aerospace Defense command center watched the Sprint-2 track straight and true toward the heart of the deadly formation. However, just as the warheads crossed over the City of Santa Barbara, one of the weapons, the one that had targeted San Diego, began to diverge from the cluster, placing it just outside the blast radius of the Sprint-2.

Reacting a hundred times faster than a human brain, the terminal computer within the Sprint's electronics compartment read the final radar scan indicating the missile had reached the center of the formation. Circuits closed and the plutonium heart of the three-kiloton weapon detonated at 60,000 feet over Simi Valley, California. A blinding fireball filled the sky over the hills of Agoura as the Sprint's nuclear blast consumed three of the four 250 kiloton warheads. The warheads did not detonate but were vaporized in the fireball. However, the deadly plutonium from their radioactive hearts would be carried by the winds, eventually claiming the lives of thousands both living and as yet unborn. Many on the ground were temporarily blinded and the unlucky few, looking at that exact point in the sky, lost their eyesight forever. Two commercial passenger jets approaching LAX Airport, each carrying over 200 souls, broke apart in flight from the blast wave, killing all on board. But it could have been worse, a lot worse. If the Sprint-2 had missed, over 500,000 men, women and children would have died in an instant and at least that same number again over the next few days as victims of third degree burns and lethal doses of radiation.

Cheers went up by men and women at all facilities watching the space age battle until the image cleared revealing one warhead was still tracking southward. Everyone held their breath, expecting the worst, at least 200,000 dead and San Diego reduced to radioactive ruins. Then someone yelled, "Look! It's starting to tumble; it's going to fall short of the city!"

Although the fourth warhead escaped the blast radius of the interceptor missile, the over pressure wave knocked it off its trajectory. The weapon's on board targeting computer's sensors had also been damaged by the burst of fast neutrons from the detonation and could not reacquire its target. The fourth nuke began tumbling end over end on a course that would take it short of the city and over the Gulf of Santa Catalina.

At 1,200 feet above the smooth deep blue waters of the Gulf, 14 miles off the coast of Oceanside, California, the warhead detonated.

Instantly a searing fireball over a mile-wide immolated a flotilla of sailboats, powerboats and yachts below; their owners and passengers out for a pleasant day of sailing on a crystal clear spring morning.

The ferocious blast wave swept up millions of gallons of seawater, pushing it toward the coast in the form of a 75-foot high tsunami. The monstrous wave towered over the condominiums and homes lining the areas west of the Coast Highway as they vanished under thousands of tons of water, sweeping everything before it inland, finally washing over Interstate Five, tossing trucks and cars like toys for nearly half a mile. Thousands lost their lives in the blink of an eye, but hundreds of thousands in San Diego and millions in Los Angeles, would go to bed that night and wake up again the next morning, thanks to the quick thinking of General Clayton Andersen and the resources of the secret interceptor missile program.

* * * *

Sung Zhao's eyes scanned the empty threat display board, searching it for incoming American missiles. "Where are they?!" Why haven't the Americans retaliated? I want that teeming scum on the surface above us wiped from the face of the Earth!"

He paced about the room, picking up and hurling objects in a fit of madness, stopping to kick the dead body of General Shen slumped over the launch console. "*Damn it!* If I cannot provoke the Americans, I can force the Russians into firing upon us!"

But as Zhao reached across the blood soaked console, the last of the winking LEDs marking China's active long-range missile sites went dark.

Gao, fearing for his own life from the raging Zhao, tried to reason with the man. "Sung Zhao, you *must* accept the fact that we have lost. We have lost the opportunity to achieve your goal … but perhaps this is far better for China and the world. You cannot punish your own people. You cannot rain death down upon humanity. Please try to calm yourself. I let you convince me of your plan's success, and I was foolishly led by you to seize the power of the Premier's office that was not mine to take. I am prepared to meet my fate. Please, Zhao, it is over. I will unlock the door mechanism, and we shall stand together to be judged as men, not as cowards in hiding, lashing out in anger. China will be a valuable member of the community of nations in the conquest of space. You shall see."

Zhao spun about with a strength fueled by his rage. Grabbing Gao Xi, he hauled him up and out of his chair. "I will *see?!* I will see *what?!* The dismantling of *my* space program? Of *my* dreams for a mighty China, smashed by the Western devils?! By the Russian filth?! Well, I want *you* to see something. Look closely at my face! Does it please you?!"

Gao Xi tried to avert his eyes. The scar that ran down Zhao's face, from his eye to his chin, was horrible to look at, like some earthquake fault line running through his flesh. Zhao, with a vicious snarl visible on the undamaged half of his face, reached his hand up grabbing Gao's jaw, forcing his head forward.

"I said … *look at my face* … how does it make you *feel?!* Does it make you ill?! Can you imagine what I feel every time I have to look upon myself in the mirror?! Do you know what it feels like to only have the pleasure of a woman that I must pay for?! Do you know what it is like to be me? *Do you Gao!?* I gave my country *everything*! I gave my entire career as well as the sacrifice of my face to China to restore her greatness. *China!* Whose ships set sail for America 2,000 years before Columbus! China that was building rockets, making paper and discovering the principals of science while the Europeans were running about like superstitious barbarians during their Dark Ages! How does it make you feel that upstart American corporations have turned China into their personal sweatshop, making trinkets, electronic parts and plastic dolls for cheap sales and huge profits! It was I, Gao ... *I* who harnessed the inflow of money from the West to build our military space program! It was I who knew that mighty China could dominate the world! That all nations would bow down before us, cowering before our might and our greatness, and now … it is over … lost… well the round-eyed devils will not have it. *Do you hear me?!* They will not!"

Sung Zhao slammed Gao Xi to the floor, walked over to the computer console and entered a code. *It was still working*, he thought, *the traitors had not yet cut his final lines of communication.*

Over a thousand miles away in the foothills bordering Mongolia, an officer in a redoubt brigade saw the red LED numbers cross his screen telling him this was a genuine transmission from either military command or party leadership. Redoubt brigades were under strict orders, punishable by death, to ignore any radio transmission that was not preceded by a verifiable set of coded numbers. They acted as long triggers in case of invasion by outside forces. Hidden in the hills and mountains, armed with tactical nuclear weapons, the redoubt brigades would strike when ordered and stand down only when the transmission telling them to do so was authenticated. Sung Zhao was now in contact with such a brigade, 200 miles from the Xichang rocket launching facility, China's spaceport.

Gao Xi pulled himself up from the floor, listening in disbelief to the words from the man who had convinced him that he would soon be the most powerful man on the face of the Earth.

"Comrade brigade leader. This is Vice Premier Sung Zhao. My authentication code is X770H. Do you confirm?"

The receiver was silent for a moment while the brigade leader verified the code, then, "Yes, sir. What are your orders?"

"Russian and NATO forces have landed and overrun the Xichang Space Center. You are ordered to use your nuclear weapons. Destroy the space center and kill the enemy. You are to disregard any further orders. Is that understood?"

With that, Zhao cut the transmission, picked up a metal chair and smashed the radio transmitter. Gao charged at Zhao, grabbing him around the neck, trying to choke the life out of him. "What have you done, you maniac? *What have you done?!*"

Gao Xi heard the blast at the same instant he felt a tremendous impact in his abdomen, knocking him to the floor. He tried to get up, but his legs were useless. He looked down at his white shirt now stained a deep red with his own blood. It was getting hard to breathe, and Gao knew he was dying, but strangely, he felt no pain, yet he had to know. "Why, Zhao? Why did you do this terrible thing? So many will die. Our great leap into … into space … you've destroyed it. *Why?*" Gao slumped back to the floor. There was a roaring in his ears, and he felt an overpowering urge the like he had never known to close his eyes and drift off to sleep, still he had to know. Softly with his last breath he pleaded, "Please Zhao … tell me why?"

"*Why*, you stupid fool?! Because I created our military space program! If it is no longer mine, then no one shall have it. *Do you understand?!*"

The sound of an explosion shook the room, knocking Sung Zhao to the floor beside the dying Gao. They were coming for him. The next blast would surely breach the door. His pistol had three rounds remaining. Sung Zhao placed the barrel into his mouth ,and as the second blast tore a hole through the steel reinforced door, he pulled the trigger.

General Liang and a squad of men entered the room. Liang's eyes caught a motion on the huge threat display board, and to his horror saw two missile tracks streak away from the Mongolian border on a direct course to the XiChang Space Center.

* * * *

The sky was turning a pale pink as the early dawn drove the nighttime chill from the air. Two powerful rockets, destined for the Moon, stood atop their launch pads. Chung Qui Noon was about to make an inspection of the fuel storage area. Everything had been on a war footing since the coup had thrust the former creator of China's military space program into the position of vice premier. Now that power had again reverted, the base was on shut down until command authority could be re-established.

Chung's eyes scanned the northern sky, and he thought he saw a hint of motion in the distance, perhaps a flash of light, the rising sun glinting off the polished metal of an aircraft in flight. Then his existence ended in two searing fireballs, consuming everything for three miles, turning the $200 billion space center into a graveyard of charred ruins and twisted metal with the ground directly beneath the twin blasts into vitrified radioactive glass.

CHAPTER TWENTY-TWO

The Chinese-Coalition Moon Base

John McGovern and Natasha Polyakova had just finished a dinner of freeze-dried chicken lo mien and rice with their Chinese hosts. Major Yuan had been speaking about his family, his wife and his little boy in Kunming, China, and had shown the two coalition pilots his personal video clips. With his right arm still in a sling, he had difficulty maneuvering his chopsticks during the meal. Later in the evening, his nephew, Sergeant Zhang, head swathed in bandages, came out from his quarters to join them.

Major Yuan spoke to John and Natasha quietly. "Thank you … thank you both for saving my life and that of my nephew. Never has the world come so close to disaster, but never has the world and the human race been given such an opportunity to redeem themselves: to put aside old grudges and begin to work together and begin to harvest the wealth of space. We can do this and do it together, but we must be ever vigilant against the ambitions of men consumed with their lust for power such as Sung Zhao."

McGovern was about to agree with him when one of the communications techs entered the dining area. "Colonel McGovern and Captain Polyakova, your countries' two presidents are in contact with us and are requesting to speak with you both."

Natasha Polyakova and John McGovern stood facing a large plasma display screen with the split image of American President Cordelier Price and Russian President Victor Simonov in front of them. A video camera mounted above that screen transmitted their images back to Earth. The conversation would suffer only mildly from the three-second delay that radio waves took to crisscross the quarter of a million mile distance.

Cordelier Price spoke first. "Colonel McGovern and Captain Polyakova, thank you for a job well done. In fact, my thanks are hardly enough to convey my, your countries' and the world's deepest gratitude for averting a catastrophe that might have ended the human race. There are truly no words to express the magnitude of what you have accomplished. As you know, a relief and re-supply mission to the *Alliance* is being organized and will launch in a few days from Northern Russia. Major Kutuzov will be flying solo, bringing up repair supplies and equipment to the space station and he will be returning with Major Vernon LaBelle to the International Space Station for further treatment and then to Earth. Major LaBelle may have been badly wounded, but he's retained his sense of humor. He threatened to sue Tom Garcia for performing surgery without a medical degree. Now, on a more serious and somber note, I'm certain that you are all aware of the number of casualties in America, Russia and China from the world's first use of nuclear weapons since the end of World War II, but what you may not be aware of yet is that Vice Premier Sung Zhao, in a final fit of insane rage, ordered a nuclear attack on the Chinese Space Center under the pretext of it having been invaded and seized by NATO and Russian troops. This has effectively cut off the moon base from any re-supply missions from China. We and Russia are working with the new Chinese government to rebuild their spaceflight capacity, but that will take several years to do so. In the mean time, NASA and the Russian Space Agency are pushing ahead with the new lunar landers as well as mounting another effort to resupply you, using the two remaining LEM landers that are currently being made flight ready. For now, Colonel McGovern and Captain Polyakova, you will serve as America's and Russia's ambassadors as well as our coalition's presence on the Moon. It will be at least six months and perhaps longer before you can be returned to Earth. That being the case, do you have any questions or requests of your governments, either the United States or Russia at this time?"

John McGovern huddled with Natasha for a moment and then spoke. "Madam President, did I understand you correctly that we will be on the Moon for six months or longer?"

"Yes Colonel, that is correct."

"Then President Price and President Simonov, we would like to request the services of a Russian Orthodox priest."

The American president appeared perplexed as did Simonov.

"Yes, I'm sure that can be arranged … but what did you have in mind?"

"Well, Madam President, with you having your hands full with the crisis and, just in case Norman Taggert didn't tell you, Cosmonaut Polyakova and I are engaged. She's pretty adamant about that institution of marriage thing, and I have to say I agree with her. We need a priest to carry out a long distance video ceremony … if that's not a problem."

On the split screen, both presidents' faces broke into wide smiles. Cordelier Price addressed the couple. "That would be wonderful, a fitting tribute to the hope for a new and peaceful future for the human race. Of course, Colonel, we will make it happen for the both of you as soon as you are ready."

Star City, Moscow, December 12, 2018

It was more than seven months before the first Altair Lunar lander set down at the Moon's South Pole to return Captain Polyakova and Colonel McGovern to Earth. First stop was the International Space Station, and then it was into the crew seats of the new Russian-built Klipper Space Plane, and down to the long runway at the Baikonur Spaceport in Kazakhstan. From there, the two were flown to Star City in Moscow for a full medical examination before being released. John McGovern had just finished a battery of invasive tests and was ready to spend a few days with Natasha, her father and her father's new wife,

Yulia. Natasha was still inside the office of the medical director of the space center, while John sat outside, waiting for her. An aide asked Colonel McGovern if he would please step into the director's office. A look of concern crossed John's face as he joined his wife and sat down across from Dr. Grechko. McGovern spoke to the man. "Is everything all right with Natasha? Why did you want to see me?"

A wide smile broke across Grechko's face and he answered John McGovern in a thick accent. "Please, Colonel, all is well with your wife. Her tests were completely normal except for one and that result should be cause for celebration. Your wife, Cosmonaut Polyakova, is in excellent health and … she is also two months pregnant."

-------♦-------

THE END

EPILOGUE

John McGovern watched President Price step up to the podium to Join Victor Simonov. With each step, she seemed to bounce a good ten inches into the air. It was July 20, 2021, the 52nd anniversary of the day that Neil Armstrong first set foot upon the Moon. Cordelier Price set a first in 2020. Not only did she become the first elected woman president, but she won with over 69 percent of the popular vote. Even her opponent found it extremely difficult to criticize the woman whose quick thinking and bold decisions managed to avert a nuclear holocaust. Now she was setting another first along with the President of Russia: the first American President not to only fly in space but to set foot on the Moon. The new Premier of China would not be joining them, but his foreign minister, who had arrived a day earlier, was just ascending the platform for the inauguration of the International Moon Base, a scientific community representing the very best aspects of the human race, in an attempt to put thousands of years of almost tribal animosity and warfare in the past. The International Moon Base would not only serve as a center for the development of the Moon's resources for the betterment of humanity, but as a stepping-stone to the planets. In eighteen months, the spacecraft currently under construction three kilometers from the base would lift off with a crew of eight, bound for the planet Mars.

The broadcast from the surface of the Moon would also make history as the most watched television event in history. At the United States Military Prison in Leavenworth, Kansas, even federal prisoners were marched into the cafeteria and made to watch the inaugural address. A guard on duty noticed one prisoner, facing away from the large TV screen, engaged in conversation with another inmate.

The guard slammed his billy club down on the table between them and addressed the man. “Hey, you, Crowley, pay attention … you’re not in some damned VIP suite anymore. Show your president some respect!”

John and Natasha sat together silently as President Price began her speech. Just as she was about to give her opening remarks, two small hands reached up into Natasha’s lap, “Pick me up, Mommy, Dianna want to see, too.”

Natasha reached down and scooped up their two-year-old daughter, placing her between herself and John on the sofa.

“Who’s that lady, Daddy?”

John McGovern smiled broadly at his small girl. “That’s the President of the United States, my little moon child. Mommy, and I took you to her house in Washington once but you were very little then.”

A grin formed on the apple pink cheeks of the little girl and she began to giggle. “Why am I your moon child, Daddy?”

“Well, I’ll tell you a little later, when you get bigger … but we named you Dianna, after the goddess of the Moon.”

Natasha leaned her head against her husband. “You’re not sorry you did not attend the inauguration of the moon base?”

McGovern shook his head. “Nope, not sorry at all.” His hand caressed his wife’s round bulging belly. You deserve to be right up there with me, but no way are you flying into space, seven months pregnant with our second child.”

She smiled and kissed his cheek. “And … you are not sorry that you turned down the command of the Mars mission either?”

“Natasha, that mission would have taken me away from you and our children for over two years. You and I, and the entire human race, have just been granted a second chance at life. I’m going to use my second chance to work on my motorcycles, make love to you, and watch our children grow … but, I do have one surprise for you. I’ve been saving it. Norman Taggert is retiring at the end of September. I’ve been asked to take over as the new director of NASA. I seem to recall just how much you loved Florida. So, what do you think?"

Natasha pulled herself closer to her husband and kissed him deeply as a little singsong voice playfully taunted, "Mommy's kissing Daddy … Mommy's kissing Daddy …"

TERMINOLOGY USED IN *RED MOON*

Airborne Laser: carried on a Boeing 747-400, first flown 2002. Range to target approx. 180 miles.

Altair Lander: NASA-proposed lunar lander for a 2020 return to the Moon. Crew capacity: 4.

Ares-I: NASA: built by Boeing and Alliant Techsystems, to carry the Orion capsule.

Ares-V: NASA proposed heavy-lift launch vehicle to carry the EDS (Earth Departure Stage).

Baikonur Cosmodrom, Kazakhstan: primary launch facility for the Russian Space Program.

Bigelow Aerospace: founded by Robert Bigelow in 1999. Commercial space development and inflatable commercial space stations.

EDS (Earth Departure Stage) NASA: proposed lunar stage for NASA's return to the Moon program, Constellation. Cryonic fuel (liquid oxygen–liquid hydrogen).

ESA: European Space Agency.

Falcon-9: built by Space-X, commercial launch vehicle, first flown in 2010.

Grumman Aerospace (Northrop–Grumman), Falls Church, Va.: Contractor for the design and manufacture of the Apollo Lunar Lander - the LEM.

Klipper: proposed, Russian-built, reusable space plane.

LEM (Lunar Excursion Modules), on display in museums, number and location:

LM-2- Smithsonian Air and Space Museum, Washington, DC

LM-9- Kennedy Space Center, Cape Canaveral, FL

LM-13-Cradle of Aviation Museum, Garden City, NY

LM-14-Franklin Institute Display, Philadelphia, PA

PLA (People's Liberation Army): the Chinese military, air, land, sea, and space.

Plesetsk Cosmodrom: Northern Russian launch facility, established in 1957.

Proton Rocket: (UR-500): Russian heavy-lift rocket. (First flight 1966), 22 tons to orbit.

Salyut Space Station: early Russian space stations in use from 1971-1982: A Salyut-7 space station with a Soyuz and a Progress spacecraft attached sits in front of the Hotel Kosmos, in Moscow, Russia.

Seawolf Class Submarine: US Navy fast attack submarine: *USS Connecticut*, launched 1998.

Sergei Korolev (b.1907- d.1966): Born in Zhytomyr, Russian Empire (now Ukraine). Founder of the Soviet Space Program.

Sky Striker-An SDI particle-beam weapon designed to destroy suborbital and orbital threats. Sky Striker is the creation of the author based upon the best available information on current military development of such defensive weapons.

Soyuz TMA Spacecraft: Russian, 3-man Earth to orbit spacecraft. First flown in 1967.

Star City-Gagarin training center, Moscow: Northern Moscow Region cosmonaut training center.

Titan IV Heavy Lift Rocket: built by Lockheed–Martin, used for deep space missions.

Type-094 Chinese Jin Class Ballistic Missile Submarine: carries 12 DF-31 long range MIRVed nuclear missiles (4-250KT warheads per missile).

Ural Night Wolf: Ural Motorcycle, Co. Irbit, Russia. Factory custom motorcycle, 750cc opposed twin.

Xichang Spaceport, China: PLA and the Chinese Space Program's primary launch center.

ABOUT THE AUTHOR

Chris Berman is the author of the popular *The Hive* and *Red Moon* books, both of which Leo has reissued from their original publisher.

Berman grew up reading science fiction novels and stories and began writing his own towards the end of 2007, after a bicycle accident. Chris's writing defies a set style, creating novels of hard science fiction, techno-thrillers, and alternate history—with each work of fiction, a unique literary adventure. He holds a Master's Degree in military history and is a member of the Society for Military History. Berman has an extensive background in spaceflight and astronomy. Chris Berman lives in Florida with his wife and daughters.

CPSIA information can be obtained at www.ICGtesting.com
Printed in the USA
LVOW041318220812
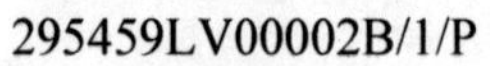
295459LV00002B/1/P